"A skilled storyteller." —*Publishers Weekly*

TERRY
JOHNSTON

OVER 2.5 MILLION COPIES
OF HIS BOOKS IN PRINT!

ASHES of
HEAVEN

THE LAME DEER FIGHT—MAY 7, 1877
AND THE END OF THE GREAT SIOUX WAR

THE PLAINSMEN SERIES: BOOK 13

ST. MARTIN'S
PAPERBACKS

U.S. $7.99
CAN. $9.99

LOOK FOR THESE OTHER BOOKS IN
TERRY C. JOHNSTON'S EPIC
PLAINSMEN SERIES

SIOUX DAWN
RED CLOUD'S REVENGE
THE STALKERS
BLACK SUN
DEVIL'S BACKBONE
SHADOW RIDERS
DYING THUNDER
BLOOD SONG

NOW AVAILABLE FROM
ST. MARTIN'S PAPERBACKS

ISBN 978-0-312-96511-2
50799

EAN

4/25

OVERWHELMING ACCLAIM FOR THE WORK OF
TERRY C. JOHNSTON

"Compelling . . . Johnston offers memorable characters, a great deal of history and lore about the Indians and pioneers of the period, and a deep insight into human nature."

—*Booklist*

"Johnston's books are action-packed . . . A remarkably fine blend of arduous historical research and proficient use of language . . . Lively, lusty, fascinating."

—*Colorado Springs Gazette Telegraph*

"Rich in historical lore and dramatic description, this is a first-rate addition to a solid series, a rousing tale of one man's search for independence in the unspoiled beauty of the Old West."

—*Publishers Weekly* on *Buffalo Place*

"A first-class novel by a talented author."

—*Tulsa World* on *Dream Catcher*

"With meticulous research, vivid dialogue, memorable characters, and a voice uniquely his own, Johnston has once again written the finest of historical fiction, seamlessly blending together both time and place to bring to life a world as real as our own."

—*Roundup* magazine on *Dance on the Wind*

"Terry C. Johnston is the absolute master at taking authentic details into the realm of gripping, compelling entertainment . . . Johnston has the astounding ability to take the reader into the hearts and minds of real Western characters, while simultaneously making the details of historically based plots crystal clear. He walks the ground before he writes, then the reader walks with him."

—Michael Martin Murphey,
Popular Western Entertainer

THE PLAINSMEN SERIES BY TERRY C. JOHNSTON

Book I: Sioux Dawn
Book II: Red Cloud's Revenge
Book III: The Stalkers
Book IV: Black Sun
Book V: Devil's Backbone
Book VI: Shadow Riders
Book VII: Dying Thunder
Book VIII: Blood Song
Book IX: Reap the Whirlwind
Book X: A Cold Day in Hell
Book XI: Trumpet on the Land
Book XII: Wolf Mountain Moon
Book XIII: Ashes of Heaven
Book XIV: Cries from the Earth
Book XV: Lay the Mountains Low
Book XVI: Turn the Stars Upside Down

ASHES
OF
HEAVEN

The Lame Deer Fight—
May 7, 1877 and the End of the
Great Sioux War

Terry C. Johnston

St. Martin's Paperbacks

This is a work of fiction. All of the characters, organizations and events portrayed in this novel are either products of the author's imagination or are used fictitiously.

ASHES OF HEAVEN

Copyright © 1998 by Terry C. Johnston.

All rights reserved. For information address St. Martin's Press, 175 Fifth Avenue, New York, NY 10010.

ISBN: 978-0-312-96511-2

Printed in the United States of America

St. Martin's Paperbacks edition / January 1993

10 9 8 7 6 5

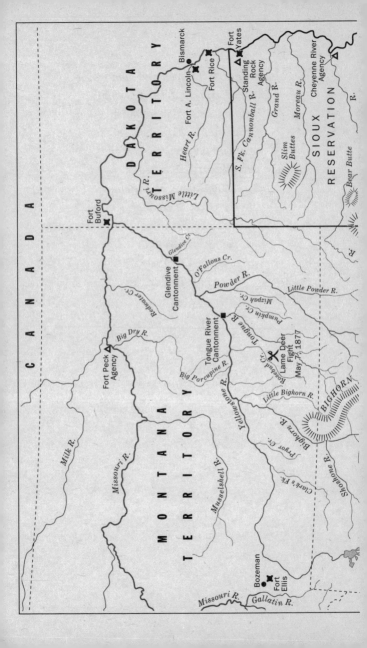

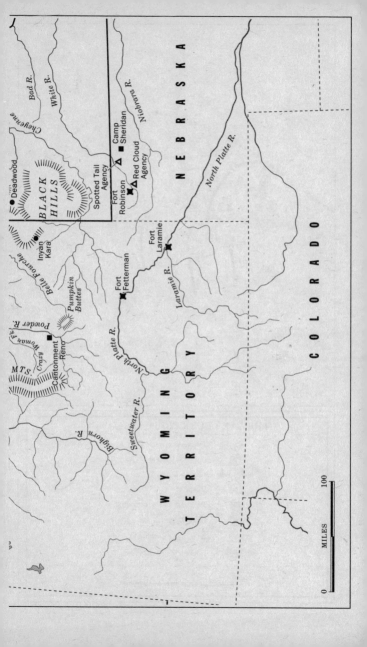

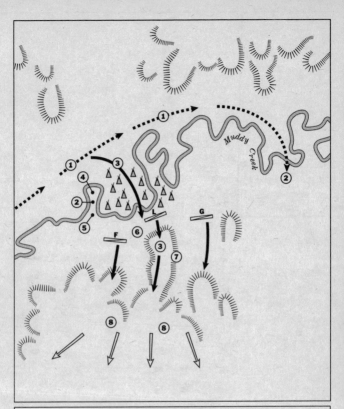

Muddy Creek

THE LAME DEER FIGHT, MAY 7, 1877

•••①▶	Troops stampede pony herd
②	Captured ponies
━●③➡	Charge of F/G/L, 2nd Cavalry
④	Hospital
⑤	Miles-Lame Deer encounter
⑥	Lame Deer's death
⑦	Iron Star's death
☐⑧➡	Route of fleeing Indians

0   FEET   2000

Ashes of Heaven
Cast of Characters

———•———

Seamus Donegan
Samantha Donegan
Colin Teig Donegan

———•———

Civilians

Nettie Capron
John Collins—   contract trader at Fort Laramie
Luther S. "Yellowstone"
   Kelly
Johnny Bruguier—   called "Big Leggings" by the
                                  Lakota and "White" by the
                                  Cheyenne

William Rowland/"Long
   Knife"
Willis Rowland/"High
   Forehead"
Joseph Culbertson
Robert Jackson
Dr. Van Eman—   civilian contract surgeon,
                                  Lame Deer Expedition

———•———

Military

General William Tecumseh   General of the Army
   Sherman—
Lieutenant General Philip H.   Commander, Division of the
   Sheridan—   Missouri
General Alfred H. Terry—   Commander, Department of
                                    Dakota

Colonel Nelson A. Miles—	Commanding Officer, Fifth U.S. Infantry
Major Andrew W. Evans—	Third U.S. Cavalry, Post Commander, Fort Laramie
Major Frank Brisbin—	Second U.S. Cavalry
Major Benjamin Card—	Quartermaster, Department of Dakota
Captain Ezra P. Ewers—	E Company, Fifth U.S. Infantry (given command of the newly mustered Crow scouts)
Captain Charles W. Miner—	G Company, Twenty-second U.S. Infantry
Captain DeWitt C. Poole—	H Company, Twenty-second U.S. Infantry
Captain Charles J. Dickey—	Company E, Twenty-second U.S. Infantry (given battalion command of the pack-train)
Captain George L. Tyler—	F Company, Second U.S. Cavalry
Captain James N. Wheelan—	G Company, Second U.S. Cavalry
Captain Edward Ball—	H Company, Second U.S. Cavalry (in command of the mounted battalion)
Captain Randolph Norwood—	L Company, Second U.S. Cavalry
Captain Andrew S. Bennett—	Company B, Fifth U.S. Infantry
Lieutenant Charles A. Woodruff—	Company B, Fifth U.S. Infantry
Lieutenant Charles E. Hargous—	Company H, Fifth U.S. Infantry
Lieutenant Oskaloosa M. Smith—	H Company, Twenty-second U.S. Infantry
Lieutenant Cornelius Cusick—	F Company, Twenty-second U.S. Infantry

Lieutenant Benjamin C. Lockwood—	G Company, Twenty-second U.S. Infantry
Lieutenant Oscar F. Long—	Fifth U.S. Infantry, Acting Engineering Officer to Lame Deer Expedition
First Lieutenant Samuel T. Hamilton—	L Company, Second U.S. Cavalry
First Lieutenant George W. Baird—	Adjutant to Colonel Nelson A. Miles, Fifth U.S. Infantry
First Lieutenant Paul R. Brown—	Assistant Surgeon, Lame Deer Expedition
Second Lieutenant Edward W. Casey—	Twenty-second U.S. Infantry (commanding a detachment of mounted infantry and Cheyenne scouts)
Second Lieutenant Charles B. Schofield—	L Company, Second U.S. Cavalry
Second Lieutenant Alfred M. Fuller—	F Company, Second U.S. Cavalry
Second Lieutenant Lovell H. Jerome—	H Company, Second U.S. Cavalry
Second Lieutenant Samuel R. Douglass—	Seventh U.S. Infantry (battalion quartermaster the Second U.S. Cavalry)
Sergeant John F. McBlain—	L Company, Second U.S. Cavalry
Private Charles Shrenger—	Fifth U.S. Infantry, orderly to Colonel Nelson A. Miles
Private William Leonard—	L Troop, Second U.S. Cavalry

Cheyenne

TSE-TSEHESE-STAESTE

"THOSE WHO ARE HEARTED ALIKE."

Old Wool Woman (Sweet Taste Woman)	*Antelope Woman*

Twin Woman   Crooked Nose Woman
    Crane Woman
    Red Hood (Red Hat)

Fingers Woman   Black Horse

OLD MAN CHIEFS:
    Morning Star   Little Wolf
    Old Bear   Black Moccasin (Limber
                         Lance)

COUNCIL CHIEFS:
    Crazy Mule   Old Wolf

White Bull (Ice)   Last Bull
Wrapped Hair   Two Moon
Wild Hog   Left Handed Shooter
Bear Who Walks on a Ridge
    (Ridge Bear)
Medicine Bear   Wooden Leg
Tall White Man   White Hawk
Old Man Coyote   Little Creek
Buffalo Calf   Snow Bird (White Bird)
Strong Left Hand (Strong
    Left Arm)
Crazy Mule   Young Little Wolf
Iron Shirt   Standing Elk
Crazy Head—Council Chief   Old Wolf—Council Chief
White Elk   Bobtail Horse
White Thunder   Black Bear
Sleeping Rabbit   Brave Wolf
Roan Bear
Little Wolf—Sweet Medicine
    Chief
Morning Star   Old Bear
Coal Bear—Sacred Hat Priest
Sacred Hat Woman   Black Wolf
American Horse   Black Eagle
Turkey Leg   White Clay

Broken Jaw
Plenty Bears
Red Owl
Magpie Eagle
Weasel Bear
Howling Wolf
Sits in the Night
Spotted Wolf
Crow Split Nose
Spotted Elk
Lame Dog

Wolf Medicine
Beaver Claws
Tangle Hair
Sits Beside His Medicine
White Wolf
Fast Whirlwind
Walks on Crutches
Elk River
Goes After Other Buffalo
Big Horse

Lakota

Crazy Horse (Tsunke Witko)
He Dog
Lame Deer—Mnikowoju *chief*
Little Big Man
Horse Road—Hump's brother
Iron Star (Big Ankle?)—Lame
    Deer's nephew
Touch the Clouds
Roman Nose

Sitting Bull
Four Horns
No Neck
Hump (High Backbone)

Red Bear
High Bear

Casualties

KILLED IN ACTION:
Private Charles Shrenger—   H Company, Second U.S.
                                 Cavalry

Private Frank Glackowsky—   F Company, Second U.S.
                                 Cavalry

Private Charles A.   R Company, Second U.S.
    Martindale—   Cavalry

| *Private Peter Louys—* | H Company, Second U.S. Cavalry |

Lame Deer
Iron Star
Heart Ghost
Shorty

WOUNDED IN ACTION:

Trumpeter William C. Osmer—	F Company, Second U.S. Cavalry
Private Samuel Freyer—	F Company, Second U.S. Cavalry
Private Andrew Jeffers—	G Company, Second U.S. Cavalry
Private Patrick Ryan—	G Company, Second U.S. Cavalry
Private Thomas B. Gilmore—	H Company, Second U.S. Cavalry
Private David L. Brainard—	L Company, Second U.S. Cavalry
Private William Leonard—	L Company, Second U.S. Cavalry
Private Frederick Wilks—	L Company, Second U.S. Cavalry

ARMY-NAVY JOURNAL quoted H.Q., Second U.S. Cavalry, in listing two more wounded:

Private John O'Flynn—	F Company, Second U.S. Cavalry
Private John W. Jones—	F Company, Second U.S. Cavalry
Lieutenant Alfred M. Fuller—	Second Cavalry
Sergeant —— Sharp—	Second Cavalry

In fact, the Great Sioux War was the only conventional war the army ever fought against the trans-Mississippi Indians. It was the type of conflict these Civil War veterans were supposedly used to, where large massed bodies of troops maneuvered for control of battlefields. Reynolds, Crook, and Custer were simply outmaneuvered and defeated in quite conventional battles. It was only when the military could return to the harassing tactics employed so successfully in the Red River War that the Indians were defeated by starvation and exhaustion.

—Paul Andrew Hutton
Phil Sheridan and His Army

Hon. George W. McCrary, Secretary of War,
. . . I now regard the Sioux Indian problem, as a war question, as solved by the operations of General Miles last winter, and by the establishment of the two new posts on the Yellowstone, now assured this summer. Boats come and go now, where a year ago none would venture except with strong guards. Wood-yards are being established to facilitate navigation, and the great mass of the hostiles have been forced to go to the agencies for food and protection, or have fled across the border into British Territory.

—William Tecumseh Sherman
General of the Army
July 17, 1877

[Lame Deer's] band commenced to surrender, in small squads from two to twenty, immediately thereafter, until at length, on the 10th of September, the last of the band, numbering 224, constantly followed and pressed by troops from the command of Colonel Miles, surrendered at Camp Sheridan. The Sioux war was now over.

—Philip H. Sheridan
Lieutenant General
October 25, 1877

The Lame Deer fight was the last battle. For better or worse, the only remaining free-roaming band was now as destitute as the rest and would have no other choice but to go into the agencies and surrender.

The Great Sioux War was over.

—Charles M. Robinson, III
A Good Year to Die

Prologue

"Crazy Horse!"

The first time he heard his name drift up from below, he thought it was nothing more than the cold, harsh whisper of the winter wind taunting him where he sat on an outcrop of rimrock overlooking the valley of the Buffalo Tongue River. The wind always howled and snarled in this country near the foot of the White Mountains.*

Here at last, near the mouth of Prairie Dog Creek, the camp's hunters had stumbled across a few poor buffalo.

"Tsunke Witko!" repeated the faint, distant voice, reverberating a little within the rocks this time.

He knew it was not the wind.

This strange man of the Oglalla looked down, tugging some of his long, brown, wavy hair from his eyes. He had never worn it in braids, never adorned it with anything more than a feather, two feathers at the most. Below him among the rocks and the dirty snow and scrub cedar he spotted movement. The figure of a man took form. He stopped, heaving for breath from the climb, then called out again.

"Crazy Horse! Are you here?"

Slowly, reluctantly, the strange one held up his out-

---

*Bighorn Mountains

stretched arm and waved it side to side. In that hand he gripped the small personal pipe he had come here to smoke among these sacred rocks of the earth, alone. During the Moon of Frost in the Lodge, he often walked away from camp to visit these high places where the wind blew cold, where he could smoke and think. Here he could pray.

But few answers came.

Below him now he made out He Dog's face.

"I am here," Crazy Horse said, hollow with despair that he had been found, and with a sour resignation that his old friend had come looking for him.

Why didn't these people just let him be? Why did this band of Hunkpatila Oglalla still depend upon him? No longer was he a Shirt-Wearer. After he had run off with Black Buffalo Woman, No Water came searching for them and Crazy Horse had been stripped of his shirt. Yet the chiefs chose no one to wear the shirt after Crazy Horse lost his honor for taking another man's woman. Only He Dog continued in the old way of the Shirt-Wearers.

A life that was dying.

"I followed your tracks," He Dog gasped breathlessly when he was close enough to speak without shouting.

For a moment Crazy Horse watched his old friend scrambling among the rocks in his wet, buffalo-hide winter moccasins.

"I did not hide my coming here."

He Dog dusted the icy snow from his hands, tightened the blanket he had belted around his shoulders, then settled back against the rock an arm's length from Crazy Horse. He looked around and sighed, "You come to be among the stones and high places more than you are among your people these days."

"Those people do not need me," he answered with a bitter sadness, staring at the snowy heights of the White Mountains. "They no longer need warriors."

"Your people still look to you."

His eyes locked on He Dog's. "If I choose to lead them in to the White River Agency,* will they follow me?"

---

*Red Cloud's agency for the Oglalla Sioux, near Camp Robinson, Nebraska

He Dog nodded. "They will follow."

The Horse gazed at his old friend a moment, then looked away again. "And if I choose to stay away from the white man's agency . . . who then will they follow?"

"These people will follow you, no matter the path you take."

Sadly, Crazy Horse remembered, "Last winter you started south with your family, He Dog—"

"It was a mistake."

Crazy Horse studied the man's eyes a moment, realizing how his friend must have felt: reluctantly leading his relations south for the agency with some of Old Bear's Shahiyela* when the soldiers attacked them on the Shifting Sands River,† starting a long and terrible year of fighting.

The Horse went back to gazing at the distant bulk of the mountains. "You must realize I leave the camps to get away from the dark, hollow-eyed hunger that has sunken into the faces of the women who suffer in silence," he whispered against the rising whine of the cold wind. "I walk into these hills so that I do not have to listen to the little ones whimpering at the pain in their empty bellies."

"You cannot blame yourself that there are so few buffalo this winter—"

"Will there be more buffalo next winter?" Crazy Horse interrupted. "Will we have enough meat to dry before the first snows?"

"No man can answer that," He Dog finally admitted. "Not even you, *mita kola*, my friend."

Crazy Horse reached out and laid a hand on the warrior's arm. "You are right: I should try no more to understand what I was not meant to understand."

He Dog's eyes narrowed in concern. "Have you slept in these seven days since we fought the Bear Coat# at Belly Butte?"@

---

*Term used by the Lakota to designate the Cheyenne tribe
†Powder River
#Name given Colonel Nelson A. Miles by the tribes of the Northern Plains who fought against him
@Battle of the Butte, January 8, 1877. The Plainsmen Series, vol. 12, *Wolf Mountain Moon*

"I have closed my eyes some," he confessed.

"Perhaps it is time to come down from the rocks. Go sit by your wife's fire," He Dog proposed. "Eat enough to fill your belly for once. Then wrap yourself inside your robe and press your skin against your woman's flesh. When you are done coupling with her, then sleep."

"Fight and eat, ride and couple," Crazy Horse said with a sad grin. "You make it sound like our old days together, *kola.*"

"I am afraid those old days are gone . . . for us both." He Dog struggled with the words.

"They truly do want to make agency loafers of us."

He Dog snorted, bobbing his head in derision, thinking of the Lakota emissary from the faraway soldier chief who had reached Crazy Horse's camp two days earlier saying that the *wasicu** agent at White River knew how the Lakota were suffering. The emissary had journeyed north with the promise of food and blankets and clothing if only Crazy Horse and the Hunkpatila would come in. "Have you decided to send Sword back to Red Cloud and Three Stars Crook† with empty hands?"

"I am not an agency loafer."

"None of us ever will be," He Dog proclaimed. "No matter how much Sword wants to entice his own relations with the *wasicus'* hollow promises."

"We may send him away, back to Red Cloud and Three Stars, but every day in our camp there are more and more who talk of surrender."

Dolefully He Dog vowed, "We will stay strong, we will keep them from leaving as we always have."

"With more of them wanting to surrender now than ever before . . . it is so hard to soldier them all—to break their lodgepoles, to cut up their lodges—when to stay on here with us offers these people so little hope."

Not knowing what to say, He Dog looked away for a few moments as the wind tormented his braids. "An old friend has come to see you."

The casual way He Dog announced this news made Crazy

---

*white man
†General George C. Crook

Horse turn to look at his friend's face. "Is this why you climbed up here to find me?"

"I came to tell you he is here to visit you."

The Horse snorted, "Another rider come from the loafers' agency proposing that I should bring these people in?"

"No," He Dog declared. "Sitting Bull has journeyed south . . . looking for you."

"S-Sitting Bull?" he echoed as it sank in, baffled by the sudden mix of excitement and trepidation from this startling revelation. "He is here?"

He Dog nodded. "Sent me to find you—"

"This is good news! The messengers we sent out found him north of the Elk River!" Crazy Horse bubbled, sensing a momentary leap of joy like the spirit-wings of the red-tailed hawk fluttering beneath his breastbone. For far too many moons there had been little to make him feel hopeful.

"Yes—our messengers found him."

Gripping He Dog's wrist tightly, the Horse asked, "Did he bring the rifles and bullets we wanted him to trade for with the Metis?"

He Dog was a moment before answering. "Sitting Bull has very little anymore. No Lakota is rich these days. The Bear Coat has chased and chased and chased him this winter. The soldiers drove him into the snow twice." He wagged his head and stared at the dirty snow between his moccasins. "No Lakota will ever be rich again."

For a long time, Crazy Horse refused to release the firm hold he had on He Dog's wrist, brooding on the words of his friend, on this announcement that Sitting Bull had come to visit. He let the gale whip the wavy, brown hair across his face as he stared beyond the broad river valley to the rumple of snowy hills on the far side, hills that climbed ever higher toward the slate-gray sky.

"Perhaps there is still hope," the Horse finally said. "If Sitting Bull came here with his people, his warriors and his weapons, without the Bear Coat catching him or turning him back, then perhaps there is still hope that we can reunite our peoples and drive the army from our hunting ground. How many lodges did he bring?"

"No more than ten-times-ten still follow Sitting Bull after this winter of too many soldiers."

He turned quickly on He Dog, a rock in his belly. "That is all?"

"Sitting Bull says there are not many of his people left. Some have gone with Gall. Others are with Crow King. But Sitting Bull has come to talk to you about what your people will do in making war on the soldiers . . . or if you will choose to ride across the Medicine Line into the Land of the Grandmother."

"What my people will do?" he almost shrieked in disbelief. "I cannot decide what these people will do anymore. How can I, when I do not know what I myself am going to do?"

"Sitting Bull is resting in my lodge until I return with you." He Dog seemed anxious to go, to be out of the wind.

Crazy Horse's eyes began to pool with tears stirred by the bitter lash of that cold wind. He blinked to clear them, but it did no good. He became aggravated that he could not see clearly with so many wind-tears. No more could he gaze across the valley, at that rise and fall of the river bluffs, and the hills silhouetted against the mountains beyond.

Not far from this place he had met and defeated Three Stars in a battle that lasted all day.* A few sunrises later he had crushed the Long Hair in a brief, terrible fight beside the Greasy Grass.†

But Crazy Horse could no longer see that far, even from the highest point of these rocks. This cruel winter wind was blinding him as never before.

Slowly Crazy Horse peeled himself from the cold ground and stood, joints and muscles stiff. He turned slightly and held his hand down to He Dog.

They stood together a moment, shoulder to shoulder, in that torment of wind.

"Come," the Horse said as he started down the snowy slope into the valley. "Let's go see if we can learn what the days ahead will bring us."

---

*Battle of the Rosebud, June 17, 1876—*Reap the Whirlwind*, vol. 9, The Plainsmen Series
†Battle of the Little Bighorn, June 25, 1876—*Seize the Sky*, vol. 2, Son of the Plains Trilogy

Chapter 1

27 January 1877

BY TELEGRAPH

DAKOTA.

About the Black Hills.

YANKTON, January 20.—An informal joint
session of the two houses of the Dakota legislature was held this afternoon to listen to ad-
dresses made by parties representing the
interests of people in the Black Hills, concerning their resources, interests, and wants . . . The
statements were all unqualified as to the rich-
ness in mineral wealth, quality of soil and extent of timber. The legislature awaits the action
of congress ratifying the agreement of the Sioux
commissioners to provide settlers with courts
and local organizations, but can do nothing until the Indian title is thus extinguished.

"By what name shall this child be called?"
Seamus Donegan took his eyes off the minister's face,

gazing at Samantha. She nodded slightly, smiling, her eyes brimming with tears.

Gazing down into the face of the infant boy he held across his big arms, the Irishman smiled himself, feeling the tears begin to pool in his eyes.

Finally he looked back into the minister's face and said, "His mother and I shall name him Colin Teig Donegan."

Behind them, Seamus overheard the quiet whispers of the small crowd. In the absence of a chapel, they had gathered in the band quarters that terribly cold morning as the wind whistled through the clay chinking between the logs, tormenting the poorly hung door. Every bench in this tiny room was filled with women and children who had come to pay witness to this christening. Around them stood a semicircle of officers, non-coms, and civilian workers too, men who had set aside everything else this morning to be here as a testament to their affection for the big Irishman, his beloved Samantha, and their firstborn child.

A gauzy wisp of fog slipped from the preacher's lips as he said, "Before this gathering and in the sight of God the Almighty, we have joined our hands and our hearts to celebrate the offering of this child to his Heavenly Father."

Turning to Seamus, the minister reached out and brought the bundled, four-month-old infant to rest across his left arm. The child's big eyes rolled to the side apprehensively, staring up as both Seamus and Samantha stepped close enough for their son to see them. Inching up to the preacher's elbow, Nettie Capron held out the small pewter bowl half filled with water. Into it the preacher dipped the tips of the first two fingers on his right hand.

"Still a bit cold," he whispered to the parents.

Nonetheless he placed the fingertips on the boy's forehead, slowly inscribing a wet streak downward from the hairline to the bridge of the child's nose.

"In the name of the Father . . ."

The minister dipped his fingers into the bowl a second time. "And the Son . . ."

Then he streaked those fingers across the width of the boy's brow as he finished, "And the Holy Ghost, I baptize you Colin Teig Donegan, child of God."

Beside him, Seamus heard the sob catch in Sam's throat. He squeezed her against his side all the more securely as she nestled her head into the crook of his shoulder and dabbed a linen kerchief at her nose.

Looking down into the infant's face, the preacher continued, "A child of God from this day onward till God calls him home—his earthly toil complete, his temporal labors come to an end."

Then the minister turned his gaze at the parents, his eyes touching them both before he asked, "Will you vow to raise young Colin Teig in a way that will please his God in Heaven?"

"Yes," whispered Samantha.

The preacher's eyes stared into Seamus's. "Will you protect him from all earthly harm as he grows right, and straight, and true?"

"I . . . I will," Seamus vowed with a croak.

"And will you see that he is brought to his manhood living in fear of the Lord?"

"We will," Samantha answered quietly, dabbing the kerchief at her eyes.

As the minister gently passed the child to his mother, he said, "Then I pronounce this a great day for God's kingdom here on earth, in this land of rich opportunity, this land of tall peaks and endless prairies. It is a great day here in the sight of God and all these friends that this man and this woman have brought their firstborn son before the maker of us all, dedicating his life to the will of God."

He nudged Seamus and Samantha around to face the congregation. "A great day," he repeated. "Let us celebrate this new life of Colin Teig Donegan!"

The back of the room erupted in spontaneous applause from the men, followed by the happy murmur of the women rising from the pews, wiping their eyes, hugging their own children, and adjusting coats and hats once more. Suddenly it seemed everyone was inching forward and talking at once, filling that tiny log building with joyful celebration.

Far from the din of battle that was the life's work of so many stationed here at Fort Laramie, Dakota Territory. Far, far from the rattle of gunfire, the boom of cannon, the cries of the wounded, and the whimpers of those drawing their last breath.

"When's a fella gonna have hisself a chance to drink his good wishes to this here man-child of yours?"

Seamus looked up at the sound of the familiar voice, star-

ing into the knots of men at the back of the chapel, finding
the face of Billy Garnett.

"Yes, scout Donegan!" another voice called out before
Seamus had a chance to open his mouth. "When do the Irish
get us a chance to celebrate with you this wonderful day?"

"Johnny Bourke!" he cried. "Bless your soul for coming
over from Camp Robinson to share this day with us!"

Bourke fought his way forward through the crowd, smiling
broadly beneath the sweep of his bristling mustache.

"I never figured you to come," Seamus said, a clutch in
his chest as Crook's favorite lieutenant came up, offering his
hand. Donegan pushed it aside and pulled Bourke into a
fierce embrace.

When the lieutenant caught his breath and pulled back to
arm's length, he said, "You think I'd let a little snow and
cold keep me away from this day, Seamus Donegan? Not
after all that we've seen each other through on the Powder
and with Mackenzie on the Red Fork!"*

Seamus pulled Bourke close again, whispering in his ear,
"God bless you for it, Johnny. It means the world to me
you're here."

Earlier that morning, Samantha had joined her husband at
the window, cradling their son in her arms.

Dawn had arrived clear and oh, so cold. For two days it
had stormed off and on, leaving close to a foot of new snow.
But it was what the winds had done with it that had made
Seamus and Samantha fear they would have to postpone
their son's christening.

The minister had come by before breakfast saying he had
gotten a fire started in the band quarters' iron stove that
would go a long way to knocking some of the chill off the
tiny room before folks began to arrive at midmorning.

"Anyone who's coming to Fort Laramie for this christening will be here already," the preacher reminded them earlier. Then he had looked out at the remnants of the recent
storm and said, "God watch over any man who finds himself
out in that."

"Are you sure you want to take Colin out in that cold?"
Seamus had asked Samantha. He figured this matter of prop-

---

*Dull Knife Battle, November 25, 1876—*A Cold Day in Hell*,
vol. 11, The Plainsmen Series

erly caring for babes was bound to be a mystery to him for a long, long time.

"I will see that he and I are bundled up properly," Sam had cooed. "He's been out in the cold before, Seamus. I'll just see that I wrap the folds of the blanket loosely over his face—"

"But you never had him out in nothing near as cold as this morning," the Irishman interrupted with a wag of his head.

"You fought your last two battles in weather like this," Samantha said as she put her unoccupied arm around his waist and buried her face against her husband's chest. "You've lived for weeks and weeks out in cold like this. I think your son and his mother can stand it long enough to cross the parade and reach the band quarters."

"So cold I don't figure there'll be many folks come out to join us," he said as he held them both in the circle of his arms. "Just don't want you disappointed when the first bench isn't filled 'cause it's so bleeming cold."

But at the band quarters the first three benches were filled even before Seamus and Sam got there—and on both sides of that short aisle!

More and more the room bustled with activity and anticipation, and finally the morning gun sounded and the great flag unfurled. Those stripes and blue field of stars slowly climbed up that huge seafarer's mast of a flag-pole at the center of the sugar-crusted parade. Here and there details of soldiers went about their business, their long, buffalo-fur coats slurring the steep drifts, tall collars turned up against the wind that whipped the snow into glittering streamers along the ground as the rosy sun climbed into the stunning blue cloudless sky. That shade of blue he had only seen here in the west with the passing of a terrible storm.

In minutes there were folks streaming toward the building from all directions like prairie ants homing in on their hill. It filled his heart to look over all those faces freshly scrubbed and shaved, faces so rosy from the terrible cold as they squeezed into every last seat on the half-log benches, then started filling the spaces along the walls and frosted windows. When the minister finally showed up, he had to squeeze in the door to side-step his way to the front of the room where he removed his coat and muffler. Then he turned and looked out upon that hushed assembly with the grandest of smiles.

"See how proud he is!" Sam whispered into Seamus's ear

off to the side of the room. "He's never had this big a crowd on Sunday!"

The preacher motioned the Irishman forward with his wife and their young child as the crowded room fell silent.

"Are we ready to baptize this boy of yours at last, Mr. Donegan?"

"W-we are," he answered self-consciously.

"Very well, my brethren," the minister replied, looking over the breathless throng. "Let's take up our hymnbooks and sing ourselves a song of this joyous occasion, a song requested by the child's mother: 'Jesus, Friend, So Kind and Gentle.'"

As soon as the preacher led off, a few unsteady male voices dared to join the many women who dived right in as if they knew the words by heart.

> *Jesus, friend, so kind and gentle,*
> *Little ones we bring to Thee;*
> *Grant to them Thy dearest blessing,*
> *Let Thine arms around them be;*
> *Now enfold them in Thy goodness,*
> *From all danger keep them free.*

On the last line, Samantha inched herself right against Seamus's side, looking up at him with a brief flicker of those bottle-green eyes.

When they had completed all three stanzas of the song, the preacher stood before them a moment, still grinning widely, then sighed. "I don't think I've ever heard such a joyful noise in this place! How wonderful!" he gushed as he flipped the page of his hymnal. "I'm so taken by this special occasion I would like to sing the very next song in your books. If you'll turn the page, I'll lead off."

> *Lord Jesus Christ, our Lord most dear,*
> *As Thou wast once an infant here,*
> *So give this child of Thine, we pray,*
> *Thy grace and blessing day by day.*

"And for our final hymn, Mrs. Donegan requested the next song in memory of the child's grandmother—God rest her soul in Ireland."

Seamus bent a little, whispering in her ear, "Thank you."
Samantha smiled at him as she began singing the words
with the others in the room, shifting the blanket-wrapped
bundle to her husband's arms. The way she looked up at
Seamus made him suddenly think on things he had long ago
pushed to the back of his mind. Here and now he wished
that his mother were still alive to know her grandson, to hold
him . . .

> *Blessed Jesus, here are we,*
> *Thy beloved word obeying.*

How Seamus wished his mother had survived those years
of blight and famine and black death in Ireland to reach this
faraway land of Amerikay with her son and brothers. Countless times he hoped that she had joined him on that stinking
ship instead of staying behind in the land of their birth.

> *Now this child doth come to Thee*
> *As Thou biddest in Thy saying . . .*

Then he wished her brothers could have been here to
stand beside him too. Ian O'Roarke—far out there in
Oregon country with his own family, a solid man given to
little nonsense, a man firmly planted in his own ground as
he had always wanted. And Uncle Liam . . . oh, Liam! That
big, raucous, footloose leprechaun of a man. Buried now
beside that nameless river where Forsyth's fifty scouts had
held out against better than five hundred of Roman Nose's
finest horsemen across nine blistering days.*

> *Let the little ones be given unto me;*
> *Of such is the kingdom of heaven.*

Seamus found himself gazing down at his son's face as the
others finished the song around them. With the boy cradled
across his left arm, he slowly became aware that the singing

---

*Battle of Beecher Island, September, 1868—*The Stalkers*, vol.
3, The Plainsmen Series

had stopped, aware that the minister was speaking in silver tones to the gathering in that chilly log and plank house.

It had been so, so hard to decide upon a name for the child as Seamus rode south from the Tongue River battlefield where Colonel Nelson A. Miles had collided with Crazy Horse in battle.* Should he name this boy after his Uncle Liam, and perhaps curse the child for all the rest of his days with the same rootless wanderlust that drove Seamus's uncle always to seek out what lay beyond the next band of hills? Or, should he name the boy after his Uncle Ian, a more solid, rooted, sensible sort? Back and forth, mile after endlessly cold mile Seamus had grappled with it as he plodded south toward the Powder River, south to Fort Fetterman, and finally to this reunion with his little family here at the army's Laramie post.

He and Samantha hadn't decided upon the name until late the night before the christening, after talking it back and forth and sideways all these days since Seamus had shown up on the hillside to the north of the fort. In the candle-lit closeness of their little room, their breath issuing in steamy vapors as they lay huddled beneath their mountain of blankets while the storm spent itself and the howling wind battered the sides of Old Bedlam, they had bent all the possibilities this way and that, front and back, until they both knew they had found the proper name for the child asleep beside them in his crib.

Colin Teig Donegan.

"A damned sight better than naming the wee lad after his father," Seamus had snorted as he finally snuffed out the candle and closed his eyes, drawing her against him.

"Wouldn't been so bad," Sam had said quietly. "A strong son carrying on the name of his dear father. If you hadn't come back, I was going to name him—"

"After me!" he interrupted. "A curse that'd been, woman!"

She playfully yanked a long strand of his hair that spilled across his shoulder as she nestled her cheek against his neck. "Proud he would have been, growing up to know who his father was."

"It's better this way," he whispered at last in the frosty

---

*Battle of the Butte

darkness, speaking his words against the tangle of her curls spilling beneath his chin like seafoam.

"Yes, 'tis better this way," she answered. "I have my husband back in my arms. And our son has a name."

Chapter 2

Hoop-and-Stick Game Moon
1877

BY TELEGRAPH

The Black Hills Treaty, Etc.

Washington, January 23.—The house committee on Indian affairs to-day agreed to recommend the passage of Seelye's bill to ratify the arrangement made with the Sioux Indians by the United States commission last October, for the relinquishment of their title to the Black Hills country, etc.

Old Wool Woman took the offered tin cup, felt its warmth in her cold, bony hands, smelled its heady aroma and bent to sip the coffee, her eyes watching the handful of white men over the rim of her cup.

This wasn't something the *ve-ho-e** did to his prisoners, was it? Would these soldiers bring her here to drink strong coffee sweetened with the white sand only to torture and kill her?

It simply could not be, she convinced herself, studying the

---

*White man

face of the Bear Coat, unless his eyes were a mask to what truly lay in his heart. Old Wool Woman could not believe the soldier chief had treachery in mind when he sent Big Leggings* to fetch her to this log lodge where a fire hissed and crackled in a metal box at the corner of the room. She and the other *Ohmeseheso*† prisoners had not wanted for warmth from the moment of their capture. Nor had they gone hungry. They had as much as they wanted to eat every day. Especially in the ten days since they had reached this collection of log lodges the soldiers had erected at the mouth of the Tongue River.

She let a smile grow inside her, thinking how much the young Black Horse ate of the soldiers' food. And when he had finished the youngster always asked the other prisoners if they had any food they weren't going to eat. He always cleaned everyone's plates. Growing, just the way her young sons had grown when they were becoming young men like Black Horse.

For a moment Old Wool Woman felt a stab of pain where the smile had been, remembering. Suddenly thrust back in time to think of sons killed by *ve-ho-e* soldiers. Forced to recall how she lost her husband in battle against Three Finger Kenzie's soldiers. Reflecting on her life as Sweet Taste Woman, raising babes and coupling with Black White Man, and wandering after the buffalo season upon season. That life was gone in the blink of an eye.

Now she was Old Wool Woman, her name changed because there was little left in her life that was sweet at all. Her name changed because all that she had managed to drag from their lodge the morning of Three Fingers Kenzie's attack on their village was an old wool blanket. Grease- and blood-stained, smoked beside many fires, it became such a source of pride for her. Despite its crust of mud and ragged edges, it had sustained her through a terrible ordeal. It sustained her still.

She sipped her coffee and glanced at Big Leggings, the one her people called "White" because of the half-breed's fair

---

*Johnny Bruguier
†Term used by the Northern Cheyenne to designate themselves as the "Northern People"

complexion. Word in the camps of the Crazy Horse people
was that he was a traitor to Buffalo Bull Sitting Down*

The previous autumn while the Hunkpapa hunted buffalo,
Big Leggings had been living with the Lakota warrior bands,
interpreting for Buffalo Bull Sitting Down when the Bear
Coat brought his soldiers after them to fight. But something
soon made Big Leggings abandon the Hunkpapa and run off
to join the soldiers. Besides speaking the white man's tongue,
the half-breed spoke good Lakota, and also managed to
make himself crudely understood in the language of the Shahiyela. On their trip north from the fight at Belly Butte, Big
Leggings would mix his Shahiyela and Lakota when he
talked with her and the other prisoners. But it did not matter
to Old Wool Woman. She understood as much Lakota as
Big Leggings did. For a long time her people had remained
close to the Oglalla: camping, hunting and fighting together,
intermarrying, raising families in both camps.

That was why Crazy Horse had managed to hurt so many
of the survivors of the fight with Three Fingers Kenzie when
they came looking for him. Behind their hands many still
whispered how the Oglalla war chief might as well have
turned them away. Without compassion, he had told the Shahiyela survivors his Lakota people did not have enough for
themselves. Besides, Crazy Horse had explained, it was plain
to him that the soldiers were hunting down the Shahiyela,
not the Lakota.

Wasn't it true that theirs was the first village the soldiers
had struck back in the Light Snow Moon?†

And weren't the Shahiyela leading the villages when the
Long Hair's soldiers attacked them on the Greasy Grass? In
fact, didn't the fiercest of the fighting occur directly across
the river from the *Ohmeseheso* village?

Wasn't it true that Three Stars Crook sent Three Finger
Kenzie to destroy the Shahiyela in the White Mountains? So
wasn't it clear to everyone, Crazy Horse demanded, that the
soldiers were making war on the Shahiyela?

---

*Cheyenne name for Sitting Bull
†Reynolds's Fight on Powder River, March 17, 1876—*Blood
Song*, vol. 8, The Plainsmen Series

Suddenly the Bear Coat was talking as he arose from behind the big wood box covered with a profusion of flat pieces
of thin white parfleche, each adorned with long lines or
strange picture writing, scratched upon their surface. He
went to the fire-box in the corner of the room and poked in
a long twig. He lit his pipe and turned back to look at Old
Wool Woman.

When the soldier chief finished speaking, Big Leggings
stood and dragged over the three-legged stool he was sitting
on. He placed it closer to her and settled himself as she
watched him intently for any signs of betrayal. She was alone
here. The two other women were back with the children tonight. As she looked into Big Leggings's eyes, Old Wool
Woman said a quick prayer to the Everywhere Spirit that
she would return to the other prisoners when the soldiers
were done with her. She prayed that even if these *ve-ho-e*
beat her, abused her, they would not kill her.

"The Bear Coat had me bring you here because you are
the oldest," Big Leggings explained, speaking haltingly in her
tongue.

"Is it easier for you to speak Lakota?" she asked after
swallowing her coffee.

"Most times," he grinned at her. "As long as you understand what I say, and I know what you say to me, we can
talk."

She glanced at the other soldiers, then brought her eyes
back to the half-breed. "If I am the oldest, why am I here?"

"The Bear Coat hopes that you will understand . . . because you are the oldest."

"Understand?"

"The soldier chief does not want to fight the Shahiyela."

Remembering the words of Crazy Horse, Old Wool
Woman asked, "Are you saying the Bear Coat's soldiers
want only to fight the Lakota?"

"No," and he shook his head. "The Bear Coat does not
want to fight any of the warrior bands. If they would come
here to surrender, he would not go looking for them. He does
not want any harm to come to the Shahiyela. He wants to
make peace with them."

When Big Leggings paused, the Bear Coat spoke as he

warmed his hands over that fire in the metal box. The interpreter turned back to Old Wool Woman.

"The soldier chief wants to ask you if there is any way you can help bring the Shahiyela in to this soldier fort peacefully so that no harm will come to them."

"May I have more coffee?"

Big Leggings grinned and stood, turning to the stove for the big, blackened pot. She was already thinking, surprised to find that she wanted to help the Bear Coat, to help the *ve-ho-e* who had killed her sons and husband. It surprised her to be sitting here among these soldiers, the one they asked for help.

Old Wool Woman took back the cup and waited as the interpreter heaped more of the sweet grains into her coffee then stirred it for her. She watched the small metal spoon go round and round in the cup, causing the black liquid to go round and round with it. She wistfully thought of her lodge, round as that cup, missing it and the life she had lived with Black White Man. Unlike the Shahiyela, the white man lived in a square world. Her people lived in a round world. Slept in a round lodge . . .

"In our village," she suddenly blurted, her eyes boring into his, "there is a lodge where all men are safe."

"All men," he repeated, "No matter if they are white?"

"All men, no matter if they are enemy or not."

Big Leggings squatted before her and licked the spoon he had used to stir her coffee. "Tell me of this lodge."

"It stands at the center of the camp crescent. It is a powerful place. A medicine lodge. It belongs to the keeper of *Esevone*."

"*Ese . . . vone*?" he echoed.

"The Sacred Buffalo Hat."

"I have heard of it. Tell me how this hat can help."

Old Wool Woman explained, "If there is fighting in the village, and an enemy jumps inside the door of this lodge, the fighting will stop. He is safe inside the lodge."

Big Leggings's eyes grew large. He looked at the Bear Coat and nodded eagerly. "Go on!" he said to her.

"Once that enemy is inside this sacred lodge, the keeper of the hat will perform the peace ceremony. The Sacred Hat Priest and the Old Man Chiefs will smoke the pipe with him. Peace is made through smoking the pipe, for the pipe never fails. It is a prayer made to the Everywhere Spirit."

The interpreter immediately turned to chatter in the white man's tongue to the Bear Coat. As she watched the soldier chief's face, Old Wool Woman saw him smile behind his dark beard, saw his eyes turn to her. He looked pleased with her news.

"The Bear Coat is very, very pleased," the interpreter said to her. "This is the way we will have a chance to talk to your chiefs and tell them of the soldier chief's wish to have peace."

"You and the Bear Coat are going to find my people's village and slip inside the Sacred Hat Lodge?"

He wagged his head and explained slowly in her tongue. "When I say we, I do not mean me and the Bear Coat. I mean *you* and me. The Bear Coat is sending you and me to find your village. He wants us to take along presents: coffee, and lots of sugar, dried fruit, bacon and beans."

"And tobacco?"

Big Leggings nodded enthusiastically. "Yes, lots of to-bacco."

"This is good," she told the interpreter, feeling a little ner-vous. "The warrior camps have not had any tobacco for a long, long time now."

Old Wool Woman sipped her coffee while Big Leggings and the Bear Coat talked with the others. She watched the smiles on their faces, their animated eyes, the excited tone of their foreign words as they talked to one another. She did not have to understand their tongue to know that what she had told these *ve-ho-e* was very, very good news.

Perhaps she really could do something to help her people. War had brought them only devastation and poverty, wan-dering and death. Perhaps she would be that instrument the Everywhere Spirit would use to bring about a just peace with the soldiers so that no more of her people had to die.

Big Leggings turned suddenly and gripped her thin, bony hands between his. Her coffee cup trembled, not from fear, but from a keen, ready anticipation. She saw the expectation firing the interpreter's eyes. Yes, Old Wool Woman did in-deed tremble from her own mounting excitement.

"Will we go soon?" she asked.

"Four, perhaps five, days. And when we find the Shahiyela camp," Big Leggings told her, his deep voice rising, "it is a matter of life or death that you help me find that Sacred Hat Lodge!"

The Lakota wolves had returned after many days of trailing the Bear Coat's soldiers back to their fort. Day after day the ten scouts, mounted on the strongest horses left among the warrior camps, had watched for a chance to slip in close enough to free the captives. Instead, the warriors could only watch the soldiers reach their fort at the mouth of the Buffalo Tongue River with their prisoners. They had little choice but to turn back for the village with empty hands and small hearts.

The *Mnikowoju** chief watched the ten slowly crossing an icy Prairie Dog Creek on their weary animals as small, icy flakes danced around them. They did not ride like victors. They looked every bit as whipped and weary as their ponies. There were only ten riders. No others. The Bear Coat still held the Shahiyela.

So much had taken place while those ten riders had been gone. Across four days Sitting Bull, Crazy Horse, and the other Lakota chiefs sat in council with Shahiyela leaders, men like Morning Star and Little Wolf, Two Moon and Old Bear, the Sacred Hat Priest. Each day they smoked and passed the pipe and talked until the sun had run its winter race across the sky. And in the end two things grew certain.

Despite what Sitting Bull had managed to trade from the Red River Slotas after the Bear Coat's soldiers had twice attacked his people, there were not enough guns and bullets to wage war on the *wasicu* as they had the previous spring and summer.

Just as certain, no longer was there the same united resolve among the warrior bands, the resolve that Sitting Bull once had tapped within each fighting man, the resolve that once made them rise up and make a stand whereas before they had only raided, skirmished, and fought long enough for the villages to escape.

It disgusted Lame Deer the way his old friends dithered

---

*Lakota for *Minnicoujou*, which is the spelling of the word as used on the tribal flag and deliberated over what, to him, was not worth argument. It angered him because there really was but one path to take. While Sitting Bull, No Neck, and others talked of fleeing north into the Land of the Grandmother, Crazy Horse and the rest discussed marching south when the weather broke, so they could slip back onto the reservations.

The Grandmother's soldiers would treat them squarely, Sitting Bull's allies said. There would be buffalo. The camps would be left in peace north across the Medicine Line.

But winter stays long in that far place, others protested. Even the summer days can be cool, and the nights wet. Besides, the Land of the Grandmother had never been our land. No matter how many Lakota go there, it never will be our land.

Why are you arguing this way? Lame Deer wanted to yell. Couldn't the other chiefs see that there was really only one choice?

In the end it deeply saddened him that none of the other leaders could see that there was a third path open to them. They did not have to flee to a faraway land where they were unwelcome strangers. And they did not have to slip back onto the agencies with their tails tucked between their legs just because the women were hungry and the children were sick.

A warrior did not give up!

"As for me," Lame Deer announced after Sitting Bull had declared he would leave in the morning for the Land of the Grandmother, "neither path you have offered suits my *Mnikowoju* people. Any lodge, any warrior from any camp who wishes to join me may come with us. We are not giving up, no matter what the *wasicu* might promise us—because we all know his promises are like dust in a strong wind."

"What will you do?" asked No Neck.

"We will hunt buffalo and elk, antelope and deer, as we always have," Lame Deer explained as he rose to his feet. "And we will continue to wander these hunting grounds our peoples have been given by *Wakan Tanka*. Never will we hold out our hands to take what the white man offers us!"

Chapter 3

27 January 1877

BY TELEGRAPH

Army Re-organization.

WASHINGTON, January 27.—The commission appointed to prepare a plan for a re-organization of the army, report to the president that there has been a very general discussion and interchange of opinions, but other important matters have so occupied them that they have not been able to give the subject that attention and deliberation its importance demands, and cannot therefore make recommendations.

Everyone was Irish today.

With the music and revelry of this celebration for young Colin Teig, everyone who came that afternoon had a touch of the Irish in them.

Both a sergeant from one of the infantry companies and a corporal from a cavalry outfit brought their scratched and scuffed violin cases. Another cavalryman brought his well-traveled banjo, while a fourth pulled a harmonica and jew's harp from the pocket of his coat the moment he stepped inside the rooms where others had hurriedly pushed all the furniture back against the walls.

How just the sight of those musical instruments made Samantha's eyes sparkle with mischief! Why, not even in Denver or Cheyenne City had the two of them listened, much less danced, to lively music. Then he remembered—they hadn't danced since their wedding day on Sharp Grover's place back in the summer of 1875 when Mackenzie's Fourth Cavalry and Miles's Fifth Infantry brought an end to the Great Buffalo War with the Comanche, Kiowa, and Southern Cheyenne.*

"May I have this dance, madam?" he asked, slipping his arm around her waist.

Samantha turned, grinning as she rarely did, her pale, slightly freckled face flush with the cold, rosy with excitement. How those green eyes did reflect her love for him. "What of Colin?"

"Here," Martha Luhn said, taking the infant from Sam's arms. "Give the li'l tyke to me and go dance with your mister!"

Seamus winked at the officer's wife. "Thank you, Martha." Then he took a step back, laid his right arm across his waist and bowed gallantly. "Mrs. Donegan, would you do me the honor of this dance?"

How she made his heart flutter as she gazed at him beneath those long eyelashes, cocking her head to the side coyly, then curtsying elegantly. "If you'll watch out for my feet with those big hooves of yours—"

Before she could finish, he seized her left hand and flung his right arm around her. He whirled Samantha out among the few who were daring enough to venture into the center of the room with that first song the fiddlers and banjo player began to scratch out.

Round and round he whirled her with crazed abandon, sensing her finally relax as she gave herself over to him while he slipped into a clumsy rhythm—twirling her round and round, listening to the thumping of other feet, the clapping of all those hands, the twang-twang-twang of the jew's harp. And with every step he made sure not to raise one of his big feet off the ground far enough to catch one of hers beneath it.

"I didn't take you fellers for Irish!" he exclaimed breathlessly as he rolled up before the musicians after a second song, Samantha clasped against him beneath an arm.

"My grandpappy," explained one who held a violin. "He taught me what I know of fiddling."

"I ain't Irish," the older infantryman admitted with a wag of his head and a big smile emerging beneath his shaggy horseshoe of a mustache. His sergeant's chevrons were well faded from many a washing, many a march beneath the western sun. "But I learned my Irish tunes during the war against the Johnnies."

Everyone was Irish today! Every last woman and child, every last man jack of them. When those fiddles started crying and that banjo began plinking, when a few of those women got out there in the middle of it all and hiked up their layers of skirts and petticoats only high enough to allow them to kick up their heels and clog until they were breathless and beaded in sweat, then Seamus knew they couldn't have had a better christening celebration in County Kilkenny itself.

From time to time Seamus would wheel onto the floor with young Colin Teig wrapped securely in his arms, where father and son would bend and whirl and spin, eliciting wild giggles from the boy as he carried him round and round, and in among the other dancers. As the pair wheeled past, all of them reached out to pinch a cheek or pat the youngster's arm. At other times, Seamus would sit in one of the simple ladder-backed chairs, little Colin propped on his knee so the youngster faced the dancers, and there he bounced and waggled his firstborn in time to the music.

"Seamus," Samantha said later. "Let me take him."

"We're doing just fine here together, him and me!" Seamus protested as Sam held out her hands.

She leaned forward to whisper, "You've got to find something more to drink, husband."

"More still?" he squeaked in disbelief. "It feels like I just got back from the trader's with that last armload!"

"Dancing works up a sweat, Mr. Donegan," Nettie Capron said at Samantha's side. "And there's a heap o' dancing going on here for your son's day!"

"For the love of the Virgin Mary," he exclaimed as he

stood, handing the boy to his mother. "I'll go see what I can haggle out of Collins now."

Samantha kissed the boy's cheek as the child twisted himself in her arms so he could watch all the action. "Where are you getting the money for all this ... this celebration in a bottle you're buying everyone, Seamus?"

"Not yours to worry about, my bride," and he smiled down at her, squeezing her against him.

"I can only imagine you had some pay built up for all that time you were away," she said, standing on her toes and speaking into his ear. "But, I can't imagine how you'd have anything left after the two dresses and that pair of new blankets, along with that cloth you bought for me to make Colin some clothes. This army must pay you much better to scout for it than it pays its own officers!"

He kissed Sam lightly, squarely on the mouth, something he rarely did in public. Then looked down into those green eyes filled with surprise. "Yes, my beautiful bride, mother of my son. The army pays its scouts well enough that I can provide for my family without worry. I'll be back from the trader's straightaway."

Bundled in their coats and mufflers and hats against the horrid cold, the men stepped out on the front porch from time to time to puff on their pipes or smoke their cheroots away from the women and children who frolicked and laughed inside. Now for a third time Seamus himself pulled on his coat and went outside, trudging quickly through the snow to trader Collins's saloon where he purchased another armload of brown and green bottles—more whiskey for the hard drinkers, as well as brandy for the ladies and those who preferred to sip their libations.

"You'll give me a fair price now?" he had prodded the trader the day before when working out their arrangement.

Collins had licked his lower lip. "You said you were paying in cash? No I.O.U. drawn against future payroll?"

Seamus had grinned and patted the lower right pocket of his worn vest. "Army scrip, trader. I'll pay you now for what we'll drink tomorrow. Now tell me, just how fair you going to make your prices for a father what has a naming to celebrate?"

Donegan did indeed have money. For the first time in his life he had no worry in buying his friends their drinks. Nor did he have any fear he would end up drinking away everything and have nothing left for Samantha and Colin Teig. General George Crook had seen to that.

The morning after he had returned to Fort Laramie, right after untangling himself from his wife's leggy warmth, Seamus had reported to the post commander's office.

"There's no doubt what you've come for, Mr. Donegan," Major Andrew E. Evans said as he shuffled through some papers atop a desk littered with duty rosters and daily reports from Camp Robinson.

Standing stiffly on the other side of the desk, Seamus glanced at the post's commanding officer. The two of them had shared the battlefield at the Rosebud, shared Crook's horse-meat march to the Black Hills. "If you mean the money that's to be waiting for me, Colonel," he replied, using Evans's brevet rank, "that's what I've come for."

"Here it is," Laramie's commander sighed, pulling out a brown envelope. Folding back its flap, the major in the Third U.S. Cavalry pulled out a bundle of scrip enclosed within a sheet of paper. Dropping the stack of army pay on the desk, Evans quickly reread the page. "Yes, I remember this now." He looked up at Donegan. "General Crook left orders that I was to hold this until your return . . . or, until the first of May."

"The first of May, Colonel?"

Setting the paper down, the major cleared his throat and said, "At that time I was to call in your missus. With orders to explain what might have happened to you. And to give her this money at that time."

"Just what Crook and Mackenzie said they'd do."

"Are you surprised," asked the officer of the day, an infantryman, as he stepped up to Evans's elbow, "that either of them would be men of honor?"

"Colonel Evans here can tell you just how much stock I put in the word of another man."

"So, Mr. Donegan," Evans began, picking up the bundle of scrip, "here you are. As guaranteed by General Crook himself. All I need you to do is to sign this voucher that you've received—"

"I don't want it all, sir," he interrupted, watching his words bring Evans up short.

"Not all?"

"Those orders left by General Crook, sir? If I could make the same request of you personally, Colonel, I'd be in your debt."

"The same request?"

"I'll take some of the money, yes, sir. To buy my bride a new dress or two. Wrangle some whiskey out of the trader, and have ourselves a proper Irish christening for my boy. The rest, I want you to hang onto for safekeeping."

"Hang onto your pay, is it?"

"Yes. I'd be in your debt if you'd hold most of it for me."

"I'm no banker, Mr. Donegan."

"And I'm no eleven-dollar-a-month soldier, Colonel." He tried to make it come out as gently as he could. "But there's still unfinished business up north, and I figure that means there'll be some work for a man who's had him some experience guiding for General Miles's army."

"Work up north, you say."

"They say Sitting Bull's north of the Missouri—likely heading for Canada where he'll be out of reach," the Irishman explained. "And Crazy Horse is somewhere south of the Yellowstone. Miles plans on going after him as soon as the rivers free up."

"And you'll be going with Miles, I assume?"

"It's what I do, Colonel. Until this land is safe for my wife and boy, until I can find another way to put a roof over their heads and food in their bellies—I'll be an army scout. Yes, sir. When General Miles marches south from Tongue River Cantonment this spring, I plan on being with his column."

Slowly a smile of admiration came across Evans's face. "So perhaps you can tell me, Mr. Donegan. How much are two women's dresses, along with enough whiskey to throw yourself a good Irish celebration, all going to cost you?"

He felt a flutter in his chest that he hadn't felt in so, so long. Rather than scraping by hard-scrabble, living with what he was given or could beg off others, Seamus Donegan could now afford the best of what he wanted.

"I s'pose I could have you give me fifty dollars of that scrip."

"And I'll keep the rest here for you," Evans said as he bent over the paper, pulled a pen from its holder, and dipped it in the inkwell.

"For me, or for my wife, sir."

The major stayed his hand a moment, then straightened and looked squarely into Donegan's eyes. "You tell me a date I should expect you back from the north country, Mr. Donegan. A date you will want me to call your missus to my office."

He cleared his throat, glanced at the two other soldiers, then stared out the frost-rimed window to the stone guardhouse in the distance. "I figure, Colonel . . . I should be back by autumn."

"Shall we make it the end of summer then?"

"Yes, sir. The war should be over then."

"All right," Evans said and went back to writing. "We'll put it down here. By 1 September 1877." When he had finished, he turned the paper around and held out the pen to the Irishman. "I need you to sign there at the bottom, Mr. Donegan. To show that I'm giving you fifty of your dollars."

Taking the pen clumsily in his big hand, Seamus suddenly felt the hot flush of self-consciousness. He rolled it over and over between his fingers, staring at it. So odd. He couldn't remember the last time he had held a pen in his hand.

"You do know how to write, don't you, Mr. Donegan?"

"Yes, Colonel," he replied, then bent over the page and thoughtfully, precisely, wrote his name. "It's just been a long, long time."

Taking up the page, the major blew on the civilian's signature as he held out a small stack of the army scrip. "Your fifty dollars."

"Thank you, Colonel."

"One more thing, Mr. Donegan," the post commander said as the civilian was turning to leave. "Am I invited to this christening for your son?"

"Yes, Colonel! By all means. We've shared the battlefield. Come and celebrate with my family! Bring your wife. *Your* family, sir." Then he quickly looked at the other officers behind Evans. "Your men as well. The more's the better to us Irish. Come and bring your families and celebrate with me and my wife."

"It would be an honor, Mr. Donegan," Evans said as he drew himself up and saluted the surprised civilian. "To attend the naming of a child born to an honorable man who sees so well to his family's needs, the same way he steps forward to play such a selfless role in his nation's business. I'll be there."

Chapter 4

1 February 1877

BY TELEGRAPH

MISSOURI.

The Ice Breaking Up Again.
ST. LOUIS, January 31.—The Steamer Belle St. Louis was cut down by moving ice to-day at St. Genevieve, some sixty miles from here, and will probably be a total loss. She was owned by the Belle St. Louis Transportation company, and had run in the Missouri river until that river closed last fall, when she went into the Memphis trade and was *en route* to that city when she was forced to lay up on account of ice . . . Most of the steamers at the levee and along shore between here and the arsenal have steam up, so that they may be ready to move with the ice when it starts, and various other precautions have been taken to insure against the destruction of river craft and property.

"You sure I can't talk you into staying for the spring campaign?"

Luther S. Kelly turned to find Colonel Nelson A. Miles approaching. "No, General," he replied, respectfully using the officer's brevet rank. "Pretty much made up my mind. I haven't been east since the Civil War."

Kelly continued to stand at the edge of the trees, watching the small detail of mounted infantry wrangle a half-dozen hardy pack mules away from Tongue River Cantonment. Two civilian riders were leading the soldiers south that cold, gray, snowy morning.

"I can understand your homesickness," Miles sympathized.

"Not so much that, General," Luther attempted to explain as he watched the riders angle up a snowy hillside in single file. "I just figure right now is about the best time for me to get back there to see what friends and family I have left."

"They won't all come in, Luther," Miles admitted glumly after a moment of silence. "No matter how sweet the plum I hold out to them."

"I don't figure they all will, either."

"And those who remain out will be the hardest of the lot, don't you know," the soldier sighed in resignation. "Those who refuse to surrender will be the toughest bastards to drive back to their agencies."

"You've been chivvying the toughest of the bastards all winter, General. Sitting Bull's holdouts up there on the Missouri. And the Crazy Horse village on up the Tongue. They don't get any more wild than them two."

"Trouble is, Luther—about all that's left are the wildest of the wild ones. The sort who won't even consider surrender and a new way of life on the reservations. I'm coming to believe we really are going to have to rub out the last of these sons of bitches."

"Yellowstone" Kelly stood in silence for a few moments, watching until the last of the pack-mules disappeared from sight around the river bluff. Only then did he say, "But I will admit that you and Bruguier are giving it one hell of a shot, General. Sending that Cheyenne woman was a real stroke of genius on your part."

"I'll say," Miles agreed proudly. "More than pale hope, I have a good feeling this operation of mine will bear fruit by spring. If that detail of soldiers can find the hostile Cheyenne camp, and if that woman can slip the half-breed into camp without getting themselves killed, then they just might have a chance of convincing their leaders that I am a fair man.''

"No better way of showing them just how fair you can be than to send the woman to tell firsthand how well the Bear Coat's treated his prisoners," Kelly replied. "They've been kept warm and dry, fed all they could possibly eat. A damn sight better those captives have had it here with your soldiers than those Cheyenne and Sioux have it in their camps right now."

"But that's what keeps nagging me, Luther," Miles confided to the twenty-eight-year-old scout. "I don't know if this terrible cold and a hungry belly will cause a war chief to surrender . . . or make him want to fight on all the harder."

Before Sitting Bull departed for the north country with his hundred lodges of Hunkpapa, he left fifty-four cases of fixed ammunition for the Crazy Horse people, bullets for hunting and for continuing the war.

No Neck and Sitting Bull planned to use those pack-mules they had taken from the soldiers and hunt buffalo come spring. Sitting Bull declared that once they had made meat and the women had robes, they would wander up to Fort Peck to trade with the Yanktonnais before marching across the Medicine Line. They were giving up. There were too many Americans pouring into Lakota land.

Their abandoning the war only served to make Crazy Horse angry. He had been arguing with himself on the best course to take, but now that the others were turning to flee to the Land of the Grandmother, did nothing but stiffen his resolve as winter continued to assault the land. Upon their arrival, the Hunkpapa had found the Crazy Horse people and Shahiyela terribly divided on whether to continue the war or sue for peace. Back and forth the headmen argued.

Back in the Mid-Winter Moon most of the chiefs had become convinced they should talk peace with the Bear Coat. But when the treaty-makers had gone to the mouth of the Buffalo Tongue River, the *Psa** had brazenly burst out of

*The Crow People

the trees and murdered five of the Lakota peace-talkers.*

After those killings, Crazy Horse, Little Big Man, and others whipped the people into a war fury once again. As the Bear Coat's soldiers marched upriver toward the village, the warriors harassed and skirmished with the column time and again until they suffered their humiliating stalemate at Belly Butte.

Now with the torment of hunger and a gnawing despair gripping their hearts, the people again began to think more and more of making peace.

In those first few days after Sitting Bull's people departed for the north, a few lodges had attempted to slip away from the Crazy Horse encampment, desiring to sneak south to the agencies.

But his camp police, the *akicita,* saw that no one limped back to the reservations. The warriors went after those who disobeyed Crazy Horse's orders, chopping up their lodge-poles, slashing their poor lodgeskins, even confiscating weapons and horses so that those who wanted to flee now had no choice but to return to the camp in shame and humiliation. The Horse was determined that the white man would not succeed in dividing his people against one another . . . against him. They would stand united.

If the white man were truly as strong as some said, if there were truly as many soldiers as some had reported, then Crazy Horse knew he had to hold his people together at all costs. Even if his people did not want to stand and fight to the end.

He let them grumble and talk behind his back. The Sans Arcs wanted to go. So did all the *Mnikowoju*—except for Lame Deer's band. But at least the Shahiyela of Little Wolf and Morning Star, Black Moccasin and Old Bear all remained strong. They, along with the Oglalla, understood what surrendering would mean.

What good was a fighting man who had given up his pony, who had turned over his weapons to the soldiers? What good was a man to his people then?

These cold days slid past slowly as the people plodded through the endless snows, the sun as pale as frozen mare's milk in a pewter sky. Beneath the new snow lay a layer of icy crust. Under that lay the breast of the earth blackened

with the fires of the previous summer.* There was little grass
for the ponies. Little feed for any game they might hope to
find. Without enough new hides, the women did what they
could to patch the lodgeskins and keep out the wolfish winds.
Men wore holes in their moccasins, then boiled them with
bones for a soup that made Crazy Horse's belly revolt.

Perhaps things would get better if they left the valley of
the Buffalo Tongue. Little Big Man had suggested they take
the village west over the divide to the upper Greasy Grass.
If not buffalo, at least they might find antelope.

Should they fail to find game there, Crazy Horse knew,
they could always push on downriver. If the hunting wasn't
very good there they would keep searching. His people
needed meat to keep up their strength. If they had no
strength, they could not fight. And if they could not fight,
then the white men would overrun this country.

But how could a man expect to find game to eat when he
could not find a single track among the endless snows? Not
a buffalo hoofprint. No sign of elk or antelope.

Not so much as the tiny tracks of a snowshoe hare.

"You deserve this, General!" Frank Baldwin exclaimed. "To
have your department enlarged to encompass the hunting
ground of the hostile Sioux, and to have Lieutenant General
Sheridan provide you with the men and supplies you're due!"

Colonel Nelson A. Miles nodded, his eyes crinkling in
proud agreement. "That's just the reason I'm sending you to
see Terry in Minneapolis, Lieutenant."

The commanding officer of the Fifth U.S. Infantry was just
getting underway his campaign to wheedle and pry what he
most desired out of Philip H. Sheridan in Chicago and Sheridan's superior, William Tecumseh Sherman, in Washington
City. After all, Sherman was his wife's uncle.

"With the success you had against Sitting Bull last December,† twice driving his village into the wilderness with only
what they could carry on their backs," Miles slammed a fist
into the palm of his other hand, "and our similar victory over

Crazy Horse up Tongue River—why is it taking so long for my superiors to act?"

"They've dealt with Hazen and Gibbon, Terry and Crook too long, sir," Baldwin groaned as he pulled his pipe from his blouse pocket.

The strikingly handsome Miles shuddered as if struck with a blast of cold. But this was a wave of genuine physical revulsion held for Crook and Terry. Plain as paint, General Alfred H. Terry back in St. Paul failed to support Miles throughout the previous autumn and winter campaigns. Why, Nelson had even gone so far as to write to Sherman accusing Terry and his Department of Dakota offices of making a determined effort to see that Miles accomplished nothing in his campaigns at best, and of criminal neglect of duty at worst.

Still, the colonel's most intense hatred was reserved for George C. Crook—a soldier who had turned in an even sorrier effort than that of Terry! To Nelson's way of thinking, Crook's bumbling and thumb-sitting, while Custer's killers moseyed off to the four winds, had accomplished nothing but give the hostiles renewed confidence! And now there were rumors that Crook was sneaking around down at Red Cloud's Agency, attempting to enlist Spotted Tail himself to search for Crazy Horse. Why, the conniving blackguard! If Crook thought such puny efforts would undermine Miles's campaign to force the tribes to surrender, then Crook was more of an incompetent dullard than he could have ever imagined!

Miles was the only one who could lay claim to fighting this war, by God! Those hostile chiefs and warrior bands belonged to Nelson A. Miles. No two ways about it. They were *his* Indians. Miles had been the one to fight them right from the moment of his arrival in the Yellowstone country last summer, his thirty-seventh, fighting the hostiles right on through the fall and into this interminable winter. He had tracked them, stalked, and harried them. Hell, the only fight Crook had with the enemy was when the Sioux caught him eating breakfast and playing whist!

No, indeed, Miles thought: the Sioux and Cheyenne belong to me. And by the heavens, Nelson A. Miles should be the one to whom those warrior bands surrendered!

"Perhaps all of my superiors being cronies of Sherman and Sheridan does explain it," Miles considered, his disgust rising like sour, bubbling acid. "There is no other logical reason for my commanders to ignore the worst management of the rear I've ever seen! If those four worthless popinjays were out of the way, why, Pope could be packed off to New York and Terry could be sent down to replace him at Leavenworth."

"But that still leaves Hazen and Gibbon here in the north, General," Baldwin reminded him.

Miles snorted and rubbed the end of his nose, brooding on the two colonels who still outranked him in seniority. "Both of them have been out here so long they'd doubtless jump at the chance to go east!" He slapped a palm down on his cluttered desk. "I promised Sherman that if he would give me this command and just half the troops now in this department, I would end this Sioux war once and forever in four months!"

"What did General Sherman say to that?"

"I'm ignored! No goddamned answer at all!" he shrieked in torment. "Why do Sherman and Sheridan ignore my reports, my requests, my exposing the utter criminality in the quartermaster corps, if not to protect their old cronies, like Crook and the others?"

"Nothing short of criminal, General!"

"If Major Benjamin Card wasn't such a thief disposed to ignore my department's needs, then my men would have what we need to pursue this campaign!" Miles growled as he sank into his desk chair. "As it is, I had to turn around and return to our base instead of chasing after that fleeing village."

"But for the want of forage and rations," Baldwin grumped in sympathy, "we could have dogged Crazy Horse until we caught him again, staying right on his tail till we whipped him once and for all."

Scratching at his heavy, black beard, Miles wagged his head. "We've got less than five months to get the job done, Lieutenant."

"Why only five months?"

"That's when Congress's new legislation goes into effect," he explained. "They've reduced the size of the frontier army by 2,500 soldiers."

His voice rising in disbelief, Baldwin cried, "Just a year

after they approved the appropriations for all the new recruits they were calling 'Custer's Avengers'?"

"The whole nation was up in arms after Custer got himself
butchered by the Sioux and Cheyenne," Miles said. "And
now with that contested presidential election causing the pos-
sibility of another revolt in the south finally put to rest—"

"Revolt, General?"

Miles waved a hand, casually discounting just how serious
the problem had been back east for the past few months.
"That situation with Hayes, and the way the southern states
contested his election so they could put an end to reconstruc-
tion. Seems the wounds still run deep down in the south, and
those wounds are still a might tender."

"So Congress will proceed with cutting our troop strength
now that we're just beginning to show some success with the
hostiles?"

"We've got till July 1, Mr. Baldwin," Miles said as he ran
his fingers through his thick hair. "So we must strike while
the opportunity is at hand."

"As soon as Bruguier returns, you'll have an idea just what
the sentiments are in those camps, General."

"Damn right," Miles agreed. "As I wrote Sherman, my
perfect spy system has enabled me to know the strength and
design of the enemy, to find, follow, and defeat him—wherever he may flee."

"What will it take to make Washington realize what you've
accomplished out here?"

"Your trip to see General Terry will be my first step in
securing all that I am due, Lieutenant."

"Enlarging your department—"

"As I explained, I've written both Sheridan and Sherman
telling them that there ought to be but one department over
this whole country the hostiles claim. One department, and
one department commander."

"You, General."

"Absolutely. But I need more good officers." He wagged
his head like a grumpy bear. "If Terry would only replace
Otis down at Glendive Cantonment, I wouldn't have to
worry about the door on my eastern flank."

"Not to mention our supply problem."

"That's the quartermaster again! Criminal neglect from
those scheming bureaucrats!" Miles roared. "I threatened

Sheridan that I would go to the press if I didn't get what I ordered for my campaigns from those crooks in the quartermaster department!"

"Sheridan hates the papers."

"Damn right he does. And he always advises against taking any correspondents along so I'm sure he knows how bad this whole thing would look if I talked to the papers. I told him squarely that only a full department command would defend me against those who are conspiring against my success."

"A success no other officer can match in this war, General."

"The Fifth can be very proud," Miles said. "We have fought and defeated larger and better armed bodies of hostile Indians than any other officer since the history of Indian warfare commenced! And at the same time I've gained a more extended knowledge of this northern frontier than any living man."

"They have no one better for the job, sir."

Miles turned to the large map he had tacked behind his chair. Tracing a finger around the extent of country between the Canadian border and Fort Fetterman to the south, the colonel said, "I told Sherman I would make the following recommendations: As the bad lands of the Little Missouri and that near the headwaters of the Tongue River afford the hostile tribes their strongholds of refuge, I would recommend that they be occupied by supply camps, where a movable command can obtain supplies; also the mouths of the Little Horn and the Musselshell, and at Fort Peck. These points, with two exceptions, can be supplied by steamboat transportation, while the others can be supplied by ox-trains."

"Not a word from the commanding general on your ideas?"

"Not a peep," he said, glowering at his desk. "I even asked Sheridan and Sherman for an appropriation to furnish wire for a military telegraph connecting Bismarck, Dakota with Bozeman, Montana. And another wire connecting the Yellowstone Valley with Fort Fetterman, Wyoming. Why, similar appropriations have been made with good results down south in Arizona, Texas, New Mexico, and Indian Territory."

Baldwin stood and stretched. "Tomorrow morning is going

to come early, General. I believe I'll be off to bed before I depart."

"Yes, by all means, Lieutenant," Miles replied. "I want you rested before you ride east to sit on Terry's desk for me."

"Yes, sir. I'll do everything I can for us so that the July 1 deadline won't mean that all we've accomplished comes undone."

Miles came around the desk and stopped almost toe to toe with Baldwin. Placing a hand on the shoulder of his trusted lieutenant, the colonel said, "I want you back here before the end of April."

"You can count on it, General. The end of April."

"There's only so much you can accomplish fighting those at Terry's headquarters," Miles growled. "And I want you here when spring comes . . . when I march the Fifth to finish what we began this winter."

Chapter 5

Early February 1877

BY TELEGRAPH

MISSOURI.

Breaking Up of a Hard Winter.
ST. LOUIS, February 2.—After being ice bound for fifty-six days, the river finally burst its bonds between 10 and 11 o'clock this morning, and ice has been passing the city but not in great quantities, ever since. Navigation southward is resumed and steamers will prepare for business to-morrow. Ice on the western side of Arsenal Island still holds fast, but it will no doubt break up and run out very soon, but in the meantime there is a sufficient channel on the east side for all practical purposes.

Johnny Bruguier was a wanted man.

But in jumping out of the skillet, he just might have pitched himself right into the fire.

Now Johnny figured he was a wanted man in two cultures. By attempting to slip the *wasicu* hangman's noose from around his neck, he might well have put the Lakota knife at his throat.

Day after long, cold day, Johnny brooded beneath the turned-down brim of his hat, squinting into the distance, his eyes constantly moving. Fear made a man a good hunter, he reminded himself. He might just have a chance if the warrior bands did not catch Old Wool Woman and him out in the open on their way to find the village, and if Johnny could get to the sanctuary of that sacred lodge . . .

If he didn't, well, to hell with the hangman's rope waiting for him back at the Standing Rock Reservation. The Lakota warriors would accomplish what those white law dogs wanted, anyway.

Johnny turned a moment, looking behind him at the old woman hunched in her blanket against the slashing wind which drove wispy streamers of icy snow along the ground. They had them a bargain, these two. He had promised her he would find the village and return Old Wool Woman to her people. And she had vowed to do everything she could to give him his chance to talk to the tribal leaders. To do that, she would have to get him into the village alive.

She looked up at him momentarily beneath the hooded flap of her thin, gray army blanket. The wind tormented the pony's mane as it struggled sideways against the brutal gale. Tugging on the rein, she kept the animal moving. She adjusted the heavy buffalo robe she clutched around the blanket at her shoulders. Then buried her head once more, hiding her face from the wind.

For but a flicker of time, as a gauzy strip of icy snow swept across the ground between them, Johnny thought she looked much like his own Lakota mother. It made his heart yearn. Knowing how hard her life had been on the Standing Rock with that drunken French-Canadian trader for a husband. But every time Johnny's heart ached for this old Shahiyela woman, he scolded himself for that softness.

It was something that just might get him killed by that woman's people. Wouldn't the Crazy Horse people consider him a traitor?

Of course they would.

He quartered in the saddle, trying to turn his right shoulder into the wind, tugging up the side of his collar. But there was really little he could do about the wind now that they had climbed out of the valley of the Tongue and crossed toward the Rosebud, following the village's westward migration toward the Chetish Mountains.* There the trail turned south by west, striking for the White Mountains, what the soldiers called the Bighorns. For generations the Lakota had been going to those slopes to cut lodgepoles at the end of every summer. But with the constant harassment and the destruction of their lodges through the previous autumn and winter, the warrior bands needed poles now. It made sense to him that they would strike out for those foothills. Even more sense when he considered how the camps must be on the verge of starvation.

A man had only to look at the prisoners. Those captives Miles had taken the day before his battle with the Crazy Horse village were all skinny, their eyes sunken, cheekbones sharp beneath the skin, as if chiseled out of red sandstone. This was a harsh winter to begin with. It had begun early and remained relentless. With the soldiers on their heels, the village couldn't have had much time to hunt, dry meat, cure hides—to provide for the little ones, and for the old.

In the past handful of days, Johnny himself hadn't seen much game to speak of. It was a good thing the soldiers brought along their army food, in packs lashed to the backs of those dozen mules.

Perhaps closer to the mountains, the village would find buffalo and the hunting would be good. That had to be where they were headed. West, right into the teeth of this wind coming off the slopes of those icy granite peaks.

Every day or so he came across signs of their passing: a patch of bottomground where it was plain to see they had camped, the hundreds leaving the frozen snow trampled, pocked with small, round, black scars marking every fire pit. Trees were left gnawed by the ponies, unable to find anything to eat when they pawed down through the trampled crust to the blackened cinders of the scorched earth the warrior bands left behind last autumn. Besides the bark of the cottonwood and the slender branches of the alder and chokecherry, there was nothing for the starving ponies to eat.

---

*Wolf Mountains

Johnny grew thirsty in the dry, wolfish wind, so he sucked on his tongue to stimulate some saliva. How this cold made him all the more thirsty than a hot summer day. The shocking cold sucked all the juices right out of a man. He tucked the loose, flyaway flap of the buffalo coat around his right chap and pressed it against the horse's ribs to clamp it down against the strengthening wind.

Big Leggings. That's what Sitting Bull's Hunkpapa called him. Johnny had been running for his life last summer when he bumped into them. General Miles said the white officials had a writ out for his arrest. With a little St. Louis education under his belt, Johnny knew what that writ meant. Murder meant hanging, especially when the victim was a white man killed by an agency half-breed.

Able to speak both his mother's Lakota and a good deal of the white man's tongue, Johnny had spent three seasons as an interpreter for the agent at Standing Rock. Then he rubbed up against the wrong white man—a teamster, a wrangler, a trouble-maker from first jump, who beat who he wanted and abused any woman he coveted.

Then came that cold day at the agency store. With eyes as dead as stones, the white man grabbed a young Lakota woman, dragging her to the door. Johnny was standing even before the woman's grandmother flung herself shrieking onto the man. But Johnny wasn't quick enough to stop the white man from beating the old woman aside. The half-breed had stepped beyond the point of retreat.

Knives pulled, the two of them danced for a moment that passed in a blur. He stood back moments later, amazed at how much blood could pour out of a man, the floor beneath his opponent slick with dark puddles and a greasy coil of gut. He had killed a white man. No matter that he had gone to the defense of the helpless. No matter that the white man had pulled his big knife first.

Johnny fled on a stolen horse tied outside the door. Racing west away from the agency, he eventually reached the Black Hills, where it wasn't hard for a strapping youngster to find work sweeping up and hauling kegs in and out of a saloon. The watering hole provided a warm place to sleep too, there in the back, among the crates of supplies and whiskey, while the noisy miners shouted and shot at one another out front.

Then the saloon owner showed him the stiffened parchment with Johnny's likeness printed on it. The English words said he was wanted for murder. The handbills were going up all over town. If they got their hands on him, a miners' court sure as hell would hang a half-breed like him. What with all the Indian troubles since spring.

He slipped down the alley and stole another horse. A big one with a blaze face and two front stockings. Behind its saddle was tied a thick blanket roll, wrapped in an oiled slicker, along with two stuffed saddlebags. Plain to see that horse and rigging were ready for the trail. They raced off to the west, somewhere the white man wouldn't dare to follow him: hostile country.

That first night beside his fire Johnny unwrapped the bed-roll and found the pair of well-oiled leather chaps inside. He was wearing them when he bumped into the Hunkpapa village. And when he studied the half-breed's chaps, Sitting Bull himself anointed Bruguier with his Lakota name: Big Leggings.

Bruguier migrated with the Hunkpapa last autumn when they crossed to the north side of the Elk River* and discovered that the supply trains moving between the soldier posts drove off the buffalo herds and ruined the hunting. At Sitting Bull's direction, Johnny wrote English words on a scrap of paper and left it tied to a stick so the soldier wagons would find it.†

When the soldier chief read the note, he ignored Sitting Bull's demand to leave the Hunkpapa hunting ground. The Lakota attacked. In a day-long running battle against the wagon soldiers, Gall's warriors accomplished little more than slowing the white man's progress. After two days of fighting, the Bear Coat arrived from his fort to the west with enough soldiers to raise the siege. And while the wagons continued west over the hills toward the Buffalo Tongue River, the Bear Coat asked for a parley with the Lakota chiefs.

In that middle ground between the two enemies, Big Leggings had settled himself between Sitting Bull and the Bear

---

*Yellowstone River
†Otis's supply train bound for Tongue River Cantonment, October 1876, *A Cold Day In Hell*, vol. 11, The Plainsmen Series

Coat, a soldier chief named Miles. Back and forth those two
strong men argued. The Lakota demanded that the soldiers
abandon their posts in that country so the villages could hunt
as they always had. Then the soldiers demanded that the warrior bands give up their claim to that Elk River country and go
in to the reservations where they would learn to be farmers.

Johnny knew that attempting to turn a warrior into a sod-
buster would work about as well as trying to tie a woman's
bustle on a boar hog. It wouldn't make the hog any prettier,
and in the end, someone was bound to get hurt.

It was no surprise when that parley broke down and the
Bear Coat's soldiers started a running fight that drove the
Lakota villages all the way to the north bank of the Elk
River. But while most of the war chiefs escaped across the
river, Sitting Bull and a few loyal followers slipped off to the
east and eluded the Bear Coat. If they could just stay far
away from the white man, the Hunkpapa mystic declared to
his people, they could go on hunting as they always had.

As a cold, drizzly autumn quickly froze with the coming of
an early winter on those northern plains, more Lakota stragglers limped in from the other camps to join Sitting Bull in the
badlands of the Missouri River. There they found buffalo,
making much meat and dressing the hides to replace the
lodges they lost when the Bear Coat attacked their village.
And in that country north of Fort Peck, the Slotas showed up
from the Land of the Grandmother, those half-breed Metis
who had ammunition and guns and whiskey to trade.

Still Sitting Bull did not seem content. He was beginning
to realize that the Bear Coat was steadily chipping away at
his grand alliance.

"This land is no longer any good," he explained to Johnny
one cold night. "The soldiers are here to stay. As much as
we might try to avoid them, the soldiers are not going away.
I am looking to the north, Big Leggings. Perhaps there I will
have peace."

If Sitting Bull took his people north to Canada, Johnny
had a decision to make: a choice between casting his lot from
here on out with the Hunkpapa in that foreign land, or trying
to make a life for himself somewhere on the frontier, where
he would always be looking over his shoulder, dreading that
someone might see the wanted poster with his likeness and
offer of reward on it.

He licked his cracked, blistered lips again now, remembering the tastes he had acquired around the agency at Standing Rock—coffee and fresh bread, strong tobacco and whiskey.

So when a contingent of soldiers came upriver to garrison the Fort Peck Agency, the Lakota bands who had once more gathered around Sitting Bull scattered to the four winds. But Johnny had stayed behind. With a blanket over his head, and that dark skin of his, he blended right in with the agency bands who camped near the agent's stockade walls.

But even in that village, he remained homesick. His heart yearned for the smells and sounds and sights of the agency, for the life he had come to know as a youngster on the Standing Rock. Just about the time he had decided he was going to stay on at Fort Peck rather than return to Sitting Bull's village, the Bear Coat's soldiers showed up from the south.

Along with Miles was that long-haired scout named Kelly, who recognized Johnny despite the blanket pulled over his head. He was cornered. Instead of arresting Bruguier, Miles wanted to offer the half-breed a bargain. While the other soldiers advised against making a pact with Bruguier, the Bear Coat nonetheless explained how they could help one another.

If Johnny Bruguier would turn his back on Sitting Bull and divulge where the warrior bands were camped, then Miles would do all he could to get the half-breed cleared of that killing back at Standing Rock. In the end, both of them had a shot at what they wanted most.

Trouble was, until Miles had those Sitting Bull and Crazy Horse bands rounded up and put on their reservations, Johnny Bruguier wasn't going to get what he wanted. Which meant that when the Bear Coat said he wanted to send one of the captives to parley with the Crazy Horse people, Johnny couldn't rightly say no. It was go along, or chance having his neck stretched.

Johnny was in too deep now. No matter how crazy the plan sounded, he had to go along.

Now dabbing his horsehide mitten against his sore, cracked, and oozing lower lip, Bruguier turned slightly and glanced at the old woman. They were a strange pair, the two of them. Once more Johnny was putting his life in the hands of another, once more in the hands of an Indian.

Maybe she had him fooled, he considered as her sad eyes met his stare. Maybe she had no intention of helping him extend the Bear Coat's offer of peace to her people. Chances were good that she might only turn Johnny over to the camp's warriors in retaliation for her capture.

Still, something in those sad eyes reminded him of his mother. He smiled back at the old woman, praying he wasn't wrong for putting his life in her hands.

Praying that the old woman really did believe she had a shot at making peace for her people.

Chapter 6

Big Hoop-and-Stick Game Moon
1877

Old Wool Woman wasn't exactly sure what moon it was. So much had happened since the fight at Belly Butte. Best she could figure, it was the latter days of the Big Hoop-and-Stick Game Moon. Not much chance that they had reached the early days of what her people called the Dusty Moon.

Hard to know, really, the way the sky stayed cloudy, day and night. Hard to know how much of the old moon was left, or if the new moon had begun to swell again in the heavens. So cold, bleak, and endless were these days trudging back up the Buffalo Tongue River behind the half-breed who the Lakota of Buffalo Bull Sitting Down called "Big Leggings." Her own Shahiyela simply called him "White."

Behind the two of them plodded six mules carrying supplies for their journey and gifts for her people. Around those mules rode the soldiers who were escorting her and Big Leggings into the traditional hunting grounds of the Northern People.

"Old woman, you would tell me if you thought I was taking us in the wrong direction to find your people, wouldn't you?" the half-breed had asked in Lakota at last night's fire. "You would help me find them?" He always signed as he slowly spoke the tongue of the *Hotohkesoneo-o*, the Little Star People.*

She knew enough of that Lakota tongue to understand this half-breed right from the first night when he had summoned her to the Bear Coat's lodge where the three of them talked of taking gifts to her people, talked of surrender and peace—when she had spoken of the Sacred Medicine Hat Lodge as the object of their quest.

"I would tell you," she had answered him.

"I am not wrong?"

"No, the camp is still moving west."

His eyes seemed to soften in the flickering firelight. It was easy to see how she had reassured him. "They are in a hurry, old woman," Big Leggings said.

She had looked back down into the fire and thought a moment before she responded. "Those people are hungry. They do not have time to journey slow. There are too many bellies to feed."

Many times since her capture she had suffered stabbing pangs of guilt because she had so much to eat. Back when the Bear Coat's soldiers first reached the fort with their captives, the wary guards had cooked every meal, then brought the Shahiyela women and children their portions. But it wasn't long before the soldiers gave their prisoners weekly rations and allowed the women to cook their own meals. Old Wool Woman hadn't seen so much food in . . . a long, long time.

In those days before she was captured, just after the Red Fork fight when she lost her beloved Black White Man, when she left the Crazy Horse people and had gone to visit Tangle Hair's village on the Pretty Fork,† she had trained herself to eat less and less so that she could give some of her food to the young ones. Many nights she went to bed with an aching belly, sucking on a short piece of chokecherry from which she had peeled the bark. That sliver of wood gave her mouth something to do as she drifted off to sleep, gave her tongue something to taste when she could give her belly very little to fill it.

---

*How the Northern Cheyenne referred to the Oglalla Lakota
†Belle Fourche River

But now she had all she wanted of the soldier food: the salty meat and hard, dry crackers. Back at the army's fort, she and the other prisoners had watched the soldiers open hard containers from which they poured strange foods onto their tin plates. Foods red, yellow, and green—all with new and pleasing tastes that Old Wool Woman quickly grew quite fond of.

But nothing pleased her quite so much as a cup of scalding coffee, strong and flavorful, sweetened with heaps of the *ve-ho-e*'s sugar. Each night spent at the fire with these soldiers, she remembered how she once was called Sweet Taste Woman. In those long ago days when life itself was sweet. As a girl those tiny white grains had tickled her tongue, had become her greatest treat.

Then came the beginning of this winter when Three Finger Kenzie's soldiers attacked their village in the mountains, driving the *Ohmeseheso* into the sub-freezing dawn with little more than what they wore on their backs. The day she kissed Black White Man goodbye before he tore away from their lodge to fight off the attack, the day she lost her last son to the soldiers. The men of her family had given their lives in that battle.

After that day, life would never again be as sweet for Sweet Taste Woman and the Shahiyela. With her scrap of greasy, fire-smudged blanket wrapped about her, she had joined the rest of the survivors who lumbered on frozen feet, day after day, in search of the Crazy Horse village. No more was this old, weary, frozen person known as Sweet Taste Woman.

Now she was called Old Wool Woman.

That greasy blanket was always at her side, wrapped tightly about her. Though the soldiers had given her a gray army blanket and a buffalo robe of her own, Old Wool Woman did not abandon the blanket that had sheltered her through all those days of freezing and hunger. She held it tightly against her as she rolled up beside the soldiers' fire to sleep each night, thinking of Black White Man. And every morning she lashed it around her waist to provide an additional layer against this winter's wolfish winds.

There were times Old Wool Woman felt as if she were dreaming through much of the days on this journey with Big Leggings, her head tucked beneath a flap of her soldier blan-

ket, the strong American horse rocking beneath her as it
lunged forward with each step, breaking through the icy
snow. From time to time the half-breed awoke her from her
reverie, pointing to a patch of ground in some creekbottom
where, it was clear to see, the village had stopped, made
camp, and rested for the night.

How reassuring it was whenever she and Big Leggings discovered such places, dismounting to walk across the ground
where her people and the Crazy Horse Lakota had camped.
Had it not been for the soldier food, she would have suffered
the same terrible hunger her people had to be suffering now.
Rarely did Big Leggings's small party encounter any game
throughout the short, cold days of this journey. Yet her belly
rarely grew empty enough to complain.

In this season of despair, Old Wool Woman hoped her
people had found enough buffalo to end their tragic search.

From the divide west of the Buffalo Tongue, Big Leggings
led them down into the valley of the Roseberry River.*
Along the wide path the village had scratched across the
snow, they encountered very few buffalo, nothing more than
a handful of old bulls here and there. In the river valleys she
reminded herself to look for the burial places—nooks and
crevices back in the rocks where her people would have
placed the bodies of those who died from the ceaseless cold,
from the starvation. She was sure the very old, or the very
young, could not defend themselves against the constant,
endless snows. Old Wool Woman knew there would be
mourning in the lodges of the *Ohmeseheso*. More mourning
than any people deserved.

Almost as if *Ma-heo-o*, the Everywhere Spirit, had abandoned his people.

Perhaps the prophecy Buffalo Bull Sitting Down had angrily delivered after their fight with the soldiers on the Little
Sheep River† had come to pass. In his fateful vision during
the sun dance held the previous summer, the Lakota leader
had been told that the warriors would be victorious, but that
none of the victorious men and women were to take anything

---

*Rosebud Creek
†Little Bighorn River

from the bodies. They were to remove nothing from the battlefield.

But suddenly drunk with their victory, the Lakota and the Shahiyela had claimed soldier weapons, stripped the bodies, torn the saddles from the dead horses—revelling in their new wealth. So perhaps the Everywhere Spirit really was punishing them for disobeying Him.

Maybe this was the reason the *Ohmeseheso*, once the single richest, most powerful tribe on the northern plains, was now the poorest—reduced to begging for help from the Little Star People, brought to the brink of begging the white man for peace.

"Tomorrow," Big Leggings said as he settled near her now beside the fire, "we will reach the valley of the Greasy Grass."

"My people call it the Little Sheep River."

"Perhaps we will see the place where Sitting Bull's Lakota and your Shahiyela killed all the soldiers last summer," the half-breed said as he bent forward and filled his cup with more coffee.

She stared at the fire for a while, then wagged her head, and replied, "That is north some distance from where we will reach the valley. Those soldiers were killed downstream from where the trail of this village will cross the Little Sheep River."

He sipped at his coffee, then said, "I am sorry to hear that. I was looking forward to seeing this place where the warrior bands saw their greatest victory."

Looking directly at the half-breed, Old Wool Woman said sadly, "It was a victory we did not learn from."

"What did your people fail to understand?" He wiped droplets of coffee from his upper lip, the firelight dancing on his dark face.

"We should have learned that the end was already coming," she sighed. "We should have been brave enough to learn how to make a strong peace . . . the way we had made a strong war for as long as we could."

"Looks to be this is the place where we turn back."

Johnny Bruguier warily flicked his eyes at the soldier who had just spoken, the soldier who was in charge of the escort

Bear Coat Miles sent south with him to find the hostile camp. Staring back down at the valley below, the half-breed's eyes narrowed in concern. Swallowing, he said, "Don't wanna stick around? Maybe to see if we make it, or if I get shot riding in there?"

The soldier shook his head. "General Miles give us our orders to turn back once we got you in sight of the village," replied the soldier with two stripes on the thick woolen shirt he wore beneath his buffalo coat. "You and the woman gonna make it the rest of the way down there on your own."

Johnny watched the man turn to the others, quietly ordering them to check the cinches on all six of the mules before dividing off two of the pack animals for their return march to the mouth of the Tongue River. On that pair the soldiers lashed their own blankets and bedrolls, along with their rations and extra ammunition for their long rifles.

Right about then Johnny wished he still had the Winchester carbine he had given Sitting Bull the previous year when the Hunkpapa chief presented him with the fine horse that had seen the half-breed through hundreds of miles of campaigning.

He dropped from the saddle and flung the stirrup fender over it, tugging on the cinch. His heart thumped just the way it had the day he rode boldly into the Hunkpapa camp.

Johnny remembered how he loped right past the first warriors who dashed out to confront him, pounding his heels into the ribs of that horse he stole in Whitewood, urging more and more speed out of it until he dismounted on the run and dashed into the first lodge he could reach. It turned out to belong to White Bull, Sitting Bull's nephew.

Would that fickle whore called Lady Luck chance to smile on him again today?

Bruguier dropped the stirrup back in place and turned to the old woman, still seated bareback atop her soldier horse. He couldn't blame her for preferring it to sitting atop one of the army's god-awful saddles. "Are these your people?" he asked in his methodical Lakota, using a little sign.

Turning to him, the woman said, "Perhaps. That is a big camp, so maybe it is my people, traveling and hunting with the Little Star People."

"Perhaps?" he asked, sensing the claw of cold apprehension rise in him, like a prairie wind shoving a thunderstorm at him out of the west.

With a shrug, the woman explained, "It has been a long time for me to be in that village. Maybe some lodges have gone for the agencies after the fight with the Bear Coat's soldiers. Maybe more Lakota lodges have come from the hills to join with Crazy Horse. It has been more than two moons since I was in that camp."

"I remember you telling me of this one night at the fire," he said as a means of apology. He drew in a deep breath to steel himself for what lay ahead below. "You said you were coming back from a visit to friends in another village when the Bear Coat's scouts captured you."

Johnny watched her dab a dirty soldier mitten at her eyes.

"Yes," the woman answered with a croak, "I have not seen my relations in a long, long time."

Suddenly a soldier's hand was on Johnny's shoulder. The half-breed wheeled around with a jerk.

"You don't need anything else," the soldier began, stepping back the moment Bruguier jumped. "We're turning back for the post now."

"You tell Miles I done what he asked?"

"You bet I will, mister. I'll tell the general you and the woman took your presents into that village. Just be sure you get their chiefs to ride back to the Yellowstone with you to surrender."

For a moment that confused him. Then he remembered the white man called Elk River by a different name: the Yellowstone. "Yeah, I bring the chiefs back with me to talk peace."

"Surrender is what the general wants from 'em," the soldier repeated as he crawled back atop his horse, the wind picking up among the sage and snow. "They don't wanna come in to give up, you be sure to tell 'em Miles is gonna keep whipping 'em until there ain't no more hostiles left in this country—buck, squaw, or papoose. You make sure they know they got the choice: they can surrender to the general, or we can rub 'em all out—one camp at a time."

All Johnny could do was nod as the soldier reined his horse about and started away. The others fell into a ragged column of twos behind him, the last pair tugging at the two mules they were taking north with them. He watched the soldiers cross the top of the low ridge and quickly drop out of sight as they pushed east for the Tongue. It suddenly grew very cold up there on the west side of the slope where the wind could get at a man and work its way through the flaps of his clothing. Johnny had been cold before, and he figured he'd been just about as lonely too.

Then he glanced at the woman, still hunkered on her horse. Her red-rimmed eyes momentarily flicked at the village down in the snowy valley, then back to him.

She asked, "We go take these gifts to my people now?"

"Yeah," he answered with something less than complete enthusiasm, swinging up into the saddle and tapping his horse into motion. "Let's go before I freeze my manhood off up here on top of this hill."

Chapter 7

7 February 1877

BY TELEGRAPH

GENERAL MILES STILL PURSUING

CRAZY HORSE.

THE INDIANS.

A Brush with Crazy Horse on Tongue
River.

CHICAGO, February 6.—A St. Paul dispatch,
received to-day officially at military headquarters here, says: The following was just received
via Bozeman and Helena:

HEADQUARTERS COMMAND ON THE
YELLOWSTONE, January 20, 1877.—I have
the honor to report that the command fought the
hostiles tribes of Cheyenne and Ogallalla Sioux
under Crazy Horse, in skirmishes, on the 1st, 3d
and 7th of January, and in a five hour engagement on the 8th instant. Their camp, some six
hundred lodges, extended three miles along
the valley of Tongue river, below Hanging

Woman's creek. They were driven through the canyons of the Wolf or Panther mountains, in the direction of the Big Horn mountains. Their fighting strength outnumbered mine two or three to one, but by taking advantage of the ground we had them at a disadvantage and their loss is known to be very severe.

Our loss is three killed and eight wounded. They fought entirely dismounted, and charged on foot to within fifty yards of Capt. Casey's line, but were taken in front and flank by Capt. Butler's and Lieut. McDonald's companies. They were whipped at every point and driven from the field, and pursued as far as my limited supplies and worn down animals would carry my command. The indians appear to have plenty of arms and ammunition, but otherwise are in a destitute condition. Some of the prisoners now in our hands were captured with frozen limbs, and were living on horse meat. The weather has been very severe, and the snow is from one to three feet deep. The command is in good condition.

Signed, Nelson A. Miles, commanding.

As the wind rattled the newsprint where he stood gripping it outside the sutler's store, Seamus quickly reread the short article emblazoned across the front page of Denver's *Rocky Mountain News*.

This time he had beaten the latest war news home.

His heart pounded faster as he began to pour over the short article a third time. Here were the names of officers he had fought beside. They and their men were the real heroes of the Battle of the Butte.

Shivering in that February wind, Donegan remembered how Captain Butler held his shaky command together in the face of a howling blizzard as their thin blue line drew close enough to the enemy to see the colors of the face paint on those warriors bristling atop the low ridge. Soldiers down to their last one or two cartridges, frightened men preparing to make that terrifying assault. Undaunted, Butler gave the order for his men to mount bayonets. Without bullets, those gallant soldiers were about to scale the icy heights and engage the enemy eye-to-eye, close enough to smell what your enemy had eaten for breakfast. No hunkering behind breastworks or a downed tree. No firing from a distance now.

Butler had them moving through the deep snow, rallying them from the back of his horse, urging them on, cheering them even to the base of the slopes. Preparing them for the meanest work of a fighting man.

Toe-to-toe with your enemy, war became more than bloody, more than dirty. War became very, very personal.

Seamus disagreed with only one conclusion in Miles's brief report. From what he had seen and experienced in those cold, snowy hours of battle far up the Tongue, the Irishman wasn't all that sure the Indians had plenty of ammunition. What they had taken off the Custer dead, added to what they had managed to trade at their agencies, along with what little they might have plundered from miners and teamsters in and around the Black Hills in recent months . . . the hostile bands had to be running low. They might well still possess those weapons—Springfield carbines, Winchester and Henry repeaters, perhaps a few high-powered needle guns ripped from the hands of a buffalo hunter—but, ammunition was another matter. There simply was no constant supply of that.

And with every extended engagement fought against the army, the warriors used up more and more of their dwindling stores of those precious bullets without any way to reload their brass.

How much longer could they fight the outfits that came searching for them in the winter snows? he wondered. How long would their resolve compel them to struggle on? How long until the buffalo were gone and the warrior bands had eaten all their horses?

How long before this goddamned war was over?

Seamus suddenly glanced up at officers' quarters nearby, then stared back down at the newspaper. Finally, he looked over at the door to the sutler's store. Should he go in and buy every copy of this issue, toss them into the heavy iron stove in the corner of Collins's saloon just so Samantha wouldn't have a chance to read about the fight?

Then Seamus realized just what a bone-headed idea that was. For a full year now she had been reading those brief newspaper accounts of the army's campaigns, just like the officers' wives who stayed behind each time their men went off to fight with Crook or Mackenzie or Miles. A year ago now he had marched off to the Powder, and the Rosebud after that. Then Donegan traipsed all the way to Slim Buttes, and back to Camp Robinson, before trudging his way north again to the Red Fork of the Powder where the Fourth Cavalry jumped the Cheyenne. Donegan had rounded out this last year in hostile country when he marched up the Tongue, only to run into Crazy Horse again.

Looking down at the newsprint rattling in his cold hands, Seamus realized this wouldn't be the first story his dear Samantha would read on this war with the Sioux and Cheyenne. He swallowed hard, knowing it wouldn't be the last story she would read about this dirty conflict either.

He straightened his back, dragging the back of his hand beneath his nose, and started for officers' quarters and that room where Samantha always waited for him to return from his campaigns, the room where she and their son held on and . . . waited.

From the big pocket on his blanket-lined canvas mackinaw, the Irishman drew out the small, tin, penny whistle. Laying his big fingers over the holes as he neared the snow-covered porch, Seamus gave the fife a tentative blow. Slowly dancing his fingertips off and on the holes, he surprised himself by making sounds with the thing.

He smiled and stomped onto the porch, kicking snow from his tall boots. He happily carried the newspaper and some hoarhound candy for Samantha this morning. And the penny whistle to play for Colin Teig while he bounced the boy on his knee.

What child wouldn't be fascinated by the sound of that tiny tin flute? Why, maybe with a couple of months' practice, Seamus could pipe a few songs for his son before riding north again to rejoin Miles and his Fifth Infantry for their spring campaign.

For this farewell, Colin Teig might just be old enough to have some limited understanding that his father would be away for some time, that his father was riding north into enemy country to finish a long and bloody war.

Finish it at last.

*   *   *

*Esevone** sat protected in a newly constructed lodge of buffalo hides that stood at its prescribed place, here at the center of the great, curving crescent of the camp circle.

While it was not as grand a lodge as the one destroyed by Three Finger Kenzie's troops on the Red Fork, this was nonetheless the finest place the Sacred Buffalo Hat had resided in the two moons since Coal Bear had escaped that doomed village and fled into the mountains with the powerful religious object.

Coal Bear laid another limb on the fire and sighed in satisfaction. He watched the thin tendrils of smoke climb toward that place where the newly peeled lodgepoles were joined with the tight wraps of rope. The buffalo hides the women used to sew together the lodgecover were so new, so white, they hadn't begun to darken with countless fires, as had the old Sacred Hat Lodge the soldier destroyed.

The frost-stiffened doorflap was pulled back and his wife ducked inside, carrying a small armload of firewood she had gathered along the banks of a nearby creek the Lakota called the Rotten Grass.† She dropped her wood to the left of the door, bent briefly to lay her hand on his shoulder, then left the lodge to continue her search for wood. Coal Bear scooted the small iron kettle closer to the burning limbs, then dropped some chunks of red meat into the steaming water.

Days ago they had stumbled across some buffalo. Thanks be to the Everywhere Spirit! They had found enough of the beasts to feed the village.

But not before some of the Lakota had decided to part company with the *Ohmeseheso*. Four Horns and his small band of Hunkpapa departed for the Elk River, hoping to find Buffalo Bull Sitting Down before the great chief crossed the Medicine Line into the Land of the Grandmother. All the Sans Arc and the *Mnikowoju* under Lame Deer had started away to the northeast, intending to wait out the rest of the

---

*The Sacred Buffalo Hat
†Their camp was located somewhere between present-day St. Xavier and Lodge Grass, Montana, on what is now the Crow Reservation

winter in that country around the Antelope Pit River.*

People said even Crazy Horse was thinking of having his Little Star People tear down their lodges and strike out for the Little Powder River.

"Maybe the buffalo have returned," Crazy Horse had declared. He was trying to explain to the headmen of both the Lakota and the *Ohmeseheso* why he was considering a return to his beloved Powder River country.

For Coal Bear, any country where there wasn't a white man, where the army did not march, that was good country.

Hunting had grown better the closer the camp drew to the foothills of the White Mountains. But the village was large, with far more than a hundred lodges, many mouths to feed, and all those ponies to graze. The headmen had begun to consider that perhaps it was time to part company now that it appeared the soldiers were no longer dogging their trail. Perhaps now there would be some security for the villages for the rest of the winter.

They had killed far too many of their ponies before they ever stumbled across the buffalo herds. Poor, gaunt, starving ponies butchered at every camp as the *Ohmeseheso* marched south, then west after their fight with the Bear Coat. For a long time they camped at the mouth of the Prairie Dog where it flowed into the Buffalo Tongue River. But with each new day the hunting grew more and more disappointing.

Now that the other Lakota bands had dispersed to the four winds, Crazy Horse's Little Star People and Coal Bear's Sha-hiyela had finally stumbled onto a few buffalo. Not in the numbers the old priest remembered from his youth, but enough bulls and cows that his hungry people would no longer worry about starving that winter. Perhaps there might be enough hides for the women to scrape and tan to replace those lodgeskins left behind, burned and destroyed by the soldiers.

In the days that had followed, the Lakota-Shahiyela camp traipsed after the herds from the mouth of Rotten Grass Creek, upstream from the Sheep River,† as the buffalo slowly migrated toward the Little Sheep River. There in that

---

*Little Missouri River
†Big Horn River

protected valley, the shaggy beasts appeared content to stay as winter continued. The *Ohmeseheso* were content to stay with the buffalo on the Rotten Grass, buffalo that were a sign that *Esevone* Herself was continuing to bless Her people. Day after day, the women raised a few more new lodges against the sky, their whiteness like brilliant cones flung against the pale, winter blue.

Besides Coal Bear and Box Elder—that old, venerable, blind prophet who had foreseen the attack by Three Finger Kenzie—all four of the Old Man Chiefs gathered here in this village that formed a great crescent: Little Wolf, Morning Star,* Old Bear,† and Black Moccasin. This north country was land the Ohmeseheso believed was their hunting ground, granted them from the time of the Great Treaty at Horse Creek.# Here they were not disturbing any white people. Perhaps, just perhaps, the fighting was over.

But, Coal Bear scolded himself: only a stupid man would believe that the soldiers wouldn't be marching come the spring grass. If the Bear Coat marched when the winter winds howled, then he would surely have his soldiers marching once the ice in these rivers and streams began to groan and creak, breaking up as the weather warmed.

But for now Coal Bear's heart was strong. His people were exactly where *Esevone* had led them—to the buffalo that would sustain them until spring.

His heart warmed with that thought, Coal Bear smiled and decided he would venture out to help his woman bring in more wood. Emerging from the lodge, he gazed into the sky at the pewter-colored globe obscured behind the thickening, gray clouds. Perhaps there would be more snow before nightfall. As he took those first steps away from the door, a loud voice stopped him in his tracks.

Coal Bear turned at the cry.

A second voice shouted in alarm.

Now some were pointing in the direction of the Little Sheep River, wagging their arms toward the low hills at the

---

*Called Dull Knife by the Lakota and the white man
†Whose village was attacked by Colonel Reynolds on 17 March 1876—*Blood Song*, vol. 8, The Plainsmen Series
#The Fort Laramie Treaty of 1851

eastern fringe of the valley. Could they have sighted soldiers?

Protectively, the priest stepped back to stand directly in front of the lodgedoor. Here again he would guard *Esevone*.

Then, out on the flat prairie, he saw them. Two riders coming slowly toward the village. Straining his old eyes, Coal Bear tried to focus behind the pair, but there were no others. Only two. One rode a saddle with stirrups, the other without. Perhaps bareback.

By now three young warriors had leaped atop their own ponies and were dashing toward the strangers. As Coal Bear watched, the two riders spotted the trio and suddenly kicked their big horses into motion. The animals burst into a gallop. As the horses raced toward the village, it became easier to see that the strangers did not ride on poorly fed, winter-gaunt Indian ponies. This pair rode on big American horses.

Horses so fast that they managed to race past the young warriors. Big horses picking up speed as their riders pointed them right for the middle of the village crescent.

They were coming straight for Coal Bear's lodge!

In the space of three pounding heartbeats the riders were nearly upon the Sacred Hat Keeper. Even before his horse stopped, one of the strangers leaped to the ground, landing no more than the length of two bows from Coal Bear himself. The priest stepped back, gazing up at the other rider who brought his big horse to a halt. The animal snorted and pawed at the icy crust of snow.

"Coal Bear!" that rider called out in the tongue of his people. "My heart is full of song to see you!"

Then the stranger pulled back the blanket from his face and Coal Bear now saw that the rider was a woman.

"O-Old Wool Woman?"

How was this? She was a prisoner of the Bear Coat—

"It is me!" she cried with happiness, her wind-burnt cheeks wet with tears.

Rocked with confusion, Coal Bear suddenly turned to stare at the other rider. His dark skin, something about his eyes—was he Lakota? If so, he was wearing the strangest clothing, white man's clothing to be sure.

"It really is you!" a female voice called out. The speaker lunged to a stop at Old Wool Woman's knee.

"Antelope Woman!" Old Wool Woman blubbered, reaching out her hand to the younger woman who held up her hands to the returned captive.

Without warning the dark-skinned stranger stepped right up to Coal Bear, yanked off his horsehide mitten, and held out his empty right hand to him. Coal Bear stared down at it a moment as the village grew noisy around them. He looked back into the stranger's face, then glanced quickly at Old Wool Woman's face, finding her happy eyes crying, before gazing behind the stranger. Warriors, women, and other head men raced up on foot.

In confusion, Coal Bear turned back to the dark-skinned man a moment before the stranger suddenly withdrew his hand. How quickly the man's black-cherry eyes narrowed in fear as they darted across all those people rushing toward them. Just as Coal Bear turned to Old Wool Woman, about to ask who her companion might be, he saw her stab her head toward the lodgedoor. A signal for the stranger.

In that instant the stranger ducked to the side, scooting behind Coal Bear to plunge into the lodge before the old man could twist around to stop him.

"Old Wool Woman?"

Coal Bear wheeled around again at the sound of Little Wolf's voice. The Sweet Medicine Chief had reached Old Wool Woman's knee, looking up at her astride the back of the tall American horse.

She was crying hard now, sobbing so hard she was unable to utter a word. Yet at the same time she was laughing as she sank from the saddle and touched the ground. Arms stretched out for her, countless arms. Other happy, wet faces emerged from the crowd, all of those eyes as teary as hers, their cheeks rubbing together in welcome as the many cried together.

"One who was lost has now returned!" Morning Star hollered above the tumult.

"One who we thought dead," Coal Bear croaked with a shaky voice, feeling the tears sting his own eyes as he stepped forward to embrace Old Wool Woman, "has come back to us alive."

She stepped into the old priest's arms, laying her leathery cheek against his chest where she sobbed and laughed, then laughed some more. Around the two of them women sang in tremolo and trilled their tongues, while children cried out

and men sang their courage songs. Such happiness Coal
Bear's people hadn't had in a long, long time.

In the midst of that joyous reunion, the Sacred Hat Priest
bent his head, putting his lips beside Old Wool Woman's ear,
and whispered, "Who is this stranger who takes refuge in our
sacred lodge?"

Chapter 8

Big Hoop-and-Stick Moon
1877

Old Wool Woman could not believe it—how she could
cry and laugh at the same time.

Antelope Woman would not let go of her hand from the
moment Old Wool Woman dropped to the ground. Patting
that bony hand, stroking it, squeezing it while so many others
pressed close, all of them chattering like a flock of noisy magpies.

She could barely speak, hardly get a sound out, there was
something thick clogging her throat. She could not remember
ever feeling this way before, at least not since that warm
night when her family heard a young man playing his flute
outside their lodge and her father told her she should go out
to listen because the flute-player was a brave, honorable
young man. No, he was not wealthy, nor would he be able
to bring many ponies to a young bride's father, but her father
said that the young one was a good man. Old Wool Woman
hadn't felt this way, hadn't sensed such utter and exquisite
joy since that night when she ventured outside her family
lodge and let Black White Man play his love songs for her.

Oh, how she wished he were here for her to return home
to. How she wished her sons and daughter were here to welcome her among her people. But her sons were dead, and
Fingers Woman was a captive at the Bear Coat's fort.

Then she realized, standing in the middle of the noisy,

pulsing knot of well-wishers that they had become her family in these moons since she had lost her husband and sons. They had protectively wrapped themselves around her wounded heart the way they were crowding around her now, cooing as they stroked her face, touched her hair, stared into her eyes to be certain sure it really was her returned from the *ve-ho-e*'s army prison.

Then Morning Star suddenly grabbed both her arms, spun her toward him in an embrace before he asked, "Who is this Hunkpapa you brought to our camp?"

"He . . . he is not a Hunkpapa," Old Wool Woman replied with a stammer.

Little Wolf leaned forward to demand, "Who is he then, if not a Lakota? He is not Shahiyela!"

"He is Big Leggings," she explained in a loud, cracking voice above the noise of the crowd around them. "The one our people call 'White.' " Behind Morning Star and Little Wolf she suddenly recognized how restless and agitated the young men of the warrior societies had become: Kit Fox Soldiers and Elkhorn Scrapers, the Crazy Dogs and Bowstrings too. All of them were goading one another into a lather. They actually believed an enemy had penetrated their camp.

"The Lakota called Big Leggings?" Coal Bear cried, staring in disbelief at the entrance to his sacred lodge.

"The same," Old Wool Woman replied.

Last Bull, the war chief shamed at the Red Fork fight, lunged forward, spitting out his words, "When Buffalo Bull Sitting Down visited Crazy Horse not long ago, he told our camp that this Big Leggings was a traitor!"

That news made her skin turn cold. "The Lakota . . . where is Crazy Horse? Is he here in this camp?"

"No, he is less than a day away," Morning Star reported.

She grew even more frightened for the delicate prospect of peace, for the half-breed's life. "Did he go with Buffalo Bull Sitting Down, still hoping to gather the Lakota to make more war on the soldiers?"

Little Wolf shook his head. "Buffalo Bull Sitting Down is taking his people north to the Land of the Grandmother . . . alone."

"And Crazy Horse is ready to start with his village to the Little Powder to spend the rest of the winter," Coal Bear finished explaining.

"I don't think there ever again will be a village big enough that we can crush the soldiers sent against us," Morning Star declared sadly. "But the white man does not bother us here, and there are a few buffalo—"

"How did you escape from the Bear Coat?" Last Bull interrupted suspiciously.

"I did not escape," she explained. "The soldier chief asked me to come speak to my people."

"About what?" Little Wolf demanded.

"To tell you what choices each of you has for your families and your children." Then Old Wool Woman raised her voice so all could hear. "Big Leggings and I left some pack animals over there in the brush by the river. Go bring them to us here."

Little Wolf ordered a few young men to hurry off to the nearby riverbank. In a matter of minutes they were back, herding a double-handful of army mules, each one laden with packs.

"What are these?" Morning Star asked.

"The animals carry presents," she explained. "Unload them here in front of the sacred lodge."

It did not take long to strip those packs from the mules, to spread out the canvas covers and expose the bags of sugar and coffee, bacon and dried fruit, along with beans and dark plugs of army tobacco. Everything taken off those ten mules was quickly stacked in several impressive piles.

Old Wool Woman stepped to Coal Bear's side and announced, "All that you see before you here is sent to you and the chiefs, sent not only to our military leaders, but also to every woman and child too . . . by the Bear Coat."

"Gifts from the soldiers?" Coal Bear asked.

"Yes, because the Bear Coat shows you how much he wants to make peace with us."

Coal Bear hushed the eager, excited crowd, then began calling out names of warriors from the societies, ordering the young men to divide the gifts equally between all the lodges. Everything, that is, except the tobacco.

"If there is anything left over from the sugar and coffee and army meat, we will use it tonight for our council meal," Coal Bear explained. "And for the tobacco—the society headmen and chiefs will use this when we smoke to consider the important matters Old Wool Woman has brought before us."

As the warriors came forward, the space around Old Wool Woman and the chiefs became a beehive of activity.

Last Bull stepped forward haughtily. "You could have brought these presents here on your own, Old Wool Woman. Why did you bring that traitor with you?"

Behind him several warriors pressed close, as if they might invade the sanctuary that was the Sacred Hat Lodge if given permission by their leaders.

"Big Leggings is here to help." Old Wool Woman sought to soothe the angry temper of the crowd inching her closer and closer to the entrance to Coal Bear's lodge. "He speaks Lakota. Most of us speak some Lakota too. He brings the words from the Bear Coat. The same words the Bear Coat told me to bring to you himself."

"If you know the Bear Coat's words," Little Wolf asked, "then why did the half-breed traitor come with you?"

She drew herself up to her full height with dignity as she sought the words for her answer, "Big Leggings came to protect me on my journey. He came to see that I made it back to my people safely. And he came to convince our leaders that we can make a good peace with the Bear Coat."

"There is no good peace with the *ve-ho-e*!" Last Bull growled.

"These are matters for us to discuss in council," Little Wolf declared, silencing most of the angry muttering. Then he held his arms high, demanding complete quiet. "Coal Bear will prepare the Sacred Hat Lodge so that the head men can meet to discuss what news Big Leggings brings from the soldier camp."

"Turn the half-breed over to us!" a voice cried out among the young warriors.

"Yes!" a second voice shouted above all the murmuring. "We will exact our revenge for the good lives the soldiers took at the Red Fork fight!"

"Give him to us, Coal Bear!" a new voice called out. "We will spill his blood the way the white man spilled the blood of Big Crow!"

"No!" Little Wolf shouted, shoving back two of the young hot-bloods eager to reach the doorway. "This visitor sits in the Sacred Lodge. No one will bring him harm. There he can eat and sleep as a guest. While he is our guest, we will listen to his words. And we will consider what the Bear Coat offers us for peace."

"The word of a *ve-ho-e* is worth as much as the dung of a coyote!"

"You are wrong!" Morning Star shouted back at the voice from the crowd. "What the Bear Coat has said he would do, he has always done. He told us that if we did not come in to surrender at his soldier camp, he would come looking for us and attack our village. The Bear Coat was true to his word. He attacked our camp. And the Bear Coat also told us he would treat his captives kindly. That he would feed them and keep them warm. Now look at Old Wool Woman. And you will see for yourselves that the Bear Coat speaks the truth."

"Yes," Little Wolf said gravely as the clamor died around him. "If the Bear Coat tells us he will come make war on us . . . we will have to sleep on our weapons, we will have to watch our back-trail, we will have to live in constant fear. Because the Bear Coat does what he says he will do."

Esevone's home is a place of refuge.

Any enemy is safe in Her home.

Johnny Bruguier kept murmuring the old woman's words over and over again as the crowd outside grew louder, their voices angrier. Every now and then he imagined he could make out Old Wool Woman's voice among all the others, but most of the time her voice was swallowed up, drowned out by louder, angrier, deeper voices.

While he did not understand most of the sharp-tongued Shahiyela words, Johnny had no trouble comprehending their meaning.

He became aware that he was finally growing warm. Dragging the horsehide mittens from his hands, Bruguier yanked at the buckle to his gun belt, dropping the rigging beside him on a pile of blankets. He slipped out of his coat, then laid the holster and belt on top of it, pistol butt positioned just so, ready. Staring at the doorflap, Johnny flexed the fingers of his gun hand. If those who spoke with sharp-edged voices outside shoved into this lodge, at least he could take a few of them before they took him.

Something caused him to turn his head, to study the back of the lodge, across the fire pit from where he crouched. There lay the bed he knew belonged to the owner of the lodge. Positioned against the lodgeskins at the head of a skimpy pile of blankets and a pair of buffalo robes stood a tripod some four feet tall. From that tripod of stout, peeled saplings hung a bundle, its wide strap embroidered with porcupine quills.

"The Buffalo Hat," he whispered, rocking forward on his knees.

He sensed a sudden anticipation rush through him like the fiery burn of adrenaline that heated his veins when danger raised its head. Curiosity made him yearn to move, yet fear of the unknown kept him riveted to the spot—unmoving, tense, and trembling. He remembered how a light came across Old Wool Woman's face whenever she spoke to him of this lodge, of that bundle, of the powerful object kept within the bundle's furry protection.

Even though many of the voices continued bitter and angry just outside the lodge—no more than a matter of feet from him—Johnny Bruguier felt himself growing calm. He sank onto the blanket beside his coat once more, and settled, not taking his eyes off that bundle. While curiosity urged him to look inside at this object these Shahiyela revered above all others, he was amazed to find that he was at peace with waiting.

Surprisingly, Bruguier felt safe right here in the middle of the enemy camp. Genuinely secure and safe from harm. No matter that there were hundreds outside who would gladly kill him because he had come here uninvited, because he was a courier from Bear Coat Miles, because he was a half-breed scout who had helped tear six Shahiyela women and children away from their people and drag them north to the soldier post at the mouth of the Tongue.

The doorflap was pulled aside and a head appeared.

Bruguier jerked anxiously, his heart rising in his throat. Old Wool Woman entered. He swallowed hard, and found himself smiling. Glad to see her. She smiled in turn and nodded as she came through the door, crouched, both arms laden with what Johnny guessed to be some of the rations Miles sent with them on the mules. Right behind her came a younger woman, small packages filling her arms as well. Her gaze met Johnny's for a long moment. He read no fear, no hatred in her eyes. She turned away and continued to the back of the lodge where she and Old Wool Woman laid their treasures on the Hat Keeper's bedding.

Old Wool Woman knelt by the fire, warming her cold hands, rubbing each joint and swollen knuckle the way he had watched her rub them over every one of their fires, morning and night. As she kneaded her sore flesh, she gazed up at him.

"You are safe here, Big Leggings," she spoke in halting Lakota so he would understand her.

"I feel safe here," he admitted. His eyes flicked over to the younger woman with the pretty face, accentuated by the highest cheekbones he had seen in a long time.

"This is Antelope Woman," the older one explained. "She has been a special friend to me for a long time." Turning to the younger woman, she spoke in Shahiyela. Then she looked back at Johnny, and said, "I reminded Antelope woman who you are, that you are here to talk peace between the Bear Coat and our people."

"What did you bring in?" he asked, pointing at the small bundles of waxed paper the two had placed at the rear of the lodge.

"The Old Man Chiefs wanted us to bring in some of the food the Bear Coat sent with us—so they can have a meal before they smoke the pipe and talk about these important words you bring from the soldier chief."

"Food," he repeated in Lakota, realizing his nervous stomach might also be very hungry. Johnny hadn't eaten anything that morning at their breakfast fire, knowing that this was the day they would catch up to the village. He had sipped at coffee, reminding his hands not to tremble as they gripped his coffee tin.

As Old Wool Woman started to rise, Johnny asked, "Where are you going?"

"We are going to help bring more wood and water here to Coal Bear's lodge," she instructed. "The meal and all the talk will last long into the night."

"You'll be back?" He surprised himself for asking what he might ask of his own mother.

How close he felt to her after their days and nights of travel. Safe near her. Secure in the truths she shared with him. Knowing that she spoke honestly, bravely. Old Wool Woman had been right all along about everything: that she could get him into the village without being harmed, that he could reach this sacred lodge where he would be safe and he could speak with the Shahiyela leaders.

"I'll return soon," she vowed as she slipped past him quickly.

Antelope Woman followed and together they left the lodge. The frozen flap slid back across the entrance about the time the loud and angry voices quieted. He sat there a few moments, listening intently to the noises. Sounds of feet shuffling away across the icy, groaning snow. The snort of one of their horses. Voices of men and women and young children withdrawing, fading off gradually.

Outside it grew so quiet that he was startled when the doorflap was pulled aside. Fully expecting to see Old Wool Woman's face again, Johnny felt his breath quicken when a man ducked inside. The flap slid back over the door and the older warrior stood, closely studying Bruguier a moment before he stepped around the fire to the back of the lodge.

There he knelt among the small bundles the women had delivered, sniffing at some of them, setting some of the parcels near the edge of the fire pit, placing others directly beneath the tripod that held the sacred bundle aloft at the head of his bed. That done, the old priest looked hard at Johnny with narrowed eyes and sighed.

"You speak Lakota, I am told," he said in the halting language of Bruguier's Hunkpapa mother.

"Yes, but I do not know much of your language."

"It is good that the old woman brought you here," the man admitted, stopping a few times to remember words, to recall just how to phrase certain things.

"She told me I would be safe in your lodge."

The older man glanced over his shoulder at the tripod and its sacred bundle. "You are safe here. *Esevone* will guard you with Her power."

"Everything the old woman told me about your people, about this lodge and you . . . everything she said is true."

The priest smiled. "Old Wool Woman has no reason to lie about the powers of the Everywhere Spirit." He bent over the fire a moment and poked at it with a small tree limb. "She tells us you watched over her on your journey here to this place."

Bruguier shrugged slightly. "I brought her here, yes. To return her to her people."

"You are a tracker for the army now?"

"Yes," he admitted.

"Will you speak to our leaders for the Bear Coat?"

"I bring his words to your chiefs."

The priest tossed the limb into the embers. "My name is Coal Bear. I am Keeper of the Sacred Buffalo Hat of our people."

"The woman said you were a man of great power."

Coal Bear grinned while gazing into the flames, as if sharing in a private joke. "It is not my power, but the power of the Hat Old Wool Woman spoke of."

They were quiet for some time until Johnny asked, "When will the others come to smoke the pipe and talk?"

"Later," Coal Bear answered. "Perhaps you would like to rest now. To sleep some before the others come."

By way of an answer, Johnny shoved his coat to the side and laid his head upon it. Then he dragged his gun belt so that it pressed against his belly.

"You are safe here," Coal Bear said, bringing his eyes from the pistol to the half-breed's face. "You will not need your gun. This is a sacred place."

Rocking up on his elbow, Johnny asked, "Do you want to keep my gun? I do not want you to think I am afraid in your home. If you say I am safe here, I will trust your words."

"No," said Coal Bear, waving his hand as if dismissing the whole matter. "I do not want to take your gun. You keep it for when you leave and go back to the Bear Coat's house at the mouth of the Buffalo Tongue River. Out there you will need a gun. But here, in sight of the power of *Esevone*, all men are at peace. All tongues speak the truth. And all hearts are set on the right path."

Johnny laid his head back down on his coat and stretched out his legs. He let out a sigh, telling himself to sleep. Listening to the crackle of the fire, listening to the noises the old man made for a long time.

After some time, Coal Bear said, "It was a good thing the old woman brought you here to this lodge."

Bruguier opened his eyes slightly, and said, "Old Wool Woman and I watched over one another, we kept one another safe on our journey here."

"Yes—but it was the power of *Esevone* that watched over the old woman, the power that kept *her* safe."

Chapter 9

Mid-February 1877

"The soldiers fed us well," the old woman told those leaders gathered in council. "We had a good place to stay out of the cold, and the guards watched us so that nobody bothered us."

Johnny Bruguier looked from face to face of those ringing the fire here in Coal Bear's lodge, eager for something that might betray what they thought of the woman's story. Some of the war chiefs and head men glanced at one another momentarily; others murmured or grunted, nodding their heads as the woman described the conditions for the Shahiyela captives at the Bear Coat's fort.

Having shown up just after dark, the leaders of both tribes had talked quietly among themselves during their meal of pork and hard bread, dried fruit and boiled white beans, finished off with cups of steamy coffee, sweetened with sugar. Then Coal Bear unwrapped his pipebowl from the skin of a mountain cougar and the long ash stem from the folds of a red-haired buffalo calf. Putting the two pieces together, he next laid out his willow bark, dried dung, and wild rosehips, mixing these with some of the soldiers' tobacco. It was clear to Johnny that the old priest had prepared more than enough for one pipeful.

With the bowl loaded, Coal Bear nodded to the warrior seated to his right. The one called White Bull scratched among the embers at the edge of the firepit and, with two small twigs, extracted a small piece of coal. White Bull placed the glowing coal atop the tobacco in the bowl and leaned back, while Coal Bear lit his pipe. The Sacred Hat Priest murmured his prayers in Shahiyela to the cardinal directions—to the earth and sky and all the sacred persons—then passed the pipe to his left, following the path of the sun. Crazy Horse was the next to take the pipe. Then one after another the rest drew breath through the bowl and stem, sending their smoke toward the sky above as they uttered their prayers in either Lakota or Shahiyela.

When the pipe reached the doorway, it was handed halfway round the lodge to Coal Bear who passed it to White Bull so that it might continue its journey. When the pipe finally reached the half-breed, Coal Bear spoke slowly in Lakota so the stranger could understand.

"You are the one the *Ohmeseheso* people call 'White,' " the priest explained. "You may smoke with us, because this is a sacred occasion. Smoke, and let your moment with the pipe be your vow that only the truth will pass your lips."

Bruguier nodded, feeling the eyes of nearly half-a-hundred warriors and old man chiefs concentrate on him at that moment. In his mind he remembered those few occasions when his mother's people had invited him to sit in on special ceremonies: a naming, a memorial, perhaps a song-making. Johnny remembered how he was taught to smoke so that each breath was a prayer uttered before the Lakota's Great Mystery. He hadn't prayed in a long time. But here tonight, he found himself praying harder than he had ever prayed before.

With each puff he waved some of the exhaled smoke back toward himself. The first time he brushed some smoke over his head, and down each side of his long hair. The second time he rubbed some smoke over his chest. On and on, with each puff he brushed some of the sacred smoke over his arms and his legs.

Once he had finished, Johnny passed the pipe back to his right. As it began its return journey to Coal Bear, the priest said something in Shahiyela. The warrior nearest the door-flap scrambled out the door, returning momentarily with Old Wool Woman, who was wrapped in her gray army blanket.

She entered and stepped to the right, settling in the last vacant place between Johnny and the door.

"Welcome to the Sacred Lodge of the Medicine Hat," Coal Bear addressed her. "Tell us all of your travels to the soldier fort."

She began to tell these leaders how well the Bear Coat and his men had treated their captives. While most of the soldiers at the post lived in canvas tents with log walls, she and the other prisoners were eventually given a place of their own inside a timber lodge almost as big as the Bear Coat's.

"While the soldiers are given three meals each day," she explained, "any time we asked for food, it was brought to us."

A special place was made for the women to relieve themselves in privacy. Twin Woman's two young children, Red Hood and Crane Woman, were special objects of affection and attention for the soldiers. Many of the *ve-ho-e* came by each day to play with the youngsters, to talk to them, to learn some of the Shahiyela tongue from them too.

"We did not feel we were at war with the Bear Coat and his men," she declared.

"But these are the same men who have made war on us," Last Bull roared, the veins in his temples throbbing. "They have made war on our villages and our families."

"But Old Wool Woman is showing us that the Bear Coat can make a strong peace," White Bull countered, "or he can make a strong war."

"Go on," Coal Bear instructed her. "What message do you bring from the Bear Coat?"

Old Wool Woman said, "He wants you to know he is your friend. The Bear Coat wants you to come in to his soldier camp and surrender."

"What then?" asked Black Moccasin. "What happens?"

"All will be well if you go to the soldier camp," she answered. "You will have plenty to eat too. No one will be harmed and the rest of the prisoners will be returned to you."

"Why did the Bear Coat keep the younger women there?" Two Moon asked. "Why did he send you?"

Her eyes dropped a moment, then came back to gaze at Coal Bear. "The soldier chief said he chose me because I was the oldest. He wants to make peace. He does not want to harm the Shahiyela. He wants to have you come in so no harm comes to you with more war."

"The soldiers will make more war as soon as the snows are gone?" Little Wolf asked.

"Until all have surrendered," she answered. "That is why the Bear Coat sent me here with Big Leggings. To say you have a choice. You leaders must decide if the People will move in to the soldier camp . . . or if we will have more war."

Several men questioned Old Wool Woman, while others questioned the half-breed, late into the night. Then Coal Bear announced it was time for the council chiefs to discuss the matter between themselves. Their discussion went past the setting of the moon and Johnny grew weary. So late was it that Bruguier was awakened by the tap of a finger at his cheek.

Old Wool Woman knelt over him. The fire burned low at the center of the lodge. The Shahiyela and Lakota leaders were standing, stretching, working kinks out of their legs.

"Did they decide?"

Wagging her head sadly, she whispered, "There are many for making peace with the Bear Coat now; so many are hungry and the horses are poor. Our warriors have little ammunition and the hunting hasn't been good. But it seems there are many chiefs who speak out for continuing the war."

"So . . . what is going to happen?"

"Coal Bear and the Old Man Chiefs have turned the matter over to the leaders of the warrior societies," she told him. "They will meet tomorrow afternoon to come to a decision."

"Tell me," Bruguier begged in a whisper, feeling the prickly rise of apprehension, "does it look good for making peace with the soldiers?"

She shrugged a shoulder and pursed her lips a moment. "I don't know how to answer you right now. I can only trust to the power of *Ma-heo-o* to watch over His people, and to have His people do what is right for them."

Antelope Woman shivered more with anticipation than with the brutal cold, while a sun, pale as mare's milk, slid off midsky.

Leading her brother's ponies back from watering at the frozen river, she suddenly stopped, turned, and gazed back at the hills, at the willow, and other trees along the bank.

Looking north, she saw the shadow of a magpie cross the crusty snow. She remembered that hot day the summer before. Back then the great village had stood not far north from where the ponies were hovering. She remembered. And her heart grew confused. How was she supposed to feel about all that was happening to her people, to her friend Old Wool Woman—about what was happening to her?

Should her people make peace with the *ve-ho-e* soldiers who had killed her nephew, Noisy Walking? She remembered: how proud he was to be one of the suicide boys who paraded through camp. It was the day before the Yellow Hair's soldiers attacked the villages clustered beside the Little Sheep River. He and the handful of others had vowed to give their lives in the fight they knew was coming.

"Look at these!" the elders had exclaimed as the boys slowly rode through the Shahiyela camp and the women cried out in tremolo. "Your eyes will not see these fighters again!"

Noisy Walking had been so proud to give his life to the Spirit Persons in such an honored way. So how would Noisy Walking feel about this talk of peace with the Bear Coat? He had laid down his life in the fight with the soldiers; so how would the young man have felt about Old Wool Woman returning to this camp with her glowing stories of how well the enemy had treated her, fed her, and kept her warm, when that same enemy had destroyed nearly everything the *Ohmeseheso* ever had? When that enemy had taken away all of young Noisy Walking's remaining days?

Many, many more Shahiyela warriors would have been killed that day had not *Ma-heo-o* caused the *ve-ho-e* soldiers to go crazy and turn their guns on themselves.

Stepping from the misty fog of the ponies' breathsmoke, Antelope Woman continued toward the village, where gray curls spiraled from the tops of the new lodges hardly browned from this winter's fires. Since the glory days of their culture, her people had watched Three Finger Kenzie's soldiers and scouts burn all but one of their lodges in the valley of the Red Fork. With nothing, the survivors limped north in search of the Crazy Horse people. Where they could, the Shahiyela crowded in with the Little Star People. Still, some of the survivors preferred to build themselves crude shelters of rock and brush that did little to hold back the winter winds. But in these days since Antelope Woman's people had come across good buffalo country, the women and girls were again busy scraping, curing, tanning the hides. One by one, day after day, these new, white lodges rose against the pale sky, arranged in the grand half-moon of the *Tse-tsehese*,* the horns of the crescent facing the rising sun each morning.

"Sister!"

Antelope Woman turned, finding White Bull riding up slowly behind her.

Bringing his pony to a halt, he smiled and said, "My horses are in good hands with you."

She watched him drop to the snow. Together they continued walking toward the lodges. "You were not in the lodge this morning when I awoke. Your horses needed water for the day so I took them down before breakfast. You must have much on your mind before the council starts."

"Yes, the council," he repeated.

"You are going to speak, aren't you?"

"That is why I was gone when you awoke this morning," White Bull explained. "Sleep was elusive last night, so I finally dressed and took my pipe into the hills before sunrise."

"Did my brother find the answer he sought?"

White Bull was a moment in answering. "There are many answers, Antelope Woman. And I thought on each one of them."

"You are not so quick to speak and act as Last Bull and some of the others—"

"Let them be," he interrupted his younger sister, a stern look of disapproval creasing his face. "If a man wishes to make a fool of himself, a wise person does not seek to stop him."

"I think you are one of the wisest, brother," she said contritely.

Shrugging at her compliment as they entered the camp crescent, White Bull said, "Sometimes . . . I do not feel so wise, young one."

"But you will speak at the warrior society council this afternoon?"

---

*Term both northern and southern peoples use to describe themselves, literally meaning "those who are hearted alike"

"This is a very critical time for our people," he explained almost in a whisper. "We stand at a crossing of trails: one black and one red."

"Old Wool Woman told me this morning she hopes the council decides to make peace with the Bear Coat."

He replied, "Yes, while so many others want us to continue walking down the red road of war."

They stopped beside his lodge where she lived with White Bull's family. He knelt and tied his pony to a tentpeg.

After a long moment she asked, "What road will you walk, brother?"

Brushing his pony's neck with his blanket mitten, White Bull said, "I will set my feet on that road the Sacred Powers told me to walk when I smoked my pipe this morning."

"What road is that?"

The warrior tried out a valiant smile on his sister. "For many winters now, I have been asked to walk the hardest road."

Chapter 10

Big Hoop-and-Stick Game Moon
1877

E ver since the days of his youth, he had been called Ice. Only in recent winters had his name been changed.

With thirty-nine summers behind him now, White Bull was considered a holy man, a powerful doctor by the *Ohmese-heso*. His father, North Left Hand, had been a powerful sha-man among the Southern People—so powerful that it had been said that North Left Hand caused the death of another man he considered a threat to him. For that North Left Hand was banished from the Southern Bands. After wandering, he was taken in by the *Hetane-vo-eo-o*, the Cloud People,* and married a woman of that tribe. They named their firstborn son Ice. North Left Hand's boy grew to be an honorable young man, well respected. It became clear from those early days in the Southern Country that Ice would have special powers to heal, given him by the Sacred Powers.

He was no more than fifteen winters old when he went into the hills for the first time to fast for four days, praying that the Powers would take pity on him. On the fourth day, as his body weakened, desperate to receive an answer, Ice was visited by one of the *Ma-heono*.† Almost unable to

---

*The Southern Arapaho
†The Sacred Powers, the Spiritual Beings

breathe because of his excitement, Ice gazed on the small, handsome man who spoke out of the great silence surrounding that place in the hills.

"Friend, some day I wish you to dig a big hole in the ground. Then I want you to get into it, and to have others put a big rock over the hole in which you put yourself," the Sacred Man instructed. "Let the rock be a large one, even if it is so big that it would take a number of people to lift it. I will be with you and help you, and I will bring you out safely."

"W—when I return to my village?" the young man croaked apprehensively.

"No. But one day," the handsome man said. "One day there will be this testing of your special powers."

The following summer Ice injured his knee in a fall from a pony. No matter what the tribal doctors did for him, no matter how many poultices he applied, or how many times he soaked it in hot springs, or what roots he rubbed on it, the leg remained swollen and sore. It remained very painful for the next two winters, troubling him to the point that he could feel the power of his spirit ebbing out of him just as surely as sweat would seep from his pores. Slowly, day after day, he came to realize the injury would eventually kill him.

So filled with despair was he that Ice hobbled before his father and said, "I know I am going to die. When I do, I don't want you to bury me in the ground and cover me with dirt. As a warrior of my people, leave me out where my flesh can be eaten by birds and animals, so that my flesh can be scattered far and wide toward all four Sacred Directions."

"You must not die this way," North Left Hand argued. "Get ready and I will outfit you for battle. You must go to war and give your body to the enemy."

"Yes, to die in battle," Ice agreed.

"Ride right in before the rest so you can count the first coup, then let them kill you. That will be dying bravely."

Soon he joined a war party riding against the Omaha in their own country. Riding his father's finest war horse, wearing his best clothing, Ice rode straight into battle, kicking his pony ahead of the others so he could be the first to strike. The first enemy he confronted fired his smoothbore at Ice, so close the young man felt the burn of the muzzle-flash. He slashed his quirt across the enemy's arms, knocking the rifle loose. Ice had struck the first coup! But a second Omaha with a bow closed on him. The arrow hissed past Ice's ear.

By that time the rest of the young men had caught up to Ice and joined the fight. In the end they put the Omaha into retreat. When the war party turned south for home, they carried with them three enemy scalps.

When the war party reached their village, North Left Hand was very surprised and extremely happy to see his son still alive. "My son! You have been to war. You have made a vow and given your body to the enemy—but have lived! This truly means you will live to be an old man! You will never be killed by an enemy!"

Ice's father began to dance as his son dismounted, chanting his prayer, "*Ma-heo-o*, I gave you my son. But you took pity on me and you sent him back to me alive so that he may continue to live upon the earth! Now I know he will have a long life."

North Left Hand leaped atop the war pony and began slowly to circle the camp of the Cloud People, calling out the name of certain people in the village, giving each one a horse. As the person called came forward, he put the pony's rope in their hand and related the story of his son's first coup. On and on he continued around the camp, giving away all his horses and repeating the story of Ice's deliverance by the Everywhere Spirit.

From that day onward, Ice never again tried to throw his life away. The Sacred Powers had prevented him from giving his body to the enemy. They had taken pity upon him.

It was becoming clear to the young warrior that the Powers were saving him for other, more important, work in the years to come. By his twenty-third spring when he and his father had journeyed north to live with the *Ohmeseheso*, Ice was already respected as a holy man who possessed powers to heal and protect.

As it stormed outside one hot night, rain slashing against the lodgeskins and lightning streaking the prairie sky, a visitor came to his lodge. Hook Nose, a young warrior also known among his Northern People as the Bat because his movements in battle were as swift and light as a bat swooping at its prey, came to ask help from the young holy man. This Hook Nose was the same Elkhorn Scraper the *ve-ho-e* called "Roman Nose." For the last few seasons the man had refused to become a chief of his warrior society, or to sit on the Council of Forty-Four. His only desire was to protect his people.

The two of them smoked that stormy night in Ice's lodge as the thunder clapped above them. That was a powerful sign from the Spirits.

Finally, Hook Nose asked, "Holy man, did you see anything that will protect a fighting man?"

"Yes, I saw something once. A war bonnet. I saw it when the Thunder came to speak to me."

"Make that war bonnet you saw for me, a war bonnet that would protect a fighting man."

For a long time Ice worked on the bonnet, its solitary buffalo horn and its double trail of feathers, in addition to that special earth paint, Hook Nose would wear whenever he rode into battle. The final touch was to sew a kingfisher skin behind the single horn. Because one of the *Ma-heono* assumes the shape of the kingfisher when he appears to man, this Sacred Being has the power to close up bullet holes. With this skin sewn to the bonnet, Hook Nose would be bulletproof. Even if an enemy's bullet struck the warrior, the wound would close up immediately.

Now it was time for Ice to instruct Hook Nose in the sacred obligations that went along with this powerful headdress.

"After you put this bonnet on your head for the first time, you must never again shake hands with anyone. If you do, you will surely be killed. When you go into a fight, imitate the call of the kingfisher. This will call up the power of the *Ma-heono*."

Then, gazing squarely into Hook Nose's eyes, the young holy man declared, "And you must be faithful to all the vows of the Contraries. Especially the law that says that you cannot eat any food that has been taken from a dish with a metal tool. If you do, you will die in battle," he warned ominously.

Now Hook Nose had been dead nine winters. Killed by the *ve-ho-e* who shot their horses on a sandbar in a narrow riverbed.*

---

*Battle of Beecher Island—*The Stalkers*, vol. 3, The Plainsmen Series

Many were the warriors and chiefs who knew of Ice's warning to Hook Nose. When the great warrior was killed by the *ve-ho-e* a short time after he ate meat prepared with the white man's metal, respect for Ice's holy powers swelled among the *Ohmeseheso*, as well as among the Northern Bands of the Lakota, especially the Little Star People. Side by side with the Lakota, Ice fought the white man, and even saved White Horse's life at the big fight on the Shell River.*

Two summers later, the *ve-ho-e* soldiers had raised three forts in the hunting ground claimed by the Shahiyela and Lakota warrior bands. Even after they had ambushed and slaughtered the Hundred in the Hand,† the soldiers still would not abandon their posts, where they cowered like frightened sow bugs beneath a buffalo chip. The Lakota and *Ohmeseheso* met to hold their respective sun dances and decide what to do to drive the white man out of the buffalo country for good. It was a time of meaningful prayers to the Sacred Powers—a time when Ice recalled his first journey into the hills to pray for a vision. During that moon, when the buffalo bulls were rutting#, the young holy man decided to carry out the wishes of the small, handsome man who had come to him in his vision fifteen summers before.

At their annual camp on the Roseberry River, his people were dancing and praying, calling out for help from the Sacred Powers. Perhaps, Ice believed, his holy strength would save the *Ohmeseheso* and the Lakota from the soldiers.

After selecting a place outside the camp crescent, Ice dug a great hole in the ground deep enough for him to sit up in. Then he gathered a group of men from the warrior societies, sending them into the hills to find a stone large enough to cover the hole he had excavated. Eventually the men returned with a monstrous sandstone slab they had to turn end over end to get down to the village. A crowd of the curious swelled in size as the stone drew closer to the hole.

People scoffed, "What is he doing?"

Others doubted, "Ice cannot move that rock by himself!"

---

*Platte Bridge Fight, July 11, 1865—*Cry of the Hawk*
†Fetterman Massacre, December 21, 1866—*Sioux Dawn*, vol. 1, The Plainsmen Series
#July, 1867

"He will die in that hole!" others cried in panic.

Quieting the crowd, Ice instructed some women to erect a great lodge over the hole, a lodge so big it required three covers. At sunset he held a huge feast inside the lodge, consisting of buffalo, dog, and dried fruit, the three foods blessed during the sun dance. Carrying a special buffalo robe he had painted with the colors of the four Sacred Powers, Ice settled himself at the bottom of that hole as darkness fell.

One of the doubters in the crowd called out, "Let no man leave who brought this stone here! If we cannot pull the rock off the hole, surely Ice will die!"

With all the Old Man Chiefs and the priests of the *Ohmeseheso* present, the leaders formed three rings of the sacred circle around Ice's hole. Then two warriors bound the holy man with bowstrings, hand and foot, before they covered him with his painted robe. He faced the east. In that sudden darkness, he could only hear the sounds of the many who strained and groaned as they muscled the sandstone slab into position. Then there were scraping noises as they moved four rocks atop the huge slab, each placed at one of the cardinal directions, and each so big it would take more than one strong man to lift it.

With that done, Ice listened as they constructed the frame of a sweat lodge upon that sandstone slab, covering the willow branches with buffalo robes just as he had instructed them to do. Eventually, the holy man heard the muffled singing begin as the priests and elders began calling out their prayers for his deliverance.

Becoming aware of the burning ache in his arms and legs, Ice realized how tightly he had been tied by people who did not believe he could accomplish this powerful thing. He told his heart to be quiet, to listen. And for a long time he sat in the darkness as the silence deepened.

After a while, he thought he heard something, then felt something brush past his side. For some unknown reason he could now see when he opened his eyes. There before him sat the little man with the handsome face. Just as he had promised in the dream.

The little man got to his feet and stood in front of Ice. "Why have your people put you here?"

"They think they are in trouble with the *ve-he-o* and they want help."

"They tied you because they don't believe you can do this thing?"

"Yes," Ice answered gravely. "I do not think many of them believe I can."

"They should learn to believe," the holy little person replied. "Shut your eyes."

The moment Ice closed his eyes, the little man slapped him on the sole of his right foot, then slapped the sole of his left foot. Moving around Ice, the holy person took Ice by the hair and pulled on it. It felt just as if he pulled Ice up a little, straightening his back.

"Now," the holy person said to him. "Open your eyes."

When Ice looked, he found himself standing outside the huge lodge. Many of the people unable to crowd into the lodge were gathered there before him. Directly in front of him stood a woman whose back was turned to him.

She called out to the priest and chiefs in the lodge. "Why don't you hurry up and sing your sacred songs before he gets smothered under that great rock?"

Her question confused him, so Ice asked her, "Who will be smothered?"

Whirling around in surprise, the woman gazed at Ice, her face filling with amazement. Her lips moved but she could not utter a sound.

"Let them finish their songs," Ice told her quietly. "Then ask them to light a fire and we will have something to eat. I am very hungry."

In that next moment, others who were standing outside the lodge turned to discover Ice among them. Some began to shout their miraculous news to those inside the lodge.

"Look under the rock to see it isn't true!" disbelievers cried.

"Move the rock and you will find his body!" others hollered.

But when the warriors went to remove the sweatlodge from the top of the slab, they found it and the four smaller rocks had already been shifted to the side of the lodge, stacked neatly out of the way. Then they discovered that the hole was empty. Atop the stones lay the painted robe, and across it lay the bowstrings that had been used to secure Ice's wrists and ankles.

From that moment on, the Northern People referred to the event as Ice's miracle. And by showing his faith in the Spirit Persons, the holy man was given a new name.

Now he was known as White Bull.

Chapter II

Big Hoop-and-Stick Game Moon
1877

BY TELEGRAPH

SERIOUS INDIAN DEPREDATIONS

IN THE BLACK HILLS.

THE INDIANS.

Lo, the Poor Indian, Devastating
Deadwood and Vicinity.

DEADWOOD, February 15.—During the last week a number of reports of Indian depredations have been coming in from small towns adjacent here, and to-day these rumors assumed an alarming aspect. Well substantiated news of simultaneous attacks in different directions leads to a belief that the Indians are surrounding this vicinity. Volen's large cattle train was captured entire near Bear Butte yesterday, and Fletcher's herd of mules was also captured in the same vicinity. The Montana ranch, a short distance from here, was attacked about the same time, the Indians capturing all the stock.

> Wigginton's herd of horses, which was near
> Crook City, were all captured, Wigginton
> wounded, and his assistant killed. Considera-
> ble stock in the vicinity of Spearfish was also
> run off.

White Bull found much to loathe in Last Bull, leader of the Kit Fox warrior society.

In the past two winters, Last Bull had grown all the more arrogant and belligerent. Long ago he had stolen the wife of American Horse, now a respected Council Chief. Everyone knew Last Bull for an overbearing bully, whipping not only the members of his own society, but having his warriors quirt and humiliate others in camp when rules were not obeyed. By the time Three Finger Kenzie's soldiers attacked their camp on the Red Fork, the Kit Fox Warriors were commonly known as the "Wife Stealers" or the "Beating-Up Soldiers."

Last Bull's arrogance had cost the *Ohmeseheso* their village, their wealth, their weapons, their very way of life. Yet instead of becoming apologetic and humble before the people he had brought to ruin, Last Bull had grown angry and bitter as the rival Elkhorn Scrapers increased their prestige and respectability in the eyes of the Northern People. Their members were legendary, men who time and again put the good of the band above their own selfish desires.

Little Wolf, as Sweet Medicine Chief, was head of all the Council Chiefs. He was an Elkhorn Scraper, not a Kit Fox Warrior.

Old Bear, the venerable chief whose winter village on the Powder River was attacked by soldiers, was an Elkhorn.

Black Moccasin, respected member of the Council of Forty-Four, was an Elkhorn as well.

Hook Nose, the one called Roman Nose by the *ve-ho-e*, who led the charge against the white men huddled behind their dead horses even though he knew it would mean his life, had been a revered Elkhorn.

Lame White Man, second only to Little Wolf in courage, a warrior who gave his life leading his people against the soldiers at the fight on the Little Goat River—an Elkhorn too.

In his fighting days, even the blind, elderly priest Box Elder was an Elkhorn.

Wild Hog, Crow Split Nose, White Hawk, Tall White Man, Left-Handed Shooter, Goes After Other Buffalo, Plenty Bears, Wolf Medicine, Broken Jaw—all were Elkhorn fighting men now grown famous among their people in this time of grave trouble with the soldiers.

Why, membership in the Elkhorn Scraper Society even spanned tribal lines. Young Man Afraid of His Horses, a revered Shirt-Wearer for the Lakota Little Star People, was an Elkhorn.

And to a man, these Elkhorn Scrapers regarded Last Bull with nothing less than a fiery contempt. More than being just an unworthy leader of one of the four warrior societies founded long, long ago by Sweet Medicine himself, the Elkhorns believed Last Bull to be little short of a duplicitous, self-serving, and conniving liar.

It made a fire smolder inside White Bull's belly to see how Last Bull strode in now to brazenly take his place among the head chiefs and little chiefs of those three warrior societies still remaining in the Northern Country this winter. One at a time the leaders of the *Ohmeseheso* entered the huge double lodge erected for this grand council to discuss the news brought them by Old Wool Woman, upon which the Old Man Chiefs could not reach agreement: the Bear Coat's demand for surrender. Gathered to listen, to argue, and to decide this most important issue were these chiefs of the Kit Fox Warriors, the Elkhorn Scrapers, and the Crazy Dogs.

Once every headman had settled four deep in that great ring surrounding the fire, the rest of the village pressed close on all sides of the great double lodge so they too could hear the deliberations. With the lower edges of the lodgeskins rolled up, the coming debate would be a most public matter.

Because of their ancient position of honor among the warrior societies of the Northern People, the Kit Foxes were allowed to speak first. Wisely realizing that their leader, Last Bull, might well poison their position if he spoke before the assembly, the Kit Fox Soldiers decided that Two Moon should instead address the gathering.

"For many summers we have fought the *ve-ho-e* soldiers while we went about our journeys, following the migration of the buffalo in our hunts," Two Moon began as he gazed about his audience, speaking with understated eloquence. He wore a large feather tied to a forelock and attached to a piece of buffalo horn. "And when each summer was done, so was the fighting. The soldiers went back to their forts and they left us to our lives. But for the last two winters the soldiers have not let us be."

There arose the first shards of angry muttering.

"The *ve-ho-e* have stalked our villages of women and children, finding our camps in the river valleys, driving our families into the wilderness with little but the clothes they wear. No more is war with the white man a summer occupation. The *ve-ho-e* promised to follow us, harass us, crush us in the snows of winter. And that is the one promise the white man has kept."

Many of the Kit Foxes were crying loud in response to his impassioned words. Beyond them, among the spectators, many of the women openly wailed, keening as they remembered the husbands and fathers, sons and nephews lost in battle after battle with the soldiers.

"While for some of you, your burning hatred of the soldiers will lead you to fight on and on and on until there is not one *Ohmeseheso* left alive," Two Moon continued, his strong voice cracking with emotion, "your burning hate will destroy us! But for me, I stand before these leaders to declare I will go to speak to the Bear Coat, to listen to his words. And if his words are straight and fair . . . I will surrender to the soldier chief at the Elk River Fort."

When Two Moon finished his long, impassioned speech, Wrapped Hair was the next to stand and recite his war deeds before this great assembly. Then he too added his voice in favor of surrender. Bear Who Walks on a Ridge spoke as afternoon stretched into evening, as the winter night descended upon their camp. Still more of the Kit Fox Warriors stood to speak, all echoing the sentiments of Two Moon.

A cold, gibbous moon had risen in the east and hung against the cold sky by the time the last Kit Fox Soldier had finished his argument in favor of surrender. At last it was time for the Elkhorn Scrapers to express their views.

Although Little Wolf and Morning Star were both members of the warrior society, as Old Man Chiefs they did not choose to speak before this council. Instead, Wild Hog stood. It was clear to White Bull to see that he was seething with the same rage that burned inside Little Wolf.

"How does the *Ohmeseheso* talk of surrender to the *ve-ho-e*?" the Hog's voice crackled with thunderous emotion.

"How does any warrior of the People talk of making peace with the soldiers who have made war on our women and children?"

Suddenly the Elkhorns came alive within the great lodge, sentiment strong and deep among those hardy spectators standing in the cold around the ring of warrior chiefs.

"We did not choose to make this war on the *ve-ho-e*," Wild Hog declared. "The white man came to our country, driving off the buffalo, killing off the game. We did not ask him to come to our country!"

Many in the noisy throng did more than grunt their approval.

Hog spoke for a long time, that place between his eyes deeply furrowed as he uttered each word the way a man might spit out a foul oath.

"The *ve-ho-e* declared war on us. He sends his soldiers to destroy everything we have. And when we have nothing left but our lives, he sends Old Wool Woman and the half-breed to tell us we better surrender or he will keep making war on us. As for me, I will tell the Bear Coat to come kill me himself!"

After the loud approval had quieted, Left-Handed Shooter spoke.

"I am a warrior of the People. Many times have I offered my body to protect those who cannot protect themselves. In all the days left me, I will continue to give my life to my enemy to save the *Ohmeseheso*. The white man will not go away on his own. He thinks this is his land when it does not belong to him. He thinks the buffalo belong to him, when the buffalo belong to *Ma-heo-o*. How can you teach such a creature what is right and what is wrong?"

"You can never teach the white man how to live like a human being!" a voice called from the gathering outside the lodge.

White Bull quickly turned in that direction, hoping to see who had cried out. He could not, but he did catch a glimpse of his younger sister. Antelope Woman stood at the edge of the gathering, a blanket clasped around both her and Old Wool Woman. On the other side of the old woman stood the clearly anxious half-breed. The fire-lit darkness accentuated the deep furrows of worry deeply chiseled into his face.

Yes, White Bull thought as another of his fellow Elkhorn Scrapers prepared to argue for war over surrender, yes; this

Big Leggings must feel like a crippled dung beetle trapped on a teeming anthill. Things did not look good for the advocates of peace.

Yet as he listened to the harsh, strident arguments of the Elkhorns, White Bull saw not the procession of speakers but the weary, hunger-ravaged faces of those spectators crowded around the war council. True enough, there were many young warriors whose eyes ignited with each renewed call to carry on the fight. Some were young men who had only come of age in the past few winters of struggle against the *ve-ho-e*. There were some who hadn't experienced war as White Bull and other older warriors had—the seasons of pain, tribulation, death, and mourning this war had visited upon the People.

But, as he recalled his own youth, White Bull realized he could not tell much of anything to a brash young warrior. For some reason, they already knew all they needed to know. It had always been that way with the young hot-bloods, and it would always be so.

While the Elkhorn Scrapers continued to denounce any talk of surrender, it was not the faces of those young men eager to carry on the struggle that drew this veteran's attention.

No, White Bull looked closely at the faces of the women—mothers, sisters, daughters, and aunts of the many warriors who had been killed in this ongoing fight with the *ve-ho-e*. There in the dancing light of the council fire, his heart was most touched by the faces of the little ones, some who were destined to grow to adulthood without knowing their fathers, some who might only have an uncle or grandfather as tutor and mentor. Those children who huddled beside their mothers or those clutched in the arms of grandmothers, yes, these members of the *Ohmeseheso* would be the ones who suffered the deepest for any difficult decision made by the wise and respected men of this council.

Next White Bull looked here and there at the deeply lined faces of the few old ones left among the Northern People this second terrible winter of war. Not nearly so many as there had been when Old Bear began his march south for the White Rock Agency the previous year.* Night by freezing night, the bodies of the old ones began to fail. With so little to eat, with so much endless cold, with so far to travel after each attack of the soldiers—one by one the spirits of those old ones simply gave up their long and valiant fight to survive.

Winter had devastated the People every bit as much as war had. Both were vicious, evil enemies that preyed not on the strong and bold of the tribe. Instead, winter and war alike preyed on the weak, the very young and the very old, preyed on those who could least defend themselves.

As White Bull looked across at those shivering within their blankets and buffalo robes at the edge of the firelight, those listening to the long harangues on war versus surrender, he heard nothing but the endless voices of those prideful, strutting prairie cocks who made war out to be a man's destiny.

Yet here in this winter of despair, what White Bull saw so vividly was that war did not make the warriors its victims . . . but rather the old, the young, and the women.

By the time the moon had set, all but one of the Elkhorn Scrapers had spoken in favor of continuing the war. The society stood foursquare against the Kit Foxes' desire to surrender at the Bear Coat's Elk River Fort. The only Elkhorn yet to speak was White Bull.

Outside the lodge in that deep cold, pricked with the distant shimmer of countless stars, outside that council lodge where nothing stirred but the frosty breath of the onlookers, the crowd now fell completely silent. Inside, the leaders of the three warrior societies remained respectful and hushed as this great and revered holy man of the *Ohmeseheso* cleared his throat after nearly a day of disuse.

"It is very, very late and we have heard so much talk already today," White Bull said to the startled throng. "My heart is very, very heavy with all that has been said. I yearn to say what weighs heavily on my mind. But because all of you must be tired, because what I have to say speaks directly

---

to the hearts of those who are surely the most weary . . . tomorrow we will gather here in this place when the sun has risen two hands above the horizon. It is then that I will speak my heart on this matter of war or surrender for our people."

Chapter 12

Mid-February 1877

Johnny Bruguier walked to the large council tent with Old Wool Woman that winter morning as the crowd began to gather. Since dawn, the sky had been hinting that the heavy cloud cover would blow on over, freeing the sun to shine at last. But for now, as a half-dozen women started the fire in the big council lodge, the sun was nothing more than a hazy pewter button climbing toward midsky.

For the past two days the half-breed had been brooding on just how smart he'd been to let himself get talked into helping the soldier chief at the Yellowstone. More than once Johnny had convinced himself that he had stepped right in it by putting himself within reach of, and at risk from, these Shahiyela warriors and their mourning women. During those long hours he spent by himself in the lodge Old Wool Woman had explained was sacred, Bruguier had time to worry, lots of time to grow increasingly more scared of just what might happen if the chiefs decided to continue to make war on the army—starting with that half-breed courier from the Bear Coat.

Although he figured the chances were slim that the young, angry warriors would actually break a taboo by entering the Sacred Hat Lodge to snatch him, Johnny nonetheless sensed no real welcome as he sat in the old priest's home. Coal Bear and his woman never spoke to Bruguier, rarely even glanced at their visitor as they came and went about their business; they ate, slept, prepared meals, smoked the pipe, received visitors, and, when the rest of the village gathered at the nearby council lodge, departed without a word.

As hard as he tried through those first two days, pressing his ear right against the scraped buffalo hides of the sacred lodge, Johnny still could not make out what the various voices said when they grew loud with impassioned argument. About all he could be certain of was that he was listening to a lot of anger. Hour after hour that second day he grew more consumed with worry that such fury might well boil over and engulf him.

After all, he was alone there in the sacred lodge, jumpy and startled each time the doorflap was pulled back, especially when the one called Antelope Woman ducked inside late the night after a long, long day of arguing among the Shahiyela. He had breathed a little easier when a second woman came in to stand by the first.

"You remember my friend?" Old Wool Woman asked in her slow-spoken Lakota, so he could understand.

Nodding to the young woman, Johnny then looked into Old Wool Woman's eyes. "What is going on with the surrender talks?"

As he watched, Bruguier saw some of the skin sag around her eyes again.

Old Wool Woman answered, "There are many who say they will go south to the White River Agency once the weather warms and the ponies are stronger."

"To surrender at the Lakota agency?"

"Yes, we are close to the Little Star People there," she nodded. "But . . . there are many voices who have strong talk against surrendering at all."

Johnny had waited a few moments, expecting Old Wool Woman to go on. When she didn't, he asked, "Are any of your people going to surrender to Miles at his fort?"

Gazing down at the small fire, she replied, "Only the Kit Fox Warriors speak of surrender to the Bear Coat."

Something in the way she said it, in the way she refused to look him in the eye, convinced Johnny that what should be welcome news might not be all that much a blessing.

"What could be wrong if the Kit Fox Warriors speak in favor of surrender?"

"Last Bull, their leader, has been shamed."

"How?"

"Because of him, because of his warriors not allowing our camp to retreat," she said, finally fixing her gaze on him, "my people lost everything to Three Finger Kenzie's soldiers."

He recalled hearing Miles's officers talk about reports of that fight. How the soldiers figured the refugees from the destroyed village had fled into the wilderness to search for Crazy Horse. So when the Bear Coat's soldiers went marching up the Tongue they had found Shahiyela warriors fighting alongside the Lakota men. If they now blamed the Kit Fox Warrior society, as well as the soldiers, for the complete destruction of their culture, then it stood to reason that most of them would now refuse to heed the arguments made by any of the Kit Fox leaders.

Bruguier scratched at his bearded cheek, worried anew that he might not make it out of this village to ride north to the Yellowstone. "Those who speak against surrender to Miles, are they truly stronger than the Kit Fox Warriors?"

"Yes," Old Wool Woman said. "Ever since the destruction of our village in the mountains because of Last Bull and the Kit Foxes, the Elkhorn Scrapers have grown stronger."

"All of the Elkhorns are against going north to surrender at the soldier fort?" he asked.

"All but one has spoken," Old Wool Woman answered. "It is so late now. So many are tired and cold from the long day of long talks."

"This last Elkhorn Scraper, he will speak against surrender when he talks tomorrow?"

"Yes," she replied. "White Bull—a powerful holy man who is a strong healer—he will be first to speak in the morning."

Johnny didn't sleep all that well after hearing Old Wool Woman's dire reading of the odds for getting her people to surrender to Miles. Back and forth he tossed beneath his blankets and a buffalo robe until the sky grayed where the poles were tied together above his bed in the Sacred Hat Lodge.

Not that he could blame these Shahiyela for refusing to give up. Never before had he seen deep snow such as these people had endured. Never in all his years had Johnny experienced such cold as this. It was plain to see that this village had survived on horseflesh until they chanced to stumble upon enough buffalo to feed the tight bellies, to sew together more lodgeskins. Everyone in this camp was cramped together, two or more families in each new lodge, so only this Sacred Hat Lodge remained a quiet refuge from those who had somehow outlasted this terrible winter. Such deep, deep suffering.

More than once he had stared in the bundle hanging from its tripod in that place of prominence at the back of this lodge.

How these people had sacrificed, even unto their lives, to protect that sacred object. Some small voice of warning inside him said that a people as stoic and strong as they would not consider surrender unless no other path was open to them. And if that powerful holy man named White Bull offered these people strength, goaded them into believing that their best opportunity rested in turning south to the Lakota agency on White River . . . then Johnny would certainly fail.

Old Wool Woman had come for him that morning after the sun came up, bringing Bruguier some meat in a kettle she set to boiling on the fire in the Sacred Hat Lodge. The four of them ate in all but total silence, except when Old Wool Woman would talk with Coal Bear or Sacred Hat Woman in their Shahiyela tongue, which Johnny struggled to follow. At times the old woman might translate something into her fractured Lakota, but most of that morning the four of them sat in silence, eating, or thinking, or tending the fire . . . and waiting.

Coal Bear finally stood, said something to the two women, and gathered up his old robe, which he flung about his shoulders before leaving the lodge. Bruguier watched Coal Bear's woman set a few more pieces of wood on the fire, then she too departed beneath the protection of a blanket.

"It is time to go to the council lodge," Old Wool Woman announced.

"You will return here to tell me what your people decide today?"

"No, Big Leggings," she said as she draped her blanket over her head. "You come with me to listen for yourself."

"They . . . your men will allow me to attend their council?'

"All my people will be there this morning, just as they have been there to listen since these talks began," Old Wool

Woman said. "Come now—we go together to hear what White Bull tells the other men is in his heart, what path he believes our people should take."

White Bull was up before the first streaks of gray brightened the sun's rising behind patchy, snow-laden clouds.

He smoked and prayed about which direction his people were to turn. To go north to give themselves over to the Bear Coat who had come hunting for them in the snow? Or to march south toward the agency where Morning Star's people often made their home among Red Cloud's Lakota? And if they did not surrender in the north or to the south, then wasn't it still a grand folly to keep on making war against the *ve-ho-e* and his soldiers?

The more he prayed, the more White Bull became convinced he already knew his answer. Had known the answer for many, many days now. Finally, at first light, he realized the most difficult part of his decision was just how he would explain it to the others who were relying upon his prestige and power to sway those who had not yet made up their minds.

"Antelope Woman!" he called in the dim light of the small fire he was rebuilding.

His sister pulled the robe back from her face.

"I want you to bring Old Wool Woman to me," he said as she blinked at him and rubbed her knuckles into her eyes.

"Old Wool Woman?"

"Bring her now. I must talk to her without delay."

He waited in his tiny lodge with his wife and older children, as well as the other family who lived with them until the women sewed together enough buffalo hides to make another lodge. By the time Antelope Woman returned with her old friend, everyone was awake in White Bull's lodge, sitting very quietly, expectantly. Something in the holy man's tone convinced them of the gravity of this visit from the old woman who was once a captive of the soldiers.

"Everything you told us two days ago was true?" he demanded as she settled beside him at the fire and let her old blanket drop from her bony shoulders.

Old Wool Woman nodded. "What is it you are asking?"

"The Bear Coat did not send you here with a false message

for us? Something to trick us into coming to his fort?"

Her eyes darted back and forth between his, her brow creasing. "No, the Bear Coat is not trying to trick you."

"They still hold your niece and your daughter at the soldier fort," he said, daring to hope that this woman could allay the last of his fears that the soldier chief would attempt some *ve-ho-e* treachery upon his people.

"Yes, Crooked Nose Woman, and Fingers Woman too."

Laying a hand on her forearm, White Bull said, "Look into my eyes and tell me that the Bear Coat is not holding your family hostage."

"Both of them, and the others are still prisoners—"

"But why did he release you?" White Bull demanded, cutting her off. "Why you? If he didn't want to keep the others, to kill if you didn't come here?"

"No!" she shouted.

"Yes," he growled. "He would kill them if you did not succeed in luring us into his trap."

The old woman's hand flew to her mouth. It trembled there, her eyes filling with dread. "No. I will not believe the Bear Coat would do that."

"Isn't the Bear Coat the sort of man who would lie to an old woman, to convince you that you came here to deliver a message for the good of your people?" he explained. "Wouldn't the soldier chief be the sort of *ve-ho-e* who would send you to bring us to his fort or kill your family and the other prisoners?"

"He ... the Bear Coat ... but he never said anything about any of the others!"

"Didn't he tell you to bring us to him or he would kill the rest of your relations? Didn't he, Old Wool Woman?"

"No," she sobbed, hiding her face in her old hands. "He does not seem to be the kind of man who would lie to me."

As soon as she looked up from her hands, he watched her face, how her lips quivered, her eyes pooled. Tears spilled down the weathered creases of her face.

Finally, in a very quiet whisper, he asked, "What can you say to convince my heart so I can believe in this soldier the way you believe in him?"

Slowly, she reached out and took White Bull's hand in hers, stroking the back of it the way she would her own son's. "I have lost most of my relations."

"Yes," he replied. "That is just the reason why I am concerned; you would not want to lose any more of your family to the soldiers. That is why I think you would do anything to keep your daughter and niece alive at the Bear Coat's fort."

Squeezing his hand, her eyes implored his. "I look at you and I see a man who wants me to tell him he really can believe . . . when he already believes. You are a good man, White Bull. You were a fierce warrior when you were young—a defender of our people."

"Yes, I remember fighting alongside your husband," he said wistfully, recalling early days. "The Cold Maker's fight at the Buffalo Creek Fort,* and the summer fight against the medicine-gun soldiers too,† when their rifles fired many bullets without reloading."

"But in recent years you have become a different sort of warrior for our people," she continued, still clutching his hand. "You have proved your power as a healer many times over. You have shown your great medicine as a holy man. In both these ways, you are still defending the People."

"That is why I must know, Old Wool Woman."

"You already know."

"Know what?" he asked.

"Know that I speak the truth about the Bear Coat, about what he offers us if we surrender to him," she said. "You already know this is the right path for our feet to walk."

Now as the long pipe finished its circle and rested once more in the hands of Little Wolf, the Sweet Medicine Chief, White Bull finally stood before the gathering. He was the first to speak this cold morning, as icy flakes began to lance down from the tumble of dark clouds rolling in from the west, snowflakes fluttering in a swirl around those who gathered just outside the great council lodge.

"I am the last of the Elkhorn Scrapers to talk to you," he began once he had recited his battle exploits. He looked upon the faces of the chiefs and warriors of both tribes, then gazed at the old men and women who had come to listen on this frigid, stormy morning.

---

*Fetterman Massacre, *Sioux Dawn*, vol. 1, The Plainsmen Series
†Wagon-Box Fight, *Red Cloud's Revenge*, vol. 2

"The Kit Foxes have told you how wise we would be to go north to the soldier fort and surrender to the Bear Coat."

He watched many of the rival Kit Fox Society shift on their haunches, as if they figured he was launching right into the very speech they expected him to make against them.

"And when I am finished, I am sure many of the Crazy Dogs like Iron Shirt and Little Creek will tell you that war still has a home in their hearts."

For a fleeting moment his eyes touched some of the Crazy Dogs chiefs, seeing how they glared at him with distrust.

"But the path for our feet cannot take us down the road to war any longer," he declared suddenly, watching how his words stunned several of the chiefs and war leaders of all three societies.

"No longer can we allow the white man to make war on our women and children, on our villages." White Bull continued. "There are too many of the *ve-ho-e* coming. I have dreamed of the desolation it will bring if we do not find a white man to believe. I have seen the People's destruction if we do not find the right path to take."

Some of the heads bowed, their eyes unable to hold the gaze of White Bull as he spoke to them of the ruin he had foreseen in their future. But there, in the crowd, beside the Bear Coat's half-breed messenger, stood Old Wool Woman. He could tell she was beginning to cry again. But she did so silently, stoically, every bit as bravely as her husband had died. Old Wool Woman looked directly at him as the tears spilled down her cheeks.

Now it was time to speak of what he had come to know.

"The path the Elkhorn Scrapers want us to take, to give up our ponies and our guns at the White River Agency, is not the path our people should walk," he declared forcefully, fighting to keep his voice from cracking with emotion as he remembered his only son.

"There are too many *ve-ho-e* near that White River Agency. Too close to the Holy Road. Too close to the sacred hills and to Bear Butte. Much too close to those white men who come to dig for the yellow rocks. The White River Agency is not in our country," he told them. "*This* is our country."

He watched how that declaration stung many of his fellow Elkhorn Scrapers, warriors and chiefs who were relying upon him to throw his weight in with the rest of his society.

"*This* is our hunting ground," White Bull repeated. "The White River Agency is home to Red Cloud's Little Star People. Not home to the *Ohmeseheso*."

For a brief moment he looked over at Morning Star seated at one of the four sacred directions around the fire. "Time was, Morning Star thought it best to take his people in to stay at the White River Agency. Had he not escaped last summer, he would be there today—without his ponies, without his weapons."

At the eastern side of the compass, another of the Old Man Chiefs, Little Wolf, clearly seethed, restless, with much to say.

White Bull pointed to Morning Star, explaining, "But if he had stayed on the White River Agency, Morning Star would not have lost his sons to the soldiers this winter."

It was plain to see from the way that Morning Star stared at the flickering flames, that he too was remembering the family he had lost to the *ve-ho-e*.

"Who among you is wise enough to say that Morning Star, a leader of my own Elkhorn Scrapers, should have stayed at the agency and let the soldiers take everything from him? Who among you can say it was best that Morning Star returned to our north country to hunt and roam and fight the soldiers—only to lose his sons?"

The crowd gathered outside the lodge was beginning to murmur, but White Bull had expected this. They were all seeking some way to express their surprise that he had suddenly thrown his weight against the rest of his warrior society who desired to march south.

"No one of us is so wise that he can say we should continue to make war because that would let the soldiers kill more of our women and children and young men," he said, his voice growing dramatically quiet. "And likewise, no one is so wise that he can say we should go south to a country that is not ours, to live with a people that are not our people, to last out our days among so many *ve-ho-e* crawling over that land."

Again, White Bull looked at Old Wool Woman. Saw how the tears froze on her old cheeks.

"As for me, I choose to walk a lonely road," he explained. "I will go north to see if the Bear Coat's words are straight.

I will look into his eyes and see if he is a man of honor who will keep his promises to my people."

For a moment, White Bull could not speak, so overwhelming was the memory of his son, Noisy Walking, still so raw was the remembrance of his death.

"Many of you will remember how my son came to be killed last summer fighting the soldiers on the Little Sheep River," he reminded them. "And some of you will remember how he was a long time dying that night after suffering his terrible wounds. Shot three times, stabbed many more than that. Not until sunset did Noisy Walking ask for water. But I told my son he could not have any because that water would kill him."

Some of the women in the crowd began to quietly keen with the terrible remembrance of what a father had to deny his dying son.

"Many times I've thought about him since that terrible day of our great victory over the soldiers," White Bull said. "How I told my son he should not drink because it would kill him . . . but he died anyway. Many times in the past two days I've thought how we are like Noisy Walking right now. How what we want most may kill us as a people."

He felt the clot gather at the back of his throat, so took a moment to lick his dry lips before continuing.

"The wounded among us want to go on fighting, just as Noisy Walking wanted to go on fighting. And that will surely bring an end to us all," he explained. "Other wounded among us want us to go to a place that is not our country, a place which will kill us all slowly, slowly."

White Bull swallowed hard against the growing lump that threatened to keep him from speaking what needed saying. "I am a doctor. You people know me as a holy man. Yet, all my powers were not enough to save my son that terrible day beside the Little Sheep River."

Again he looked at Old Wool Woman, finding her smiling courageously behind her tears now. And he realized she was right. He had always known what he had to do.

So it was that this holy man told the leaders of the Lakota and the *Ohmeseheso*, "Even if I have to walk this journey alone, I will go north to talk to the Bear Coat about surrender in my own homeland."

Around him, the crowd was murmuring in shock, in utter surprise.

"Last summer all my powers were not strong enough to save my son," he explained gravely. "I pray that now, in this winter marked by so much death, that my powers will be strong enough to save my people."

Chapter 13

Late in the Big Hoop-and-Stick Game Moon
1877

With less than half of the village now on its way east toward the Buffalo Tongue River, which would take them to the soldier fort, Old Wool Woman struggled through each day's journey with the rest of the old people. Like so many of the adults, she carried a little one through the snow as long as she could, then rested beside the trail. Only when she had recouped her strength did she pick up the child and continue in the wake of the village as it struggled on in its winter journey.

While each day seemed a little longer than the last, they nonetheless became colder as the women fought to drag the hides off the poles every morning, fought to raise their shelters every afternoon as the sun slid down behind the peaks of the White Mountains. Most everyone was still tired when they arose and broke camp, all the more weary when the young warriors came back along the ragged procession to announce that a place had been selected for their camp that night. They stumbled with cold feet and leaden legs onto a sheltered stretch of bottomland where the wind might not harass them, where they might find enough wood for all the fires, where they could chop through the ice for themselves and the ponies.

More than once a day Old Wool Woman reminded herself that she had lived through two ordeals worse than this. At least this time they had some lodges and food, buffalo robes and blankets. This time, they had a little hope. Unlike when the soldiers attacked Old Bear's camp on the Powder River, or when Three Finger Kenzie's soldiers discovered them in the mountains and drove the village into the winter wilderness to seek out Crazy Horse a second time, the *Ohmeseheso* now had reason to hope that they would never again be forced to endure a winter march such as this.

Never again.

At times during those frightful days she would stop, turn, and look upon their back-trail, hoping to see the faces of old friends, thinking she had heard them coming. But each time Old Wool Woman slowly realized it was nothing more than the cruel wind keening through the skeletal trees and the naked willow. No, it was not the voices of those who had followed Morning Star and Little Wolf and Standing Elk south for the White River Agency.

Now the *Ohmeseheso* were divided.

She could not remember a time when her people had chosen to walk more than one path. But never before had there been such a relentless enemy like the *ve-ho-e* soldiers.

Old Wool Woman's heart grew heavy when she thought how divided her people were. This is how the white man had truly defeated them. Not in battle, no—because no matter how heavy their loss, the women always fled and the warriors covered the retreat. After a time of mourning, the *Ohmeseheso* were ready to move on with their lives of war and wandering, chasing after the buffalo herds with the rotation of the seasons. No, the soldiers had not defeated her people in war. The white man had divided the survivors of that constant war, pitting them one against another.

More than half of the Northern Bands had started away from that camp on the Rotten Grass toward the White River Agency where they would go to live with Red Cloud's Little Star People. Less than half had chosen to follow the holy man White Bull to the soldier fort on the Elk River.

She had had to tear herself from so many friends as the two camps spoke their farewells, as the mounted guards reined away and moved out in two different directions, as the warrior chiefs called for the march to begin, as the women wailed and the little ones cried, as family and friends were torn asunder. Hearts cold and small, hearts shattered by the *ve-ho-e*.

But, she promised herself, just as White Bull had told them that first afternoon of their journey as they were going about setting up their camp for the night; while their hearts might be wounded, their spirits would remain unbroken.

The white man would never defeat their spirits.

After White Bull had spoken on the morning of that second day, the voices of the Crazy Dogs were heard. It seemed clear that warrior society was split: some agreed with the holy man that they should surrender to the Bear Coat, while most agreed with the Elkhorns that they should go in to the White River Agency. All day and into that second night the warrior chiefs debated, but without resolution. Unable to reach the one mind required if the question was to be settled for all the People, the warrior chiefs had no choice but to hand the matter back to the council of chiefs.

"Whatever the chiefs decide," Left-Handed Shooter declared, "the warrior societies will support."

That third morning the headmen of the *Ohmeseheso* met once again. They passed the pipe, praying for wisdom in this most troubling of times, praying for a vision to choose the right path for their people. For another day and into the cold night these older men pulled the issue this way then tugged it that way. And finally recessed due to the weariness that gripped them all.

On the fourth morning, the chiefs and headmen gathered anew, hopeful that on this sacred day they would arrive at a consensus, that they would discover a path that all could take together. But as time ground by and the sun fell past midsky, Old Wool Woman grew less hopeful that the chiefs would be of one mind. True, the three Old Man Chiefs all agreed they should take the village south to the Little Star agency. But it was still just as clear that some still believed in listening to what the Bear Coat had to offer to the north.

As the shadows lengthened that fourth afternoon, it became plain that young Two Moon was growing more frustrated with the agency talk of the Elkhorn Scrapers. It did not surprise Old Wool Woman when Two Moon stood suddenly, there among the back rows of the little chiefs of the warrior societies, interrupting the Council Chiefs as politely as he could.

"I want to echo White Bull's words," he blurted out.

Stunned into silence, Little Wolf, Morning Star, and Standing Elk all turned to stare at the brazen warrior. This was a brave thing, to ask to speak in a council where he was not a member.

Little Wolf, the Sweet Medicine Chief, growled, "You should not interrupt. This is not acceptable—"

"These are unusual times," Two Moon blurted. "The trouble before us requires behavior that is not always acceptable."

"Please," White Bull pleaded with the Council Chiefs, "let Two Moon speak. If all our talk in more than three days cannot change your minds . . . what is the harm in listening to what this passionate warrior has to say?"

For a moment the three Old Man Chiefs looked at one another. Finally, Morning Star relented, "Tell us what you have to say, Two Moon. The Chiefs' Council will have ears for your words."

"Two days ago, White Bull told you what rests in his heart," the warrior began. "Even though it is clear that the rest of the Elkhorns are prepared to move into the White River Agency, this holy man has told you why he does not believe it is a wise move for our people to travel south.

"I have been there as well," Two Moon said. "You chiefs know that. Our eyes have seen the same sights there. Most of the Little Star People there have witnessed the white-topped wagons snaking their way past, heading west, or heading north to the Sacred Hills. Like White Bull said, there seems to be no end to the *ve-ho-e*. There are so many that they are all over that country. They are like ants boiling out of an anthill.

"That is not our country. We must share it with the Lakota. But it never was *our* country. Even when we were at that White River Agency last summer,* the white man known as Long Knife,† the white man who has married one of our women, warned me that many *ve-ho-e* are coming.

---

*Before the breakout that would precipitate the skirmish at Warbonnet Creek, *Trumpet on the Land*, vol. 10, The Plainsmen Series
†William Rowland

Not this winter perhaps, maybe not even next winter—but he said they would come soon in numbers we cannot imagine. It is just as White Bull has said it.

"Perhaps the holy man is right," Two Moon continued. "Maybe we should learn to be friends with the white man. Maybe we should make a treaty with the *ve-ho-e* while there are still any of us left."

Drawing himself up, the warrior laid his hand upon his chest and said, "I will go north with White Bull. I will go to the soldier fort on the Elk River to see what the Bear Coat has to say about surrender, about an agency in our own country. Any warrior, any family who wants to come with White Bull and me should join us! And those who do not want to see what the soldier chief has to say can choose where they want to take their families."

It had suddenly become so clear, Old Wool Woman remembered, that there was not going to be one consensus for the People to follow. It was plain their camp was divided, and would stay divided. The white man had succeeded in tearing the *Ohmeseheso* apart.

With Two Moon's declaration, Crazy Head, a little chief with the Crazy Dogs, had suddenly bolted to his feet. As the council began to stir and murmur, he raised his voice to say, "Two Moon is right! There are too many whites for us to fight. It is impossible to kill them all! We must find a way to live with them before there are no more of us. I will follow White Bull and Two Moon!"

"You will give up to the soldiers?" Standing Elk challenged from his position on the southern end of the sacred circle.

"War has brought us nothing but death and ruin," Two Moon said before Crazy Head could respond.

Suddenly Old Wolf stood in that circle of chiefs, declaring, "I too will join White Bull."

Then Medicine Bear got to his feet. He had carried *Nimhoyoh*, the Sacred Turner, into their fight against the Bear Coat's soldiers at Belly Butte when a cannon ball struck his pony in the battle. "And I will join you. My people will go with White Bull to the soldier fort."

Distress blanched the faces of Little Wolf and Morning Star, nothing less than black-bellied anger crossed the face of Standing Elk.

He stood now, holding his short warrior's staff in one hand, slapping it against the other palm. "Very well," he growled in a low voice that showed how difficult it was for him to contain himself. "Like White Bull, Two Moon has made his decision to join with the soldiers, to make another treaty. You have heard my words. I have refused to make another treaty with the *ve-ho-e*. I still say I will not go to the Elk River post. Instead, I will lead everyone who wants to go to the White River Agency to join the Lakota.

"Not so long ago, in the memories of most men here," Standing Elk explained, "our chiefs decided to live together like relations with the Lakota people. The Lakota claim this land we are standing on right now as their hunting ground. If I must choose whose land this is to be . . . I say it belongs to the Lakota and the Shahiyela. It does not belong to the *Ooetaneo-o** and the white soldiers!"

No longer was that council a quiet affair—excited and angry voices were now raised above a whisper. A line had been drawn in the icy snow, and every man had to choose a side.

Standing Elk concluded, "I refuse to listen to any offers from the Bear Coat! As for me, I go to the agency to stand with the Lakota!"

After four days of debate and argument and council-making, all that the chiefs could decide was to go their sep-- arate ways. While friends and relations started south with Little Wolf and Morning Star, camp criers instructed those who would go north with White Bull and Two Moon to pre- pare to leave the following morning.

It took four days of trudging east before they struck the Buffalo Tongue. Four days during which Old Wool Woman kept glancing back, hoping to find someone from the other camp hurrying to catch up on the back-trail of White Bull's people.

Four days now, and it was finally clear they were few and alone in their journey to surrender to the Bear Coat.

Few and alone beneath an endless, crushing sky.

*   *   *

---

*The Crow People

"Will we camp tonight at the mouth of Suicide Creek?"*
young Wooden Leg asked as he brought his pony alongside
White Bull's at the head of the march.

"Yes," the holy man answered. "There is wood and water
there, and the people are already weary from the last four
days of travel."

"I wish to go in search of the place I buried Big Crow after
our winter fight with the soldiers."†

White Bull nodded. "You can go, as long as you and the
others keep a wary eye open for any patrols. The soldiers
may still be out and scouting for warrior camps. Do not get
yourselves in trouble."

"We will watch like a hawk on high," Wooden Leg promised. "And meet you at the mouth of Suicide Creek by the
time it grows dark."

The young warrior reined his pony about and raced back
down the line of march, crying out for his friends to join him.
In a matter of heartbeats there were six who had joined up.
The seven eager horsemen kicked their horses into a lope,
riding past the head of the march, angling up the snowy
slopes that rose on the east bank of the Buffalo Tongue
River.

As they rode farther and farther to the north, Wooden Leg
constantly assessed the rise and fall of the narrow valley,
searching for familiar landmarks that would show the young
warrior the place where he and two Lakota warriors had
buried Big Crow in their retreat after the fight with the Bear
Coat's soldiers.

"There," he finally declared, pointing toward the tall,
rocky cliff to the east.

Yes, there where the valley wall jutted straight up toward
the sky. At the base of that wall he and the two Lakota had
found a niche in the rocks where they could bury the courageous hero of that fight at Belly Butte.

It had been inspiring to the other Shahiyela warriors, who
were atop the battle ridge that cold, terrible morning with
Crazy Horse and his Lakota, that Big Crow decided to make
four sacred bravery runs in plain sight of the oncoming en-

---

*Present-day Hanging Woman Creek
†*Wolf Mountain Moon*, vol. 12, The Plainsmen Series

emy. Not far below them the Bear Coat's soldiers were approaching, sometimes stopping to kneel and shoot at the warriors firing back, warriors busy erecting breastworks out of the sandstone, busy warming their hands and feet at the many fires blazing atop that low ridge.

This was powerful medicine for so courageous a warrior as Big Crow, especially for a warrior who wore such a large and striking war bonnet that he would make a perfect target of himself for those soldiers clearly within rifle range below. As Wooden Leg watched in awe, Big Crow came out from behind his protective breastworks and began to dance and cavort in clear view of the enemy. At times the chief would fire his rifle at the soldiers struggling through the deep snow toward the base of the ridge where he goaded them with his bravery.

After that first run, Big Crow had ducked behind the rocks, kneeling there, huffing loudly to catch his breath in the dry, shockingly cold air. Swallowing a mouthful of snow, the warrior chief suddenly leaped to his feet again and went out to perform a second dance before the soldiers, taunting them, whirling this way and that, firing his rifle until his repeater was empty.

Big Crow came back a second time to catch his breath behind the breastworks, to reload, and to suck on the icy snow. Then he made a third taunting dance before the enemy. But after another brief rest to catch his breath, a soldier bullet caught Big Crow squarely in the chest.

As soon as Wooden Leg and the two Lakota warriors reached the fallen chief, they could see he had received a mortal wound: too much blood turning the snow crimson beneath the brave warrior's body. Ultimately they dragged Big Crow behind the breastworks. When Crazy Horse began his retreat, and with the two Lakotas' help, Wooden Leg managed to drape the body over the back of a pony.

After fleeing many bullet-flights up the valley, Big Crow had regained consciousness, but with it came the great pain. He had asked to be left to die in a proper place for a Shahiyela warrior. With sadness, Wooden Leg had complied, curling the war chief's body into a crack in the rocks before carefully setting many small rocks over Big Crow to form a protective cairn.

Now this afternoon Wooden Leg grew confused as he

looked across the rocky wall for that niche. Where he had gone first to look, there was no body. In desperation he continued north along the ledge for some distance. Finally he returned to the others, muttering to himself that he was sure he had been right in the first place.

"This is where we buried Big Crow."

"But there is no body here now," one of the warriors said.

And a second remarked, "Maybe the soldiers came and found the body and took it away."

"Yes," agreed a third. "See how the rocks have tumbled down from the wall."

Wooden Leg was all the more confused by the appearance of that cleft in the rock wall, by the jumble of stones below it. "Those had to be the rocks I placed over his body—"

"Look here!" shouted another who had hung back upon his pony. He pointed to the brush sticking up through the snow.

Hurrying over, Wooden Leg and the others inspected the clumps of sage. It was true—some of the branches were broken and others disturbed. Perhaps this was sign of what had become of Big Crow.

"Did you and the Lakota crush those branches when you brought the body here?"

"I don't think so," said a member of the group. "The snow was deeper that day." He stood a distance down the slope. Now he pointed at the ground.

"Big Crow crawled this way," Wooden Leg declared after he trudged over, inspecting the site.

Together the seven followed the path scratched through the snow between the clumps of sage until they could see the patch of buckskin emerging from the windblown snowdrift plastered at the side of a small stand of stunted pine. They knelt around that snowdrift and carefully began to scrape away the icy ridge of frozen snow that had formed around the body. The more they cleared from the corpse, the more it became plain how Big Crow had crawled down here, as if making his way to the river.

Having dragged with him the buffalo robe Wooden Leg had buried him in, Big Crow had propped himself against a large clump of cedar there among the stunted pine as if to rest, to catch his breath as he had been doing when he was making his bravery runs before the enemy.

"He looks as if he is sleeping," one of the others said as Wooden Leg brushed the last of the icy snow from the dead man's face.

Indeed, it did appear as if the brave warrior chief were only sleeping: his right arm was raised and propped behind his head, his left hand simply laid across his bloody breast.

Without a word among them, the seven spread out, some venturing downhill, while others went uphill in search of enough stones to form a new burial cairn. Then, with Big Crow's frozen body laid out within that small stand of stunted, winter-gaunt pine, the young Shahiyela warriors buried the revered leader beneath those yellow and red sandstone slabs once more. They smoked their pipes over his grave and asked the Spirit People once again to accept this brave warrior onto the Star Road.

Then the seven arose from the snow, climbed onto their horses and slowly moved down into the valley, continuing on their path to the mouth of Suicide Creek.

Only once did Wooden Leg look back at that windswept hill and what little vegetation grew there to protect the holy place from the howling winds.

Big Crow had crawled there to die after he was alone. There beneath the wide sky where *Ma-heono* and the eagles could look down, he had given up his spirit.

The ground a brave man had chosen for his final resting place.

Chapter 14

18–19 February
1877

BY TELEGRAPH

Territory of the Black Hills.
WASHINGTON, February 16.—The senate committee on territories had a long meeting, devoted to the consideration of Senator Spencer's bill to create a new territory out of the Black Hills country, which it was proposed to call Lincoln territory . . . The committee decided to lay the matter over till the next session of congress for the reason that the bill ratifying the treaty made last summer with the Sioux Indians has not yet been passed by the house, and because legislation being so far behind now, it would be impossible to secure the final action of the senate this session.

With the descent of the sun, the wind had picked up in the valley of the Tongue River. Johnny Bruguier tugged at his worn woolen scarf, once more covering his raw, red nose. The army horse between his legs chose its footing carefully, slowly. The animal was nowhere near as strong as it had been back at the first of the month when he rode away from the soldier fort. It had begun to grow weak almost from the moment the soldier escort turned around for the post, taking with them that supply of horse feed stowed away on the pack animals.

Once more the half-breed could understand why the warrior bands always told the soldiers they would do this or they would do that, when their ponies were stronger. Winter took its terrible harvest on the horses too: those animals that didn't die before spring were nothing but crow-bait bags of bones by the time the snows began to melt and the first shoots of grass emerged from the frosty ground. Bruguier only hoped the army horse between his legs would have enough bottom left in it to cross these last miles in to Tongue River Cantonment.

Again he offered the best prayer he knew that the Shahiyelas' ponies would have enough strength to cross these last miles before they reached the Bear Coat's lodge.

Just before dawn that morning, Bruguier saddled up to begin this ride northward in advance of the village. The cold seemed all the more intense as he grasped wrists with White Bull, nodded to Old Wool Woman, then took the reins to his horse from Two Moon.

"Tell them I will come out from the fort to meet them," Johnny explained to Old Wool Woman as he settled atop his saddle. "They do not have to worry about the Crow scouts murdering them this time."

Old Wool Woman stepped up to the horseman, and grabbed his stirrup. "Tell the Bear Coat I am bringing my people to him. Just as I promised I would."

"He will be happy with this news," Bruguier assured her just before he turned his horse about and gave it his heels.

It hadn't gotten all that much warmer after the buttermilk sun rose in a pewter sky. But at least the wind wasn't blowing. That is, until now that the sun was easing down after a long, lonely day of pushing everything he could out of the army horse beneath him.

Squinting ahead with the failing light, the half-breed studied the valley north of him, recognizing some landmarks. Now, more than ever, he hoped to cross these last few miles before dark. Better that he ride into the Bear Coat's fort before the full fading of the afternoon sun. Too good a chance that a dark-skinned man like him might well be taken for a hostile warrior slipping out of the gloom as another winter night approached. Johnny knew Miles would have wood-cutting parties out until that last hour before sunset. He just didn't want to stumble onto any soldiers who would take him for the enemy. Not when he was this close.

Not when he had come this far to take that hangman's rope from his neck.

Less than half of them had followed him north from the Little Bighorn. He hoped Miles would not be angry with less than total success. More than half of the fighting bands of the Shahiyela refused the Bear Coat's offer to talk of peace and surrender; they were on their way south to live with Red Cloud's Lakota, down in General Crook's country.

And if they ended up surrendering all those warriors and guns and ponies to Crook, then Johnny Bruguier knew in his bones the Bear Coat was going to be furious.

Yesterday Johnny figured that if he delivered some good news about White Bull's band to Miles then perhaps the soldier chief would not be near so angry. So when the village made camp no more than a day's ride from the mouth of the Tongue, Bruguier decided he would hurry ahead to carry his momentous announcement to Miles.

Nervously glancing over his left shoulder, the half-breed saw how the sullen, winter sun was just then settling upon the hills to the southwest. He didn't have long now. What was the Lakota prayer his mother would have spoken at a time like this?

Angrily, he cursed himself for forgetting the words in his youth, replacing his mother's language with the rich profanity of the white man. Hanging about the sutler's cabin and cavorting with the soldiers had served only to drive the woman's prayers out of his memory. And those were prayers he figured he ought to be mouthing right about now—

He smelled woodsmoke.

Looking up, Johnny squinted into the deepening afternoon light, a ragged shred hung above the trees far, far ahead, tatters of pale smoke streaking the paler sky. Another glance at the sun and Johnny jabbed his heels back into the flanks of the big American horse. It lunged ahead a few steps, then settled back into its lethargy. Without grain for so long, Bruguier figured he would be lucky if the animal got him to the fort, no matter the speed. Still, he clucked and tapped his heels repeatedly as the smell of woodsmoke became all the stronger.

Off the hillside where he had been riding just below the crest, the half-breed pointed the horse toward the Tongue itself. Down into the bottomland where the cottonwoods grew tall and thick, surrounded by a profusion of willow and alder, chokecherry and sarvisberry—enough cover for a dark-skinned man slipping up on a soldier post. He might just make it before dark.

When the voice called out behind him, Johnny froze.

"Stop right there!" it cried with shrill alarm. "Sergeant!"

Bruguier yanked back on the reins and raised his empty left hand encased in the horsehide glove.

"What is it?" a second voice boomed from the brush ahead.

The scared soldier was stepping out of the trees, coming up behind Bruguier, his long rifle pointed squarely at the half-breed's back.

"Injun!"

The second man's voice was close now. "Only one, eh?"

"I'm Bruguier," Johnny announced to the man ahead of him, turning around in the saddle. A handful of soldiers came up to stand behind the sergeant who dropped the butt of his Springfield to the snow and draped his wrists across the muzzle.

"That's right," the older man declared with a grin. "This here's the general's scout."

"That's the one did the talkin' for that ol' red-belly Sittin' Bull back to last fall," announced another.

"I reckon he's seen the error of his ways," the second man replied as he stepped forward to get himself a good look at Bruguier. "Thought you rode off with that old Cheyenne woman more'n two weeks back."

"She's a day behind me," Johnny said, licking his swollen lower lip, less nervous now that they knew who he was.

Another man stepped up to the side of Bruguier's horse. "We heard you found the camp of them hostiles. Escort boys told us when they come back."

With a nod, Johnny said, "I'm bringing in a bunch of them warriors to surrender."

"They're gonna give up?" a soldier shrieked.

"I need to ride on in to tell the general all 'bout it," the half-breed explained. "They'll likely make it here by this time tomorrow."

"By gonies, boys!" the second man bellowed loud enough to roust some crows from nearby branches into noisy flight. "That's good news this here scout's bringing the general! This here war's over for us!"

The older soldier stepped right up to the half-breed's horse, yanked off a mitten and held the hand up to Johnny. They shook. "You done good by the general, scout."

Bruguier gave his horse a nudge as he pulled his gauntlet mitten back over his right hand, more anxious than ever to reach the fort. Having stumbled across this wood-cutting detail, and with the woodsmoke growing strong in his nostrils—the very taste of it scratching the back of his throat—Johnny didn't figure it would take him long at all to reach that clearing where the log huts and humble canvas tents stood against this winter's unrelenting onslaught.

Among those poor shanties looming ahead, soldiers in their long buffalo coats and muskrat caps spotted him, turning and slapping the next man until it seemed nearly the whole post was turning out to watch the half-breed bring that worn-out, broken-down army horse back to the fort. While many of them whispered among themselves as he plodded by, it wasn't until he neared the commander's office that a soldier actually raised his voice.

"Scout's coming in, General!" the man hollered as he took off in an ungainly lope across the trampled crust of snow ahead of Bruguier. "Tell the general his scout's coming in!"

"By damn, if he ain't still alive!" shouted one of the two men standing on either side of the low door to Miles's office.

The second guard turned and pounded the loose-fitting plank door with the side of his balled-up mitten as Johnny gently drew back on the reins and stopped his weary horse. "General Miles, sir! Your half-breed's back from the hostiles, sir!"

No sooner had he unwrapped himself from the half-robe tucked around his legs and dropped to the ground, worrying how his stiff, frozen knees would hold him up, than the noisy plank door flew open. The door was drawn back with a scrape across its jamb by Miles himself, who nearly filled the opening.

"Bruguier!" he roared as he stepped into the fading light.

That exuberant voice, the shaggy mane, as well as the full, unkempt beard, reminded Johnny of a great black bear. "By the stars—it is you!"

He grabbed the half-breed's hand and squeezed it, immediately tugging Johnny toward the door. "C'mon, c'mon! We're going to warm you up inside by the stove and then you're going to tell me about your journey."

Miles suddenly stopped there at the low threshold and turned to look across the snowy quadrangle. "Where are the rest? Did you bring anyone else? Where's the old woman? Did she elect to stay on with her village?"

"You got any coffee, General?" Johnny asked the instant Miles paused to take a breath in that rapid-fire hailstorm of questioning.

"Of course! Of course!" the colonel roared, turning again to one of the soldiers who were pressing close. "Have the officer of the day get us some fresh coffee over here. And dig around for some tins of fruit too. Let's get this man's belly filled so he can start wagging his tongue for me!"

The morning after Big Leggings left to hurry north for the soldier fort, White Bull and the other warrior chiefs did not spur their people to break camp before dawn. Already they had traveled long, difficult days through the deep snow to reach this camping spot beside the Buffalo Tongue River, less than a day south of the Elk River post. White Bull felt the hidden scars from this war: the way the cold and hunger had carved deep into the hearts of his *Ohmeseheso*.

A holy man was he, cursed with seeing that which other men would never see.

White Bull's people had only what dried meat they had when the encampment broke up and dispersed to the winds. In that burnt-out country west of the Buffalo Tongue, they found little game while they limped west after the snowy fight at Belly Butte. Coming here from that country of the Little Sheep River near the White Mountains, again little game was found.

The holy man prayed the Bear Coat would be true to his word, prayed he would offer food for hungry bellies, blankets for shivering children, an opportunity for the old ones to rest without fleeing. White Bull wordlessly spoke his prayer throughout that short winter day, even after the Shahiyela made camp for the night and the severe cold settled low in the river valley, clinging to the cottonwood and the brush and laying close in among the lodges.

By the time a sulky sun had climbed close to midsky the following day, White Bull figured he and the other leaders had to be drawing near to soldier fort.

Fearing that the soldiers or their Crow People scouts would again shoot at the sight of the Shahiyela warriors, White Bull, Two Moon, and the other chiefs decided that no more than a delegation of headmen should ride in to talk with the Bear Coat.

"We must all go to see if the soldier chief talks well," White Thunder said.

"No, some of you must stay behind," White Bull argued. "If we are made prisoners by the Bear Coat, or if the soldiers' scouts lay in wait to ambush us again just as they did before,* then we need a few strong chiefs to quickly lead our people out of danger. Chiefs who will watch over and protect them until the *Ohmeseheso* can decide what to do when there is no one left to trust."

"What are you saying?" asked Sleeping Rabbit. "Are you really suggesting that some of our leaders stay behind?"

"Yes," White Bull answered. "If our chiefs are murdered by soldiers or soldier scouts . . . then we must be sure some of our leaders survive to lead the People."

"Who is to stay?" Medicine Bear asked.

White Bull turned to look at the man. "You will stay. You will watch over these people. I trust no one more than I trust you, my friend. I will count on you to hurry this village away if we do not return."

"I will go north with you," announced Hump, leader of the few lodges of *Mnikowoju* who had resolutely stayed on with the Shahiyela when the rest of the Lakota departed with Crazy Horse. Behind this leader, also known as High Backbone, stood several of the warriors of his clan. "Because I am the only Lakota chief here, I owe it to my people to talk with the Bear Coat myself, to see if his words ring true."

"Good," White Bull answered. "And if we are murdered by the Crow People, or if the soldiers take us prisoner, then

---

Wolf Mountain Moon, vol. 12, The Plainsmen Series

you must have your people flee with Medicine Bear."

"Agreed," Hump replied. "We have chosen to take the same path in reaching this place. My people will stay on that path the Shahiyela have chosen."

As the only two Council Chiefs still among them, Crazy Head and Old Wolf rode at the head of the procession that left the village behind that morning. Following them were the older, honored warriors: Little Creek and Iron Shirt, Black Bear and Crazy Mule. Behind them rode Two Moon and White Bull, both of them riding on either side of Old Wool Woman. Joining them were White Thunder and Sleeping Rabbit, the great Shahiyela physician. Protecting the rear of the delegation were Hump, his brother Horse Road, and several of their Lakota kinsmen.

This delegation drove their weary ponies as fast as they could through the crusty snow, halting only once at midmorning to water the horses and let them blow. After that short rest, the riders hurried on, anxious to learn if they could come to trust the Bear Coat as Old Wool Woman had . . . or to know at last if this was nothing more than a *ve-ho-e* trap using the old woman to lure the chiefs into the snare.

If so, White Bull kept assuring himself, at least a few of the People would survive. Medicine Bear and the other leaders would hurry them south, away from the soldier chief's deadly trap. The men could hunt, the women could tan the robes, and their children could grow to become warriors and mothers, knowing the soldiers would eventually come looking for them.

If not that winter, then perhaps in the spring.

If the Bear Coat's word was nothing more than a breath of foul wind, then Medicine Bear and the others left behind in the village would stand little chance of surviving another winter, even if they fled into the fastness of the mountains. Three Finger Kenzie had shown them that. Even in the mountains the *Ohmeseheso* were not safe.

Their survival rested less and less on how resolutely White Bull's people made war against the soldiers, but more and more on how bravely his people could make peace with these strangers who had come to take everything that belonged to them. The land. The rivers and streams. The buffalo.

So many lives lost and still the Northern People hadn't turned the soldiers back. The time had come to talk of surrendering with honor to the soldier chief. Time to make a courageous peace before there were no more *Ohmeseheso* to carry on the names and the old stories and the glory tales of long-ago battles, before no one was left to tell the little ones about the days when the buffalo ran free across the hills and the prairie, when the People rode free with those buffalo.

Before the coming of the *ve-ho-e* and his soldiers.

White Bull reminded his heart he had to believe that the Bear Coat would be a man of honor.

If not, the glory days of the *Ohmeseheso* truly were like ashes on the wind.

Chapter 15

Late in the Big Hoop-and-Stick Game Moon
1877

Old Wool Woman could sense the danger felt by the men around her. Strong in her nostrils, so palpable she could smell it on the wind, it was almost as strong this day as it was when they fought Three Finger Kenzie in the Red Fork Canyon.

These were brave men, she thought as she gazed around at them this cold, clear afternoon. While she alone seemed convinced that all would be good with their going to the Elk River fort, she clearly realized that these *Ohmeseheso* and Lakota chiefs and warriors around her had nowhere near the confidence she had in the Bear Coat's intentions.

Yes, these were the bravest of her people, she reminded herself. The others, even great chiefs like Little Wolf and Morning Star, were nowhere near as brave as these men. Those who led the way south to the White River Agency were taking what they believed to be the easiest path—perhaps to slip into the reservation without alerting the soldiers or the *ve-ho-e* agent. Sly those leaders would try to be.

And those few who had refused to go either north or south but instead rode away with some of the Crazy Horse warrior bands—they simply didn't have the courage it took to make the toughest decisions regarding the future of the *Ohmeseheso*.

But these who rode behind Crazy Head and Old Wolf toward the Elk River post were the bravest of any simply because they dared take a chance on peace for the good of their people. Easy it was to run away until they were surrounded like the white man's spotted buffalo. Easier to keep on fighting until there were no more Shahiyela left. Easiest to close one's eyes and keep on starving until hunger claimed every last one of your relations.

She sat up a little straighter and took a deep breath of the cold air, thankful the sun had appeared today after so many gray days in a row, strung together like knots on a rope—

Magpies burst into flight, rising from the trees to her right, up ahead along the west bank of the river. Startled by the sudden movement, some of the ponies shied as the shadows flitted low overhead. Great jets of steam issued from the horses' round, flaring nostrils, as the men brought them under control.

Then Old Wool Woman saw two riders appear out of the cottonwoods ahead.

Old Wolf threw up his arm, halting them. The rest of the delegation clattered up on either side of him and Crazy Head, arrayed in one broad flank should trouble prove unavoidable, should treachery raise its ugly head as it had for Packs the Drum and four others the last time peace-makers came to this place.

On either side of her American horse streamed in Hump's Lakota warriors, hurrying to fill the gaps on that line of courageous men, to take their places on the solid phalanx that arrayed itself in front of the enemy.

"It's the half-breed called White!" shouted White Bull.

"Is it a soldier with him?" Sleeping Rabbit asked.

With a flat hand shading his eyes, White Thunder answered, "I cannot tell for sure—but he does not ride like an Indian."

Old Wool Woman shaded her eyes as well and gazed at the distant riders who had frightened the magpies into flight. Bruguier pushed back the front brim of his hat to expose more of his face, then raised the arm high in greeting. He called out her name in Lakota.

"Big Leggings!" she cried, with the relief of a mother welcoming her son who had gone off to face much danger. Old Wool Woman urged her big horse between the ponies ridden by Two Moon and Crazy Mule, then halted in front of that wide line of men, waiting for the half-breed and his companion.

"The rest of the village stayed behind?" Bruguier asked when he had come to a halt before her.

"Yes," she answered in Lakota. "Have you been to the fort and seen the Bear Coat?"

"Yes, yes," he answered, flush with renewed excitement. "The soldier chief wants you all to come talk with him. It will be safe. No soldiers will harm you."

"Are we far?" White Bull asked Old Wool Woman, who translated.

"No, not far," the half-breed assured them. "Tell the chiefs and these warriors that the Bear Coat wants them to dress up in their finest war clothes before they reach the fort."

"War clothes?" Iron Shirt asked after Old Wool Woman translated.

Crazy Mule demanded, "Why would we wear our war clothes if we are going in to talk of peace?"

"Big Leggings says the white man wants us to wear the clothes for a grand show," she explained. "The Bear Coat told the half-breed that he will put his soldiers in two lines when we get to the fort. We will ride between the lines of soldiers. The soldier chief will come out to shake hands with some of you then."

"Be sure to tell the chiefs they must choose a few of their number to ride forward and shake hands with the Bear Coat," Bruguier reminded her.

As soon as Old Wool Woman explained the request to the others, there arose some nervous mumbling about that demand: fresh in their memories were the five ambushed by the Crow People scouts. She could tell the men around her were growing more fearful of a trap.

"There is nothing to fear from the soldier chief," she tried to assure them. "Those who volunteer will ride forward to meet the Bear Coat in the middle and shake hands."

Turning back to look at the half-breed, Old Wool Woman watched something gray cross his face.

"I believe I should tell you something important," Bruguier disclosed. "The soldier chief owns two horses. If he rides out to meet you on the white one, it means he will talk of peace. But if the Bear Coat comes out to meet you on the roan—that is his war horse."

For a moment she didn't know how to explain that to the others, these Shahiyela leaders who were looking at her, waiting for her to translate the half-breed's words. Would this bit of news ruin every hope she had been nursing for so long? Had she come this close to the Elk River fort with these men the Bear Coat sent her to bring back, only to learn that the Bear Coat might yet be a man who held war in his heart? Had she been deceived? Had she been made a fool?

Her lips quivered slightly as she reluctantly translated.

"The Bear Coat will ride his war horse to take us prisoner!" Iron Shirt shrieked in dismay and anger.

"He called us here in peace," White Thunder bellowed, "but once we are close enough that we can't turn back, he speaks to us of war!"

"Big Leggings!" Old Wool Woman shouted in the midst of the growing uproar. "Is this talk of the two horses true?"

"The Bear Coat has two horses," Bruguier affirmed. "I have seen them with my own eyes so I wanted these chiefs to know. The soldier chief rode the roan when he went after Sitting Bull's village last autumn. Again when he came down the Tongue after the Crazy Horse village"

"But did the Bear Coat say you were to tell us about his horses?"

As she spoke the words in Lakota, Old Wool Woman watched the half-breed's eyes twitch. The way a man might attempt to hide a flinch.

"The soldier chief owns these two horses and he could ride either one—"

She interrupted, "Did the Bear Coat himself tell you that he might ride out to meet us on his war horse?"

Without speaking, Bruguier shook his head sullenly. "No, he did not mention the horses when he told me he would talk with the chiefs. He told me if they surrender to him, there will be peace. If they do not surrender, there will be war."

"What did this one say to you?" Black Bear Shirt demanded of Old Wool Woman.

She explained what the half-breed said in Lakota, then added, "It is the same message the Bear Coat asked me to bring to you myself. If you want to talk of surrender, you can come to his fort and he will talk peace with you. But if

you do not want to surrender, he will put his soldiers on the
trail of our village."

"Until he drives us onto the Lakota agency at White
River!" Little Creek argued.

"No," White Bull said calmly. "Perhaps if we surrender to
the Bear Coat in this northern country, the soldier chief will
give us our own agency in our own land."

Crazy Head declared, "This must be. If we are to surrender to the soldier chief, he must give us our own agency on
our own lands—where we will always be close to the bones
of our grandfathers."

"Tell the half-breed we will follow him to the soldier fort,"
White Bull instructed Old Wool woman. "Tell him we come
to talk to the Bear Coat about surrender, to talk about an
agency in our own country."

This was the ninth day of their journey north from the
valley of the Little Sheep River. Too long a trip only to turn
around and flee now. Too great a distance, so deep the cold.
So little to eat, so little warmth. So very much to hope for.
A white horse or a roan horse. Surrender and peace rode
one animal while war and desolation would ride the other.
Old Wool Woman's heart was in her throat as the delegation
followed Bruguier and the stranger north those last steps to
the Elk River.

It wasn't long before she smelled fires, heard the distant
ring of axes as wood was being chopped. Thin veils of smoke
stained the winter blue sky. Then she spotted the first soldier
ahead. He turned to shout at the clearing beyond him, waving a small piece of cloth tied on the end of the long knife
attached at the muzzle of his rifle.

More soldiers appeared, stopping to stand and stare as if
incredulous, disbelieving.

Old Wool Woman watched many of these chiefs and warriors stiffen, their faces set stoically for what now confronted
them, as they slowly rode into the arms of the enemy.

A horn blared in the distance as she spotted the tops of
those wooden lodges and canvas tents where she and the
other prisoners were held, where the soldiers lived, where
the Bear Coat told her he was offering peace to her people.
Many of the soldiers were shouting now, mixing their voices
with the clatter of metal striking wood and the thump of
hundreds of feet pounding the hardened, snowy ground.

Of a sudden a flood of soldiers appeared in front of the *Ohmeseheso*, streaming left and right as some of the *ve-ho-e* shouted orders. In their long, buffalo-hide coats and big fur hats, pulled down over their ears, the soldiers were forming themselves into what appeared to be a battle line.

While Crazy Head and Old Wolf and the others slowed their gait slightly, they did not halt, despite this display of warlike might from the Bear Coat's soldiers. Closer and closer their ponies slowly carried them toward the log lodges, toward the tall pole where the soldier chief had hung his medicine symbol with its stars of white and its bars of red. Toward that line of *ve-ho-e* standing stiffly, each one clutching a rifle with its long knife attached—those weapons pointed at the sky and ready for war.

Still more shouting continued behind that first rank of soldiers as more of the white men appeared, forming themselves into second and third rows, strengthening those first walls of the enemy.

Didn't they understand she had brought them men of peace? Old Wool Woman thought. Didn't these soldiers realize this was a group of brave men come to talk of surrender? Didn't these *ve-ho-e* see how quickly they could wipe out these courageous chiefs who put themselves in the palm of danger?

"Make up your mind now, Two Moon," White Bull spoke low to the warrior riding beside him, just in front of Old Wool Woman. "Have courage . . . for here we are to be killed."

She swallowed hard, her heart thumping loudly, as Two Moon nodded once and both men stiffened—their backbones rigid as if to ready their bodies to receive the impact of soldier bullets.

She could not have made a mistake, Old Wool Woman told herself. The Bear Coat had promised her. She had looked into his eyes and believed.

Then suddenly out of the shouting and wavelike movements of soldiers in their long buffalo coats, she saw the top of his body, recognized that thick wool cap he wore. He was so tall, his head rose above the others.

The air was sucked out of her as she realized he was on horseback behind those rows of soldiers, that horse carrying him toward the *Ohmeseheso* delegation.

Row by row by row the soldiers parted as she held her breath, waited for her heart to beat again. There he was as the last soldiers opened a path in their ranks for him. The Bear Coat was riding the whitish-gray horse!

"He is riding the horse of peace!" she announced out loud even though every one of the chiefs could see it for themselves. He was wearing a short bearskin coat, the tails of which spilled across the back of his saddle.

"The half-breed spoke wrong?" Two Moon asked, leaning slightly as he whispered to White Bull and the entire delegation came to a stop.

"I think the half-breed wants to have his joke on us," the holy man said grimly, his eyes narrowing on Bruguier's wide back.

Holding his bare right hand aloft in greeting, the soldier chief came to a halt right in front of the delegation. He said something to Bruguier. Then the half-breed turned to speak his Lakota to Old Wool Woman.

"The Bear Coat will shake hands with the mighty warriors of the Shahiyela and Lakota to welcome them. He will have his soldiers put up some canvas lodges for you to sleep in while you are here. And he has ordered a meal prepared for all of you. When you have eaten, the soldier chief will call you to come talk with him at his lodge."

Then Bruguier turned back to the Bear Coat and spoke in the white man's tongue again.

The soldier chief nudged his horse forward, stopping at the center of the line where he held out his bare hand to Crazy Head. But instead of gripping the chief's hand as Old Wool Woman knew these white man favored doing, the soldier chief momentarily gripped the Council Chief's right wrist in his hand, then released it, smiling all the while.

In front of her the chiefs and warriors began to murmur among themselves. She understood why all too well. Among the Indians of the plains, this quick gripping of the wrist was the sign for *prisoner*.

Turning from Crazy Head, the Bear Coat performed the same gesture with Old Wolf, then moved on down the line, briefly gripping the wrists of each one of the delegation. Still smiling was he.

Old Wool Woman was confused more than ever. Did he know this was Indian sign for something bad? Or was the soldier chief merely clumsy in his enthusiastic greeting of these warriors?

No matter, she supposed, as she looked around in those moments while the Bear Coat finished his wrist-grab greeting. She and the warriors were now surrounded the way she and the other women and children had been surrounded by the Bear Coat's scouts on that wintry day near Suicide Creek. They were prisoners as much today as they were that afternoon before the Battle of Belly Butte. So many soldiers, so many guns, and nowhere to run, even if they could escape now.

The *Ohmeseheso* had been prisoners all along, she figured. Prisoners of the winter, captives of the wandering, and the cold, and the hunger.

What difference did it make now if the Bear Coat broke his word and made them prisoners of his soldiers?

Chapter 16

19 February 1877

In less than three weeks the half-breed and the old woman had returned in success! They had managed to convince many of the Cheyenne to ride north to talk to him.

Nelson A. Miles sensed a giddy surge of elation through his every vein. Now Sherman and Sheridan would have to drape him in glory! Now those mealymouthed superiors like Terry and Crook would be shown for what bumbling, indecisive, incompetent fools they were.

Now Miles would get what he had wanted all along: his own damn department!

The colonel was beside himself with self-congratulation at his genius in sending for the leaders of the warrior bands. The only thing that might in any way threaten to dampen his mood was the fact that Crazy Horse and his headmen hadn't joined this delegation. As soon as the courier had reached the post, Miles had asked about the war chief and his village.

"They are on their way to the Powder," the half-breed explained as he was handed a steaming tin of coffee.

"To the Powder?" Miles's voice rose an octave. "Why?"

With a shrug of one shoulder the scout first sipped at his coffee, then answered, "This Crazy Horse not going to surrender easy."

"No," Miles had replied, his enthusiasm sinking. "I didn't think Crazy Horse would make it easy on any of us."

Like stepping from the sunlight into the shade on a bright autumn day, Miles felt a bit colder for that news. It meant he had some chasing and harrying and fighting to do before he would stand ramrod straight to have those general's stars pinned on him. Word had it Sitting Bull was already out of reach, somewhere north of the Yellowstone, closing on the Missouri despite the winter weather, and making for Canada as fast as the latest storms would allow his impoverished people to move. And now Crazy Horse was just beyond his grasp as well.

"To the Powder you said, Bruguier?"

He wiped some coffee from his mustache with a forearm and answered, "East is the best guess for that bunch. Powder. Maybe for the rest of the winter. That's his country."

Irritated, he pressed on, "Surely Crazy Horse realizes by now that we know he favors the Powder River country."

But the half-breed only drank his coffee.

Miles had turned and looked at the crude map hanging behind him in the tiny commandant's office. Running a fingertip down the Tongue River, south by west, he rested it near the star he himself had drawn after returning from the fight at Battle Butte. Looking east from there to the Powder, he brooded. Then his eyes moved west, to the country of the Rosebud.

"Isn't Crazy Horse a man smart enough to attempt to fool me with some underhanded jiggery?"

When Bruguier again failed to answer, Miles looked about the room at the officers crowded in there with him. Captain Andrew S. Bennett, lieutenants Charles E. Hargous, Oscar F. Long, and Edward W. Casey all nodded their heads, murmuring in agreement with each other.

"He's for sure going to give us the slip by scooting west, just like you say, General," Captain Ezra P. Ewers declared, using Miles's brevet rank long ago awarded for courage under fire.

"Yes—but we can catch the bastard on the Rosebud," Miles had assured them. "Still, for the present, we're going to have our plates full with these Cheyenne and Lakota coming in to surrender."

Now that he had accomplished just what he told his superiors he would do, sleep had been difficult for him. The night after the half-breed showed up, he only dozed off and on, his mind busily composing letters to Mary, many more telegrams to Sheridan in Chicago, others to Sherman in Washington City. After all, wasn't he due a moment of gloating and self-congratulation?

And when that morning sun climbed unobstructed by snow clouds, his spirits rose with it. He was finishing his fourth cup of coffee when Bruguier stopped at his office door and the guard announced his arrival.

Miles stepped out into the bracing cold, glancing a moment at the rising sun, bright and splendid in all its radiance. "Going to be a glorious day, Johnny."

"Yeah, General."

"Bring those chiefs here to me, Johnny," he instructed as his cup steamed in the cold.

"I get them Injuns here for you, then you fix my trouble over to Standing Rock?"

Leaning a shoulder against the jamb of the open doorway as he watched the half-breed step into the saddle, Miles said, "Soon as these warrior bands surrender and I don't have to go chasing after them anymore . . . then I'll see that those charges against you disappear. You keep on doing what I've asked you to do, Johnny, and I'll do what you've asked of me."

He had watched Bruguier rein away without uttering another word, watched the scout's back until the half-breed was tangled in among all the cottonwood that framed the Tongue on its path south.

That day dragged as few had before. Miles jumped at every approaching set of footsteps, his ears perked up at every loud voice outside—believing each new noise heralded the return of Johnny Bruguier and the Cheyenne leaders. Waiting, waiting past his midday dinner and on into the afternoon.

When the first word came in, adjutant George W. Baird had Miles's horse ready, that gray beast with the faintest brushes of white in his coat. A clayish-white coat dominated by a huge head—And oh, how the beast loved to prance. There never was but one choice of horse for Miles to ride out to meet the chiefs when they showed up. He would awe them with his splendid appearance astride that magnificent animal he had paddle-wheeled north from Leavenworth the previous summer. Those Cheyenne would get themselves a good, close look at the Bear Coat, the soldier chief who had given them no quarter and now demanded their surrender.

There atop the great gray beast he had perched himself regally, while they came before him—hungry-eyed, poorly dressed in winter's rags, every one of them riding a half-starved Indian pony that was no more than skin and bones—come to sue for peace.

He had no doubt that these enemies would be impressed by his sudden appearance from behind his men formed in ranks—he, on horseback, seated imperially above file upon file of an infantry that had twice driven Sitting Bull into the wilderness, the very same infantry that had put Crazy Horse and these war chiefs to flight just the month before.

He remembered how his mouth went dry when the momentous cry echoed across the parade and the officer of the day ordered the bugler to sound assembly. Miles had taken one last glance in that cracked mirror he had carried from Leavenworth in his small chest of personals. Among them were a gilt-edged cabinet photo of Mary, a small locket of her hair, which he had carried up the Tongue in a vest pocket, and some sweet-scented letters of her most daring confessions of the flesh. He had always been resolute, enduring their forced separation.

"General?"

Miles looked up now and found his adjutant standing stiff and expectant before his desk. "Yes, Mr. Baird."

"I've come to report the Cheyenne have finished their supper."

"And their coffee?"

"Yes, sir."

"Very good, Lieutenant. Have the sergeant of the guard escort them here, and tell the officer of the day to fetch up Bruguier and the prisoner called Old Wool Woman so we can have our translators at my side."

"Of course, General," said Baird, snapping a quick salute before turning for the door.

My, but they did look magnificent in their own wild and feral way, Miles mused as the chiefs entered his small office one at a time. Each man first acknowledged him with a glance, then let their eyes roam over everything. Old Wool Woman busied herself with each chief as he came into the office, gesturing toward Nelson, plainly telling her people they could settle themselves on the floor in front of the Bear Coat's desk.

"I imagine they've never been inside a building before," he whispered to Bruguier who slouched beside him on the edge of the small, cluttered desk. "This must be a wonder to them."

When the visitors had all been seated row upon row on the crowded floor, there was barely enough room for his officers to stand, pressed against the walls. A palpable tension had seized that small room. Nelson's men had no weapons visible for this conference, but he had ordered them to have their sidearms ready beneath their unbuttoned coats. Neither he nor his officers were innocents when it came to dealing with these war chiefs. Only a stupid recruit, or a dead man, would believe the chiefs didn't hide pistols and rifles beneath the blankets they wrapped around themselves.

Despite the air of suspicion and fear of treachery, Miles grinned hugely as their eyes came to bear on him. He nudged Bruguier forward beside him two steps, then halted.

"Ask them if they would like a drink of my whiskey," the officer instructed.

After translating, Bruguier shook his head. "None of them want your whiskey, General."

"Well, now—perhaps that's for the better," Miles replied. "Tell them I am very glad that they came to see me and that I will get to know all their names very soon," Miles promised, and waited for the half-breed's translation. "I understand there is a Sioux chief among them."

Toward the back, a man stood.

"He is called Hump," Bruguier said. "With the Sioux, he is a brave warrior, a smart chief."

Both alarm and excitement flushed through Miles. "Why is this man here with the Cheyenne chiefs?"

Johnny asked for Hump's answer, then repeated it. "He says he and these Shahiyela are related. Many of them marry each other. They hunt together, they fight the white man and the Crow together. Now, he says, he comes with his friends and relations to hear what the Bear Coat says about making a strong peace and giving their people a country of their own for all time."

"Why didn't he go with the other Sioux?" Miles asked. "With the Crazy Horse village?"

"Hump says all the leaders went their own way after making up their own hearts. Some chiefs went one way, some another. Lots of directions, like the winds off the hills come spring. Hump and his people have followed his heart to hear if the Bear Coat speaks true."

"Tell Hump, tell them all, the Bear Coat speaks with one tongue," Miles instructed. "Tell Hump I welcome him here with his friends, the Cheyenne."

When the Lakota chief had settled at the back of the room among his brother and their warriors, Miles turned to ask Bruguier, "Should we smoke the pipe now?"

"It is a good thing," Johnny answered. Then the interpreter knelt before Old Wolf and Crazy Head, in the middle of the assembly, and made sign.

Old Wolf turned to a warrior behind him, who handed the chief a pipe, its bowl already filled. Bruguier shuffled over to the Sibley stove and poked a twig through the slots in the door. With it burning, the half-breed returned to hold the twig over the bowl of Old Wolf's pipe. It took only a moment for the fragrant smoke to fill the room before the chief handed it over to Crazy Head. When he had smoked, Crazy Head held it up for the Bear Coat.

Having watched every detail of their ceremony, Miles puffed on the pipe-stem four times, then two more to finish before he passed the pipe down to the warrior seated at Old Wolf's right hand. The handsome, dark-skinned man smoked, then handed the pipe on. More and more of the heady smoke rose to the low log beams over their heads as the pipe continued its crawl from man to man. When it came back to Old Wolf, the chief passed the pipe over his shoulder to the warrior behind him, then spoke.

Bruguier whispered to Miles, "This one, he's one of their Council Chiefs. Important man. He'll talk first."

"All right."

"Old Wolf wants to know why he should surrender his people to the Bear Coat. Why the Shahiyela should surrender at all. They are a strong people. A powerful people with many warriors. In their camps are more fighting men than you have soldiers at this fort. They could bring their village up and attack this fort, so Old Wolf asks why he should surrender his people to you at all."

"A fair question," Miles replied, drawing himself up, and

glancing over many of those dark, luminous eyes reflecting the glow of the oil and bacon-grease lamps. The stove, the lamps, and all those bodies were making it warm in his small office. And he could smell the animal grease—what he had heard warriors smeared in their hair.

Miles could tell bluster for what it was. Of course they would try to talk tough, he brooded while studying the faces of those men who had been his enemies since the arrival of his Fifth Infantry on these northern plains. They would size him up as quickly as he would size them. If he showed the slightest weakness, they would likely capitalize on it. Instead, the colonel vowed he would show these war chiefs nothing but an iron hand. Perhaps one wrapped in the velvet glove of mercy, but an iron hand nonetheless.

His very future depended upon it.

"Here you are in my house," he began. "I have called you here to talk with me. You came to talk surrender to me. I didn't come to talk peace terms with you. This is *my* ground."

After waiting for Johnny to translate his words for Hump and Old Wool Woman, he then had to wait for her to translate them into Cheyenne. He paused after every sentence or two so that he wouldn't get so far ahead that all understanding was lost on this singularly important occasion.

All of a sudden, Bruguier's face flushed, and he leaned close to Miles, whispering tensely. "The one called Little Chief—I think he just told the young men to put something in their guns."

"In their guns?" His eyes darted across the stony faces of the Cheyenne.

They all studied him as he watched their hands.

"Gentlemen," Miles called to his officers in a calm tone of voice, "our interpreter here says we should be watchful of treachery. They've been told to put something in their guns."

"I knew it!" Bennett grumbled. "Sonsabitches brought weapons to a goddamned peace conference!"

"And so did we," Miles said, still wary, but with growing confidence since not one of the delegates had moved to load, much less expose, a weapon.

"In some ways, I am a mean man," he declared. "In other ways I am a good man. I want you to bring your people here to surrender to me. I want you to give up your weapons—

rifles and pistols. And you must give up your horses, your ponies. Your animals must be turned over to my soldiers when you surrender."

"If they do all this for you," Johnny translated Crazy Head's question, "what will you do for them?"

"If they and their people do as I tell them to do, I will be a good man to all of them," Miles vowed. "I will see that they get their own reservation, anywhere south of the Yellowstone."

"But if they don't give you their guns and ponies," Bruguier inquired after another of the Cheyenne had spoken, "what then?"

Realizing how every last one of them was staring directly at him, Miles took a dramatic pause, conscious of the nuances of expression on his face, the import of his furrowed brow, the forthright, determined glint in his eyes.

"If you chiefs do not surrender your weapons and ponies to me, then . . . yes, I will be mean to you," Miles promised. "The war will go on. I will hunt down your camps. I will make it so you have no time to hunt. Your children will cry with hunger and your women will weep because I have made them widows without husbands. Your camps will be filled with children without fathers. I will be mean to your people until the last survivors obey me and surrender."

As Miles patiently watched, several of the men in the front row conversed in low tones until one of them finally spoke to Old Wool Woman. She related something to Bruguier. Then the half-breed spoke.

"They say they've heard your words and now they're going to talk about it among themselves."

"Among themselves, yes, yes," Miles repeated. "Tell them that's good, Johnny. Explain that they can return here in the morning to tell me what they have decided to do."

After the last of the Indians had departed in the dark toward their two large tents, Miles stayed on, staring out that single small isinglass window at the parade ground illuminated beneath a cloudless, moonlit sky. If nothing else came of this conference, even if the war chiefs left and did not return with their village, at least he now had information as to the location, numbers, and condition of those hostile bands.

Nearby, he thought he could hear the wailing cry of one

of the women. Perhaps the old woman had returned with some bad news for one of the other prisoners. Every now and then the wail rose to a pitiful screech that made the skin across the back of his neck crawl. Against the eerie cry, the sergeant of the guard called out while making his rounds of the pickets, his random footsteps stomping across the squeaky snow.

Tomorrow Miles would find out if these chiefs were going to surrender to him, or if he would have to continue his war on their villages. If they decided to turn in their weapons and horses, so much the better. What a feather in his chapeau that would be!

And if the chiefs told him they thought they could do better than his kind and generous offer, then he would carry on with his war against them. Perhaps he might even start by taking the chiefs prisoner—to hold them hostage. After all, they were fighting men, and leaders of fighting men. He had never promised any of them sanctuary if they came to talk to him, so he would not be breaking an oath.

Tomorrow morning might well be just another day of the horrid war in this frozen wilderness . . . or it might be the first day of peace on the northern plains. That would make Ol' Bill Sherman and Little Phil Sheridan sit up and take notice like they never had before.

Tomorrow.

The woman continued her skin-crawling wail as Nelson A. Miles closed his eyes to sleep.

Chapter 17

20 February 1877

"Them's the finest two I got right now, Seamus," the trader explained, standing behind the wide wooden counter of his Fort Laramie store. "Fact be, I can't recollect seeing two finer dresses in all my years."

Donegan dithered with this sort of thing. On anything else it was pretty much an open-and-shut matter. If he sorely needed something and had the money, he simply bought it. Ammunition, a belt knife or scabbard, a new pair of britches or boots, perhaps a heavier coat when autumn winds began to blow through the thin, worn places in his old one. There was no deliberation to it, no confuscating deliberation to it at all!

But having to decide between the two dresses was another matter altogether. This was damned important, buying gifts to make Samantha feel again like more than just a mother. Something to tell her he saw her as a woman.

"Hold this'un up on you again," he instructed, handing John Collins the pink gingham.

Exasperated, the trader sighed and reluctantly took the dress from the Irishman, dragging it back across the top of the counter.

"Step out here where I can see all of you again," Donegan demanded.

He waited while Collins came around the end of the

counter, unaware that he was really pushing his luck by asking the trader to model the dresses for him. Thoughtfully
scratching his chin whiskers, the Irishman wagged his head,
looking the dress up and down, from hemline to neck ruffle.

"Now the other'n," he ordered.

Collins carefully spread the first across the counter, then
seized up the second and held it against him as Donegan ran
a finger along the length of his nose, brow furrowed as if he
had just been asked to calculate the number of fools it would
take for the army to fill up this Indian country before there
would be a lasting peace struck with the warrior bands.

"By the Virgin Mary!" he exclaimed with a snort. "If I
don't like 'em both!"

"Damn your hide, Seamus!" Collins roared, whirling toward the counter with that second dress billowing around
him like seafoam. "You've had me *wearin'* both of them
bloody dresses for you for the better part of the afternoon
and you still can't make up your mind—"

"Trader Collins!" the voice boomed as the door flung
open. "Never knew just how pretty you looked in a spring-
time dress!"

"Colonel!" Collins gulped as Major Andrew Evans entered the store. Red-wattled with embarrassment, the trader
flung the second dress across the counter then hurried as far
away down the counter from those dresses as he could get
and still be in his own store.

"Don't give him none of your guff now, Colonel," Donegan growled and winked as he patted one of his two belt
pistols. "The poor man had him no choice. I threatened Collins with my persuader here, made him hold them dresses up
so I could make a choice."

"Ah," said Evans, "you're selecting a new spring wardrobe
for your wife?"

"Aye, Colonel. But I can't decide—like 'em both."

"Men aren't meant to have any business in matters such
as this, Mr. Donegan."

"How so?"

The major rubbed the end of his nose with a philosophical
air. "My experience only, you understand—but every time I
choose a dress for my missus, damn if I don't learn she would
have picked the other one! Was a time I figured I'd picked
just the right one for her, then I remembered she always

chose the contrary. So, I did likewise and chose the other. But, lo—when I went home with that box I learned she'd had her eye on the first one I'd picked but left back to the store!" He wagged his head dolefully. "There's just no figuring womankind, is there, Mr. Collins?"

Pressing himself back into the corner behind the counter, the trader gulped. "I wouldn't know, Colonel. Not being a married man like you two."

Suddenly Seamus stepped over to the counter and picked up the first dress. He begged, "Which of 'em would you pick, Colonel?"

After due consideration, Evans answered, "That's a tough one. I'm glad I'm not standing in your boots, Seamus."

"By the saints, my Samantha needs a new dress," he exclaimed as he ran his fingers over the fabric of the two garments. "Nearly every dress she had when we come up here from Texas she's let out while she was carrying the boy."

"What fits womankind before sure don't fit 'em after they swell up with child," the major observed.

"So I want her to have a new dress, something she hasn't had to sew and sew again just to fit into."

Perplexed, Seamus sighed as he looked at one, then the other. In his big, clumsy hands, this matter of a woman's things was nothing more than devilment to him.

Of a sudden Evans stepped up to his shoulder and suggested, "Did you ever consider buying your missus both dresses?"

As the Irishman turned to stare at the officer, thinking Evans had plainly gone daft, Collins hopped behind the dresses spread across the counter.

"That's it, Seamus!" he bubbled, eyes bright and luminous. "You won't have to bother with deciding any more!"

"B-both?"

Evans nodded. "You've got the money, don't you?"

It struck him like a cold slap of the wind. "Yeah . . . yeah! I've got the money, don't I?" He looked up at the trader, grinning hugely. "All right then, trader! Wrap up both them dresses for Mrs. Samantha Donegan, by God!"

When Collins turned away and Seamus had stepped over to pick up one of the toy tin fifes from a wooden crate, the major stopped at the Irishman's side. "You still want me to hold onto your money, Mr. Donegan?"

"Yes, Colonel. It's safer with you."

"Bullshit. You're not the sort to go have yourself a spree and burn through it all."

Donegan smiled wickedly. "Time was, Colonel. If only you'd knowed me then. Time was."

"Perhaps—but not now that you've got a family."

Nodding, Seamus said, "That's why I like it just this way. I know where the money is if I truly need it. And, you have my instructions to turn it over to my Samantha if ... if I shouldn't make it back."

The officer gripped Donegan's forearm. "Then it is true, isn't it?"

"What's that?"

"I've heard talk that you've planned on riding back north to Miles's post on the Tongue River this spring."

"Talk does make its way around Laramie post, don't it?"

"It's true?"

"Aye," he sighed. "I gave my word that when General Miles marched out come spring, I'd be there to scout for him."

"Don't you realize how far that is from here?"

"You remember, Colonel, I rode down here from the Tongue."

"Yes, yes you did," Evans replied with a wag of his head. "But with spring coming on, the Indians will be up and moving about again—hunting, raiding, letting the wolf out to howl—"

"Tell me, Colonel. Does George Crook have any scouting wages to pay a working man back there with him in his Omaha offices?"

"Can't say I've heard any word of Crook planning a spring campaign."

"So does Mackenzie have something for an idle man to do over to Camp Robinson?"

"There might be something you could scare up to do around that agency, what with all the talk that Crook is busy convincing Spotted Tail to go bring Crazy Horse in—"

"Bleeming, bloody damn!" Seamus whispered harshly, glancing over the major's shoulder as Collins went about neatly folding the dresses, preparing to tie them in brown paper with coarse baling twine. "If I had to wait for those mights you've throwed at me, had to wait on all the could-be's the army promises a man, why—I'd still be damned poor and my wife wouldn't have had that grand celebration the day we named our son. And I sure as hell wouldn't have enough money to buy her the dresses she deserves, Colonel."

Evans nodded reluctantly. "But there's always work to be done here—teamster, blacksmith—something rather than chancing your way north through the hunting bands, something better than to keep on fighting just when things are quieting down."

"Things ain't going to quiet down enough for my wife and that little boy until they're quiet enough all the way north into Montana Territory, Colonel. I intend to go there to find an old friend I've lost track of over the years. And together we'll do us some digging."

"Gold?"

"I pray it's gold we dig up," he replied. "But to do that, I've got some work to finish. And so has the army, Colonel. All them warrior bands ain't gone in yet. Which means Mrs. Donegan and her boy are sitting right here till her mister helps get things settled down."

"Will there be anything else now, Seamus?" Collins chirped, tying a knot in the twine he had wrapped around the second package.

Donegan held up two tin fifes. "A pair of these, my friend. One for the wee lad, and one for his pa. I'll take one along with me to the north country and learn to play it so I can teach the boy when I return."

"You're dead set on riding back into that Indian country, are you?" the major asked.

The Irishman's eyes glimmered softly as he stuffed the two small fifes in a big patch pocket on his canvas mackinaw coat. "I've got a family to support now, Colonel." He stuck the fingers of his left hand through the twine on both packages and raised them from the counter. "I'm too old and set in my ways to join your bleeming army. And I'm too proud to dig latrines, to hammer shoes on your horses, too proud to slap the backs of wayward, cantankerous mules."

"Give me time, I'll find something for you to do here instead of you sticking your neck out—"

He laid a hand on the officer's shoulder, stopping Evans midsentence, then explained, "I know what work I'm good at, Colonel. It's honest work and I get paid a fair wage for it. After all, I've got a family I love more than life itself."

Evans nodded in resignation. "Because you've got a family to support."

"The older I get, it seems, the less opportunity jumps up in front of me . . . so when General Nelson A. Miles tells me he'll pay good wages for an Irish scout—by God, I'll ride as far as it takes, eat all the beans and hard-bread I can shove down, and I'll help him find the last of them warrior tribes, sir."

"The Bear Coat speaks with straight words," Two Moon declared, the first to talk that morning after their first night spent under army canvas. Army food lay in their bellies, army coffee and blankets had warmed them after their long journey.

White Bull and the others had asked Two Moon to speak for them. After breakfast and coffee, after they had passed the pipe among themselves, Two Moon stood now and talked as he looked at the Bear Coat, pausing frequently while Old Wool Woman translated for the half-breed, while Big Leggings translated for the *ve-ho-e* soldiers.

From the moment the soldier chief had begun to speak to them the night before, White Bull had begun to feel more certain he had made the right decision. And after their council with the Bear Coat was over, when the Lakota gathered with Hump in one tent and the Shahiyela gathered with Old Wolf and Crazy Head in another, most of the leaders admitted they were beginning to feel more confident that they had come north.

"We see what you have in your heart," Two Moon continued. "It is well. We have decided to go back to our village, still a day's ride up the Buffalo Tongue River. Our chiefs will bring the village down so we can move right into the post. And we will surrender to you."

When the half-breed spoke his white man words to the Bear Coat, the translation made the soldier chief smile. The other soldiers in the small room slapped themselves on the back, leaning forward over the seated chiefs and warriors, extending their arms to the Bear Coat. One after another they all gripped the soldier chief's hand and shook it in that white man way. So different, White Bull thought, from the way the Bear Coat shook our wrists yesterday.

That gesture told us we were his prisoners—not a happy

thing. But this gesture among the white men this morning was one of unmistakable joy. These soldiers treat us so differently than they treat one another, when we are all warriors. All family men with wives and children. All men with hopes . . .

How White Bull hoped the good word of today would still be the good word of tomorrow.

Then Bruguier was talking to Old Wool Woman in Lakota as the soldiers grew quiet. A moment later, she was speaking to White Bull and the others.

"The Bear Coat is glad you have chosen to surrender to him here at his Elk River post," she explained. "He says it's a very good thing that you will return to our village to bring them here to surrender. So the Bear Coat wants one man to stay with him while the rest travel to bring up the village."

"One man?" Two Moon echoed.

"Yes. This man will be as I was while I stayed with the Bear Coat," she instructed. "If the rest return, that man will be released. But if the village flees and does not come to the Bear Coat, then that man will be the soldier chief's prisoner."

"He will not hold you captive as he did before?" asked Sleeping Rabbit.

"No. I am free to go back to my people," Old Wool Woman said. "To return here with them to surrender."

"He wants a man to stay as hostage?" asked Crazy Mule.

"A warrior leader," she explained.

Then Two Moon turned to the group who sat around him. "Who among our young men will do this for our people?"

White Bull watched their eyes drop. They were fearful of treachery. "How quickly our young men talk of fighting," the holy man chided them. "But when our leaders ask them to do a truly brave thing, these warriors lose their tongues."

"One among you, surely," Two Moon prodded the others. "One man to stay here with the soldiers, to stay with the women and children until we return with the village."

"I am not a woman or a child!" retorted Brave Wolf.

"Yes!" agreed Roan Bear. "A warrior does not make a prisoner of himself unless he is willing to give his life over to his enemy."

On and on they argued that morning, back and forth, looping all around the question, and still Two Moon could not convince a single young warrior to stay behind when the others left.

Just past midday in that cramped office, an exasperated Two Moon confided to Old Wool Woman, "Tell the Bear Coat that we cannot decide who will stay as his prisoner. We are going to talk among ourselves some more and when we have our answer, we will come to the soldier chief's house again."

They filed out, tromping back to their tents where the *Ohmeseheso* and the Lakota sat around their fires and talked in low tones as the sun fell and night eventually spread across the land.

Two Moon spoke to the young men again the following morning, when all were up and had relieved themselves. Time dragged on and on, but still not one of them volunteered to stay with the soldiers as a prisoner. It became plain to White Bull that this was a matter of nothing more than pride. The simple, vulnerable pride of men who have agreed to surrender, but never entertained the idea they would be made prisoner.

"Old Wool Woman," White Bull said, standing beside the fire as he handed his tin soldier cup to Iron Shirt. "I want you to go tell Big Leggings my words for the Bear Coat."

Hump, his younger brother Horse Road, and their Lakota stepped in close around the Northern People seated in a ring at the fire.

"Tell the Bear Coat that I will stay," White Bull continued as the group fell silent. On all sides many young warriors quickly put their hands to their mouths in amazement.

"You will stay?" Old Wool Woman repeated.

"Yes," the holy man said. "I do not know what the Bear Coat wants with me, I do not know what the soldiers will do with me . . . but I will stay."

Two Moon quickly came to stand before the older man. "You are certain you should do this?"

"If none of us will stay, then we are all prisoners," White Bull explained to them quietly above the crackle of the fire. "If we are to make peace with the Bear Coat, then one of us must stay while the village comes to this place."

"Surely, one of our younger men can step forward now and do this brave thing!" Old Wolf scolded the warriors.

"No," White Bull declared, waving his hands to quiet the

hubbub. "I have decided this is for me to do. If we are to believe in the Bear Coat, then the Bear Coat must believe in us. This is the only way we can make peace for our people. Go now—make your plans to return to the village. They are cold. They are very hungry. Bring them here where we can feed them and make them warm."

Leaping to his feet, Iron Shirt began dancing in a tiny circle at the edge of the fire, singing his war song. Other men began chanting theirs. This was good and powerful medicine that enveloped White Bull at this moment of his courage. This was like a bravery run.

Surely what he had agreed to do was like *four* bravery runs!

No—this giving of one's self over to the soldiers for the good of his people was like something no man of the *Ohmeseheso* had ever done before!

Chapter 18

*Mid-February
1877*

"THE NEW GOLD FIELDS"

THE BIG HORN COUNTRY LOOMING UP.

AN EXPEDITION TO START IN APRIL.

AN OUTFITTING POINT WITHIN 150 MILES.

Best Route, Etc., Etc.

An expedition of from 200 to 300 miners and prospectors will leave Rawlins for the Big Horn country between the first and the tenth days of April, 1877, headed by the oldest miners and mountaineers in the west. It is desired by those going to increase their number as greatly as possible in order to secure safety and success in prospecting . . . All persons should go prepared to outfit themselves with a saddle-horse, pack-horse and prospector's outfit. There are large stores at Rawlins where everything required for

a complete outfit can be bought cheaper than
parties could take the goods there. The mer-
chants have agreed to furnish this expedition
with their provisions at the actual cost of them
laid down at Rawlins. Horses are plenty and
can be bought at from $30 to $75. Any person
desiring information will receive a prompt answer by writing to any of the following committee:

DR. T.M. SMITH,
P.J. FOSTER, Merchant,
JUDGE H.F. ERRET,
G. CARL SMITH, Attorney
at Law, Rawlins, Wyo.

Seamus could tell by the way the newspaper was folded
and creased just so, that Samantha had intended for him
to read that newspaper advertisement.

This was no casual dropping of the paper after she had
read this latest edition of the *Rocky Mountain News*,
freighted up from Denver with provisions bound for Fort
Laramie. She had purposely wanted him to discover it here
this morning after she and some other wives had gone next
door.

Didn't she know how long the gold sickness had burned
in him? As far back as those youthful days when he'd first
come to Amerikay, listening to the overblown tales of the
great California gold rush. Then just when he figured he
might be old enough to strike out on his own for the Colorado hills, the Great War had come along and swept him up.

As soon as Appomattox had ended that horrid war and he
was mustered out, why—Seamus had thrown in with a seasoned veteran and started for the gold diggings of Virginia
City and nearby Nevada City. But he and Colonel Sam Marr
had run afoul of Colonel Henry B. Carrington's army, and
bumped right up against the Lakota of Red Cloud.

One of these days, Seamus had promised himself, he would
get up to the gold diggings. If Virginia City had played out
. . . he'd heard some of Tom Moore's packers talking about
Last Chance Gulch. The last time he'd received word from
Sam Marr years ago before heading out for Oregon Country

and Captain Jack's war,* Last Chance Gulch was where Sam
had staked a claim. Maybe he would have his own last chance
after all up there in Montana Territory.

Oh, sure and begora, Seamus realized he could have ske-
daddled west to Salt Lake City with Samantha long ago,
headed north from there on a much, much safer route than
that bloody Bozeman Road.

But there had been this job to do. And it was honorable
work for a man more used to making his daily bread with
the strength of his back than by the power of his wits. Scouting was something he could do and do well. On this dirty,
winner-take-all frontier he could have done a lot worse to
feed his family.

By the Virgin Mary! Hadn't he done well by Samantha
and the boy? They wanted for nothing . . . except perhaps for
his being there a wee bit more from time to time.

Did Samantha really think it would be better for him to
be off chasing gold than off chasing the last of the hostiles?
At least he had made himself a handsome purse now and
then by stalking those warriors, while he never did find any
of the gold that lured him west in '66, the same gold he was
bound and determined to find when he brought her north
from Texas in the fall of '75 just as this bloodbath of an
Indian war was fixing to erupt.†

He read through the advertisement once more as he sat
there on the edge of their tiny rope-and-tick bed. Seamus
wondered if Samantha understood that he couldn't leave this
before the job was done. And he wondered if Sam understood it really wasn't a matter of army pay versus Rocky
Mountain gold. This was something that ran as deep in him
as a vein of gold in the high country. Something much, much
deeper than a matter of making a living.

This was where the Irishman knew he belonged. Here, in
this rugged country thrust up against the far purple mountains. And until this war came to an end, this land wasn't
going to be safe for any woman, any child.

No matter if that woman were Samantha and that child
were his son, Colin Teig Donegan, neither one was safe until

Devil's Backbone, vol. 5, The Plainsmen Series
†*Blood Song*, vol. 8, The Plainsmen Series

this war was brought to a close. No matter if it were some Lakota woman or some Cheyenne child caught in some sleeping village when the army charged down on them.

For now no one was safe in this country the Irishman had come to claim as his home. And too much blood had been shed in his own front yard.

The time had come.

This war had to be brought to a close before Seamus Donegan and his family could get on with their lives.

Old Wool Woman could see how nervous the soldiers were as soon as the warriors mounted their ponies that morning and rode across the new snow to present themselves at the Bear Coat's log lodge.

The *Ohmeseheso* chiefs and Hump's Lakota formed a crescent in front of the door at least three riders deep.

From the window of the lodge where she and the other hostages were staying, Old Wool Woman recognized the fear on the faces of the two young soldiers standing at the Bear Coat's doorway. Other soldiers barked and snapped, ordering more of the *ve-ho-e* out of their warm places, into their buffalo-hide coats and the sub-zero temperatures, to hurriedly form a phalanx between the riders and the hut where the soldier chief lived.

"I should go outside and tell them," Old Wool Woman said to her daughter, Fingers Woman. The two women stood together, shoulders butted, their noses pressed against the frosted windowpane.

"Tell them what?" Fingers Woman asked.

Old Wool Woman turned from the window and swept up her blanket. "Tell our chiefs that they have frightened the soldiers into lining up the way they do when they are ready for a fight."

Then she dashed out the door, speeding across the frozen, trampled snow toward the scene.

"Two Moon!" Old Wool Woman called as she reached the rear of the horsemen, her voice all but buried beneath the growling of the soldier leaders.

"Do these *ve-ho-e* want to fight us this morning?" Old Wolf turned to ask her as she pushed her way between the ponies to reach the front row.

"I think they believe *you* want to fight," she said, a little breathless from her sprint in the cold, dry air.

"We have come to tell the Bear Coat our farewells," Crazy Head explained.

"I know," she replied, gazing up at the old chief, then pointed at the soldiers arrayed between the horsemen and the log hut. "But these soldiers don't know why you have come here."

"Tell them we want to see the Bear Coat," Two Moon said to her.

"I cannot speak their tongue," she confessed. "Cannot make them understand me—"

The door behind her suddenly dragged open across its timbered threshold. Some of the soldiers turned with a jerk, yanking up their rifles as White Bull appeared in the doorway, his buffalo robe clutched about his shoulders.

"Two Moon," the holy man called.

"White Bull," Two Moon gave his greeting. "Is the Bear Coat inside with you?"

"He must still be sleeping," he admitted. "I have not seen him this morning. I slept by the Bear Coat's small fire-box last night."

Just then a pair of soldiers pushed up through the others and stood shoulder-to-shoulder in front of White Bull, facing the holy man, barring his exit from the log lodge. Behind the pair a single soldier appeared, shouting over White Bull's head into the darkened interior.

"They do not want White Bull to walk free," Two Moon announced gravely.

Sleeping Rabbit agreed, "I think the soldiers are afraid we have come to take White Bull back."

"To steal him away and flee from this place," White Thunder added.

"These soldiers are too nervous," Two Moon declared to White Bull. "Perhaps you shouldn't stay behind with them, my friend. I think it is better if you come with us back to the village this morning. We will all return here together—"

"I gave the Bear Coat my word," White Bull interrupted. "If he cannot trust my word, then there is no common ground for us to make peace together."

At that moment the two soldiers retreated one pace and stopped as the soldier chief appeared beside White Bull. He gently nudged the holy man aside and stepped into the new day's light, speaking to his soldiers. A heartbeat later, the half-breed loped up, his big coat flapping, rubbing his gritty eyes.

After the Bear Coat grumbled at Big Leggings, the half-breed turned to Old Wool Woman and said, "What is happening?"

"The chiefs came to say goodbye to the Bear Coat."

"Is that why they are here?" he asked. "On their ponies, with their rifles out?"

She turned to quickly look over that front row of chiefs. "They came here to this place on their ponies and with their weapons. They will ride back to our village on those ponies and with their weapons."

"Why are they showing their weapons?" Big Leggings demanded, still rubbing one red eye. "That is not a good sign to the soldiers."

"I think you should tell the soldier chief that the men of my people haven't surrendered to him yet. Those ponies still belong to the chiefs. And those are still their guns."

"What they did made the soldiers scared—"

"Two Moon and the chiefs vowed they would return and surrender."

Wagging his head in consternation as he stepped up beside the Bear Coat, the half-breed said, "The rifles still scare the soldiers."

"I think some of these soldiers would get scared if a magpie shadow crossed over them," she observed wryly. "Tell the Bear Coat these chiefs mean no harm. Say that they have come to offer their farewell before returning to our village."

"They will bring the village here?"

For a moment she pursed her lips, and finally said, "Big Leggings, you were there when these men stood against the others, stood against the Elkhorn Scrapers and the Crazy Dogs, and promised they would seek peace with the Bear Coat. These are honorable men. I am glad they do not understand your thoughtless, wounding words."

She watched his eyes flick up and Old Wool Woman knew he was looking to see if Hump had been listening to their talk in Lakota.

"I made a mistake by questioning their promise," he said.

Immediately the half-breed turned to talk with the soldier chief in the *ve-ho-e* tongue. Then he turned back to Old

Wool Woman. "The Bear Coat and his men understand. He says he knows the word of your chiefs is straight and true, that they will return here with their ponies and weapons, with the rest of the village. He knows they will keep their word to surrender to him even though some of Sitting Bull's Lakota promised they would surrender last autumn, then ran away."

"We are *Ohmeseheso*," Two Moon replied after Old Wool Woman translated. "I do not know about those Lakota the Bear Coat chased last autumn. Perhaps they had very good reason to run away from his soldiers. I am reminded that it takes two sides to make a peace, Big Leggings. Not just those who surrender to stop the killing."

He waited for the double translation, then Two Moon continued, "Here we are, all ready to go back to our village. The Bear Coat asked for one man from our party to stay with him, and White Bull has agreed to stay."

When he heard the translation, the soldier chief smiled and said, "I am happy White Bull will stay at my fort. Last night I told him, 'Come inside my home and rest until the others return with the rest of your people.'"

Two Moon dismounted and passed his rifle off to another warrior before he stepped up to the soldier chief and the holy man. "I want to go inside this place where you will keep White Bull. I want to go inside to tell him my goodbye."

The soldiers before the doorway parted as the Bear Coat turned and went inside. Behind him went two more soldiers, the half-breed, then White Bull and Two Moon. Old Wool Woman was the last to step into the shadows of the log lodge.

When he had turned and leaned back against the big wooden box covered with papers, the soldier chief said, "I will do no harm to this man you are leaving with me. I want to enlist him now as a scout for my soldiers."

Two Moon repeated, "A scout for you?"

"I have learned there are some Indians who will not go in to their agency," the Bear Coat explained. "They are Indians who will not come in to surrender to me. I must go find them. They must go to their agency or I will have to fight them."

Nodding, Two Moon said, "We know there are bands of warriors who will not agree to come in."

"I need a man like White Bull to lead me to these warrior bands," the soldier chief explained.

"You want me to be your scout to find these Indians?" White Bull asked.

"I will pay you to be my scout, White Bull. You will have a horse and a rifle. I will feed you and give you a soldier uniform to wear since you will be leading my army."

For a moment the holy man considered it, then said, "Once I was a warrior all the time. Now I am a priest of my people. But if you want me to be a scout for you, I will scout for the Bear Coat."

When the translation had been made, the soldier chief smiled and pounded his hand on White Bull's shoulder. "This is good news! Welcome, White Bull!"

Still, Two Moon appeared grave. "You must remember that I do not wish to have White Bull killed or hanged while he stays with you. He should die like a warrior in battle. He is a good man and is my friend. I would rather see him shot than hanged, so his soul can be free in death."

"I would not kill my new scout, White Bull," the soldier chief exclaimed in dismay at the translation. "He is my friend and is going to help me find the Indians who do not understand that the fighting must end."

"This will be good I think, Bear Coat," Two Moon said. "When we return, we will march our village right through the middle of your soldier post and camp on the bottom-ground above it."

"My soldiers will help you all that we can," the Bear Coat promised. "I know the people in your village must be very hungry.

"It has been a hard, hard winter for the children and the old ones."

The Bear Coat continued, "If you and the other chiefs will return to your tents for awhile, I will have my soldiers bring you food to live on while you ride back to your village. And a little food to take back to your people. This is my gift to show you that I mean to help your people. That I do not want to punish them anymore."

Chapter 19

Cannanpopa Wi
1877

Lame Deer knew he would have to ration this last of his agency tobacco. What little remained would have to last him until they had a chance to trade, or until he found some stuffed in the pockets of a white wagon driver or one of those yellow-rock diggers they might happen to come across.

More than at any other time, he always liked smoking here as the fire burned low and the camp fell quiet. Everyone but him was asleep now.

It hadn't been all that long since half-a-hundred lodges of his *Mnikowoju* had followed Crazy Horse away from the great hunting camp of Lakota and Shahiyela in the Greasy Grass country. South by east, the great village had been traveling toward the Powder River country, long a favorite of Crazy Horse. Every day meant looking for game, along with sending out the young men to search for sign of the soldiers everyone knew were roaming. With so many people, the big village made short, daily marches, stopping early to camp before the winter sun fell.

Eventually the Lakota camps began to talk of going their own way as well. The hunters had to range farther every day to find enough game for all the hungry bellies. And to find enough buffalo. For the first time in the memory of any of the old men, there wasn't enough buffalo meat to dry, not enough hides to make all the shelters and sleeping robes they required.

More and more each day, Crazy Horse had become like a man confused, truly the Óglallas' strange one. Increasingly he spent his time away from the camps, going alone to the hills. Where, no one knew. To do what, Lame Deer could only guess. The man's leadership was needed now more than ever. But Crazy Horse was rarely seen in camp.

At this crucial time, Lame Deer believed the Lakota needed a leader who would not flee to the north like Sitting Bull was doing. The *Titunwan* needed a fighting man to lead them, not someone who rode off alone into the hills to talk to the trees and stones and clouds above. The Lakota needed a man to stand at the center of his people, gather them to him, and stare the *wasicu* soldiers in the eye.

"No more will we run from the white man," Lame Deer had vowed when the camp leaders spoke of splitting apart. "Those who will stay in our country to fight the soldiers should lock themselves together like the fingers on our hands intertwine to make one all-powerful fist."

Brushing his fingers along the well-rubbed stem of his pipe, here in the red glow of his low fire, Lame Deer thought of the stories of how *Wakan Tanka* brought the Sacred Pipe down to earth and presented that sacred gift to its First Keeper, Buffalo Standing Upright. To smoke was a spiritual act. *Cannunpa iha wacekiya.* His people prayed with the pipe.

Many nights when the village fell quiet and the wind moaned outside the lodges, Lame Deer stuffed a little of his precious tobacco and bark mixture within his pipebowl and smoked it slowly, thoughtfully. Winter was indeed a time of thought for a considerate man who weighed all things very carefully.

At first he had wanted to know why the old ways were disappearing. Gone were those easy days when the Lakota wandered and hunted, coupled and celebrated, the days when they raided other tribes and the few white men who ventured through their country. No more were there any easy days. And the decisions came harder.

Sitting Bull had brought ammunition and announced he was taking all of his people north into the Land of the Grandmother. No one disputed his right to go there, but neither did anyone say what Lame Deer himself wanted to shout.

"Don't you realize that if you flee with your Hunkpapa across the Medicine Line that we will never again unite in numbers strong enough to crush the *wasicu*? Don't you realize that you are abandoning the rest of us to the white man?"

But at least the rest of the Lakota who had stayed on with Crazy Horse could count on the Shahiyela to stand beside them against the white man. Twice the Shahiyela had limped into their camps after the soldiers had attacked. Twice the Crazy Horse people had sheltered and fed their old friends. So despite the fact that the Hunkpapa were abandoning the struggle for the Land of the Grandmother, there were still plenty of Indians willing to fight on.

As winter continued to batter the north country, Crazy Horse and He Dog, Heart Ghost and Lame Deer, along with the many other war chiefs, decided that the combined village was too large. Too many hunters and too few buffalo, not to mention no elk and no antelope. And the women and children were forced to range far to scare up enough firewood. It was better that the chiefs had decided to part company with the Shahiyela for the remainder of the cold time.

From that big hunting camp on the Greasy Grass, Crazy Horse led his people toward his favorite country in the valley of the Powder River. There they would be sheltered, and the snows would not be near so deep. Nor would the cold bite all the way to the bone as it did farther north.

His ears caught the sound of distant voices outside his lodge, and he wondered who might be up this late, unless it was an old man who had to leave his lodge several times a night to relieve himself.

But these were young voices, two of them at least.

Lame Deer set his pipe down on the altar he had made with two forked sticks by the low fire, snatched up his blanket, and ducked out the doorway.

The dim moonshine reflected off the bluish snow, making the lodges dark tripods against the steel-gray sky as his eyes adjusted to the lack of light. He heard the voices again, finding the three men with his ears more than his eyes.

"Lame Deer!" one of the trio turned and called out as the three heard the chief's moccasins crunch and whine across the icy snow.

It was his nephew, Iron Star. But Lame Deer did not recognize the other two who stood clutching the reins to their ponies, heaving with exhaustion, their heads hung low as they shivered in the cold.

"Visitors?" he asked, sensing no alarm from his nephew.

"Shahiyela," Iron Star announced.

"We come from our camp nearby," one of the men began, speaking his unaccustomed Lakota slowly.

"I am concerned that you have come here so late," Lame Deer commented.

"We saw the smoke from your fires near sunset," the first man explained. "We were still a long way off, but the thought of reaching your village tonight appealed to us much more than a night of curling up beneath a cedar tree. We pushed our ponies hard—"

"You bring us bad news?" Lame Deer asked.

Iron Star turned to him and explained, "They say they come to tell us the Shahiyela are breaking apart."

"You mean the big camp of the Northern People is splitting up because the hunting is so poor?"

"No," said the second visitor who only now spoke up. "We bring news that our Council Chiefs and the chiefs of our warrior societies cannot decide on one path to take—to continue the war, or to make peace with the white man."

"Make peace?" Lame Deer echoed in disbelief. "Don't you realize the soldiers will not follow us any more this winter? We fought them again and got away. They have scurried back to their burrows like gophers and prairie dogs. We will not have to worry about them until the grass is green."

"The old woman, and the Bear Coat's messenger—"

"Big Leggings," Lame Deer snarled, remembering the half-breed Sitting Bull had taken in out of the softness of his heart. That act of treachery reminded a man of what to expect when dealing with a white man. Even a *half*-white man. "This Big Leggings . . . he brings empty promises from the Bear Coat. That's why Crazy Horse and the last of our warchiefs are not going north or south."

"But the soldier chief convinced many of our people to go to his fort on the Elk River," the second Shahiyela explained. "Still, like us, many more of our people are following Little Wolf and Morning Star in turning our backs on the Bear Coat's words."

Lame Deer sneered, "So where are Little Wolf and Morning Star now?"

"They are moving south," the first man answered. "They sent us to bring word to the Crazy Horse people, asking that we all travel through the rest of the winter together, safe from the wandering soldiers, so that we won't have to surrender our ponies and guns to the Bear Coat."

"But Little Wolf and Morning Star are taking your people to the White River Agency. Don't they remember what happened to Red Cloud? Three Finger Kenzie forced Red Cloud and the Lakota leaders to give up their ponies and weapons last fall!" Lame Deer scolded. "The White River Agency is no place to be safe. Little Wolf and Morning Star are making a mistake."

The second Shahiyela drew his hand over his face as if trying to wipe away the despair. "What will the Lakota in your camp do, if not go in to Red Cloud's agency?"

Lame Deer snorted, "We have no intention of going to an agency. We have always hunted and raided, and we will go on doing the same this spring, in spite of the soldiers they may send against us. We will fight them all. Some we will kill."

"What of those you cannot kill?"

"We cannot kill all of the *wasicu* at once," Lame Deer declared, "so we will flee with our villages and fight another day."

"There are too many—"

"Just as there are many coulees and ridges for my people to hide behind," Lame Deer interrupted, scoffing. "And there are many trees. The soldiers cannot look behind every one. Besides, the *wasicu* won't be out looking for us—not with Old Crow giving up on the Tongue River, and with Little Wolf and Morning Star sneaking onto Red Cloud's Agency. Don't you see? We are very safe! No soldiers will come looking for us with everyone else surrendering!"

The weary visitors glanced at one another. "We are tired now. Tired of fighting, tired of running. Tired from our journey."

In looking at their faces, Lame Deer could see more than fatigue and bone-numbing cold written there. All around him the warrior bands were giving up and going in. He sighed, "My nephew will find you something to eat, and a warm place to sleep tonight. Tomorrow you can tell the rest of our leaders this sad news you bring of the Shahiyela splintering both north and south."

"We thank you for your hospitality," the second man said quietly.

"You will always be welcome in my camp of *Mnikowoju*," Lame Deer said to cheer them. "When your chiefs have all given up, when your leaders have all gone in to surrender to the Bear Coat or at White River, then you must bring all your warriors to the camp of Lame Deer. Fighting men are always welcome here . . . for fighting men my people will always be!"

Two Moon and the others did as the Bear Coat asked of them. They went back to their tents and waited out the morning around the fire they rekindled.

But White Bull remained behind at the log lodge because the soldier chief wanted him to stay.

After Two Moon and the others started back to the tent camp, the soldier chief turned to the holy man and said, "Now, White Bull, I want to make you my scout."

"How do you do this—making a scout?"

"I am sure your people have ceremonies when a man becomes a warrior," the Bear Coat explained. "We have a ceremony when a man becomes a soldier, our warrior. But, I have a special ceremony to perform when a man becomes a scout."

"I will do this ceremony with you," White Bull replied. "Is there a bravery test for me to complete?"

When the holy man's words were translated, the soldier chief grinned. "No. I already know you are a very brave man. Two Moon said you volunteered to stay here with me when no one else would. Such a brave man I want for my scout, White Bull." Then the Bear Coat turned to one of the other soldiers. "Captain Ewers, I want you to run over to the quartermaster's cabin and get me a uniform."

"A uniform, General?"

"Britches and blouse. For White Bull, my new scout."

Later after they finished a cup of coffee, Ewers returned with a pair of pants and a long, dark-blue shirt hanging over one arm of his buffalo coat.

Laying these clothes atop a pile of papers with tiny marks scratched on them, the soldier chief asked Big Leggings to have White Bull stand. Then the Bear Coat said, "Have White Bull raise his right hand."

"Why do I raise my hand to you?"

"You are making a very solemn promise before your Creator."

"All right," White Bull answered. "I take this vow on my life as a holy man of the *Ohmeseheso*, here before the eyes of *Ma-heo-o*, the Everywhere Spirit."

When he had raised his arm, the Bear Coat held up his own right hand and said, "Bruguier, tell him to repeat his name for me.

When White Bull had complied, the soldier chief continued:

> *I have volunteered this day at the soldier fort on Elk River...*

> *To serve as an Indian scout for the white soldier army...*

After each phrase, the holy man repeated what came through the double-translations made by Big Leggings and Old Wool Woman.

> *I will accept a horse, weapons, and food in return for my service...*

> *I will serve against the enemy I am asked to fight under the rules of war...*

At last the soldier chief finally lowered his right arm and held it out, shaking hands with White Bull. "Congratulations! Tell him how happy he has made me, Bruguier. He is now one of my loyal scouts!"

Midday came and went, but still the soldiers hadn't delivered the promised food to Two Moon and the rest at their tent camp. Near midafternoon, just when White Bull was sure the warriors must be growing very anxious from all the delay, the Bear Coat finally asked his newest scout to accompany him to the visitors' camp. Behind the two of them walked a line of soldiers carrying heavy sacks over their shoulders.

At the Bear Coat's order, those sacks were dropped at the feet of the *Ohmeseheso* and Lakota warriors. Some of White Bull's friends knelt, untied the coarse twine, and peered inside the bags. With no little excitement they pulled out packages of crackers, and wrappers containing some of the white man's meat.

Stepping up to Two Moon, the soldier chief suggested, "Since it is so late now, I think you and your men should wait until tomorrow morning to begin your journey back to the village. You can start early, after a good breakfast."

"Yes, we will go in the morning." Two Moon nodded, then smiled as he turned to study the holy man's new clothes. "You look good in the soldier's uniform, White Bull. What does this mean?"

"I am a wolf for the Bear Coat now."

Sleeping Rabbit asked, "You are going to scout for the soldier chief?"

"If the Bear Coat trusts me to be his wolf, then I can trust him to do what is fair for my people."

White Thunder stepped up, rolling the fabric of the jacket between a thumb and forefinger with admiration. "If I become a wolf for the Bear Coat, he will give me a soldier uniform like this one?"

White Bull smoothed his hands down the front of this long, dark-blue blouse of heavy wool, his fingers brushing the row of shiny brass buttons. Pulling up the bottom of the blouse he tugged his breechclout aside to show his friends the alteration he had made in the soldier britches: removing the seat and crotch so that they more resembled a warrior's leggings.

"The *ve-ho-e* coat fits good, but when I put on the pants these white men wear, I could not stand to walk around, or sit. So, I cut them with my knife to make them into something more proper for a warrior scout."

"White Bull is the most handsome scout the Bear Coat has working for him!" Hump stepped up to cheer in the Shahiyela tongue. "Perhaps I should stay with him now and get a uniform of my own."

"I will stay with White Bull and my brother too!" cried Horse Road, Hump's younger brother.

Turning to Old Wool Woman, the holy man said, "Tell the Bear Coat that he will need more soldier uniforms for his new scouts."

"More scouts?" the soldier chief echoed in surprise at the translation as several more of the delegation stepped forward, all offering to stay with White Bull, offering themselves as scouts.

While more of the men came forward to present themselves to the soldier chief, White Bull glanced to the left where the three captive women stood, looking on. Fingers Woman was the daughter of Old Wool Woman, and Crooked Nose Woman was Old Wool Woman's niece. But the holy man felt his heart flutter when he caught the third one watching him with special eyes. Twin Woman she was, the young widow of Lame White Man who had been killed in the fight with the soldiers at the Little Sheep River.

A woman such as her should not have to live without a man, he thought. She would make a good wife for him, and a good friend for his first wife. He could provide for two women, White Bull decided, feeling her eyes locked on him, admiring his new blue soldier clothes.

Then suddenly he became aware of another man who had been watching how Twin Woman's eyes remained fixed on White Bull. Little Chief strode out of the crowd and stopped before the Bear Coat.

"I too will be a scout for you," the war leader declared. "I will wear your soldier uniform and fight your enemies for you."

It was plain as the winter sun that Little Chief, half-*Ohmeseheso* and half-Lakota, who was leader of his own independent band of people from both tribes, was equally taken with Twin Woman and was not about to let White Bull claim the widow without a contest.

"Very good," the Bear Coat said. "Big Leggings tells me your name is Little Chief. I will make you a scout like White Bull." He added with a sweep of his arm, "I will make you all scouts for me."

It was a good thing, White Bull thought as he looked over the eight others who volunteered to stay with him at the fort. Then he slyly sneaked another glance at Twin Woman, hoping that someone like Old Wool Woman would explain to the widow how he had been the first to volunteer to scout for the Bear Coat, the first to say he would stay behind when the others left for the village.

He hoped Twin Woman would come to know that he had been the first to offer up his life for the good of his people.

Chapter 20

Light Snow Moon
1877

BY TELEGRAPH

DEADWOOD.

More Indian Raids and Fighting.
DEADWOOD, D.T., February 26.—A courier
from the military camp forty miles north of this
city to-day reports that Lieutenant Cummings,
Fifth cavalry, attacked a small Indian camp on
the 23rd. The Indians fled through the ravines,
leaving seven ponies and all their property.
Lieutenant Cummings captured a large herd of
sheep, a small number of cattle, sixteen ponies
and Indian robes and blankets. After the soldiers had gone into camp at night, the Indians
returned and made an attack, which was
promptly repulsed. One Indian was killed, no
whites injured. Indian signal fires were seen in
all directions. The command is moving southward to-day to meet the supply train which has
been ordered from Camp Robinson and has not
yet arrived.

Those who had volunteered to stay behind at the soldiers'
fort, those who had offered to act as scouts for the Bear

Coat, stood now with Old Wool Woman as the rest of the delegation mounted up, preparing to leave for their journey south to the village.

Besides White Bull and Little Chief there were five others. Hump, the Lakota chief, and his brother, Horse Road, and three more of Old Wool Woman's people stood with her, gazing upon those who sat atop their ponies around Old Crow and Crazy Head.

She felt Crooked Nose Woman brush her elbow as she sadly turned away. Old Wool Woman watched her niece trudge off, her shoulders slumped as if she refused to tear her eyes from the ground. Ever since that day the delegation had arrived at the fort, Crooked Nose Woman had grown increasingly despondent, pining in that broken-hearted lover's way. She was still so young, only twenty-two summers, Old Wool Woman thought. Too young to believe she would never love again.

True, ever since their capture by the soldiers, Crooked Nose Woman had grown deeply depressed. Held prisoner at the Elk River fort, she had despaired of ever seeing her people again. But when the delegation from the village appeared, she perked right up. Then as soon as she learned that her suitor had not joined the group coming to talk with the Bear Coat, Crooked Nose Woman began to sink again.

The old one felt sorry for Crooked Nose Woman, but realized they would all be back among their people very, very soon. All things would be better then. There would be shelter from the remaining snows, and food enough to fatten the little ones. There would be blankets for the old ones, and at long last there would be an agency for the Northern People.

But while Old Crow and Crazy Head were the acknowledged leaders of the group who would return to the village, it was Two Moon who shook the Bear Coat's hand and spoke through Big Leggings. "Do you see that trail up the Buffalo Tongue River?"

The soldier chief stared into the distance a moment. "Yes, I see that trail my soldiers took to fight at the butte. I see the trail your people followed in coming here."

Two Moon nodded, saying, "That is the trail I will return by. I have picked out a camping place for the village, there— in the thick timber above your soldier fort."

"I wish you God's speed, Two Moon," Miles replied.

"I shall not make a crook in my trail coming back here," Two Moon concluded, "but will come straight."

Moments later, Old Wool Woman stood watching the delegation disappear among the trees in the mid-distance.

She raised her left arm, holding it aloft. Praying they would hurry back here with the village—

The gunshot surprised them all. And it scared Old Wool Woman down to her roots.

For a moment, she thought White Bull's group was under attack by the soldiers. Then she feared for the departing riders. But in an instant, Old Wool woman realized only one shot had been fired. A sharp crack—unlike the boom of a rifle.

Immediately White Bull and the others whirled on their heels and sprinted toward the sound. Soldiers were coming from everywhere, guns adorned with those long knives clutched in every pair of hands. A sudden shrill scream erupted from the same direction they had heard the shot.

The crowd surged to a stop right in front of the log and canvas hut where the Bear Coat kept his prisoners. Inside, that shrill scream was growing. It sounded like Fingers Woman, Old Wool Woman's daughter.

Pulling at the soldiers' arms, jabbing with her hands, shoving with shoulder and hip, Old Wool Woman fought to pierce the cluster of soldiers milling outside the prisoners' hut. The moment someone shouted English words, the soldiers moved back, parting to allow her through. Leaping through the open doorway, she discovered Fingers Woman on her knees, crouched over Crooked Nose Woman.

Her daughter screamed, clutching Crooked Nose Woman against her as she rocked. Old Wool Woman collapsed to her knees beside Fingers Woman. She took her daughter in her arms and stroked her head.

"You aren't hurt?"

Fingers Woman sobbed. "No. But Crooked Nose woman is dead."

That much was plain to see. The dead woman still clutched an old pistol in her right hand. The bullet hole in the middle of her forehead oozed a trickle of blood.

"Is this her gun?" Old Wool Woman asked.

"Yes," Fingers Woman croaked.

"Where did she get it?"

"From her brother, Wooden Leg," she explained. "Some time ago—when we left for our journey to Tangle Hair's band on the Pretty Fork."

Old Wool Woman could not believe it. "She's had that gun all this time?"

"Yes—she kept it hidden from the soldiers under her dress, inside a legging—"

Turning, Old Wool Woman recognized the loud voices. The soldier chief and Big Leggings were pushing their way against the door where they stopped suddenly and stared at the scene below them.

"Is the woman dead?" the half-breed asked.

"She is dead by her own hand," Old Wool Woman explained. "This is her pistol, which she had on her when we were captured."

The Bear Coat's eyes narrowed as Big Leggings translated her words. Old Wool Woman was sure the soldier chief realized what danger he had been in all that time one of the prisoners had concealed a pistol. He said something to the half-breed.

Bruguier nodded, then knelt and retrieved the pistol from the dead woman's hand. He turned it over to the soldier chief who spoke again.

The interpreter said, "Why would she kill herself? If she had this gun all this time, and she didn't try to break free with it—why would this woman kill herself?"

Old Wool Woman turned to her daughter, holding Fingers Woman there in her arms. "Can you tell us anything that will solve this mystery?"

She nodded her head once, then swiped her hands across both cheeks. "Crooked Nose Woman wanted a lover to come for her. She did not want to be a prisoner any longer and when he did not come for her with the others . . . she knew he did not love her."

"Her husband?" Bruguier asked.

"No—a man she hoped she would marry. A man she hoped would love her the way she loved him—more than life itself," Fingers Woman replied. "She asked the other peace talkers who came to see the Bear Coat, asked them about her lover. But they told her the man did not seem to care for her, that he went off hunting instead of coming to see her."

Bruguier asked, "This is why she killed herself?"

Fingers Woman nodded. "Since the man did not come for her with the others who came to talk to the Bear Coat, she said life was not worth living any more."

"When did she tell you this?" Old Wool Woman asked.

"Yesterday afternoon when White Bull became a scout and the Bear Coat gave the rest some food to take with them to the village," Fingers Woman explained. "Then she talked about it again last night when we laid here in the dark and all the rest of you were asleep. And finally . . . she said she would kill herself again just moments ago when she walked in here crying, lifted up the bottom of her dress and pulled the gun from the top of her legging—"

"I will go catch up with the others," Old Wool Woman said as she started to get to her feet. "It would be good for me to ride back to the village with them, so I can tell her family what has happened here."

"She killed herself because the man she loved did not come for her?" Bruguier asked again, apparently having trouble understanding the senseless suicide.

This terrible winter had claimed one more life, Old Wool Woman thought as she stepped from the cabin door onto the noisy snow.

With a cracking voice she turned back to the half-breed and said, "So many of my people have died in this war . . . I pray this peace we are making with the white man will put a stop to the killing."

BY TELEGRAPH

THE INDIANS.

A Band of Sioux Surrenders.

CHICAGO, February 27.—A dispatch received at military headquarters from the Cheyenne agency says that 230 Sioux arrived there yesterday from the hostile camp on Tongue River. They surrendered their arms and 300 ponies.

The Shahiyela called him Long Knife.

His wife's people gave him that name more than twenty winters before, back in 1851 when William Rowland came west along the Great Platte River Road, a young man hungering for adventure. When the west was still wild and free—and so were the warrior bands. Back when more than ten thousand of them came to Horse Creek near Fort Laramie to make a treaty with Broken Hand Fitzpatrick. That very same autumn the Cheyenne split into two bands: one that lived south of the Moon Shell River,* and the other that roamed the Northern Country.

Not long after he had hooked up with that half-breed French trader named Bordeaux, Rowland took a shine to one of the Cheyenne girls who always seemed to be hanging around the trader's canopy, smiling at him. She was the daughter of Old Frog, one of the chiefs who had refused to sign the treaty.

Rowland made the young woman his wife, and took to the blanket with relish. Because of the huge "Arkansas toothpick" he had come by back along the Mississippi, his wife's people gave him that proper Shahiyela name—Long Knife. Oh, all that he had seen in his years out here: even happened to be in a nearby camp close to Laramie when that stupid Lieutenant Grattan marched in, aching to show some bluster and bravado, and got his entire detail wiped out.

Rowland took up the wandering ways of the Shahiyela: hunting buffalo, trading robes with the civilians who set up shop on one creek or another in western Nebraska, or what was then called Dakota Territory. His large extended family was close at hand in the autumn of 1858 when his woman gave Rowland his first son. They named the boy Willis. Two winters later, James came along.

Things had been pretty quiet during the War of Rebellion back east. None of that mattered a lick to William. He didn't have anything left back there anyway. Not any family. Not a piece of ground. Nothing more than dim memories before coming west to this new life.

But when that war ended, the white man got interested all over again in the west. Like most of the northern bands of

---

*The Platte River

the Shahiyela, Rowland managed to stay out of the army's way for the past ten years. Then one terrible day last winter, word came that the pony soldiers had attacked Old Bear's camp. With soldiers starting to stalk the north country, the lone white man somehow managed to convince his wife's relations they would be safer living on Red Cloud's reservation. He took his family south where he began to pay for his keep with odd jobs around the agency, even interpreting when the agent or the army needed to understand a little of the Cheyenne tongue.

But his work was good, and he spoke straight to both the whites and his wife's people, so General Crook and Colonel Mackenzie came looking for him, when they offered some of the agency's Shahiyela a chance to earn back their firearms and a pony or two in exchange for riding north in search of Crazy Horse. It was good money, this scouting for the army.

Those two soldiers never got a whiff of Crazy Horse's people, but as things turned out, some of Rowland's blood relatives captured an Arapaho youngster and learned of the existence of a big village of Shahiyela back in the mountains. It was Long Knife who Mackenzie sent to talk with Morning Star that cold day in the valley of the Red Fork. Rowland knew it must have made many of Little Wolf's warriors angry to see so many of their own people come with the soldiers to make war on a Shahiyela camp. And those who weren't angry must surely have been consumed with despair as they set off on foot into the teeth of a winter storm.

Like his Cheyenne relatives, Rowland realized the end was near . . . now that Shahiyela hunted Shahiyela for the army. Now that family fought family.

The squawman returned to Red Cloud's agency when Crook's winter campaign fizzled out on the Belle Fourche and arctic cold closed down the high plains.

Reports started to drift into Red Cloud's agency that the war factions in the distant camps were no longer as strong as they had been. The constant fighting, the endless hunger, and the terrible cold convinced band after band that making war came at too high a cost. Word came floating in that many of the *Mnikowoju* and Sans Arc bands were abandoning the Crazy Horse camp, then said to be wintering somewhere between the Little Bighorn and the Rosebud country. These first deserters had headed east for the Little Missouri region. But for the time being, word had it the Shahiyela were sticking with Crazy Horse.

Then news reached the agency in February that the Burnt Thigh chief named Spotted Tail had wrangled himself a deal with Three Stars Crook that would guarantee the roaming Lakota some liberal terms of surrender if they came south to give themselves up. If he decided to undertake this mission, Spotted Tail demanded that he be allowed to take along a strong force of armed Brulé headmen and warriors to insure that he would be received with honor in the distant camps. In return, the chief convinced Crook that he alone could bring in his blood relative, Crazy Horse.

Ah, that was the prize, wasn't it? Rowland brooded.

As soon as he heard Spotted Tail and his delegation were being issued weapons, ammunition, and rations, Rowland realized the Shahiyela never camped very far from the Crazy Horse people. So it didn't take any urging for him to ride over to Camp Sheridan at Spotted Tail's agency to ask the army's permission to go along with Spotted Tail when the Lakota peace delegation marched north.

Since the government officials figured the squawman could help when it came time to make the same surrender offer to the Cheyenne, Rowland was told he could accompany the Sioux, but at no more than a yeoman's wages. The money really didn't matter; Bill figured it was time for young Willis to get out of the lodge and find his own way in the world. He told his son to pack a couple of blankets and some extra socks because the young man was going to ride along, if only to get them both out from under his mother's feet for a few weeks.

Less than three moons after Mackenzie's fight had destroyed the richest warrior culture on the northern plains, Bill Rowland and his eldest were on their way to the north country to convince the Shahiyela to surrender when the Lakota came in to the reservation. After all, this quest was nothing more than what he had promised his wife he would do.

Bring in her people—before there were no relations left.

Chapter 21

Light Snow Moon
1877

BY TELEGRAPH

DAKOTA.

Jack McCall Executed.
YANKTON, March 1.—A quarter past 10, Jack McCall was executed, under direction of the United States marshal, for the murder of John B. Hickok (Wild Bill) in the Black Hills, the 2d of August last.

When their village first abandoned the Buffalo Tongue River camp, Antelope Woman was frightened. Then she grew sad.

Almost from the moment Old Crow's peace delegation departed the *Ohmeseheso* village a day's ride south of the Elk River, other voices began to rise in pitch and tone. With those who most professed a desire to make peace with the Bear Coat now gone from the camp, those who stood for continuing life in the old ways gained in power.

No more than two days passed before the other chiefs decided the village should migrate east from the Buffalo Tongue toward the Powder in hopes of remaining close to the Crazy Horse people. At the very least, the new powers declared, they could follow the scarred trail left by the Little Star People. After the *Ohmeseheso* had been twice attacked by the soldiers, after they had twice fled in search of Crazy Horse's village, after his people had twice sheltered the Shahiyela, Antelope Woman could not blame these Northern People for wanting to be near the mysterious Lakota war chief.

When all was said and done, some of the *Ohmeseheso*'s finest warriors, leaders and holy men had gone north to talk with the Bear Coat. Chances were good they were all dead by now. If not dead, then chances were better than good those men were prisoners like Old Wool Woman had become. Why should they keep the village anywhere close to that soldier fort, where the *ve-ho-e* could strike quickly, without warning . . . again?

Antelope Woman could almost believe the arguments that compelled the camp to pack up and move east, abandoning the Buffalo Tongue. She could almost believe those leaders who declared it might well be better to go in search of Lone Wolf and Morning Star to reunite the Northern People. Almost believe that they would be all right at the White River Agency.

Almost, but for Antelope Woman's brother, White Bull.

She was certain he would never allow himself to be captured by the soldiers, certain he could not be killed by the *ve-ho-e*. Most certain that White Bull would not have fooled himself about the Bear Coat's intentions.

The fighting had been going on for too long. It was time to believe in peace.

Not long after striking the Powder River, they caught up to the village of the Little Wolf and Morning Star people. Nearby lay the camp of Crazy Horse. Together, the *Ohmeseheso* and Little Star People continued south at a leisurely pace.

Then yesterday as they slowly moved up the Powder, the migrating village passed by the remains of Old Bear's camp attacked by Three Star's pony soldiers more than a year ago.* In that Light Snow Moon the *ve-ho-e* had burned

---

Blood Song, vol. 8, The Plainsmen Series

everything they could before they retreated. Lodges and
poles, meat and hides, weapons and powder, all of it gone
the way of smoke. But now, the earth had been at work a
year to reclaim that terrible site. No more were there burnt
rings and the carcasses of a few soldier horses. Now they
found only a few scattered bones not dragged off by scav-
engers. Just about the only sign Antelope Woman found of
where each lodge once stood, were the short stubs of charred
lodgepoles lying here and there, their blackened nubs poking
from the crust of endless snow, where that lodge had been
burned to the ground.

Each dark stub was like a jagged, broken bone, obscenely
protruding from a wound, each one like a ceremonial marker
commemorating an *Ohmeseheso* death in this year of dying.

That night they camped a short distance upstream from
that tragic place, near the ground where the soldiers had
butchered the People's ponies before the *ve-ho-e* retreated
any farther. Both the site of the burnt-out village and this
graveyard of bones were brutal reminders to the People of
just how much they had lost to the white man.

Reminding the Northern People just how much was asked
of them when the Bear Coat told them they must surrender.

Near the mouth of the Little Powder, Spotted Tail's impressive party ran across them. This chief of the *Sicangu* Lakota had with him an escort of 250 armed warriors and a
pack-train of army mules sway-backed beneath many gifts
from the white agents at the southern agencies. Explaining
that he had already visited the Sans Arc and *Mnikowoju*
camps of Red Bear, Roman Nose, High Bear, and Touch the
Clouds on the Little Missouri near the sacred *He Sapa*,*
Spotted Tail called together a big conference of the *Ohmeseheso* and Lakota leaders.

"Where is my nephew?" he asked impatiently, not finding
Crazy Horse among those who gathered for the council.

"He is away hunting," He Dog apologized. "Perhaps it is
better that he isn't here to listen to these words you bring of
surrender."

"A leader of his people can no longer decide things for

---

*The Black Hills

only himself," Lame Deer said. "If Crazy Horse wishes to hunt and fight alone, then I will let him."

"Spotted Tail," a voice called.

Spotted Tail turned away from the stone faces of the Little Star warriors and found the man who had called him—Crazy Horse's father. "You have something to say for your son?"

Worm reached out as he stepped forward to touch Spotted Tail's hand. "Crazy Horse left a message for me to tell you. He touches his uncle's hand through mine . . . and promises that he will bring in his people as soon as the weather makes that possible."

"No! This cannot be true!" He Dog snarled.

Calmly, Spotted Tail replied, "I will send one of my people, He Dog, along with one of yours, to go find my nephew in the hills. They will take my gift of tobacco to him and ask him to come see me himself."

Once the two couriers had started away to find the solitary hunter, Spotted Tail continued. "Three Stars Crook promises the Crazy Horse people a northern agency." This elder who was some fifty-three summers old now began to use on the eager hundreds just those words that might give them all hope. "Somewhere you choose: in the Powder River country."

"We can stay in our own land?" Lame Deer asked.

Iron Star was suspicious, having heard rumors of what the white man wanted to do with all Indians on the agencies. He asked, "They will not send us all back to the *Mnisose*?"*

Spotted Tail shook his head and looked upon those chiefs benignly. "The soldier chief tells me you do not have to give up your horses, or turn over your guns. He realizes a man needs a gun to hunt, needs a pony to hunt—needs both to feed his family. Three Stars makes you a good offer."

Lame Deer asked, "If we do not go in?"

"More soldiers will come. And there will be more grieving in Lakota lodges."

Always, more soldiers.

Then Spotted Tail looked over at the father of Crazy Horse. "I want you to tell my nephew to bring his people

---

*The Missouri River

in—so there will be no more hunger, no more fighting, and no more dying."

After a second day of talks, most of the chiefs joined in promising to bring in their people once the weather moderated. But still, Crazy Horse had not shown up to speak with his uncle.

Before leaving, Spotted Tail again touched hands with those friends he had not seen in many, many seasons, then turned south with his escort and a few lodges of the Shahiyela who were ready to turn themselves in. The chief was eager to tell the soldier chief and agents that he had the warrior bands' vow they would come to surrender peacefully before summer.

And it was here on the Powder that the peace-seekers gone to see the Bear Coat finally found them two days after Spotted Tail had started back for the southern country.

"Where is my brother!" Antelope Woman shrieked as soon as the delegation got close enough for her to see that White Bull was missing from their number.

The village had turned out to watch the return of Old Crow, Crazy Head, and the rest. Pandemonium reigned as the People pushed close to the riders.

"He stayed behind!" Two Moon cried at her in the tumult.

She lunged to the side of his pony. "He is safe there with the Bear Coat's soldiers?"

Two Moon smiled down at her and caught her hand in his, squeezing it gently. "He will be safe."

As Old Wool Woman dismounted, Antelope Woman turned to her. "Is this true? My brother is safe with the soldiers?"

"Yes," a trail-weary Old Wool Woman answered, "because he is now one of the Bear Coat's soldiers."

"White Bull? A soldier? For the Bear Coat?" She clamped her hand over her mouth at this shocking news.

"When I last saw him," Two Moon explained, "White Bull was wearing a soldier uniform. The Bear Coat said he would take your brother on the war trail this spring."

"White Bull stayed behind?" Wooden Leg lunged up from the throng.

Both Antelope Woman and Two Moon turned to find the young warrior coming to a stop between them. His face was turning red. "Yes," Two Moon said.

"This is true?" and Wooden Leg shook his head. "He is wearing a soldier uniform?"

Two Moon explained, "Yes. All is true what we have told you."

Several other young warriors were gathering at Wooden Leg's shoulders, noisy in their protests.

"I cannot believe that he would commit such a treason against our people!" Wooden Leg shrieked.

"He is not against our people!" Old Wool Woman declared.

Then Two Moon added, "Perhaps it is all right for a man to surrender to the soldiers if the man feels that is best."

"White Bull decided long ago that his feet should stay on the path to peace," Antelope Woman declared about her brother.

Wild Hog stepped up. "I am baffled at why a holy man of the People—who has fought long and hard for the *Ohmeseheso*—would now give himself over to our enemies."

"White Bull has a special medicine," Antelope Woman tried to explain as more of the Elkhorn Scrapers came up to get in on the debate. "If his medicine told him to become a scout for the Bear Coat—"

"He can surrender if he wants to!" Wooden Leg shouted, his eyes glaring in anger. "But when he offers to help the soldiers go in search of killing our old friends, then White Bull has a bad heart!"

Left-Handed Shooter, an older man, clamped his hand on Wooden Leg's shoulder and said, "Perhaps White Bull is still grieving the loss of his only son."

Antelope Woman knew no one would mention Noisy Walking by name. He was now among the dead—ever since that afternoon the pony soldiers came riding down upon that great encampment beside the Little Sheep River.

"Perhaps you are right," Iron Shirt agreed. "But White Bull seems very much at peace about his decision."

"I think White Bull wants a new wife," Roan Bear said. "I saw how he looked at Twin Woman while we were at the soldier fort."

"Twin Woman?" Antelope Woman asked. "My brother wants to make a wife out of Lame White Man's widow?"

"Yes," White Thunder answered. "Both he and Little Chief have eyes for her."

"Then White Bull is guided only by what is stuffed in his breechclout!" Wooden Leg sneered. "Not by what is in his heart!"

She started for the young warrior, her eyes narrowed into slits, her hands brought up like claws. "You take those words back and swallow them again!"

But Roan Bear and White Thunder caught her, held her so she could not fling herself upon Wooden Leg.

"This is strange," Wild Hog said. "What White Bull has done to help the soldier chief is very, very strange."

Oh, how Antelope Woman wanted to believe that White Bull truly had done the right thing. How she wanted to believe that her brother's powerful medicine was still as strong as the day the *Ma-heono* raised him out of that hole in the ground without moving that huge boulder. In this terrible time when the *Ohmeseheso* had nothing more than one leader or another to believe in, Antelope Woman wanted so badly to believe in her brother.

But Old Wool Woman had returned with even worse news for many in that village. "I was not going to come back with the others," she explained as a large circle of women gathered around her. "Instead I was going to wait at the soldier fort with those who became scouts."

"Your daughter, Fingers Woman—she is healthy?" a voice asked.

"Yes, but my heart is heavy and cold because Crooked Nose Woman has killed herself."

"Killed herself!" Antelope Woman shrieked. "Aiyeee!"

All around them women began to wail and pound their breasts, pulling at their hair while Old Wool Woman told the story. "I caught up to the peace-talkers headed back here. To tell them the story. I thought it best to come tell all of you the sad news from my own lips."

"Shahiyela do not kill themselves!"

"This is an evil omen!"

But Old Wool Woman tried to console the terrified crowd, "She was an unhappy woman only because her suitor did not come with the others to the soldier fort."

Like so many others at that moment, Antelope Woman wanted desperately to believe that such a terrible thing was not an evil portent of things to come.

But—as if all of that news wasn't enough, as if the spirits

had arranged recent events to shake her faith and trust in both White Bull and his bedrock faith that things were bound to get better—the following day seven *Ohmeseheso* horsemen showed up at their camp. These riders had come all the way north from the White River Agency! Like Spotted Tail, the seven emissaries bore gifts of tobacco for the Council Chiefs; they had come to tell their people they should surrender only at their old agency. Not at the Elk River fort. Not at the Spotted Tail Agency either.

"No one there has been punished for fighting the soldiers," one of the couriers declared.

"You have nothing to fear!" explained a second rider.

Crazy Mule asked, "They are not taking away your ponies and your weapons?"

"See here!" a messenger cried, holding up his rifle in one hand, the reins to his pony in the other. "Do you see a man before you with no weapon and no pony to ride?"

The crowd laughed, but it was a good laughter—one washed in relief. Many began to murmur that perhaps Little Wolf and Morning Star had been right all along to want to go south to the White River Agency. Far better than surrendering at the Elk River fort, it would be a place they already knew. In addition, the Little Star People would be sharing the agency with them. The *Ohmeseheso* had many friends and relations among the Little Star People, had even intermarried with them. Yes, it would be good to be close to them once more.

"But we should see if the Bear Coat will promise us as much!" Sleeping Rabbit declared.

"Yes," echoed White Thunder. "If he will give us what Three Stars Crook will give us, then we do not need to go south any farther."

Two Moon offered, "I will go back to the soldier fort with some other chiefs. We will see if the Bear Coat will give us all of what Three Stars promises."

One after another the chiefs and headmen and warrior society leaders declared they would accompany Two Moon to the soldiers' fort to see what concessions they could wrest from the army there. Soon there were more than ten leaders for every one of Antelope Woman's fingers who said they would go north to talk to the Bear Coat.

They would surely get the soldier chief to give them what

the Three Stars had offered them in the south.

But if the Bear Coat could not . . . then all of the *Ohmeseheso* would have no better choice than to march for the White Rock Agency together, abandoning the Northern Country.

Leaving her brother a prisoner on the Elk River.

Chapter 22

18–23 March 1877

BY TELEGRAPH

THE INDIANS.

General Sheridan Coming West.
OMAHA, March 6.—General Sheridan, accompanied by Colonel Sheridan, of his staff, arrived here today, and proceeded west on the Union Pacific train to Cheyenne, whither the general goes to perfect the spring campaign against the hostile Indians. The river at this point is rising rapidly.

"Who's that white man with the chiefs?" Nelson Miles roared at his officers. "Could he be a renegade mercenary?"

Minutes ago the cantonment's soldiers were put on alert with the arrival of more than 160 Cheyenne and Sioux from the wandering village located somewhere in that country between the Tongue and the Powder. Outside the log hut that served as his office and private quarters, the situation was tense as nearly all those warrior horsemen remained on the backs of their ponies, while only their chiefs dismounted to stride purposefully toward the crude log headquarters hut.

White Bull suddenly burst from his wall-tent, quickly shoving the big brass buttons through the holes in his tunic as he prepared to meet old friends.

"General Miles!" the white stranger cried as he came to a halt with the chiefs and held out his hand.

"Yes, I'm General Nelson A. Miles," he said guardedly as his officers flowed up on either side of him protectively, watching every movement made by the stranger's hands.

"I'm William Rowland, General," the man declared. "Come north from the Cheyenne agency down on the White River to talk the bands into surrendering."

"That makes you an agent of General Crook."

The man smiled, finally dropping the hand he had been holding out. "No, I came north with Spotted Tail on my own. I'm married into the tribe. Got Cheyenne relatives—my wife's people and all. Our son came with me too."

Now he really felt a prick of anxiety. "Spotted Tail? The Sioux chief?"

"Yeah, that's the one," Rowland agreed, and went on to explain how the Brulé leader had marched north from the reservation with 250 warriors and all those gifts from the agents for the Sioux and Cheyenne holdouts.

"Gunpowder too?"

"Yep, powder for their guns, General. But it weren't the army sent that powder with Spotted Tail. And it weren't the agents neither. It was the traders—"

"Damn those traders!" Miles roared. "They're always going to make sure these war chiefs come in close enough to trade for more, aren't they?" Then the colonel whipped his arm in a wide arc across those chiefs arrayed right before him. "So, what brings you with these men to my doorstep?"

Rowland rubbed a red eye, irritated by the glare of sunlight glancing off the bright snow. "When these leaders wanted to see if you could give 'em good as Crook offered 'em, I figured I'd come north to translate . . . if you want me to."

Miles glanced at Bruguier. The half-breed shrugged and went back to chewing on the piece of hard-bread he held.

"All right," Miles replied. "Let's have us another talk with these chiefs and see just what it is Crook's using to bribe them."

After the ceremony of smoking the pipe and offering some food to his visitors, Miles slowly wagged his head, growing exasperated as the squawman explained just what the hostiles had been offered to surrender with the Sioux down in Nebraska.

"And Spotted Tail told them they wouldn't have to give up their ponies or weapons?"

"That's what they was promised."

"How can Crook really offer them an agency here in the northern country?" he grumbled, turning to his cadre of officers who stood against the walls of the hut. "This isn't his department—so it damn well isn't his land to commit!"

Taking a step closer to the colonel's desk, Rowland explained, "General Miles, these leaders don't know nothing about that. They only come to see if you can give 'em good as they was offered to surrender down south."

"I know, I know," Miles declared, waving a hand at the white man. "It's perfectly understandable that these chiefs should want to go where they think they will be best treated. I can't blame them." He pounded a fist into his open palm. "But it's plain as thunder there's something else afoot here."

For the next few moments, Miles gazed over the Cheyenne and Sioux chiefs who had come to wrestle more concessions out of him, after he had unequivocally spelled out the army's terms of surrender. On their last visit, these leaders had led him to believe they were going to return to effect their surrender!

Now that elation soured like milk left out in the sun. Anger roiled inside him, but not so much an anger at these chiefs. His was a deep, abiding resentment for George C. Crook, for Alfred H. Terry back in St. Paul, for the quartermaster corps downriver who, all winter long, had seen to it that Tongue River Cantonment was deprived of nearly everything it took to provision a post of such strategic importance.

Finally his eyes fixed upon White Bull, sitting there among the others in his army uniform, his braids topped with a black slouch hat. The Cheyenne holy man looked grave.

I'll bet he understands the seriousness of the dilemma I'm facing, Miles thought. He's turned himself over to me as a hostage, and sworn in as one of my scouts. Now he finds his people might not surrender here to me, after having given their word they would.

Miles felt a sudden flush of sympathy for White Bull.

"Rowland," he said suddenly, "tell these chiefs I will talk with them again in a couple days."

"Couple days—"

"Two, maybe three. Explain that I want time to consider the import of what they've asked of me. I've already spelled out terms of surrender, but I will nonetheless reconsider their case. Tell the chiefs, while I will not feed or house the warriors who accompanied them here, I will provide tents and food for them while they are waiting for our next parley."

After angrily brooding on the situation that had been dropped in his lap, Miles met with the chiefs three days later. In that time some of the warrior society headmen had become surly, growing indignant at being made to wait by the Bear Coat.

"They say they're free men, General," Rowland translated as everyone in the tiny office settled in for the conference, after the pipe made its rounds. "Most of them young bucks don't figure they've got to hang around waiting for you to come up with something as good as what they was already promised down south."

"You tell them they will not dictate terms of surrender to me!" Miles snapped, feeling the first fracture in his restraint. "Tell them they are a defeated people, and as such, *I* am the one who will dictate terms to them!"

It was plain to see how Rowland's translation affected the leaders. The warrior society headmen began to murmur and shift about outside the log hut as those at the doorway passed on what was being said between their leaders and the soldier chief.

Miles glanced over at George W. Baird. "Lieutenant, I want you to calmly, and without showing alarm, excuse yourself and alert the units that we may have ourselves some trouble coming to a boil."

Rowland started, "Go slow at this—"

"What're your orders, General?" Baird interrupted the interpreter.

"Ready their weapons, and prepare to surround the Indian camp at a moment's notice. Now, move calmly, and don't give any of these Indians a reason to be alarmed by your departure."

As the adjutant slipped from the hut and made his way across the open ground, threading his way through more than 150 warriors, the squawman continued to translate, "General, they said maybe they won't go in either place. Maybe they'll go on hunting. Winter's going to be over soon and Spotted Tail told 'em your soldiers aren't going to be up here much longer—"

"Won't be here much longer!" Miles bellowed like a branded calf. "Where the hell did they get that idea?"

Rowland admitted, "Someone down at Red Cloud told Spotted Tail this isn't a fort, that your soldiers are here for a short time, and they'll be gone come spring—"

"You tell them that if they don't start south for Red Cloud's Agency," the colonel growled between gritted teeth, fuming, "and they won't surrender here—I'll come looking for them! And we'll have ourselves another fight like we did in January. You tell them I'm ready to be mean to them in war . . . or I'm prepared to be nice to them in peace."

But Miles knew he wasn't prepared, either way.

After the chiefs huddled together, they told Rowland that they would wait some more, while the Bear Coat deliberated on just what he could offer them if they surrendered to him. The emergency with the warrior society leaders was over, for the moment.

Yet Miles had to acknowledge he was sitting squarely on the horns of a thorny dilemma. For the next two days he brooded on what faced him no matter what the Cheyenne and Sioux decided. If they ignored his threats of continuing his war on them and took off to return to wandering with their village for the spring hunt, Miles realized he couldn't muster enough rations and supplies for both man and beast to sustain even a five-day march to chase the enemy. And, if they agreed to bring in their people and surrender to him at the cantonment, he did not have the manpower, the rations, or the facilities to manage all those who would give themselves up to him.

And the reason behind his frustrating dilemma was General Alfred Terry's poor management of the department, coupled with the low esteem Sherman and Sheridan both held for him and his regiment, as well as the neglect his men were suffering at the hands of the quartermaster corps. He was being hamstrung, prevented from prosecuting this war to its end. The way Miles saw it, as the only commander on these plains who was doing a goddamned thing about bringing the enemy to bay, it was nothing short of criminal what was being done to Nelson A. Miles!

For another two days he struggled with his options, counting and recounting his stores of supplies, listening to the suggestions of his officers, and spending time dashing off letters to his Mary. But while he admitted to her that "the management of these people just at this time, considering the condition of my command, is a difficult question," the colonel ultimately decided he could not back down from his initial demand of unconditional surrender of the enemy.

Time and again he and his men had defeated these warrior bands. And while he might not have enough supplies to pursue the enemy in the next few weeks, spring would come, and he had faith he would find a way, find the necessary stocks that would allow him to prosecute this war all the way to victory. If supplies would not arrive from downriver when he was ready to march, then by God he'd get his hands on what he needed from civilian contractors in Bozeman City. Come spring, an answer would present itself.

Miles called the Cheyenne and Sioux leaders back to his office on the morning of the twenty-third.

"Rowland, tell the chiefs exactly what I have to say," he stated tersely. "Word for word, as close as you can make it. And, Bruguier—you translate it into Sioux."

He waited as both men nodded and turned toward their audiences, then the colonel drew in a breath, set his jaw, and began.

"The Bear Coat's soldiers have driven Sitting Bull north of the Missouri and he's running for Canada.

"Two months ago I whipped Crazy Horse and all of you in our fight up the Tongue River.

"So you know that I am a man who can make war on you and your villages.

"You know me as a man who will fight you if you want to make a fight of it.

"If you don't already, you will come to know me as a man of my word. I will not lie to you—I won't tell you what you want to hear simply to get you to surrender to me. I speak to you with one tongue, whether you like the sound of my words or not.

"You will trust me as a friend, or trust me as an enemy. But I will not be among those white men who will lie to you."

As the words were translated into both languages, those two voices bouncing off one another as the interpreters delivered the colonel's stern admonition, Miles watched how many of the dark eyes lost their haughtiness, how some of the heads began to gently nod in resignation. *If nothing else*, he brooded, *they will know me as a man who deals honestly with them.*

"Weeks ago I gave you your terms of surrender," he continued. "You are in no position to come back and attempt to dictate new terms of that surrender to me. As I told you then, I can be a good man, or I can be a bad man to your people. What I said before still stands, no matter if it is winter or spring, or if I have to follow your villages into the summer and fall. You will surrender.

"You will surrender at either of the agencies south of here, Red Cloud's or Spotted Tail's; or, as some of you have already decided, you will come here to surrender to me. But, you must surrender one place or the other. The only other choice for you . . . will be war.

"If you do not want my soldiers to trail your villages, if you do not want any more of your women and children to suffer because you decide to pursue this war, then you must surrender to me without conditions. You must turn over your ponies to me. You must turn in all your firearms and other weapons as I will require. Only those among you who I trust to be scouts will be allowed to keep their ponies and their weapons."

Several of the chiefs turned briefly to glance at both White Bull and Little Chief who already had become scouts for this post. And that reminded Miles of a final point he wanted to impress upon these leaders.

"Spotted Tail was wrong and you must not believe him when he talks about me."

He waited while those words were translated before continuing.

"Yes, Spotted Tail was very wrong when he told you that this fort and my soldiers will be leaving soon. You cannot believe him. I am standing here to tell you that I will stay in this country until my job is done. My soldiers will be here until all of your bands have either surrendered, or I have made war on your villages. You will surrender, or you must fight me. And if you fight me, I vow that I will kill you before I leave this place.

"This fort will stand. My men will remain. And I will lead them against you if you refuse to surrender.

"Believe in my words. I tell you the truth. I can deal with you honestly in peace, or you can trust that I will kill you in war. It is up to you to decide."

Miles turned slowly and stepped back to his crude desk. He leaned against it, crossed his arms over his chest and waited while both interpreters finished. As silence settled over that hut, and the crowd of warriors pressed close outside, all of them being slowly surrounded by soldiers, the colonel watched the faces of those Indian leaders. For the first time in all the sessions he held with them, these headmen did not immediately begin to confer among themselves. Instead, the chiefs either stared at him, or fixed their gazes on the walls or the floor in front of them—every last one deep in their own thoughts.

For the first time, Miles brooded, *I believe they're really searching their souls on just what course they should take from here.*

Two minutes passed and still not one of the Indians stirred. At three minutes no chief had risen to speak. Four minutes passed and the only sound from his visitors was an occasional, muted cough. Then five ticked by in that uneasy stillness.

At last Little Chief, the half-Sioux, half-Cheyenne leader of his own band, slowly stood, then stepped into the small patch of open floor between the chiefs and Miles. There, with solemn dignity, he threw back the front of the painted buffalo robe, which spilled from his shoulders until it hung from his waist where he had it belted. That act reminded Miles of how one of Caesar's men might fling back part of his toga before addressing the Roman Senate.

"I am a chief, Bear Coat," he began, with Bruguier translating.

"For many generations my fathers have been chiefs before me. For a long, long time my ancestors have lived in this country, hunted the buffalo, made our fires beside the rivers, and drank of these waters. We have given birth to our children, and buried our old ones in this land."

Miles had to admit, this was an impressive man. Tall, sinewy, and muscular, Little Chief was no less than an archetype. As the colonel listened to the half-breed's translation, he studied the piercing scars across the Indian's chest, the four slashing scars across each of his upper arms.

"Ever since our people can remember, this has been our land," Little Chief continued. "You are the invaders here. You have come here without our invitation, or our welcome. The white man has wronged us, come to our home to take what is not his."

Miles watched these strong, unvarnished words cause a ripple of emotion to course through the assembly. If they hadn't been ready before, Miles prayed his soldiers stationed outside the hut were ready now for an outbreak.

"The white man has run off our game, killed our buffalo, made his camps on the sacred land of my people," the tall Sioux leader declared. "And when we would not be driven off like the beasts to slaughter, the white man sent his army against us."

This Indian had an eloquence that stabbed Miles to the quick, a dignity that struck him with the poignancy of the man's words. The colonel found his sympathy pricked as Little Chief continued.

"We did not make war on the white man. The white man came here to *our* country, to make war on *us*."

Miles thought, *If this man stood in the assembly halls of our Congress, he would surely arouse an unbridled passion for his cause.*

"But we are weak, compared to you and your forces," Little Chief suddenly admitted with finality. "We are out of ammunition. Our people cannot make a rifle, cannot make a bullet, or even a knife. In fact, we are at the mercy of those who are taking possession of our country."

Holding out both hands before him at the waist, palms up, the Indian concluded, "Your terms are harsh and cruel . . . but my people are going to accept them and place ourselves at your mercy."

Without ceremony, Little Chief turned away and settled again to the floor.

What a tremor of joy shot through Miles at those words! All his hard work here on the northern plains hadn't been

for naught! The toils and sacrifices of his men had not been
in vain!

"Rowland, tell these chiefs that some of them can go to
Washington City, there to meet the leaders of this country,"
Miles gushed, happiness awash in every ounce of his being.

One of the older Cheyenne chiefs rose and responded to
that invitation. "Tell the Bear Coat I have been to this Washington before. There they showed me a map with this land
on it. They pointed to all the country that the white man said
was his and told me the Indians must keep off that land.
Then they showed me a small piece of ground off in the
corner of the map. Here the Indians were to go and stay,
and the white people could not go there."

The old man's red-rimmed eyes showed great sadness as
he continued, "But the white men who told me this many
winters ago lied to us. The white man did not keep off the
land he said belonged to the Indian. The white man wanted
that land too."

Miles saw how the eyes of the other chiefs now showed a
similar sadness as the chief continued.

"The Bear Coat has not lied to us yet. So I am going to
try you. I am going to come in here to the Bear Coat's fort.
I am going to surrender to you."

As the old man sat again on the floor, Little Chief stepped
forward once more.

"I say these things to the Bear Coat before I shake his
hand in peace," he declared with great solemnity, while Bruguier translated.

"Some of my people want to go down to the southern
agency to surrender because their relations are already there.
And some of us will surrender to you here and remain on
the Elk River with your soldiers."

Little Chief drew himself up, holding out his hand to Miles
as he said, "This war between our peoples must not go on.
I say this to you: the killing is over."

Chapter 23

Light Snow Moon
1877

BY TELEGRAPH

THE INDIANS.

Sitting Bull Heard From.
ST. PAUL, March 7.—A Winnipeg (Manitoba) special to the Pioneer-Press says information has been received there of the arrival of Sitting Bull in the mountains of the British possessions. He had 1,000 horses and mules captured from the United States forces. A force of mounted police was sent out to interview him.

With long faces and empty hands the peace delegates returned from the Elk River.

At first, they told those in the great village, the Bear Coat had grown very angry at Three Stars for making the offer he had. Then the soldier chief told the peace delegates that he could not change the army's terms of surrender. *The Ohmeseheso* and Lakota would have to turn over their weapons and ponies. They would have to surrender themselves as prisoners of war.

So when the men gathered the following evening to begin discussing if their camp would continue on south with Lone Wolf and Morning Star who were going in with the Lakota, or if they would start north to surrender to the Bear Coat, the arguments raged once more. As was the custom among the Northern People, every man had his chance to speak—from the Council Chiefs in the front row to the warrior society headmen seated behind them. After much passionate debate, it was once again plain to see that there would be no consensus.

The chiefs sent a crier through the village to proclaim that they would announce their decision. Antelope Woman joined the others crowding around the council lodge to listen in a hush.

"Each man is free to decide on his own whether or not he will surrender . . . and where he will go in to give himself up."

So it was that among the small warrior bands gathered there beside the Powder, among the clan relations, inside every family's lodge, the grave discussions began. Every war chief, leader, and family head had a crucial decision to make. Although he would hear from all those he was responsible for, in the end it was his decision alone to make. By the fourth day it became clear that the wound first suffered by the *Ohmeseheso* beside Rotten Grass Creek still festered and oozed.

Little Wolf still smarted from White Bull's rebuke the previous summer beside the Little Sheep River. White Bull had demanded to know why Little Wolf was not in their camp when the soldiers rode down upon them to that great victory. Now the Sweet Medicine Chief flatly declared that he would never go anywhere White Bull took his family.

Antelope Woman's people were once again tearing themselves apart.

Warrior society by warrior society parted company; clan by clan the Northern People said farewell to one another. Even some family members went their separate ways.

Old Bear, Little Wolf, and Morning Star—the three Old Man Chiefs—again announced they would continue south to the White River Agency. When Coal Bear learned of their plans, he proclaimed that as the Sacred Medicine Hat Keeper, he would stay with the Sweet Medicine Chief and go south as well. In fact, the majority of chiefs stated they would join the procession south: Black Wolf and American Horse, Black Eagle and Standing Elk, Turkey Leg, Medicine Bear, and White Clay.

Predictably, most of the warrior society headmen decided to follow those Old Man Chiefs. Five of the seven leaders of the Elkhorn Scrapers, who were still alive after these many moons of bloody fighting, declared they would follow Little Wolf south: Wild Hog and Tall White Man, Plenty Bears, Broken Jaw, and Wolf Medicine.

In addition, the four Crazy Dog chiefs chose to follow the Sacred Hat Priest to the White River Agency: Red Owl and Snow Bird, Strong Left Hand and Beaver Claws.

At the end of the discussions the only Dog Soldier Chief living with the *Ohmeseheso*, Tangle Hair, stated he would follow the majority south so that he could stay with Little Wolf, a warrior whose bravery he greatly admired.

This exodus left very few who would be turning back for the Elk River to accept the Bear Coat's offer of good treatment.

Leading that small group would be several respected men. Among the most notable was Black Moccasin, the fourth Old Man Chief, who decided that he would lead his people north to the Elk River to surrender with his nephew, White Bull. Joining them would be the families of Old Wolf, Crazy Head, and Magpie Eagle. Coming along would be the mixed Shahiyela-Lakota clan of Little Chief.

Of the Kit Fox warrior society chiefs who had survived a year of devastating warfare, only four chose to journey north to the Buffalo Tongue River fort: Ridge Bear, Wrapped Hair, Sits Beside His Medicine, and Weasel Bear. Among the Crazy Dog chiefs only three elected to surrender to the Bear Coat: Little Creek, Crazy Mule, and Iron Shirt. In those moments just before the procession would start north, Left-Handed Shooter decided that he would join White Bull at the soldiers' fort. The two of them would be the only Elkhorn Scrapers to surrender at Elk River.

On that bitterly cold, snowy day the *Ohmeseheso* again tore themselves apart. A few prominent warriors finally decided they simply couldn't take their families south to the White River Agency—a place far from the homeland of the Northern People: Brave Wolf and White Wolf, White Elk and Howling Wolf, Sits in the Night and Fast Whirlwind, along with a very sad Walks on Crutches, who was Wooden Leg's uncle.

Antelope Woman felt a small but growing measure of happiness as the next few winter days drifted past and the small village plodded on for the Elk River soldier post. She kept thinking of seeing her brother again, imagining him clothed in that blue soldier coat, a *ve-ho-e* hat pulled down on his braids.

It surprised her that many of those who were headed north were so critical of White Bull after learning that he had become a scout. A few even talked behind their hands, saying that White Bull was either letting his manhood flesh do his thinking for him now that he had eyes for Twin Woman . . . or that he was not thinking clearly because of his deep grief at the loss of his son on the Little Sheep River.

She did her best not to listen to the poison in those whispers, not to notice the way others peered at her with their pitying eyes.

Antelope Woman still wanted to believe in her brother. Wanted to learn for herself why he had become a wolf for the *ve-ho-e* soldiers. Why he had joined the enemy.

ARIZONA.

Damning Proof—A Witness Against
Brigham Young.

TUCSON, March 28.—The Star prints the following: The following is a correct copy of the original order given concerning the Mountain Meadow massacre. The order, with three affidavits authenticating it was found among the papers of the late ex-Chief Justice John Titus, of Arizona, and formerly chief justice of Utah.

SPECIAL ORDER: SALT LAKE CITY, April 19, 1857. The officer in command of the escort is hereby ordered to see that every man is well prepared with ammunition and to have ready at the time you see these teamsters, a hundred

miles from the settlement. President Young advises that they should all be killed to prevent
their returning to Bridger to join the enemy.
Every precaution should be taken to see that not
one escapes. Secrecy is required.

By order of General DANIEL H. WELLS.
JAMES FERGUSON, A.A. General.

This war had reaped a terrible harvest, Old Wool Woman
brooded as the ragged procession cleared a stand of tall cottonwood and moved into the open.

This war not only left a swath of dead and wounded—not
only those who had starved or frozen to death—but it had
taken a devastating toll on the spirits of so many of her people. Like a hidden, unseen enemy that had stealthily crept
into the lives, hearts, and souls of the *Ohmeseheso*, this endless war against the white man had changed the People for
all time.

For days after she returned to the village, many had
mourned the death of Crooked Nose Woman. It was a be-
wildering, heart-rending death that touched so many because
Crooked Nose Woman was loved by all.

And in that time of grief, Old Wool Woman thought more
and more of how this war with the *ve-ho-e* had changed those
closest to her. Not only Crooked Nose Woman, but her
brother-in-law, White Bull.

Ever since she had returned with the peace delegates, the
talk had centered on the despicable thing White Bull had
done. People asked how the holy man could have turned his
back on everything he had been.

How could a man who had spent his whole life as a warrior
and healer of the People—protecting the *Ohmeseheso*
against the whites, a man whose only son had been killed by
the soldiers—now be willing to don a soldier's uniform, to
give his oath and become a scout for those soldiers, to turn
his back on all that he once fought for?

Old Wool Woman was sure this was something White Bull
would never be able to explain to their people. Just as her
new beliefs were certainly something she could never make
others understand.

In her own heart she felt the rightness of surrendering for

the good of her people, to protect the lives of those most helpless in war against the *ve-ho-e*. Time and time again the white man had shown his willingness to make war not only on the warriors, but on the villages of women, children, and old ones.

Yet there would always be those who believed the *Ohme-seheso* could fight on and on against the soldiers.

In her heart, Old Wool Woman knew better. If the Northern People did not surrender, this war might well spell the end of the *Tse-Tsehese* for all time to come.

In the mid-distance she now recognized the ridgeline. Old Wool Woman trudged through ankle-deep snow, struggling to catch up to the pony Black Moccasin rode.

She grabbed the animal's buffalo-hair halter and pointed. "Beyond those hills lies the soldier fort."

"We should be there before dark," the chief responded.

"I want to go ahead and see your nephew," she pleaded. "See that White Bull is all right since we have been away."

Black Moccasin's eyes softened in the winter light. He turned to look behind him in that procession of winter-gaunt ponies, a scattering of travois holding what little they owned, and all those men, women, and children tramping through the snow on frozen feet.

Cold vapor steaming from his lips, the Old Man Chief called out, "Antelope Woman! Come here!"

It took no time for the younger woman to lunge up through the icy drifts to reach Old Wool Woman's side.

Looking down from the back of his pony, Black Moccasin told her, "I think you will want to go ahead with Old Wool Woman now."

"Where are you going?" she asked, looking at her old friend.

Old Wool Woman smiled. "I am in a hurry to see White Bull."

"Oh, yes!" Antelope Woman cried, throwing her arms around Old Wool Woman. "Take me with you!"

Turning to gaze up at the chief, Old Wool Woman asked, "It is all right that we run on ahead of the others?"

Black Moccasin tipped off the back of his pony and landed on the crusty snow, which whimpered beneath his thick winter moccasins. "Here," he said, handing the single buffalo-hair rein over to Antelope Woman. "Take my pony and go see my nephew for yourselves. See that he is safe, and tell him I want him to come out to meet us before we reach the soldier fort."

Old Wool Woman sputtered at this great honor, "R-ride . . . your pony?"

With the corners of his eyes crinkling in a smile, Black Moccasin said, "Get up there, both of you! Go now to bring my nephew back along this trail to see us."

Bending slightly, the Old Man Chief interlocked his fingers and made a step of his hands. When Old Wool Woman set a snow-crusted moccasin in his palms, he raised her onto the bare back of the pony. Then he helped Antelope Woman to climb up behind her.

"Tell my nephew his family is coming!" Black Moccasin called after the two women as they set off.

At times the weary pony lurched clumsily on the uneven, icy ground. But on they lumbered down the Buffalo Tongue, into that gap splitting the last of the low hills, then rode onto the flat bottomland. Smoke struck her nose. Columns of wispy gray ghosts rose in the distance against the cold sky. Then Old Wool Woman could hear the faraway voices muffled among those winter skeletons of the grand trees, the ring of axes from a wood-cutting crew.

When she reached the outlying guards surrounding the soldiers' camp, a handful of the *ve-ho-e* rushed up. Old Wool Woman halted her pony. Although she did not understand the words spoken loudly to her by one of the white men, she could see they recognized her. Impatiently, she nodded her head and smiled when the soldier waved the women on.

One by one the curious white men turned, stopped what they were doing, and stared in fascination as the two women reached the outskirts of the muddied tents and log lodges. From side to side they turned, their eyes searching for White Bull. Old Wool Woman recognized many faces among them. Then at one of the doorways she saw Little Chief appear. He turned and yelled at those inside.

White Bull appeared at the door, squeezing himself out through the narrow gap beside Little Chief.

"My brother!" Antelope Woman chirped in excitement. "He looks so handsome in his soldier uniform."

Lunging across the trampled snow, White Bull raced for them. In a matter of breaths the women were standing on the ground with him, all three hugging at once, tears running down Old Wool Woman's face.

"I was afraid," she admitted as she touched her brother-in-law's face.

"The Bear Coat is a man of his word," White Bull said. "I am his scout. No harm will come to me here."

"I was still afraid." She whimpered it this time. "You are still one against many."

His eyes looked into those of his sister. "The Bear Coat asked me to lead him against the Lakota who won't surrender."

Antelope Woman pulled back from him and swallowed hard. "You are going to lead the soldiers to find our friends?"

"The war is over," he explained. "Now it is time to make a good peace. I want to lead the Bear Coat's soldiers so that I can save some lives."

"How can you save lives by leading the soldiers to the camps of our friends?" Antelope Woman asked.

"The soldiers will go after the Lakota with or without me," he explained. "If they go without me, there will be many dead. But if I lead them to the camp of our friends, maybe I can convince the Lakota to give up instead of sacrificing their lives in a war they have already lost."

"Your uncle is coming at the head of the march," Old Wool Woman said, gripping White Bull's forearm affectionately. "He wants you to ride out there to meet him."

With worry in his voice, he asked, "What of the rest of my family?"

"Every one of your relations came north," Old Wool Woman replied, squeezing his arm. "Your wife and children. They are very near."

His face brightened. "Did you bring a big group?"

Old Wool Woman shook her head. Sadly she apologized, "Our group is even smaller than before."

He stared at the crusty snow beneath his feet. "Most followed Little Wolf and Morning Star."

This time Antelope Woman tried to explain, "So many decided to stay with the Medicine Hat Priest—"

"It does not matter," he said, looking up at them and bravely trying to smile. "I am happy you are here. Come with me while I go tell the Bear Coat that my family is drawing near."

When the soldier chief heard the news, he turned to one

of his young soldiers and said something that sent the man from the room.

Turning to Big Leggings, Old Wool Woman asked, "Where is he going?"

The half-breed said, "Miles just told that soldier to catch up eighteen of the white man's spotted buffalo from their herd."

"What for?"

"For White Bull to drive south when he goes to meet your people," Bruguier explained. "It is the Bear Coat's welcome gift."

"Eighteen," she repeated the words in Lakota.

Then she began to raise fingers for her brother-in-law, one at a time. When she held up the fingers of both hands before him, she realized she did not have enough. So she added in the fingers of another hand, but that was still not enough. It took three more from the other hand!

"Eighteen!" they all repeated together, joy sweeping over them.

White Bull quickly shook hands with the soldier chief and hurried for the door. Turning to the half-breed, he roared, "I'm going to take those spotted buffalo to my uncle and my people, myself! Tell the Bear Coat that I will be back to-morrow morning . . . bringing in the all of those who are coming to surrender!"

Chapter 24

Early April
1877

BY TELEGRAPH

BLACK HILLS.

Crazy Horse Coming In.
DEADWOOD, April 5.—Crazy Horse and
1,500 warriors encamped north of Bent Butte
creek last night on their way to Spotted Tail
agency. They are in a destitute condition and
anxious for peace. They state that Sitting Bull
will accept no terms of surrender and is making
for the British possessions.

The cold, spring breeze teased the loose waves of hair that
surrounded Samantha's pale, drawn face that early morning as she and her husband stood against the porch railing
at the front of officers' quarters. She wore a look he had
come to recognize through so many farewells, so many painful partings. It hadn't gotten any easier. That first time he
and Sharp Grover reined away from the old scout's home-
stead down on the Staked Plain,* he could understand why

Shadow Riders, vol. 6, The Plainsmen Series

she might convince herself that he wasn't ever coming back.

But he had.*

And he had given Sam a ring before he said goodbye the next time, marching off on Crook's Powder River campaign† that cold winter of 1876. Seamus came back to her a second time, and a third after Crook finally tired of trying to corner the hostiles through a spring campaign that eventually fizzled out as the fickle spirits of earth and sky conspired that autumn.# After returning to her arms from the army's grand winter campaign with Ranald Mackenzie's Fourth U.S. Cavalry,@ Seamus figured Samantha ought to know that he would ride through hell itself to return to their simple, unadorned life together.

But this morning, unlike so many before, there was not the clamor and clatter of regiments and supply trains, teamsters and troopers and foot soldiers setting off on campaign. No, this morning Fort Laramie went about its normal business as Seamus Donegan prepared to set his life adrift again upon the winds of fate . . . alone.

"I have something for you before you go," she said quietly, looking up at him with those red-rimmed eyes of hers.

"I thought you gave that to me last night," he bent to whisper in her ear. "And again this morning too."

Samantha's cheeks flushed, and her eyes darted left and right to assure herself no one heard him. "You are so naughty, Mr. Donegan!"

"Only with my wife, Mrs. Donegan."

He watched her stuff a hand into the pocket gathered beneath those pleats at her waist, there under that muslin apron she had knotted around herself. Sam pulled out a small box, wrapped in a wrinkled butcher paper he knew she must have talked out of Collins at the trading post, and secured both ways with three colors of her knitting yarn for a makeshift ribbon.

"F-for me?" he stammered, aghast as he took the small

Dying Thunder, vol. 7, The Plainsmen Series
†*Blood Song*, vol. 8
#*Trumpet of the Land*, vol. 10
@*A Cold Day in Hell*, vol. 11

box in his big right hand, then swallowed. Caught speechless, stunned by the suddenness of this surprise.

For a moment Seamus gazed down at the boy lying across his left arm, looking up at his father.

"Here, let me take him, Seamus," Sam said, lifting Colin from her husband's arm.

The baby whimpered as soon as his mother put him to her shoulder. Samantha turned Colin around so that he could watch his father tug at the ends of the yarn bows she had carefully tied around the package. For now the infant seemed content, staring at the tall gray-eyed man about to set off for Indian country once more. Although a stranger to his son in many ways, Seamus nonetheless believed that in some unfathomable measure the boy did know him as his father.

Stuffing the strands of multicolored yarn into the left pocket of his heavy canvas-and-blanket mackinaw, the Irishman yanked the paper off and crumpled it in the pocket too. Then he raised the lid of the small box. Inside lay shreds of hemp packing material, the sort that cushioned rifles and pistols shipped from the eastern states to this far western frontier.

His hands came to a rest and he looked up at her. "What is this you've done?"

"You've got to find out for yourself, Seamus," she replied, lightly bouncing Colin in her arms as he fussed.

"Where'd you get—"

"From Collins!" she shrieked with exasperation. "Will you look at your gift, for God's sake!"

"All right, all right!" he soothed then chuckled as he stroked her cheek with his fingertips. "You've caught me flat-footed, you know that—don't you, woman?"

She dragged a finger beneath a teary eye and said, "See what we've given you."

"*We*, is it now?" he replied, starting to push aside some of that coarse hemp packing, much of it tumbling out of the small box to the porch planks below. "Colin had a hand in this, you're saying?"

"Yes, he did," she replied, then bent her head to plant a kiss on the boy's short, soft hair tossing in the cold breeze.

"Oh . . . Sam," he croaked, unable to shove any more sound from his throat.

"You like it?" she whispered, peering into the box with him. "You really, really like it?"

Seamus snagged his free arm around them both and crushed her against him for a moment. In her ear he said, "I love you so."

Then he stepped back, winking at the boy who gazed up at his father with wide eyes filled with awe.

Carefully lifting the big pocket watch from its cradle of packing hemp, Seamus found a sixteen-inch silver chain hooked to the watch ring. At the end of the chain hung a small key.

As he inspected the key, she explained in a hurried gush, "It's to wind the watch. To set it too. Don't lose that key. You might need to wind it this morning. Wind it now before you go—"

"I've never owned a watch before," he interrupted her quietly, gazing into her eyes. "But... how did you buy it from Collins?"

"Your wife's set some money back since last summer's campaign," Samantha declared proudly. "A few pennies here, a few pennies there—"

"And you've never done without?"

"Only without you, Seamus," and she pressed her cheek against the front of his coat.

He clutched her to him again, looking down at the face of the watch, reading the tiny words: *Elgin Nat'l. Watch Co.*

"Collins gave me a good price on it."

"He should have," Seamus grumbled, "as much as we've supported him lately."

"It's two years old, he told me," Sam continued.

"Don't matter none to me that it's used."

"Oh, no—it's not used," she explained, wagging her head. "Just that it was made in 1874. It's brand new. Only come out here recently."

Suspending the shiny silver watch from a few inches of its chain, Donegan turned it round and round for the boy who reached out to touch its glittering surface.

"You don't recognize it, do you?" she asked.

"Is it—"

"It's the one Collins told me you've been eyeing ever since you came back from the Yellowstone," Samantha admitted.

"He told you, did he?" Donegan replied. "Collins shouldn't have told you. Man don't really need a watch where I'm going—"

"If my husband wants something special for himself, then I'll get it for him, by damned!" she shut him up.

"Samantha Donegan!" he chided. "You, cursing, right here in front of our—"

"As if he won't hear the very same from your lips—and likely worse!"

He bent his head and kissed her long, surprising Sam at first—her mouth going slack before she kissed him back hungrily. Then he planted a kiss on the boy's cheek and before Colin, pressed his lips against Samantha's again.

"I'll think of your beautiful face every time I look at this watch's face in the days to come," he told her, feeling the salty sting betray his eyes.

Moving one step closer to press against him, Sam said, "When you put the watch to your ear and listen, Seamus, I want you to think of the beating of my heart. How it sounds when you lay your ear on my breast."

His vision was getting fuzzy as he croaked, "And all those stars I'll see up there in the sky each night when I make my camp . . . I'll remember how your eyes sparkle at this moment."

Donegan looked down at that watch again now even though the light had grown so dim he could barely read the narrow hands. It didn't really matter what time it was. He had been in the saddle before sunup every day and hadn't made his cold camp until after sunset, for better than two weeks now. Gone from Laramie sixteen days and the aching for the two of them hadn't lessened.

Down the dark slope below him lay the Tongue.

He figured if the horses could find their footing, he'd ride on into the night as long as they had the strength. Then he'd find a place to lay out the day when the horizon started to gray. He hadn't seen much sign of the warrior bands. No fresh trails, no columns of smoke, no restless or stampeding buffalo herds . . . but this was Indian country after all. Had been Indian country ever since he crossed the Powder.

He was plunging into the bloody maw once more.

Seamus kissed the face of the watch, closing his eyes and conjuring up her face. He squeezed the watch fiercely, then stuffed it back into that pocket sewn inside his mackinaw as the breeze stiffened with twilight's approach. He would hold onto as many pieces of her and the boy as he could through

every day of this journey—what he prayed would be the last
of this terrible war against the Lakota and Cheyenne.

Praying the eternal God would once again sustain this
lonely, simple man and see him back to the bosom of his
family.

Sustain him long enough to see this bloody war through
one last fight.

BY TELEGRAPH

Dull Knife and His Band Sur-
render to Crook.

THE INDIANS.

Dull Knife's Band Surrenders.

CAMP ROBINSON, Nebraska, April 21.—
Eighty lodges of Cheyennes under Dull Knife
and Standing Elk, surrendered to General
Crook at 11 a.m. to-day. The village comprises
about five hundred and fifty persons, eighty-
five of whom are fighting men. They turned in
six hundred ponies, sixty guns and about thirty
pistols. They are completely destitute of all the
necessaries of life, having lost everything when
their village was destroyed in November last.
They have no lodges, but simple shelters of old
canvas and skins, very few blankets or robes
and no cooking utensils. Many are still suffering from frozen limbs. It is surprising that they
have been able to hold out so long under these
circumstances, and their doing so proves the
fortitude of the American Indian under priva-
tion and hardship. This makes about 780 Cheyennes who have surrendered here since the first
of January. The latest advices represent Crazy
Horse as still en-route for this agency.

As things turned out, it was a good thing that the half-breed hurried along after White Bull.

When the holy man leaped atop his pony and scampered away for that herd of the white man's spotted buffalo, the soldiers standing guard on those animals couldn't understand a word White Bull tried to say in his pidgin-English, and didn't even comprehend any of the sign he made for them in his utter excitement to be off with those eighteen head.

Why, didn't he wear the same uniform as those *ve-ho-e* soldiers!

Didn't he say the white man's words—*Bear Coat*—well enough in his imitation of the soldier's tongue?

But the herd guards were growing visibly exasperated by the time Big Leggings rode up. The half-breed evidently explained everything well enough to the soldiers by the time he turned to White Bull and said, "Take your eighteen, holy man. And be sure to remind your people they are a gift from the soldier chief who will greet them tomorrow when they reach the fort."

"Thank you, Big Leggings!" he roared, then urged his pony away toward the spotted buffalo.

In his enthusiasm and eagerness to be under way, it didn't take White Bull long to cut eighteen of the animals from the rest and get them lumbering south toward the low hills. These creatures were dull-witted, he thought. Docile, easily herded. Not at all like the buffalo—a cantankerous, mercurial beast.

He wasn't but four or five arrow-shots from the soldier camp when he heard horses coming up behind him. He was concerned the soldiers had come to reclaim their animals. Both the *ve-ho-e* who approached on his back-trail wore three chevron stripes across the sleeves of their blue jackets. White Bull thought those gold slashes were pretty, and wondered if the Bear Coat might give him some for his own uniform.

As the soldiers drew closer they slowed to match the plodding pace of the cattle, one reining off to the left, and the other flanking to the right. Both began shouting, whistling shrilly, slapping coils of rope against their legs, making as much noise as they could as they urged the animals along the trail. And Big Leggings wasn't far behind them, coming up at a lope. He and these two soldiers ended up staying with White Bull for the rest of the afternoon, all three hollering at the creatures as if it were the most fun in the world. White Bull enjoyed yelling at the dumb animals too. Great fun—this white man way of yelling at stupid beasts.

Only when the first headmen leading the village procession came into view off in the distance did Big Leggings and the two soldiers leave their posts at the side of the herd and ride up to White Bull, all three shaking the holy man's hand in turn.

"These *ve-ho-e* sure do put a lot of value on this matter of shaking hands," he told Big Leggings when the half-breed held out his own to him.

"It is because you are a soldier like them now," Big Leggings replied. "We see your people up the trail now. So we go back to the fort for the night."

As soon as they had touched their soldier caps, the pair turned about and disappeared beyond the trees with the half-breed, all three riding for the fort.

White Bull didn't think he would have any trouble getting these animals the rest of the way by himself.

"Nephew!" cried Black Moccasin from among those in the lead.

"Is that truly you, Uncle?" he called to the old man.

"Are you truly White Bull?" he yelled back. "I see a soldier, dressed in a soldier uniform!"

As he halted his pony beside that of Black Moccasin, White Bull said, "I am a soldier scout now. Didn't the others tell you?"

"Yes," he told his nephew as the spotted buffalo milled on either side of them. "I am very proud of you. But what are these creatures you are following?"

"These are gifts from the Bear Coat! Call up the young men," White Bull turned aside to tell Crazy Head. "Get the hunters to take out their bows. They should kill these animals just the way our people kill buffalo!"

"This is a good place to camp," Old Wolf declared. He waved his arm at Fast Whirlwind. "Tell our people to make camp here. Our hunters will kill these strange animals, and our women will butcher them as soon as the shelters are up."

That evening White Bull sat with his relations near the center of that noisy camp beside the Buffalo Tongue River. It had been a long, long time since he had seen this much

happiness in an *Ohmeseheso* village. Not since they had defeated the soldiers on the Little Sheep River. Even though
some young warriors like his own son had been killed in that
fight, there eventually was an unheralded celebration.

So when had the tribe's unhappiness begun?

Not until the morning Three Finger Kenzie destroyed
nearly everything the Shahiyela owned. Since that day,
nearly five moons now, White Bull's people had teetered on
the brink of disaster, starvation, freezing to death. Five
moons of growing despair: watching family and friends slowly
die. With little game and no time to cure the hides, everyone
dressed poorly. On and on they had limped through the winter in their tattered shreds of clothing. Their bellies pinched
in hunger, their limbs blackened with frostbite, their wounds
festering.

But for the first night in a long, long time, White Bull
heard laughter. Lots and lots of laughter. There was drum-
ming and singing that night, but it was the laughter that made
the wings of his heart unfurl and take flight.

This was a good thing, he reminded himself. No more war
now. Tomorrow they would surrender to the Bear Coat.
These people would have enough to eat, enough blankets
and tents and shelters. And the *Ohmeseheso* would have
their own agency here in their own country. Not simply
adopted orphans taken in on the Oglallas' White River
Agency.

This was the last night of true freedom—with the war behind them, with surrender yet to come. This was the last
night of greatness for the *Ohmeseheso*.

"The sad days are behind us, Nephew," Black Moccasin
said as White Bull settled beside him at a fire in front of the
Old Man Chief's lodge. "Are you happy to again sleep
among your own people tonight?"

"Yes," he sighed, content in this one last moment for his
people. "After so many, many nights, I am among my own
again."

"With the *ve-ho-es*' meat, White Bull, you have brought
these people happiness."

"Look around you, Uncle," he choked with sentiment.
"Look at their faces. Not only are their bellies full tonight,
but I think their hearts are full again too."

Chapter 25

25 April 1877

"Tell them to raise their right hands," Nelson Miles instructed Johnny Bruguier. "Have White Bull tell them they will swear on their honor just as he did weeks ago."

He waited while the translations were made in that stuffy room with the door flung open wide to admit as much of the spring breeze as possible. His headquarters staff and a gaggle of Fifth and Twenty-second infantry officers stood with their backs pressed to the wall in that crowded office. More curious soldiers stood staring in at the open door, along with at least a half-dozen faces gathered at that solitary window.

Waving his arm at the eight others who had stayed behind at the post with White Bull to become scouts, Miles said, "All of them have already given their oath, Bruguier. Tell the warriors just in that, like these eight, they too will get their uniforms, weapons, and supplies when they have been properly sworn in."

Again there were translations given, both in Cheyenne and in Lakota because Hump, his brother Horse Road, and a few of their relations were now standing among more than a dozen of Black Moccasin's men, all of them volunteering to become the Bear Coat's scouts.

Once the arms were all in the air, Miles snapped the crisp page of foolscap before him and cleared his throat. This was a truly momentous occasion. Weeks before he had sworn in

White Bull and eight others as scouts. And here this afternoon, three days after they had formally surrendered to the army, thirty more had requested to be enlisted into the army.

"Rowland, Bruguier—tell them to repeat their names for me," Miles instructed.

That took a few minutes in itself, but he waited patiently until the room fell quiet again.

"I do hereby acknowledge to have volunteered this twenty-fifth day of April 1877 at Tongue River Cantonment, Territory of Montana, to serve as auxiliary scout in the Army of the United States of America—" Miles wondered how in hell the half-breed and the squawman were going to translate *auxiliary* for the Sioux and Cheyenne, when neither man likely understand the term.

"Better you tell them this," he explained when both interpreters' brows knitted; it was plain enough now that they were having trouble with that word. "Just say: to serve as warrior scout in the Army of United States of America."

And he waited while the two nodded, turned away, and continued their translations.

"For a period not to exceed six months," he said, and then thought better of it. "Instead, tell them, for no longer than six moons, unless sooner discharged by proper authority. That will be me, fellas. Unless sooner discharged by me."

After waiting until the translations were done, Miles continued. "I do also agree to accept such bounty, pay, rations, and clothing as are, or may be, established by law for volunteers . . . er, for such warrior scouts."

He went on reading from the page he held before him in the afternoon light, "And I do solemnly swear that I will bear true faith and allegiance to the United States of America, and that I will serve honestly and faithfully against all her enemies or opposers whomsoever; and that I will observe and obey the orders of the President of the United States, and the orders of the officers appointed over me, according to the Rules and Articles of War."

Phrase by phrase, line by line, sentence by sentence—they had gotten through it again. He, Bruguier, and Rowland, along with these thirty Cheyenne and Sioux warriors.

Chances were good that among these volunteers were fighting men who had stymied Crook at the Rosebud. Warriors who had crushed Custer's command. Among these thirty were enemies he himself had fought at Battle Butte while a blizzard descended upon them all.

But now they were his. They had seen that resistance was futile. To carry on the war would only mean the destruction of their people. They must have realized that to flee to Canada with Sitting Bull was to abandon their homeland. In the end, they had heard the honor in his words, and decided to surrender to him.

Five days ago, exactly four weeks after his first council with the peace delegates at the cantonment, the half-breed Bruguier brought in the *Mnikowoju* leader Hump along with his clan's warriors. They had come to give themselves up, and surrender their arms to the soldier chief.

Then two days after, when the weather again turned cold, blustery, bearing an icy snow in its bite, forty-five lodges of the Cheyenne limped in with their chiefs Old Wolf, Crazy Head, and Two Moon. What a sad, sad scene that procession had made: those three hundred men, women, and children, dressed in rags, many in nothing more than bloody, bare feet, trudging painfully along behind their leaders, sitting proudly upon their emaciated ponies. Behind them all young boys wrangled a herd of several hundred more of the ribby, winter-gaunt horses.

It was plain to read the despair and hunger in the eyes of every one of those who now turned their lives over to him.

Miles had immediately ordered that some cattle be handed over to the newcomers as they erected their camp near the mouth of the Tongue. He had watched the faces of the hundreds as they moved past him, those dark, black-cherry eyes ringed with fatigue and hunger—understanding why every last person among them wanted to get a good look at the Bear Coat. He had defeated them, commanding respect from these powerful warrior bands of the Northern Plains.

Near midmorning the following day, the twenty-third of April, squawman William Rowland and his son Willis escorted the Cheyenne males from their camp to the parade where Miles had formed up his companies. There, in a ceremony painful for any old warrior to witness, the Cheyenne dismounted and watched soldiers lead their ponies away. Then one by one by one, the warriors laid their rifles, carbines, and pistols on the cold, soggy ground.

No more were they warriors who would fight for hearth

and home against the army. No more were they men free to follow the great herds of buffalo and challenge any who might usurp their claim to this hunting ground.

Now the Cheyenne belonged to him.

Even these thirty-some warriors who had just enlisted as scouts belonged to Nelson A. Miles. Exactly as George Crook had first used Apache against Apache down in Arizona Territory, just as Ranald Mackenzie had used Sioux and Cheyenne to hunt down and locate that Cheyenne village on the Red Fork, Miles was now going to use these warriors to find the last of the holdouts.

He was sure they were out there. Those north of the Yellowstone surely had already scampered across the Missouri with Sitting Bull, and would likely reach Canada in safety now. And White Bull said the majority of the Northern Cheyenne were pushing south to surrender to Lieutenant William Philo Clark, one of Crook's damnable protégés.

So it would be up to his department to sweep the country clean. His men—these Indian scouts and his campaign-toughened doughboys—they would be the broom Miles would use to sweep up the last of the stalwarts. There wouldn't be a coulee those hostiles could hide in, not a tree or rock to hide behind, once Miles turned his scouts loose on the trail—

"General!"

Miles looked at the door where Charles J. Dickey had called. "Yes, what is it, Captain?"

All around him at that moment his staff and other officers were shaking hands with every one of the newly sworn-in scouts. Lord, how these Indians took to ceremony!

Dickey turned away a moment, and flung his arm to the south as voices from the parade grew louder. "A rider approaching, sir."

"Rider? One?"

"Yes, General. Only one."

"By the stars—is it another Cheyenne coming in?"

Then Dickey laughed. Deep and lusty. "No, it isn't a Cheyenne! Not an Injun, sir!"

More voices were calling outside. Singing out their happy greetings. Hallooing and huzzahing. A damned celebration going on right outside as he stepped toward the doorway. Then he glimpsed the rider—

It couldn't be, he told himself. Although something tried

to convince him otherwise. No, it simply couldn't be. Even though the man had vowed to return . . .

Miles reached the door, peered into the distance, anxious to know for sure. "If not someone surrendering—who's coming, Captain?"

"It's that by-God Irishman, General! The one what went south to Laramie after our fight," Dickey roared. "Raised right up from the dead himself, sir! Raised right up from the blessed dead!"

BY TELEGRAPH

Manifesto of the Czar—

Intense Excitement.

Two Men Killed in a Deadwood
Street Fight.

New Complications Arising on
the Rio Grande.

DEADWOOD.

**Seven Men with Six-Shooters—Only
Two of Them Killed.**

DEADWOOD, D.T., April 23.—This afternoon a dispute arose in which seven persons engaged, concerning the title of a town lot in South Deadwood. After some harsh language all hands drew six-shooters and commenced firing. The result was that Dan O'Bradovitch, of Eureka, Nevada, was killed, Steve Corsich, of the same place, mortally shot, and N. Millich slightly wounded. Another disturbance, caused by town-lot jumping, occurred to-day, during which several shots were fired, but nobody hurt.

"By the stars above—it really is you!" Miles roared, bolting from the doorway just as Seamus dropped to the ground, the reins still in his glove.

All around Seamus jostled those officers who he had guided up the Tongue in January until Crazy Horse stopped retreating. Those men he had joined at the base of the butte, where gallant soldiers had run out of ammunition and their officers ordered them to fix bayonets.* The crowd parted in a wave as Miles lunged up.

"In the ever-livin' flesh, General!" Donegan cried.

"I was afraid some war party would have eaten you alive before you got anywhere close to Laramie," said Miles, holding out his hand. As they shook, the colonel pounded Donegan on top of the shoulder.

"Didn't see a feather," Seamus admitted. "Colder'n a Welsh miner's lunch bucket, it was—but had me no trouble with Injuns."

Captain Poole jumped in to ask, "You got back to your family?"

"Aye," he said, grinning hugely in that full, bushy beard. "Even christened me boy too."

"What'd you name him?" asked Lieutenant Cusick.

"Colin Teig Donegan."

"That's a fine name, Mr. Donegan," Miles replied with approval. "Strong and sturdy."

"A good Irish name!" Captain Butler roared. "Can I get you something wet and we'll drink to your lad's christening?"

"Something wet? By the Virgin Mary!"

"It is that homely Irishman for sure!" a familiar voice called out.

Seamus turned to watch Bruguier step up, holding out his hand. "Good to see you're still here, Johnny."

"We going to scout together again?" The half-breed flicked his eyes at Miles.

"Looks that way, don't it?" Donegan replied. "Need us a good interpreter along."

"You damn bet I'm going along, Irishman," Bruguier declared. "Not going nowhere else till this soldier chief gets that rope off my neck."

For a moment Donegan gazed at Miles, then said, "I figure the general here to be the sort of man to do just what he says he'll do. If he says we're riding after the last of them hostiles, then we're going. And, when the general's officers go and offer me a drink, I damn well better take 'em up on it!"

The group roared with laughter. Miles snagged Donegan's elbow as the civilian started to turn away. The rest of the group stopped, falling silent as the colonel went stone serious and said, "I wouldn't have put money on you making it back."

"Didn't take me for a man of me word, General?"

"No, Mr. Donegan. Not that at all. It's just that there's . . . a lot of open country between here and there. Going and coming. I just want you to know how glad I am that you came back for our spring push."

He flicked his eyes around at those hardy officers who had tracked and battled the hostile bands all the way from the Missouri River on the north down to the headwaters of the Tongue on the south. "Your outfit has a job to do, General—and for sometime now it seems yours is the only outfit doing a bleeming thing. Damn right I'll throw in with you till we get this Sioux War over and done with."

"Good to have you riding scout with us," Adjutant Baird said.

"Where's Kelly? You got him out on some errand, General?" Seamus asked.

"Kelly took himself a leave to go back east," Miles explained.

That struck him hard. Friends and comrades in arms they were—sharing all the miles, the cold, the terror, sharing the passion of living there on the verge of dying.

"Kelly, gone east," he repeated as if in disbelief. "Not gonna be back soon enough to go along?"

The colonel wagged his head. "We're preparing to set out on the first of May. Kelly said he wasn't planning to be back before fall."

"We're pushing off first of May?" Donegan asked. "How soon is that?"

"Less'n a week now!" cheered Lieutenant Charles E. Hargous, clearly anxious to be on the trail.

"How you fixed for scouts?" the Irishman inquired.

Miles laid his hand on the tall man's shoulder and turned the civilian to the left. "There, you see those Cheyenne just coming out of my office? And there's some Sioux among 'em too."

"They your prisoners?" he asked, his brow knitting.

"They're your scouts, Mr. Donegan."

"*M-my* scouts?"

"You did ride all this way from Laramie to sign up to scout for me again, didn't you?"

"Yes, General—"

"Then I've just made sure you're going to have the best trackers in this country, Irishman. If we intend to find the most stalwart of the holdouts, then I want you to have the best eyes and ears in the territory. Warriors who know every ridge, every hillock and coulee, every tree, and creek, and bush."

"Haven't you ever worked with Indian scouts before, Mr. Donegan?" asked Captain Cusick.

"Lots of times," he explained. "But they was never Injuns I just been fighting me own self. Not no bucks I done battle with."

Miles cleared his throat. "You have misgivings, Mr. Donegan?"

Seamus turned and regarded the colonel a moment before answering, "No more misgivings than the next man what's been fighting these warrior bands since the summer of sixty-six."*

"Are you or are you not volunteering to ride with my scouts, Irishman?" Miles pressed on.

"Long as we can make sign—me and them—we'll be able to talk," he said, a dull edge of reluctance flattening his voice. "Just like I give you my word: I come here from Laramie to do what I could to find the last warrior bands still out there, General."

The colonel said, "My outfit needs men like you to help us finish the job others started. I want to know if you're in."

"I'll ride for you, General," he declared. "I need the work."

"And I need *you* because I want to trust these warriors,

Sioux Dawn—vol. 1, The Plainsmen Series

Mr. Donegan," Miles said as if sharing a confidence. "I'm going to need someone to tell me if I can trust them."

At long last, Seamus smiled hugely and said, "And you figured me for that someone, eh?"

Miles pounded him on the back as the entire group set off for the low-roofed cabin that served as a cramped mess hall. "Now, shall we go drink to our new civilian liaison of scouts, gentlemen?"

Chapter 26

Spring Moon
1877

BY TELEGRAPH

The War in Europe Underway
Already.

More Indian Murders Reported
in Wyoming.

Wyoming.

An Indian Attack and Murder.

CAMP BROWN, April 26.—Barney Hall, a prospector, has just arrived here badly wounded by Indians. He and two others were attacked near Bad Water on the 16th, and after a sharp fight the Indians killed his two partners. Three others from the same party have not been heard from.

Box Elder turned his face toward the emerging sun, feeling its newborn power. Although his rheumy, matted, watering old eyes could not see, he knew the sun was rising.

He had been waiting for it.

Sitting here that dawn, he listened as the temperature of the air subtly changed, hearing those first whispers of the earth as it warmed, feeling across his skin the talk of the wingeds, the crawls-on-their-bellies, every fragrant perfume of re-awakening life, the fertile conversations of the individual blades of grass, each tiny leaf budding on the choke-cherry. Box Elder paid attention to all that his senses told him. For most of his life, this stooped and wrinkled old man had been blind, yet, he could nonetheless see things other men with normal vision failed to see.

For the moment he was alone, brought to this hilltop in the darkness by his new apprentice. Lame Dog, son of Spotted Wolf, had already left, returning to the small camp their group had made upon reaching Beaver Creek three days ago.

"Do you see that ridge east of our lodges?" he had asked Lame Dog the evening before.

"How did you—"

"If you don't know the answer to your own question, then I am failing to teach you all I can teach you," he said, his face crinkling with a smile. "The top of that hill, take me to it after the moon has set tonight."

"In the dark?"

"Yes," Box Elder had explained. "Then you can return to our shelter and go back to sleep."

Lame Dog had awakened him as the moon sank out of sight. After wetting the bushes nearby, Box Elder held out his arm and it was seized by his young apprentice who led the blind man slowly through the brush, loose rock, and patches of old snow, then up the sharp slope to the top of the ridge.

"Do you need anything more?"

"Only for you to leave me alone now," Box Elder had instructed. "Come for me when the sun is two hands off the earth."

"I will return for you in the morning."

Box Elder listened while the sound of the young man's moccasins faded down the rocky slope. Then he was alone with the last of the night, the vestiges of this inky darkness, the final gasp of that coldest time of the day. Alone with the expectation to feel, to hear, to know.

By the time the sun had risen off the earth and was finally

climbing into that spring sky, Box Elder did know.

It was time for them to turn north.

When the *Ohmeseheso* first broke apart on Rotten Grass Creek, this wizened, blind prophet had elected to stay with the Sweet Medicine Chief, Little Wolf, and the Sacred Hat Priest, Coal Bear. Better was it for the Northern People to concentrate as much of their power within one village.

Then the peace delegates returned from their first visit with the Bear Coat at the fort on the Elk River. Box Elder grew troubled, less sure of his decision to follow the others south. He had never visited one of the *ve-ho-e* reservations. Over time he had grown uncertain that the land chosen for the Lakota Little Star People was truly the place the *Ohmeseheso* should live.

"I will take those lodges that follow me west to the Roseberry River," he had explained to Little Wolf, Morning Star, and Coal Bear many days ago when he knew he must set his own path. "I don't know yet where I am to go, but I am certain it is not to the White River Agency. I will wait for sign to come to me, then I will put my feet on that path."

On that terrible day when the multitude set off for the south behind their great chiefs, when Crazy Head and Old Wolf led their smaller group north for the Buffalo Tongue River, Box Elder turned his face west. As he held *Nimhoyoh*, the Sacred Wheel Lance, high over his head in those first, faltering steps, he was joined by Spotted Wolf, a great war chief, and Elk River, a noted horse catcher, along with their families. Days later when they reached the upper waters of Beaver Creek, the old man instructed the others to have the women make camp.

"For how long, Box Elder?" Spotted Wolf had asked.

"I don't know," he admitted. "It might be days. I only know that after all our traveling alone, it is here I will be given a sign."

For three mornings they had stayed there beside Beaver Creek as afternoon tempests raged over them, soaking the lodgeskins and those poor canvas shelters where the families huddled cold and wet until the raging spring storms had passed. Now, on this fourth morning, he knew.

"Is that you, Lame Dog?"

The young one huffed to a stop at the top of the ridge, "Who did you expect, old man?"

"Come, come get me," he directed as he stood on unsteady legs. "Take me down off this hill. I have much to tell the others."

When Box Elder and the young apprentice neared the camp, Lame Dog began to holler like a camp crier. "Gather yourselves! Drop what you are doing! Our prophet has important news!"

He heard their moccasins, heard their murmurings, felt them pressing close as Lame Dog brought him to a halt. Sensing the sun's warmth full on his face, Box Elder explained what he had come to know.

"I am going in to the Bear Coat's fort. Those of you who do not want to go with me are free to follow your hearts. You can join Little Wolf's village on their journey south. Or you can follow your hearts and wander—there are Lakota still wandering, staying out, refusing to go to their agency. Spotted Wolf or Elk River may lead you—"

"I am going with you, Grandfather," Spotted Wolf interrupted, addressing the old man with that term of deepest respect.

Elk River instantly agreed, "Where you go, Box Elder, my family will follow."

How his tired old heart leaped in his chest, as if on the broad wings of a blue heron catching wind beneath it. "I have been shown this will not be an easy thing we are going to do."

Spotted Wolf said with a gulp, "The easy times are in the past."

"Yes," he told them quietly. "I am certain we have many dark days yet to come, my children. Many, many dark days yet to come."

Despite the unknown, they had followed him. Despite all that he warned them of, the chiefs and their warriors followed with their families. There were no easy places to go anymore. There was nowhere safe for their women and children and elders. Their lives had changed and Box Elder told them they would have to find some way to accommodate that change.

Walking beneath *Nimhoyoh* across all those miles, he remembered those first *ve-ho-e* who came to the *Ohmeseheso* generations before, when he had been but a little one himself. The hairy faces who came, and went again. Those few did not stay in the land of the Lakota and the *Ohmeseheso*, but merely moved through it. Yet ever since the fight of the Hundred in the Hand near the Pine Woods Fort* the *ve-ho-e* had come to stay.

Box Elder knew the finest days of his people were in their past.

All he could strive to do now was to assure that his people survived. If they were not rich in ponies and lodges, weapons and plunder, winter robes and quillwork, then the *Ohmeseheso* must survive into the next generation. And the next. And hopefully the next.

Of all the roads Box Elder had walked, even that climb out of the Valley of the Red Fork when Three Fingers Kenzie crushed the Shahiyela and they stumbled into the unknown winter wilderness, this was the hardest.

Day by day he walked on foot with those at the front of the march, just behind Spotted Wolf and Elk River on their ponies. Their young men rode watch on either flank, ranging ahead so they would not be surprised when they finally struck the Buffalo Tongue. For two days now they had journeyed north along its west bank, sensing they must be getting close. Now they had stopped for midday, with the spring sun high, while two of the young men scouted far ahead, probing for some sign of the soldiers and their fort.

Over these last two days Box Elder could tell that Elk River had grown even more anxious. He was not quite himself anymore. The holy man called the chief to sit with him as they rested.

"Elk River, I think you have grown unsure that you made the right decision to follow my medicine."

When he finally answered, the war chief said, "Yes, it is true what you say. My heart grows heavy to give the *ve-ho-e* all our horses, to give up all our weapons as the Bear Coat demands of us when we surrender."

"The war is over," Box Elder reminded him. "Our days of fighting the white man are done, but I cannot leave this north country. I cannot leave this land. I cannot leave the bones and burial ground of my ancestors."

"A man should not leave his ancestors," Spotted Wolf said.

Box Elder continued, "Now it is up to us to see that there are *Ohmeseheso* to live, to make a peace with the soldiers—to last beyond the seventh generation."

"I hear what you say in here," Elk River said, tapping a finger against his temple, "but my heart aches so for what was."

"Elk River," Box Elder commanded, "is your daughter near?"

"Yes."

"Do you see her?"

"Yes, I see her, Uncle."

"Look at your daughter, Elk River," Box Elder directed. Then he called out in a loud voice, holding out his arm. "Bear Woman, come take my hand!"

Without hesitation, the young woman stepped up and knelt beside the old prophet, allowing him to clasp her hand in both of his. "I am here, Box Elder."

"Bear Woman, you tell your father that your family will live on into the generations to come. His blood will not die. You say this to your father now."

"I know my daughter will marry one day," Elk River interjected.

"No, she will marry soon," Box Elder replied, wagging his head. Then he turned his sightless eyes to the young woman again. "Your heart must be light, Bear Woman. Going to the soldier fort will bring a great change in your life. Where we are going, you will meet a young man."

"One of White Bull's people?" she asked.

"No," Box Elder said.

"A *ve-ho-e* soldier?" Elk River snarled.

"No," the old prophet assured. "I do not see Bear Woman with a soldier. But, the ways of the heart are rarely known to man."

Squeezing the old one's bony hand, Bear Woman asked, "What are you saying to me, Box Elder?"

"At the fort, you will fall in love with a man. The two of you will marry within a few days. . . ."

Through the brush stabbed the sound of oncoming voices, the hammer of pony hooves. Box Elder could tell the scouts were returning.

"The soldier fort!" came the cry.

"It is not far!" another voice took up the call.

"We will be there before the sun sets!"

All around Box Elder the others were standing. He could sense the fear in them. Excitement too. As the old man arose beside Bear Woman, he clutched her hand very tightly. More than anything, there was among these people a dread of going on.

"Walk with me, Bear Woman," he said as he felt his sightless eyes sting and the tears spill down his weathered cheeks.

The two of them set off slowly, parting the crowd as his feet felt their way north, into the unknown, into their future.

"I am afraid," she whispered.

"So am I," he admitted as he felt Lame Dog come alongside him, felt the *Nimhoyoh* placed in his right hand.

Bear Woman asked, "You are afraid too, Grandfather?"

"Yes," he finally admitted. "But my heart is filled with hope . . . for you and I will lead the rest into this new day for our people."

"White Bull says that old man out in the front has much power," the young Cheyenne half-breed explained to the Irishman.

Seamus nodded, watching the small procession inching closer to the outskirts of Tongue River Cantonment to surrender. He and Willis Rowland stood in the midst of more than thirty Cheyenne and Lakota scouts who had volunteered to serve Colonel Nelson A. Miles. All around them stood the women and children, the hundreds of soldiers who were turning out for this surprise arrival. The Bear Coat planted himself at the center of the long, colorful, noisy gauntlet, there among his officers as he finished shoving the last of his big brass buttons through the holes on his dress coat, draped with resplendent braid and adorned with glittering hash on the cuffs.

"What is that the old one's holding over his head?" Donegan asked.

"The scouts say it is the Sacred Turner," Rowland declared. "I've never seen it myself down south, but my mother has told many stories about it. My mother's people call it *Nimhoyoh*. They say it has the power to make them invisible to an enemy that wants to do them harm."

"They're afraid," Donegan whispered.

Not even Rowland heard him say it, but he felt his heart sink as this grand old man entered the far end of the long gauntlet of Cheyenne and soldiers greeting them. They were afraid of being murdered.

Stooped and bowed with age, the old man holding aloft that sacred object was helped along by a young man steadying one arm, a young woman on the other. *The old man must be some powerful priest*, he figured. *That priest must be very, very afraid, having to hold up that object to protect his people from the soldier bullets, walking here between two long rows of soldiers.*

"Two chiefs are bringing in their clans with the old holy man." Rowland translated what some of the Cheyenne scouts were saying as they greeted the newcomers. "There ain't many of 'em, is there?"

"Can't be many big groups out there no more," Seamus said. "Does White Bull know who them two are helping the old man?"

"Lame Dog is the young man. He's going to become a medicine man too," the half-breed youth said. "But White Bull says he don't know why the one called Bear Woman is walking up front too."

"Perhaps that's the safest place to be," Donegan observed as the procession stopped and Miles stepped forward. "If that Turner really is going to protect them from bullets."

Then Miles turned, waving Willis Rowland up. The colonel turned some more, finding Rowland's white father in the crowd. William Rowland nodded in approval. The colonel smiled and put his arm around the young half-breed, who reached his side to begin translating the Bear Coat's greeting for the new arrivals.

Moving to the elder Rowland's elbow, Seamus said, "Some stroke of good fortune brought you here, Bill."

Rowland glanced at the taller man. "A long time coming, this day."

"There's more of 'em still out there."

"I know," Rowland agreed sadly. "Soon as we heard reports Spotted Tail was on his way to talk 'em into coming in to the agency, Willis and me set off."

"You wintered up at Red Cloud after Mackenzie's fight?"

Scratching at his leathery cheek, the interpreter said,

"Agent or army always needs someone to talk for 'em."

" 'Specially after we helped Crook take the ponies and weapons away from Red Cloud's bands,"* Donegan said. "What makes a man leave the agency in the dead of winter like you done?"

Rowland stared at the icy ground, grinding at it with a boot heel. "Man gets old, winter stabs him to the bone. I ain't young as you, Irishman. I ought'n be moseying home to a fire and my woman."

The crowd was beginning to break up. Soldiers heading off in a hundred directions, Crazy Head's Cheyenne swarming around the new arrivals, leading them toward their camp north of the fort. Horses whinnied, men sang, and drums were beaten. Children laughed and women cried as they greeted old friends.

"Will you look at that, Bill?" Seamus asked as Miles passed by with some of his officers, joined by a few of the Cheyenne leaders and that old blind man who had just arrived.

Young Willis Rowland walked slowly beside the young woman who maintained her unwavering hold on the blind shaman's arm. It was plain to see that Willis was already smitten. Almost as plain to see, by the way the young woman glanced coyly from the corner of her eyes at the young half-breed, that she too was taken with the interpreter.

"I figure the boy's been bit," Rowland said as his son moved past with the others, not even glancing over at his father. "About time too. He just turned eighteen earlier this spring."

"She's a handsome woman, Bill," Seamus said as he turned back to the elder Rowland. "Your boy could do a lot worse."

"Always wanted him to find a Cheyenne gal like I did," smiled the father. "Figured he'd do better that way, than him trying to break in a white gal . . . Willis being mixed-blood and all."

"I'll wager you're right on that account," Donegan declared. "But you didn't bring Willis this far north just to get him hooked up with no Cheyenne woman."

---

*A Cold Day in Hell, vol. 11, The Plainsmen Series

"No, we could've turned south with Morning Star's village if all we was doing was to find him a wife," Rowland said as he took a plug of army tobacco out of a coat pocket and bit off a sliver. "You're right about another thing, Irishman. There's more out there. You know that, don't you?"

"How many you figure?"

"Nothing Miles can't handle," Rowland said. "But . . . the last ones gonna be the real hard cases."

"Always that way, ain't it?" Donegan asked. "Them what can read, but still won't pay no heed to the writing on the wall."

Chapter 27

Spring Moon
1877

BY TELEGRAPH

SPOTTED TAIL TO BE MADE A
COLONEL IN THE ARMY.

THE INDIANS.

Surrender of More Cheyennes.

RED CLOUD AGENCY, NEB., April 26.—
Nine Cheyenne warriors surrendered this
morning. They report thirteen lodges to follow
them in a few days. These will make twenty
lodges that have come in since the main body
of Cheyennes arrived. It is reported by these Indians that forty lodges of Cheyennes are moving toward the mouth of the Tongue river, to
surrender there. Crazy Horse was, at last accounts, on this side of the Belle Fourche, coming this way.

It took Wooden Leg a long time to do anything but grieve
for his sister.

When the peace delegates found that big village on the
Powder River, Old Wool Woman was carrying the terrible

news that Crooked Nose Woman shot herself in the head at the soldier fort because the man she wanted for a husband hadn't been among the delegates with White Bull and Two Moon. At first Wooden Leg was very angry with Shoots Twice for his sister's death, but then he realized he could not blame the man. Shoots Twice had already been gone hunting for days when the delegation started for the Elk River fort to talk surrender with the Bear Coat.

After the peace-talkers found the village on the Powder, the camp broke apart again. But this time, Wooden Leg didn't continue south for the agency with the majority. Instead, he steadfastly remained with his Kit Fox Society war chief.

"Those who want to surrender are free to surrender," Last Bull told his warriors.

It was plain to him that Last Bull still licked his wounded pride. Most of the Shahiyela continued to blame Last Bull and the Kit Fox men for not allowing them to escape, not even letting them prepare a defense against that devastating attack by Three Fingers Kenzie.

"As for me, I will not surrender anywhere," the chief declared to his loyal warriors. "Not while the grass grows tall and our ponies are fat."

In addition to Last Bull's wife and children, four other married men—Dog Growing Up, Many-Colored Braids, Little Horse, and Black Coyote—brought along their families. Joining those five lodges was a mixed group of thirteen unattached young men from all three warrior societies. At each camp these bachelors slept in the open, or made themselves shelters from willow and brush. By and large most of them did their own cooking, but Wooden Leg slept in Last Bull's lodge, as a member of the chief's family. Ever since Wooden Leg had helped protect Last Bull's wife and children during the Powder River fight,* the warrior chief had treated the young man like a nephew.

Once Wooden Leg's father decided he would follow Little Wolf and Morning Star to the White Rock Agency, Last Bull took him in. It had been good for him to have family around him as they moved west from the Powder River, hunting

---

Blood Song—vol. 8, The Plainsmen Series

each day, slowly moving from camp to camp, keeping on the watch for the Crow People or for the Shoshone, always wary of soldier columns.

A few days later a young warrior reached one of their camps, asking to join Last Bull's band. Although Yellow Eagle had wintered with his relations at the White Rock Agency, the moment the weather began to warm he said his farewells and headed for the north country alone to locate the wandering bands.

"I happened upon Little Wolf's people," Yellow Eagle explained to the Kit Fox Warriors. "But when I learned they and Morning Star's people were going in to the agency where I just left, I asked them where I might find any who were staying out."

"You want to stay free with us?" asked Yellow Hair, Wooden Leg's brother.

"Yes. I came a long way from the reservation to be free," he declared. "And free I will remain."

It wasn't long after they parted company with the big village that Black Coyote's wife gave birth to a son. Well known among the *Ohmeseheso* for her bravery, Buffalo Calf Road Woman had acted with great courage in rescuing her brother during the fight with Three Stars on the Roseberry River the previous summer.* In those final hours of Buffalo Calf Road Woman's labor, the wife of Many-Colored Braids assisted as midwife and medicine woman, delivering a healthy, strong-lunged boy who raised his first battle-cry to the spring skies.

"This is another good sign," Last Bull told them as soon as they heard the newborn's first wail from the birthing lodge. "New life for him means that we will continue in our old life!"

Inside the birthing lodge, the medicine woman tenderly rubbed the tiny boy's body with milkweed down, then cut the umbilical cord, saving a portion of it for the child's mother. In the following days Buffalo Calf Road Woman would encase the cord in a leather amulet cut in the shape of a turtle. After it was decorated with beads or quillwork, this revered symbol of the sacred Grandmother Turtle—the

---

creature who had helped *Ma-heo-o* create Mother Earth—
would remain with the child for many winters to come.

Across the days that followed the birth, four other women
helped the new mother by taking down or setting up her
lodge. Daily thunderstorms forced them to seek shelter early
every afternoon, storms of rain and cold that kept the hunting poor in the country of the upper Powder, later as they
reached the headwaters of the Buffalo Tongue country. Always when the weather turned cool and wet, the deer and
antelope bedded down and were hard to flush out. But those
rains caused the grass to grow tall and lush; in little time their
ponies would fatten after a harsh and long winter.

Last Bull came to Wooden Leg and said, "In the morning
I want you to go scouting for buffalo."

He loaned Wooden Leg one of his strongest horses and a
packsaddle to lash the meat upon. The young warrior headed
into the hills alone, hopeful. He had the rifle he had taken
from a dead soldier, after the fight on the Little Sheep River,
and a good supply of ammunition for it. Three nights he
stayed out, without sign of buffalo. Although he spotted
some game off in the distance, when Wooden Leg caught up
to the others he was empty-handed, but for two turkeys.

Never before, Wooden Leg told them, had he seen that
countryside so bare of deer and antelope, elk and buffalo.
He realized it wouldn't be long before hunger would return
to the eyes of the little ones. How it made his heart ache to
look about those three-times-ten in Last Bull's camp, to see
how every man, woman, and child's clothing had worn beyond repair. And not nearly enough skins to replace their
tattered garments.

Long gone were the blue coat and breeches he had taken
from that dead soldier beside the Little Sheep River. Even
his leather shirt and the wool leggings he had been wearing
since early winter now hung ripped and ragged. The only
decent article of clothing Wooden Leg still owned was the
wide-brimmed white hat he had captured during the Roseberry River fight. It alone had survived not only the heavy
snows of the previous winter but the drenching downpours
of spring.

While Wooden Leg had been off searching for buffalo
sign, a despairing Last Bull reluctantly dispatched two of his
warriors to the White Rock Agency to sniff out the condi-

tions of those who were surrendering. Yellow Eagle, who had recently come out from the reservation, took White Bird south with him. A few long and hungry days after Wooden Leg rejoined the camp, the two scouts returned from their journey.

"Morning Star's and Little Wolf's people have made it there," Yellow Eagle reported. "They told me they were being treated well."

Last Bull asked, "They have not been punished?"

"Not yet. The *ve-ho-e* haven't come for their guns and ponies yet," the scout said. "There is a good soldier chief there the Little Star People call White Hat. He knows how to talk to Indians with his hands. And he has seen that the agent has plenty of food and blankets and supplies for those who come in. White Hat says he is very happy the northern Indians came in to surrender to Three Stars."

When Last Bull asked his people who wanted to stay out and continue their search for buffalo in the old way, and who wanted to start south for the agency—all of those with families said they would go where they knew they could find food for their children.

"But more of our people will come to hunt with us now that spring has come," Yellow Hair told those ready to surrender. "Just like last summer, when the hunting camps grew crowded and all was good once more!"

"I have been a long time coming to my decision," Last Bull explained. "I do not think very many Indians will ever come again to this country."

"Give them time to come, Last Bull," Yellow Hair chided. "It has been a very wet spring—"

Buffalo Bull Sitting Down has run away to the Land of the Grandmother and he won't be back with his Hunkpapa," Last Bull growled. "And now reports tell us that Crazy Horse has started for the agency with his Little Star People. Never again will there be many people in this country, not as long as the white man keeps pouring in to take up all the space, to run off all the game and kill off all the buffalo."

In the end, many of the young men chose to follow Last Bull to the agency. Only four of the single warriors—Yellow Hair, Meat, Growing Dog, and Medicine Wolf—declared they would continue to hunt.

"Perhaps you will see me again soon," Wooden Leg said

to his brother the morning after he had decided to go south with his chief.

"I will look to the southeast every morning, and again every afternoon," Yellow Hair replied. "I will watch for you to rejoin us."

As those four bachelors turned west to start their search for the Lakota village of Lame Deer, reportedly hunting in the valley of the Roseberry, Last Bull started away from the north country with the last of his people.

Days later a few of the older men and women began to recognize some of the country they had reached. One of them announced they were getting close to the agency. Last Bull's band hadn't gone much farther when Wooden Leg and the others at the front of their march spotted three horsemen in the distance. The closer they got to the strangers, the more the horsemen looked to be soldiers.

But as the trio approached, it was evident from their long, unbound hair, and the feathers attached, that they were Indian. Last Bull's warriors grew anxious, frightened of an ambush. Hurrying into a broad line that put the women and children behind them, the men drew the covers from their weapons, cocking the hammers on pistols and rifles.

"Stop and tell us who you are!" Last Bull demanded.

The trio halted immediately and explained in sign that they were scouts from Red Cloud's agency. They had heard some more Indians were on their way from the north country and the White Hat told them to come out to help the new arrivals find their way. When Last Bull's warriors finally allowed the three close enough to converse, they discovered that one was a Cheyenne, one a Lakota, and the last a Cheyenne-Lakota named Fire Crow.

"Is it true that no one has been punished at the agency?" Wooden Leg asked Fire Crow that night.

The scout nodded, staring at the fire. "No one is punished."

"Did you ride with Long Knife's* scouts last winter?"

"I rode north with him, yes," the man answered sadly.

Wooden Leg growled, "You must have helped Three Finger Kenzie attack Morning Star's village!"

---

*William Rowland

Fire Crow finally responded, "I did not shoot my rifle in anger and I did not kill any of my people, if that is what you are asking. But you must know that I helped Long Knife and the soldiers talk to the chiefs. We tried to get Morning Star, Little Wolf, and the others to stop fighting so the women and children could surrender."

For a long time Wooden Leg gazed into the flames. Then he eventually said, "I am sorry I became angry with you, Fire Crow. Nothing is served by making old wounds bleed."

The army scout replied, "We did what we thought best for our people."

"Our leaders always do what they think best for our people," Wooden Leg agreed quietly. "And tomorrow . . . our warriors will bring in their women and children—to surrender."

Like Last Bull of the Kit Fox Society, White Hawk decided he wasn't ready to surrender north or south.

When the great *Ohmeseheso* village began to break up on the Powder, this little chief of the Elkhorn Scraper warrior society announced that he would wander west, looking for the hold-out bands of Lakota reportedly in the valley of the Roseberry River. Fifteen warriors swore their allegiance to White Hawk, seven of whom brought wives and children with them as the band set off on their own to hunt. They left during those wet days of early spring, while lacy collars of snow still clung to the slopes, back in the shady places, gathering round the trunks of aromatic cedar and juniper and stunted pine.

White Hawk remembered the words some Little Star friends of his told him the winter before when the Red Fork survivors joined the Crazy Horse village. They said Buffalo Bull Sitting Down had claimed he was the last real Indian. When they heard that, White Hawk and his warriors all had a good laugh. Buffalo Bull Sitting Down the last real Indian? By now the man was probably already far to the north in the Grandmother's Land—country that wasn't even Lakota hunting ground.

"No, he is not the last," White Hawk was quick to say. "There are still a few real Indians left in this country. Indians who haven't gone in to the *ve-ho-es*' agencies. Indians who haven't surrendered and become scouts for the soldiers like those in so many tribes, like our own people who came to fight us on the Red Fork, like White Bull and the others who have disgraced the Shahiyela.

"There are still a few real Indians left," he told those loyal to him. "And we will join together with them to fight the soldiers when they come for us."

What made a people give up, decide to become either prisoners or servant dogs of the *ve-ho-e*, decide to remain captive on their reservations summer after summer? Even Crazy Horse was said to be slowly limping south with the last of his stalwarts. What had happened to their hearts? White Hawk wondered. Was it the cold of winter? The desperate hunger?

"An end comes to every winter," White Hawk sermonized to his small clan. "And if there is no longer enough buffalo to feed all the northern bands, then there are enough buffalo to feed the last few real Indians who will be hunting the beasts in the old way. There will always be plenty of meat to fill our bellies for generations of hunters to come."

In the days to come, when it finally suited him, White Hawk declared they would search for the camp of Lame Deer, the *Mnikowoju* who had vowed never to go in to an agency.

"Like this Lakota chief," White Hawk said as his people moved into the valley of the Roseberry River where it was reported Lame Deer's people were hunting, "I will die before the *ve-ho-e* drives me to a reservation."

Some distance to the south, he and his warriors spotted the smudge of smoke. Enough to indicate a village. Not a small camp but a sizeable village.

"That can only be Lame Deer's people," one of the men said.

Another agreed, "Everyone else in this country has already headed south by now."

"Come," White Hawk instructed. "Let us go join these Lakota who would rather live free and die like warriors . . . than be scrap-eating dogs for the *ve-ho-e* on the reservation!"

Chapter 28

Spring Moon
1877

Not long after they left the Powder with the greater part of the village, the two Old Man Chiefs agreed they should divide their people for this journey to the White Rock Agency. Little Wolf announced his party would hurry ahead on the best of what ponies the People still possessed. Morning Star's larger group would follow along at a slower pace, with those seriously wounded in the Red Fork Fight and the battle at Belly Butte last winter. There were still many travois dragged by the horses.

Although he found his own body much slower to heal after all these winters of life, Little Wolf had miraculously survived the six wounds he took in the battle with Three Fingers Kenzie. All the *Ohmeseheso* agreed this was proof certain that their Sweet Medicine Chief was blessed by *Ma-heo-o*!

Perhaps it was so, Little Wolf thought. And if he was truly blessed by the Creator, then he prayed the Spirits would let the blessings flow through him to his people.

So much had been lost in this war with the *ve-ho-e*: every family had lost relations and friends, not to mention the decades of their cultural history. All of it had disappeared in an oily, black smoke that slammed against those low-hung snow clouds to make a profane, dirty smudge across the heavens as the soldiers put a torch to everything that had once been a way of life for the Northern People.

Finally, with winter's end in sight, after running and hiding, after fighting only to run again, Little Wolf reluctantly decided the time had come to take his people in to the agency. There they would have enough to eat. There they would be among their old friends, the Little Star People. There the *Ohmeseheso* had lived before . . . and could live again.

Historically, the Sweet Medicine Chief always put the good of his people before his own. Their lives sprang from his, and he protected them with his life. Now he was taking his people where they would have nothing to fear from the soldiers, where they would have enough to eat and blankets to stay warm.

Day after day this journey had been one of the great struggles of the Shahiyelas' experience. An ordeal filled with despair and physical misery that tested every last one of them as they battled Cold Maker's final onslaught. Steadfastly they trudged on into the first of spring's gloom. When they began this journey south, Little Wolf's people had battled deep snow that formed huge, crusty ice sculptures across the land. They clawed their way up one snowy slope, slipped down the next—yet they persevered.

Then as the air warmed a little more each day, a new misery confronted the *Ohmeseheso*. What had once been snow and ice now turned to a cold, soppy slush that soaked their torn and tattered clothing. Tendrils of icy mud plastered to the ragged bottoms of their leggings, to their moccasins, caked on their bare feet like clumps of buffalo glue.

This past winter there had been little chance to cut new poles for their lodges, to replace those burned by the soldiers. Instead for several moons now these Northern People had dragged with them the half-burnt stubs they had salvaged from the Red Fork fires, along with what tree branches and limbs they could trim and put into service. Over these they draped what scorched and ratty hides they still owned, patched now with burlap bags found abandoned at soldier camps, or a few canvas flour sacks brought in from the agencies.

Little Wolf looked upon the widows and orphans with great sadness gripping at his heart. Once these proud women wore their hair tied neatly in braids. But now the hair of so many hung in rough-shorn clumps crusted with the mud and ashes of mourning. Wild tangles of it whipped this way and that, with the cruel, capricious winds slashing at their tear-streaked, sooty faces. Exposed arms and legs showed the wounds: long, blood-clotted slashes that rendered mute testimony of their profound grief.

As Sweet Medicine Chief, he had sworn to protect these widows, their orphans, and those old ones who had no one to provide, feed, and shelter them from want and winter and white men.

For far too long game had been scarce. To many of the hunters returned to the evening camps with empty hands. Once again his people were being tested. Once again only the strong would survive this surrender march. Only those who could endure under these destitute conditions would reach the agency. Only those who—

"Little Wolf! Little Wolf!"

He blinked and realized he had been dreaming; his spirit had flown away to that world between this and the next, neither seeing nor hearing, nor sensing much of this world as they plodded toward that band of striated bluffs topped by pines which signalled they were nearing the agency.

A pair of riders came hollering, whipping their ponies back toward the head of the march. Even as the young men brought the snorting animals to a halt, Little Wolf could see how the two smiled.

"You have seen it?"

"The log lodges!" one of the riders gasped, then gulped, almost as breathless as his winded pony.

The other nodded and blurted, "We saw them from that ridge!"

"So we are close," Little Wolf sighed, feeling the flutter of apprehension fire his veins.

Never in battle had he been as concerned as he was at this moment. To fight as a leader of the People, to die in battle if he was to give up his life—that caused him no real, tangible fear. But this—to face this unknown future?

Turning on the bare back of his pony, the Sweet Medicine Chief called the other leaders forward, "Old Bear! American Horse! Turkey Leg! Black Wolf!"

And he called forward all the rest of the chiefs, summoning them from the ranks of those who had hurried away from Morning Star who would follow with the wounded and the rest of the village. Without a murmur, those chiefs spread themselves out, flowing to either side of Little Wolf where they waited quietly. There could be no mistake why their Old Man Chief had called them forward at this point in their march.

They were about to enter the reservation. They were about to surrender to the *ve-ho-e*. They were about to turn their lives over to the soldiers at the White Rock Agency.

None of them knew anything of tomorrow, or the day after, or the coming seasons. But together they would look the future in the eye.

In anticipation of this crucial event, each chief and warrior took those precious few minutes to don what few articles of good clothing he might still own after the soldier fires in the Red Fork Valley. Quietly the rituals began, chants softly emerging from the throats of a few of the older men as they altered themselves into young warriors once more with these battle raiments. Proud people were these who had followed Little Wolf here to surrender. Yet what these older men sang were not war songs, nor those of battle. Instead they sang their pipe songs, the songs of peace.

"Elkhorn Scrapers!" Little Wolf now called to those warrior society headmen, waving his right arm and pointing behind the wide line formed by the chiefs.

"Crazy Dogs!" Little Wolf cried next, pointing with his left arm behind the chiefs.

When these headmen were in place both left and right behind the old chiefs, he announced in a bold voice, "All you fighting men—protect the flanks of our march! Ride now to protect the lives of our women and children with your own lives!"

He waited while the young men stripped covers from their shields and pulled leather cases from their rifles, spreading up and down both sides of the procession, then Little Wolf rode to the rear of the column where he raised his commanding voice again.

"Tangle Hair!"

"I am here, Sweet Medicine Chief!" the war leader responded, raising an old lance.

"Your men will guard our back as always, Tangle Hair!"

"No enemy will dare slip around to attack us from behind!" the chief bellowed proudly as the handful of his men stretched themselves left and right at the back of the wide column. "We offer our lives to save the helpless ones!"

It has always been that way, Little Wolf thought to himself. As far back as any of them could remember, the Dog Men always brought up the rear of any march, always protected the village in retreat, always were the last to leave a field of battle, these men who pulled the bodies of relations and friends away from the enemy . . . and gave of their own blood to protect those who could not defend themselves.

There weren't many Dog Men left these days.

Little Wolf's eyes quickly counted the six who separated themselves into thin lines on either side of Tangle Hair. Thin but as strong as a rawhide bowstring.

At that very moment an old man and woman emerged on foot from that mass of nervous, snorting ponies and quiet, restive people anxious for this march to resume. Some dogs snarled as the peace songs continued, and a pony whinnied close by. But for the singing, the People were respectfully quiet as Little Wolf waited for that old man and woman to reach the horsemen arrayed at the front of the column.

Coal Bear and his wife, Sacred Hat Woman.

She limped painfully a few paces ahead of the old man. By tradition the woman was allowed to ride a horse only in the event of an emergency. All but crippled after this horrendous wilderness ordeal, the footsore Sacred Hat Woman had walked every step of the three-hundred-mile journey. Across her back she carried the bundle. Inside rested *Esevone*, the Sacred Buffalo Hat.

As he trudged past Little Wolf, Coal Bear glanced up and nodded. To symbolize his respect for the old priest, the Sweet Medicine Chief removed the pipebowl from the satchel at his waist, fitted it onto the long stem of his pipe, and rested this sacred object across his left elbow while the couple limped by. Moments before both of these old people had painted their faces and hands with the sacred red ocher. That flesh they exposed to the Creator.

When the holy couple were well ahead of the procession on the jagged prairie, leading them toward those distant, pine-covered ridges, Little Wolf finally spoke, his words carried on the spring breeze.

"Come, Northern People! Be proud! We ride into the future!"

Somehow they kept their nervous ponies at a slow walk,

allowing the old couple to set their own pace as Little Wolf's band crossed this last distance between the *Ohmeseheso* and the unknown. They were not surrendering as the *ve-ho-e* understood surrender. No, these were a proud people who simply found themselves unable to maintain any more resistance against the winter, against the hunger, against the overwhelming white tide.

They were not surrendering to those who had vanquished them. Instead, these *Tse-ĭsehese* came here so that they would survive.

Slowly, slowly now the Northern People marched toward the White Rock Agency, singing their peace songs. Before them rode Little Wolf and his headmen.

In front of those chiefs walked the holy priest, painted in that most sacred of colors.

But ahead of them all went the old woman carrying *Esevone*—that most powerful symbol of the Creator's power and life blessing—leading Her people into seasons yet unborn.

When Box Elder brought his people to the Elk River fort, the old man told White Bull that the power of the *Ohmeseheso* had been splintered, perhaps never to be repaired again. To the four winds they had scattered, perhaps never to reunite.

Little Wolf and Morning Star led their people south to the White River Agency.

Big Horse and Spotted Elk had hurried along the base of the White Mountains* to rejoin their relatives among the Southern People in Indian Territory.

A third band marched southwest, intending to settle among the *Sosone-oe-o*† on the Wind River Agency.

And now the people of Two Moon, Crazy Head, and Old Crow had turned themselves over to the soldiers who promised they would teach the People to become farmers, to grow their food instead of chasing the buffalo.

Had he done the right thing? White Bull brooded as the tempo of preparations accelerated around him. Perhaps he

---

*Bighorn Mountains
†The Shoshone

should have stayed out as a few of the *Ohmeseheso* had done, some lodges going this way, a few heading off in that.

Yet again and again he came back to the same conclusion: it would still be no more than a matter of time before they would be captured, or killed. This enemy from the east was not only powerful in numbers, but powerful in their war medicine.

The Bear Coat had made sure that Long Knife Rowland explained everything he wanted to say to the Shahiyela leaders. One morning the soldier chief and interpreter had taken White Bull and the others out among the white man's spotted buffalo. Standing there in the middle of that peaceful, grazing herd, the Bear Coat explained that his soldiers were going to sell the ponies the Shahiyela had turned in, and with the money they would purchase many of these spotted buffalo for White Bull's people. The holy man understood making a trade, but he did not understand the rest of the soldier chief's talk about the virtues of raising these slow-witted, docile animals for meat so the warrior bands would not have to depend upon the hunt.

Perhaps acquiring these dumb brutes was a good thing, White Bull decided. If a man of the People could not hunt the wild buffalo with a rifle from horseback, then he would have to depend upon a docile animal that never ran off, an animal that stayed close by chewing its grass contentedly, not aware of its eventual fate.

White Bull did not want to think about his fate, about next winter. Or the following spring when the lure of the old ways would run hot in the veins of the young men. This was a hard road to walk, but walk it he would.

Through Long Knife Rowland, the Bear Coat had explained that come warmer weather, men like White Bull could begin to tend their own garden plots at the outskirts of the fort grounds. Most of the Shahiyela had never been to the agency where the hang-abouts there planted and harvested their food.

"Tell the Bear Coat I want to raise my favorite food," White Bull declared that morning among the spotted buffalo.

The soldier chief asked, "What food is your favorite?"

"Raisins!" the holy man gushed. "I have tasted the white man's raisins and that is the best food I have been able to find among your people—so I want to plant raisins in the ground."

The Bear Coat laughed with the other white men, saying, "I will do what I can to see that you grow raisins!"

Then the soldier chief explained how the soldiers would cut at the ground with their horses and plows to prepare it for the *Ohmeseheso* to plant their seeds once the snows had receded and the air warmed without fear of frost.

Ever since he had elected to stay, and had raised his arm to swear his allegiance to the Bear Coat, White Bull had enjoyed the daily performances by the soldier band. How they blew on their bright, brass horns and thumped on their rattling drums, while marching in step around the fort grounds! And after every song ended the other soldiers clapped and whistled and called out lustily, hooting for more. Naturally, White Bull learned to clap and yell at the musicians after each song too. He quickly came to like their soldier music, especially diverting during those long, cold days while he waited for his people to reach the fort.

When they finally arrived they were issued tents and stoves, blankets and kettles. The families who had stubs of lodgepoles and scorched lodgeskins still used them, while the unmarried men put the canvas tents to good use, erecting them with the soldiers' help, right among that crescent of poor lodges.

But in that first, happy blush of reunion, many of the women had begun to wail and moan, asking Old Wool Woman to lead them to the grave where the soldiers had buried Crooked Nose Woman near the fort. Such sadness heaped upon sadness . . .

Then two days ago an acrobatic troupe stopped for a short visit to the fort and gave two performances. How the Shahiyela laughed and laughed at their antics. It was truly amazing how those white people bounced and jumped and balanced themselves in all sorts of contorted positions! These *ve-ho-e* were amazing creatures.

More than once Rowland and his tall, gray-eyed friend, who stayed at Long Knife's elbow, showed White Bull and the other leaders complex drawings that adorned the pages of the white man's books and magazines, some of which Long Knife explained came from far across a distant ocean, wider than any water the Shahiyela had ever seen.

White Bull wondered how many *ve-ho-e* there were beyond that ocean. And why they had ever come here to this land. Why didn't the white man just go back to where they came from so everything could return to the way it had been before?

But he knew it could not be the way it had been before. Too much had happened. Too many were dead, and too many were orphaned and widowed.

He would have to walk this white road. But the journey down that road would not be easy, for the Bear Coat was readying his soldiers and scouts to go after the Lakota reportedly camped on the Roseberry River.

Now the Shahiyela were told to hunt down the Lakota. Once again, old friends would face one another on the battlefield.

Chapter 29

1 May 1877

The tides of destiny wait on no man, but man must abide by the whims of fortune.

How Seamus grinned now as Tongue River Cantonment became a blur of man and mule, bull and wagon, preparing to launch into the wilderness once more after the wildest of the holdouts.

For the better part of half-a-year Nelson A. Miles and his Fifth Infantry had survived here on the Yellowstone without a resupply from downriver. Once the Missouri froze last fall, the Quartermaster Corps wasn't moving a thing north to the high plains. While the men supplemented their meager diet with occasional game and fowl, their animals suffered the worst of it. What with the way winter battered this country, it was a wonder Miles and his men had been able to find any forage for the horses, mules, and the once-hardy oxen they steadfastly nursed through the winter on what scant grass they could find, as well as all the cottonwood bark the men could peel. The Fifth Infantry's beasts sure were a gaunt, winter-poor lot, and not in the least fit for the trail.

As much as Miles wanted to put his outfit to the hunt, it would have been plain to a blind man that his soldiers would end up killing their stock if they hurried after the Sioux.

Then three days ago, on the twenty-eighth of April, pickets to the east began to holler shortly before noon. Not only were there riders approaching from downriver, but they were escorting the first wagon train of the season!

Donegan yanked on his mackinaw, swilled down the last of his coffee and dashed out with the rest to lunge through the trees on foot toward the Fort Buford Road. There at the edge of the clearing he stood watching Miles's hardy veterans. Twice in this damnable Montana winter these dough-boys had caught Sitting Bull napping, and twice they had flushed that cagey old chief into the wilds with only what his people could carry. Then they had marched up the Tongue after Crazy Horse's camp, and given that strange man of the Lakota his last fight with the army.

Now the soldiers stood shuffle-footed, pounding one another on the back, hallooing and hurrawing until their throats were sore and their eyes were wet with joyous tears. By God, it was a supply train from civilization!

And who should be riding at the head of the column? Lieutenant Frank D. Baldwin himself!

"What the blazes are you doing back up here, Irishman!" the lieutenant bellowed as he drew close enough to recognize Donegan while shaking hands and saluting old comrades.

"You say that like you didn't expect me back, Lieutenant!"

Baldwin smiled in that bushy two-week-old growth of his. "I didn't. I truly didn't. Thought you had more sense than to come north when you could be snuggled up with the missus."

"What? And miss your abuse, Lieutenant!" he roared as he trotted beside the officer's horse, holding up his hand.

They shook, and Baldwin said, "We'll catch up tonight after mess."

As that weary army horse trudged on past, Seamus slowed to a halt and sang out, "What'd you bring with you in them wagons?"

"Everything, Irishman! Everything precious to a soldier but the faces of loved ones. And forage too!"

That announcement elicited a deafening cheer from the men who were swarming around those wagons, working loose the knots in the ropes that secured the heavy, oiled tarpaulins covering every load, anxious enough to look inside at the new supplies that many trotted alongside the train, rumbling those last three hundred yards into Tongue River Cantonment.

Forage. Grain for their horses and mules, and those huge, horned, ribby brutes the teamsters were now backing into the single-trees with grunts and curses enough to turn the Montana air blue, harnessing the last of those bull oxen to yokes. By damn, now Miles could put to the trail, Seamus thought. Now he could be about ending what others weren't equipped to end. Miles and the Fifth Infantry were the only ones to bring this bloody Sioux war to a close.

So eager for the hunt had the colonel been that he gave his outfit no more than one day of unlimited grain for every last animal they would cajole south down the Tongue before climbing the divide for the Rosebud.

The braying cacophony of mules and men was deafening, sheer excitement slathered in every *hee-raw* and *goddammit* as this army was about to embark upon the unknown. Ah, these truly were the second sweetest sounds in the world to an old horse soldier. Next to Samantha's sigh of contentment each time he returned home to her, that is.

"Seamus!"

He turned now as Miles called his name.

The colonel stopped before him, feet spread apart, his fists balled on his hips in that manner of a man immensely proud of himself. "You'll take the supply train south, Irishman. I imagine we'll catch up to you by the second day out."

"The way these oxen of yours love to lollygag, I don't doubt that we'll be seeing the rest of you fellas real soon!"

Miles nodded, grinning. "Don't lollygag yourselves. Keep them moving from first light till it's time to go into camp for the night. I'm sending you because you're the sort of man who can find those teamsters a safe camp in enemy country."

"I'll mother 'em like they was me own kin, General!"

"Be off with you then!" Miles stuck out his bare hand even though the day was blustery and about as raw as a Montana spring day could be.

Miles and his officers had decided to send the slow-moving supply train off first, using the best of the mules and oxen that had come upriver with Baldwin, all the way west from Fort Abraham Lincoln and the depot at Bismarck. From what the arriving bands had explained, the enemy Miles sought wasn't that far away—no more than a matter of a few days. But to make a victory of this strike at the holdouts, the command would need this bull-train.

And Seamus Donegan was the man to see that the teamsters and Lieutenant Cornelius Cusick's F Company, Twenty-second Infantry, escorted the balky oxen and mules upriver as far as they could before Miles and the rest could catch up to them. Once they rejoined, it would be an overland chase, cross-country after the last of the hostiles refusing to surrender, refusing to be driven in to their agencies, celebrating this last season of freedom.

Swinging into the saddle, he adjusted the reins in his left glove, then saluted Miles, Baldwin, and the others who took off their hats and hollered as the Irishman gave his mount the heel and set off at a prance. Behind him the civilian teamsters growled their own princely commands and cracked the air with their twenty-foot black silk whips, each one snapping like a cottonwood popping in the depths of a winter night.

South. Up the Tongue. Alone with but one company of soldiers and these hardy teamsters, going in search of the very same Sioux warriors who had stymied Crook at the Rosebud, butchered Custer on the Little Bighorn, then disappeared like smoke on the wind as autumn descended upon the Little Missouri country.*

He had no idea why, but something stuck down in his craw told Seamus that these holdouts the army was stalking were likely to be the toughest of them all.

BY TELEGRAPH

ILLINOIS.

Crook on the Indians.

CHICAGO, May 2.—The Post has an interview with General Crook concerning the Indian question, the substance of which is that General Crook considers the Indians are like white men in respect to acquisitiveness; that if they are

---

Trumpet on the Land—vol. 10, The Plainsmen Series

given a start in the way of lands, cattle and agricultural implements, they will keep adding to their wealth and settle down into respectable, staid citizens.

"You should have let me kill him, Uncle!"

Lame Deer saw the fury in his nephew's eyes, the flush it brought to Iron Star's cheeks. "Perhaps."

"I could have gone after him," Iron Star snarled, "if you didn't want me to shed his blood in our camp."

The *Mnikowoju* chief gazed at the army revolver clutched in his nephew's hand. If he had the half-breed here right now, he wouldn't mind spilling that turncoat's blood himself. But regrettably, the one called Big Leggings was gone. Many days ago the half-breed had turned to the north, leaving their camp of Lakota and Shahiyela, returning to the soldier post on Elk River.

Big Leggings had shown himself at the crest of a nearby hill, bearing a white cloth knotted to the end of a long, bare limb. There the half-breed stayed atop his horse close enough to be seen and perhaps to make sign, but far enough that he had a good lead on any young warrior who might attempt to run him down for a coup, a scalp, and the half-breed's army weapons. Big Leggings remained watchful and nervous until Lame Deer and some of the other headmen walked out under their own white flag and invited him off the hill.

The Lakota were a people of honor—and the half-breed knew that. If they accepted the courier into their camp under the white flag, no harm must come to the man. There were times Lame Deer stood aghast at the complete insanity of an honorable people fighting this terrible war against an enemy who had no honor. An enemy who reaped destruction upon the villages of women and children. An enemy who refused to live up to his own promises.

Who would be rash enough to fault Lame Deer if he had indeed slaughtered Big Leggings while they parleyed in his lodge? Especially since this half-breed enemy was himself a man without honor . . .

This war with the *wasicu* had stirred up so many questions in Lame Deer's heart, questions truly without answers, matters that troubled and vexed this leader who wanted only to be left alone to hunt and live free on that land given to Red Cloud and the other chiefs almost ten summers ago, when Lame Deer was still only a warrior. Now the soldiers were taking back their word, brutally driving the Indians off that land, butchering all who resisted. Perhaps there really was no honorable war with such an enemy.

Iron Star might be right, Lame Deer thought.

To fight such an evil enemy a man had to make use of every ploy at his disposal. Every trick and ruse he had learned in all those years of raiding the *Psatoka*, those People of the Big-Beaked Bird,* the *Susuni*,† and others. To survive in this life and death struggle against an enemy without conscience, Lame Deer figured he might well have to set aside this matter of honor unto death.

If he were going to protect the many who had flocked to him once Spotted Tail tried to convince the Crazy Horse people to come south with him, in all those days since the big village broke, clan torn from clan, Lakota drifting off to the four winds to unite no more as they had in that summer of their greatness... he might have to put survival before honor.

In recent days Lame Deer's wandering village had more than doubled in size. Encompassing sixty lodges now, with some brush arbors for those unattached young warriors who no longer lived with their families, even some whose families had decided they would go south to the agencies, while they themselves would stay on in the north country and fight to the end.

When the Crazy Horse village broke up, the *Mnikowoju* and Sans Arc bands set off for the familiar country between the Little Missouri and the sacred Bear Butte. It was there Spotted Tail reached them, convincing most to start south. From there Spotted Tail and his entourage marched west, determined to find the camp of his nephew, Crazy Horse. So while the rest of the chiefs and their bands reluctantly set off for the reservation, Lame Deer made for the Powder with fewer than thirty lodges.

From the Powder they journeyed on to the upper waters

---

*The Crow People
†The Shoshone

of the Buffalo Tongue where a few more warriors brought in their families along with some young men eager to continue to live the old life. Near the mouth of Hanging Woman Creek here in the *Pehingnunipi Wi*, the Moon of Shedding Ponies, the Shahiyela had reached them—White Hawk and his fifteen lodges.

"We won't be going south with Little Wolf and Morning Star," the Shahiyela chief had declared to Lame Deer's village.

"We hear some of your people are giving up the fight, going north to turn themselves over to the Bear Coat," Lame Deer chided.

"And the rest are going south," White Hawk said bitterly with a wag of his head. "But I came here to your camp, hoping to find those who would have the heart to keep fighting. I cannot give my pony and weapons away to the soldiers we fought at Belly Butte."

Lame Deer had smiled at these good friends of his, these Shahiyela, then Lame Deer cried, "*Was-te*! This is good! Like me, you are a man who would rather die with your weapon in your hand!"

Chapter 30

3 May 1877

BY TELEGRAPH

INDIANS.

Red Cloud's Party Coming In.
CAMP ROBINSON, NEB., May 4.—A courier just in brings a letter from the Red Cloud party, which will reach this point early on Sunday morning. It's camp to-night is only twenty miles north of here. Forty-seven lodges have gone into the cantonment on the Yellowstone to surrender to General Miles.

Sitting here beneath a large scrap of oiled canvas that served to protect him from last night's rain, now two days out from Tongue River Cantonment, Nelson Miles clutched the small cabinet photo of his Mary, no bigger than the palm of his hand. She and the wives of a few officers would be arriving at Tongue River with the first steamboat of the season. Oh, how he wished she were there to fling his arms around at this moment!

Mary always teased him about his longing for her, saying that he must surely have so much to occupy his time, what with his regiment and the campaigning, that he simply didn't have a spare moment to find himself missing her. But she was wrong. All of that activity crushing in on him for some eighteen or twenty hours a day only made those few hours he had alone with his thoughts all the harder to endure.

Male faces, male voices, the sharp taste of coffee and salt-pork, the bitter tang to the spring wind—they made him miss the sound of her voice, the smell of her smooth neck, the taste of her warm, wet mouth all the more.

"One day soon, my dear wife, I promise you I will no longer be separated from you," he whispered as he gazed down on that much-handled tintype. "We will be in Washington City together, and this will all be but a memory to us both. But for now, I learn from Phil Sheridan that I may have a larger command. You know I would prefer a small command with the means of placing supplies where I know I will want them rather than having a large command, forced to have it supplied by the incompetency or indifference of others."

Not only had General Terry, his department quartermaster in St. Paul, along with Hazen at Fort Buford, seen to it that no supplies reached Tongue River all winter, but Terry even refused to grant permission to Miles to acquire the critically needed beef and other provisions from civilian suppliers up-river, like the Diamond R Ranch.

Sherman and Sheridan had to do something about Miles and the war before this brief window of opportunity slammed shut. There wasn't another man out here who could accomplish what needed doing. No one else now that Custer lay under a couple of spades of prairie earth somewhere on the Little Bighorn. Certainly not Terry or Colonel John Gibbon, those venal bastards who had delayed long enough to allow the enemy to wipe out Nelson's old friend, along with 260 of his men.

And surely not Crook! The underhanded, back-stabbing son of a bitch that he was. Sitting on his thumbs while Custer was butchered, then sitting on them some more while Custer's murderers slowly slipped away to the east. Crook wasn't interested in confronting the real power in the enemy. Instead the coward always sent in his underlings: like Reynolds on the Powder or Mackenzie on the Red Fork. The only time Crook fought was when caught flat-footed, with no other choice but to defend himself or get swallowed up, as he had done the morning Crazy Horse surprised him at coffee and cards on the Rosebud.

That one always made Nelson smile.

No, Crook wasn't a fighter. Crook was an administrator, a finagler, a bureaucrat, not much more than a goddamned delegator who left the real fighting up to others—whether those officers were up to the job or not. And now the man was finagling with Spotted Tail and Red Cloud down south, hurrying them north to meddle with Miles's Indians.

He has no business coming up here to convince them to go south, Miles thought, *when I am the one who has labored long and hard all winter to convince the enemy they have no choice but to surrender under the harshest of terms!*

So Sherman and Sheridan damn well better give me my own Department of the Yellowstone, along with the regiments of cavalry and foot I require, as well as the supplies the quarter-master is so niggardly about. If I had the men and the rations and the ammunition, I could end this war before summer.

The day after his return to the cantonment following his victory at Battle Butte,* Miles had shifted his political campaign into high gear.

Waiting for him at Tongue River was a notice from Division Commander Terry that Congressional cutbacks compelled Miles to release all but two of the cantonment's civilian scouts, as well as letting go all his packers, Indian guides, teamsters, and blacksmiths. In addition, Miles was ordered to send all his wagons downriver to Fort Buford at the mouth of the Yellowstone for the remainder of the winter.

It was enough to make a fighting man feel like a gelded bull.

He fired off an angry letter to Mary, then one to her uncle, William Tecumseh Sherman, as well. "Shame should fall on Terry for the outrageous way he has failed to support me. I do not believe he ever reads my reports or pays any attention to my requests. His directive, moreover, virtually compels me to abandon the campaign when my regiment is on the verge of total success!"

Wolf Mountain Moon—vol. 12, The Plainsmen Series

Then he implied that Terry was tinkering politically with the prosecution of the Sioux War. "There seems to be a determination that this war shall not be ended this winter, or that it shall not be ended by this command."

Perhaps that summer soldier, Alfred Terry, desired nothing better than to journey west again come June to wrap up the conflict himself!

"If I have not earned a command, I never will," Miles lambasted Sherman, "and if I have not given proof of my ability to bring my command into a successful encounter with Indians every time, I never will."

Then he confided something vital to Mary's uncle, something Miles hadn't even expressed to his wife: the post he really coveted was Secretary of War.

For the meantime, Miles realized if he didn't have the manpower, or the supplies to keep him in the field for the rest of the winter, the time would still not be wasted. Instead of expeditions against the hostiles, the colonel had pressed his campaign with his superiors. Besides laboring to convince Sherman and Sheridan that he deserved the next brigadier generalcy that fell open, Miles began firing off a series of letters to Washington City influentials, seeking testimonials from both army and congressional power-brokers to advance his cause.

In his typically unvarnished, hard-nosed correspondence with both Sheridan in Chicago and Mary's uncle in Washington that spring, Miles wrote:

> *Despite bitter cold and rugged terrain, I have cleared this region of hostiles until forced by the* criminal neglect *of scheming bureaucrats to take winter quarters. Only a full department command will enable me to defeat these intractable foes and overcome those in both the army and in civilian quarters who would conspire against me. Among them, (Lieutenant Colonel Elwell S.) Otis (in command at the Glendive depot) and Major Benjamin Card (Quartermaster for the Department of the Dakota)—they are to blame for my predicament.*

In addition, Miles leveled some of his sharpest criticism at Colonel William B. Hazen, commander at Fort Buford, accusing Hazen of stabbing him in the back and doing as little as possible to assure the success of his Fifth Infantry in their continuing winter campaigns.

> *Certainly you must understand that I do not relish the thought of going to plead my case in the national press, but if this situation is not improved and these wrongs are not righted, then I have but little choice.*
> *I have fought and defeated larger and better armed bodies of hostile Indians than any other officer since the history of Indian warfare commenced, and at the same time have gained a more extended knowledge of our frontier country than any living man. Give me what I need and let's bring this war to its conclusion.*

Miles went on to recommend the army establish supply camps for expeditionary forces in the country of the upper Tongue as well as the country of the Little Missouri, right where the last of the hostile bands were at that moment hunting and taking refuge. Furthermore, he declared three supply depots should be constructed at Fort Peck on the Missouri, the mouth of the Little Bighorn, and the mouth of the Musselshell. In addition he declared the army should install a telegraph wire west from Bismarck to Bozeman, a second line between the Yellowstone south to Fort Fetterman. Communication was the key element to tracking, pursuing, and defeating the hostiles.

Then Miles laid his best hand on the table. "If you will give me this command and one half the troops now in it, I will end this Sioux war once and forever in four months."

With that bitter tone he took when backed into a corner, his hands tied, Miles asked both Sherman and Sheridan, if they did not approve his requests, to remove his regiment from Montana and return it to Fort Leavenworth.

Every officer in the frontier army knew full well the stakes in this war. The task of defeating the Sioux had to be wrapped up before the first of July, at which time Congress had mandated the army to reduce its manpower by 2,500 men. Miles had two months to finish the job no one else had the skill or the stomach to do.

That urgency wasn't lost on his superiors either.

While both Sherman and Sheridan were weary of Miles's

shameless and incessant self-promotion, the two nonetheless were quick to recognize the talent, the energy, and the dogged determination Miles threw into every campaign. Back in Washington last winter, General Sherman read Crook's report on the disappointing end to his campaign when he failed to receive supplies on the Belle Fourche, and was therefore forced to turn back to Fetterman where he disbanded the expedition.* The commander of the army threw up his hands in exasperation at Crook's defensive sniping, grown impatient with Crook's unproductive campaigning. Sherman wired Sheridan that he thought one officer should be placed in charge of the entire Sioux campaign rather than having it fought by two conflicting departments.

"I think General Miles is in the best position and possessed of the most mental and physical vigor to exercise this command." Perhaps Miles could get the whole thing cleaned up by June, Sherman concluded, lobbying for Sheridan's support.

But from Chicago the little general, who was an old, battle-scarred friend of Crook's, wired Sherman that he believed such a responsibility was too much to lay on Miles's shoulders.

"Spring will be the time to press our suit," Sheridan wrote. "The Indian ponies will be weak from the long winter, and the Missouri and Yellowstone will be navigable for manpower and supplies. But to turn over the entire operation to Miles would be a mistake.

"Nonetheless, I firmly agree that we should expand his Department of the Yellowstone to include the Powder River country presently under Crook's nominal control. In doing so, we will need to give Miles two and one-half cavalry regiments, with two and one-half infantry regiments, along with the Pawnee scouts of the North brothers,† as well as authority to ignore all administrative boundaries when pursuing the hostiles."

Sheridan went on to propose that Colonel Ranald S. Mackenzie of the Fourth Cavalry be ordered to patrol along

---

*A Cold Day In Hell—vol. 11, The Plainsmen Series
†Black Sun—vol. 4, and A Cold Day In Hell—vol. 11, The Plainsmen Series

Miles's eastern flank, in the country of the Little Missouri and Belle Fourche rivers, preventing the hostile bands from fleeing in that direction.

"To assure the colonel will have a free hand in this aggressive cleanup of the last of these hostiles, General Alfred Terry will be assigned to stay in St. Paul to ensure Miles receives what supplies he needs. As well, Crook will stay in Omaha, no closer than Cheyenne City, to supply Mackenzie's column."

As spring warmed the northern prairies and melted the deep snows, Sherman did all that he could to reassure his quick-tempered nephew-in-law that no conspiracy of any stripe was at work to hamper the circumstances of the Fifth Infantry. "The severe winter weather, which has tied everything down from St. Louis to Bismarck, from Chicago to St. Paul, along with the nation's recent focus on the disputed presidential election, has been the real cause of your dilemma."

In that wire Sherman did agree with one of Miles's repeated proposals. "There ought to be but one Department over all that country, but I cannot at present accomplish so radical a change. I advise you not to tarry but to work hard this year, for whoever brings this Sioux war to a close will be in the fairest way to promotion."

If Miles didn't already feel the spur goading him into action this spring, then surely he felt the jab of Sherman's rowels in his flank. So when Baldwin arrived with those grain and field rations, Miles realized Sherman himself had moved heaven and earth to get those supplies north the moment the rivers opened for steamboat traffic. Mary's uncle wanted him to succeed, wanted to reward him with that general's star. Miles believed Sherman had said nothing less in his latest correspondence from Washington.

He was sure Sherman understood that it was the Fifth Infantry's presence on the Yellowstone this past winter, that it was his regiment and their tenacious engagement of the enemy despite winter's terrible onslaught, that had thwarted the reunion of the warrior bands who had defeated Crook and Custer last summer. Despite the agonizing weather, and ignoring the objections of his superiors, the colonel had accomplished more since October than the rest of the army had managed to accomplish since March of 1876, when

Reynolds bungled his attack against the enemy's village on
Powder River.

And now all those months of fierce, unremitting struggle
by his Fifth Infantry were beginning to bear fruit. Only recently word had come that Washington was relinquishing the
manpower Miles had been demanding since last autumn. For
this spring campaign his forces were bolstered by two more
companies of the Twenty-second Infantry who were transferred up from Glendive Depot. In addition, four companies
of the Second Cavalry had come downriver from their duty
station at Fort Ellis near Bozeman City. But due to his own
illness, their commander, Major Frank Brisbin, was forced to
turn back to Ellis after reaching Tongue River on 23 April.

No matter, Miles already knew exactly what he would do
with every weapon and every man sent him for this final
mop-up.

And when the last of the hostiles were rounded up and
herded back to their reservations, then he would see to it
that two more posts were constructed in the disputed region
so that there would never again be a resurgence of the hostile
warrior bands. In fact, just before leaving the cantonment,
Miles had learned that eleven companies of Custer's old regiment were headed his way from Fort Abraham Lincoln. Ordered to man posts in his new Yellowstone District, the
Seventh Cavalry would be arriving by early summer to begin
construction of the new forts, along with four more companies of the First Infantry who were at that moment marching
west from Fort Sully in Dakota.

Additionally, six companies of the Eleventh Infantry, reas-
signed duty from the Cheyenne River and Standing Rock
agencies, were coming west to construct a post at the mouth
of the Little Bighorn, no more than fourteen miles from the
site of Custer's battlefield, under the command of Colonel
George P. Buell of Red River War fame. To maintain contact with that new post, Miles had ordered construction of
not only a road between Tongue River and the Bighorn forts,
but also a system of semaphore and heliograph stations that
would allow communication across the hundred-mile distance in no more than fifteen minutes' time!

All of those reinforcements would soon bring Miles more
than two thousand men in uniform to end the hostilities and
pacify the region for settlement.

But for the moment, these four companies of cavalry and his trail-hardened doughboys were all he would need. At long last Miles had marshaled an impressive force to finish what others had so far bungled.

Somewhere up the valley of the Rosebud they were bound to find the Sioux camp Bruguier had spied upon.

No more than a handful of days from now, Nelson A. Miles knew this Great Sioux War would be nothing more than a memory.

Chapter 31

5 May 1877

BY TELEGRAPH

INDIANS.

After Sitting Bull Again.
CHICAGO, May 4.—The Seventh cavalry, with 1,100 members, has left Fort Lincoln and gone in search of Sitting Bull, who is supposed to be north or south of the Yellowstone, with some 500 warriors. The command will hunt him down and bring in the hostiles, when found, to the agencies.

Seamus had to admit that Miles wasn't the sort to hunker up for the winter.

From all that he had learned after reaching Tongue River, the colonel had done his best to keep his Fifth Infantry occupied—scouting for sign of hostile bands, cutting ice for the dugouts where perishables would be stored once warm weather crept north to the high plains, repairing their crude log huts and eventually starting construction on new, more permanent buildings, within a new military reservation the

colonel had laid out to the west of the infant community of
Miles City.

Reining up, the Irishman squinted into the bright, spring
light of that Saturday, the fifth of May, gazing along his back-
trail. There, just easing around the brow of the hill, he spotted the headquarters group and the first of the cavalry.

Second U.S. The namesake of the outfit Donegan rode
with during the rebellion of the southern states.

Because of late winter storms and poor road conditions,
those eight officers and 315 troopers hadn't reached Tongue
River until the twenty-third of April, only two days before
Seamus himself had returned for the spring campaign. But
the Irishman didn't have to wait long before Miles was ready
to move. On that Sunday, the twenty-ninth, he had led Lieutenant Cusick's escort of the Twenty-second to guard the
bull- and mule-drawn supply train up the Tongue.

The following day eighty-one more men comprising G and
H companies of the Twenty-second departed the cantonment
under command of Captain DeWitt C. Poole to catch up with
the slower train marching south.

It wasn't until sunup on the morning of 1 May that the
balance of the command marched away from the Tongue
River post. Under the command of Captain Charles J.
Dickey, four companies of the Twenty-second and two companies of the Fifth, along with the cavalry, moved out to
rendezvous with Poole's outfit already on the trail. Miles and
his staff—First Lieutenant George W. Baird, adjutant, and
Lieutenant Oscar F. Long, engineering officer—did not get
underway until 1:00 p.m. that Tuesday. When the entire command had rejoined two days later, counting both Indian and
civilian scouts as well as teamsters, the colonel had put a
force of more than twenty-one officers and 450 men in the
field to finish the Great Sioux War.

The afternoon before Seamus started south with Cusick's
supply train, Johnny Bruguier had returned to Tongue River
from his fruitless errand. Upon surrendering at the post,
White Bull's Cheyenne had informed Miles that there was a
growing band of Lakota holdouts intending to hunt throughout the spring somewhere up the Tongue. The colonel sent
the half-breed off to find that camp under a flag of truce,

giving them one last chance to come in or turn south for the agencies. Instead, Johnny found the mixed camp of Cheyenne and Lakota defiant, their chief declaring he would have scouts and guards out, daring the Bear Coat to catch them unawares. Many of the young warriors had sneered at the half-breed, begging permission of the chief to take Bruguier's scalp.

Again, Johnny had escaped with his life.

Off to Donegan's right now one of the Cheyenne trackers was waving to him from down at the wide cleft at the bottom of a grassy swale. On the slope above the Indian, pockets of old snow lay back in the shadows. Seamus tore the big brimmed hat from his head and signalled in turn the head of the column, indicating the direction he was going before he gave heels to his claybank and disappeared off the brow of the hill.

At the bottom, two more of the Cheyenne quickly joined the first, and a moment later Bill Rowland broke from the trees. None of the Indians offered to speak as the Irishman came up and dismounted. It appeared they preferred to wait until the squawman reached them. Donegan knelt beside the clutter of hoof- and footprints left in what had recently been sodden ground. Pulling the leather glove from his right hand, he gently brushed the edge of a hoofprint with a fingertip. Then he turned to the impression of a moccasin track. Small enough; it had to belong to a woman, maybe a young boy. He stood and worked his tense, aching back muscles as Rowland came up and dismounted, one of the Cheyenne speaking low to the squawman.

"White Bull says he's found the Lakotas' trail," the older white man explained as he handed off his reins to one of the young trackers.

Looking over at the Cheyenne warrior who had discovered this trail, Seamus nodded and smiled. White Bull returned with a grin of his own. Back at Tongue River Rowland had explained just how keen these scouts were to go after the last of the Sioux. Seemed White Bull and the others were angry as spit-on hens at the hold-outs, fearing what trouble the Lakota were likely to stir up might well be blamed on the Cheyenne, thundering depredations down upon the Cheyenne, just as it had twice before on the Powder and later

on the Red Fork. When those nose-thumbing Lakota stirred
up trouble, the soldiers would come looking for the Cheyenne village, finding their women and children.

As a means of protecting their own families, the Cheyenne
had eagerly volunteered to serve as trackers, as scouts, as
men-at-arms to fight these last of the Lakota.

When Crook and Miles turned Indian against Indian,
friend against friend, they had begun to write the last pages
of the great warrior bands.

Seamus liked White Bull's smile—open, genuine. "I'll say
he's found their trail, Bill. I think you ought to go on back
yourself and tell the general that we've crossed a pretty fresh
trail here."

The squawman nodded, reaching for the reins to his horse.
"Moving west, ain't they?"

He watched Rowland clamber into the saddle, then peered
into the hills that rolled upward toward the divide separating
the waters of the Tongue from those of the Rosebud. Seamus
said, "But from the looks of it, this bunch ain't running."

With no more than a nod, Rowland reined completely
around and set off at a lope.

Turning to the Cheyenne warrior, Seamus made sign.
"Good work, White Bull. You find this trail—good job."

He rubbed an eye and with a heavy accent repeated the
white man words, "Good work." Then added, "Yes, White
Bull do good."

By the time Miles trotted up with his staff and inspected
the trail for himself, the sun was already sliding off midsky.
The colonel ordered a brief stop for the rear units as they
caught up with the head of the march. Falling out to one side
or another the soldiers dropped their rifles and flung off their
haversacks before collapsing onto the knee-high grass. They
began digging into their packs for a square of hard-bread or
perhaps some chewing tobacco while they rested.

Seamus was relieving himself in the bushes when he heard
Adjutant Baird's distant call, as the lieutenant rode through
the noontime bivouac making his announcement without the
brassy blare of a bugle.

"Officers' call! Officers' call!" he cried, pointing up the
gentle slope of the hill. "Under the general's flag! Officers'
call!"

Jabbing the buttons through their holes in his canvas

britches and adjusting the braces across his shoulders, the Irishman stepped from the brush and started back for the spot where Rowland and the Cheyenne were spread across the ground.

"C'mon, Bill," he said, wagging his hand. "Let's see what's about to shake out now that Miles has his trail."

They waited among the officers, both infantry and cavalry, until Lieutenant Baird gave the colonel word that all were present and accounted for.

"I'm told by our engineer that we've come a little more than sixty-one miles," the commander began. "And I imagine it's no mystery that we've found us a hot trail," he continued, flinging his arm up the slope where a wide swath had been carved through the trampled grass between the stunted trees, where crusts of dirty snow still clung. "The enemy should be no more than a matter of a day, surely no more than three, from where we stand."

For a long moment, the colonel continued to stare up the slope, almost as if seeking to divine just how far ahead the hostile camp really was. Then he suddenly turned back to Baird and the officers.

"Lieutenant, do you have the time?" he asked in a gush. Watching Baird fumble at his vest, Miles impatiently asked the others. "One of you—any one—what is the time?"

"Just past 1:30, General," answered Captain Charles W. Miner, the big turnip watch filling the palm of his hand.

"Very good," Miles sighed with satisfaction as he gazed at that veteran of October's skirmishes with Gall's warriors.* "We'll take an hour to make final preparations, then form up our attack battalions and be off by 2:30."

Baird stepped up beside Miles, dabbing the stub of his pencil on his tongue, prepared to write down the disposition of the troops in his small ledger.

Briefly the colonel peered over his company commanders, then began, "I'm leaving the wagons with companies B and H of the Fifth. I'll also leave G Company of the Twenty-second. That's you, Captain Miner. These bulls and mules are simply too slow to keep up with the rest of us now that we have a hot trail to follow."

---

*A Cold Day In Hell—vol. 11, The Plainsmen Series

"General," Captain Dickey said, "are we going to take a pack-train from here?"

"Exactly," Miles replied. "See to it that two mules are fitted out for each company departing with me and the scouts. You will take along enough rations for six days, and sufficient ammunition for your outfits."

"One hundred rounds, General?" asked Captain Poole.

"Yes. And for their pistols, the cavalry will carry an additional twenty-four rounds. I plan to have the Second lead the way, followed by Lieutenant Casey's mounted infantry. Companies E, F, and H of the Twenty-second will protect the rear of our march."

Lieutenant Cusick moved forward a step and asked, "Sir, do you want me to bring the supply train along your back-trail?"

"By all means, Mr. Cusick," Miles answered. "I understand you will not be able to move with the same dispatch as our attack column, but I do want you to follow our trail across to the Rosebud, where the enemy trail leads. I expect you will be a day or so behind us, but within striking distance should we have need of resupply."

"Very well, General," and Cusick saluted. "We'll be able to communicate with you by courier."

Miles cleared his throat as he scratched nervously at his chin, then said, "You men know what is expected of you. Are there any questions?"

With that the colonel waited a moment longer, seeming to make eye contact with nearly every one of his officers, those who were departing with him, those who would follow with the pack train, and those who were staying behind with the supply wagons.

"Very well, gentlemen. Go now to prepare your outfits for the trail. Dismissed."

Seamus watched the officers turn on their heels and scurry off to their commands. Then he stepped over to Miles.

"General, not far south of here is a narrow pass in the hills," Donegan explained.

The colonel peered into the distance. "Something that will take us to the Rosebud?"

"It's where the Indian trail will lead you."

"We'll catch them on the Rosebud, won't we, Irishman?"

"Upstream."

"You know that country?"

Seamus replied, "I was through there a couple times with Crook. Likely gonna look familiar."

"All right, Irishman. Give your horse and your saddle sores a little rest," Miles said with a grim look of determination creasing his face. "I want you to lead us out in an hour."

The scent of the enemy was strong in his nostrils.

Lame Deer figured that soldier chief called the Bear Coat surely had to be on his way by now.

The chief stood staring north into the face of the winter-maker that evening as the shadows deepened and the small wingeds began to buzz at his ears. Most of them did not annoy him, but a few bit hard enough that they left red welts where his blood was drawn.

He swatted a forearm. The soldiers had to be on their way by now—marching slow but nonetheless relentless as they always did. Still, his warriors would swat them as easily as he had swatted that annoying insect, crushing its body against his skin. The way the *wasicu* bodies would be crushed and bloody against the brown of the earth mother's breast if they attempted to attack Lame Deer's camp.

It seemed darker this twilight, perhaps because of the dark clouds clotting along the tops of the ridges to the west. There would be rain before morning. Then another cold, dreary, bone-chilling day before the sun finally dispelled the clouds and dried up the puddles dotting the thirsty prairie.

That morning Lame Deer sent out hunters and wolves as he had every day. Most had already returned, including those from the north and east—the directions they had to fear. No danger had been spotted.

But the wolves he sent out to the south were late in reaching camp. Perhaps the Bear Coat had become a wily fox and was sneaking his soldiers around to the south. Perhaps the scouts would not return until they could safely slip around the Bear Coat's men. Once more the Lakota would have the jump on the *wasicu*.

Just as they had at the Rosebud when Crazy Horse led the many to confront Three Stars. And again when the Long Hair had blundered down onto the great encampment beside the Greasy Grass. While the Bear Coat brought his men up the Tongue River to strike the camp of the Crazy Horse people, the Lakota had been ready for the soldiers. Even the weather had conspired against the Bear Coat, allowing the village and the warriors to slip away in the blizzard. A blessing from the Great Mystery!

Just then a gust of chill wind tugged at his blanket, making Lame Deer shudder with cold.

Perhaps this last of the seven great council fires of the Lakota hadn't yet burned itself out. Once all seven burned brightly—producing much heat, throwing out intense light in their constellation of glory. A time not so long ago when the Lakota warrior camps lived a life so sweet, so like heaven on earth. But now those other bands who hadn't fled with Sitting Bull to the north had instead chosen to extinguish their fires and surrender at the agencies in the south. Even Crazy Horse was on his way south to his uncle's prison.

One by one, the great Lakota council fires had been snuffed out. Not a flame, not so much as a warm coal remained. Nothing but ash. Cold, dead ash.

But here in this country, Lame Deer vowed, there would always be an unquenchable fire where true Lakota could warm themselves, replenishing their strength to continue this struggle against the *wasicu*.

Starting back down the hill, Lame Deer looked over the many lodges nestled in the tight horseshoe of the creek, every one of them lit with warmth for the coming night.

These people of mine, he brooded, *they are the last of the brave ones—both Lakota and Shahiyela. Like the last of the leaves clinging against the late autumn winds to the branches of a tree, they are clinging to Lame Deer, the trunk of that tree. They are the last, those who will never surrender. The strong hearts have congregated around me and this last fire of the Lakota nation.*

The light from our fire will never be dimmed, never go out. My people will never be conquered. Together, he swore, *these brave hearts will make their final stand.*

Here.

This, our ancient hunting ground. This, the land where the bones of our Lakota ancestors have decayed beneath the cry of the undying winds.

Here, where this heaven of ours will never turn to ash.

Chapter 32

6 May 1877

BY TELEGRAPH

European War News—Very
Great Activity.

The Bombardment of Kars to
Begin To-day.

Snow at Deadwood—Indian
Matters—Washington
News.

Indian Affairs.

WASHINGTON, May 5.—Brigadier General Crook had a long conference to-day with the secretary of the interior and the commissioner of Indian affairs, in regard to the removal of the Sioux agencies to the Missouri river, and on the Indian question generally. Secretary Schurz and

Commissioner Smith entirely concur with General Crook in his view that the Indians should be compelled to work for their grub, and the conference to-day was mainly with a view to ascertain how the labor of the Indians could be utilized in the interest of both the Indians and of the government. No definite conclusion has been reached as to the precise location of the new agencies, but it seems certain the Indians will not be removed until next autumn, as during the warm season the Indians will be disposed to straggle off on hunting expeditions, but will be easily collected on the approach of cold weather.

The colonel's Indian trackers led them along the enemy's trail that Saturday afternoon, through that narrow cleft in the divide west of the Tongue for some eight-and-a-half miles until they finally crossed over into the valley of Rosebud Creek near the site where General Terry's column had bumped into General Crook's command the August before.*

Recognizing a few landmarks, Miles had to grin—recalling how he had managed to convince Terry that it was time for the Fifth Infantry to turn back to the Yellowstone and establish their cantonment for the winter just as Sherman and Sheridan had ordered. *Had that ever been a stroke of luck!* he ruminated now. *Freeing myself of the dawdling, pensive, professorial department commander just the way Custer must have chafed to be free from Terry in those days before the Seventh galloped up the Rosebud and into destiny.*

"As it's turned out, Armstrong," he mouthed a whisper now, "I've driven one of your murderers into Canada and the other one is racing to reach his agency before he'll be forced to confront me again. If only they would stand and fight me—I could avenge your death, old friend."

As it was, Miles prayed this last of the warrior bands would not run. Instead, he pleaded with God to give his men a

---

Trumpet on the Land—vol. 10, The Plainsmen Series

chance to drench themselves in glory with this last fight of a
long and most inglorious Sioux War.

He gave them a brief rest there along the banks of the
Rosebud as the afternoon aged and the sun sank toward the
west behind darkening clouds. After the horses were watered
and the men got their land legs back, Miles ordered them
back into the saddle. After moving upstream another three
miles, the scouts had them cross the Rosebud and continue
west, following another small creek into the increasing gloom
that ballooned around them with the coming of night and the
approach of storm clouds.

When his weary men had urged their reluctant animals in
single file up the creekbank, each man listening for the clank
of a tin cup from the man ahead of him, Miles himself was
ready to call a halt in the dark.

"What time are you posting in the record, Mr. Baird?"
Miles asked his adjutant as he landed on the ground and
jarred his knees, both of them sore from the long, tortuous
night's ride.

With no moon or starlight to speak of beneath the hoary
clouds sluicing sheets of rain upon their column, the young
lieutenant desperately tried to light one lucifer after another,
until Miles himself went over to provide more of a wind-
break. In one brief flare of light, the colonel was able to see
the hands on the pocket watch Baird dangled from a soggy,
shivering glove.

"Just past 2:30," Miles reported as he straightened. A gust
of wind blew out the match and the darkness swallowed them
once more. "You've kept your timepiece wound, Lieutenant?"

"Yes, sir, General."

"Then we've been marching for twelve hours since breaking off from our supply wagons," the colonel replied, weigh-
ing their accomplishment in his mind. "I'd estimate we've
covered something close to forty miles. Go now, and tell the
company commanders to rest their men until it's light enough
to resume our search."

If it hadn't been for those Cheyenne scouts, Donegan knew
in his gut this army would have been little more than a wandering band of tinkers and drummers—stumbling about in

the rain and the gloom with little chance of following the enemy's trail.

As it was, White Bull, Brave Wolf, and the others led the Irishman, with young Joe Culbertson and Robert Jackson, at the head of the column throughout that drenching ride as the cold sheets of rain lanced sideways at them, carried on the back of a chilling wind. Now Seamus sat huddled in the darkness with the others, reins wrapped around one hand, his other holding that big watch against his ear. Listening to the steady, rhythmic beat of Samantha's heart in his soul.

Somehow that unwavering pulse kept at bay the cold, the blackness, the crushing solitude of the night. Water continued to sluice off the wide brim of his hat, some of it spilling inside his collar, raking down his back like the path of a cold, iron box-nail. The canvas mackinaw coat had nearly soaked through, so steady was the unremitting storm. Frosty vapors clotted in front of every face, creating gauzy streamers at the nostrils of every horse and mule.

The older he grew, the quicker this damp cold stabbed him to the bone, making him weary in the saddle. What with the way it settled in his joints, stiffening them like uncured rawhide, Seamus had begun to wonder just how long he would have the strength to ride out the better part of a day, covering more than those last forty miles in some twelve hours. How long could a less-than-young man take the sort of beating this land dealt those who came to test themselves against it?

Beyond the high ground to the east, over yonder in the country of the Powder and of the Tongue, a thin, mica-shaded grayness was a'birthing, faintly reflected along the edge of the hills. Its coming gave him a small measure of relief. Perhaps the storm had spent itself. With the coming of this new day's light, they could be back at their task of tracking the Lakota. From the trail-sign, he could tell the village wasn't a big one, not like many Seamus had seen. But then, the enemy camp might be as small as the one Reynolds had jumped on the Powder more than a year back. As small as the one Frank Grouard and Captain Anson Mills bumped into last September.

But nowhere near as big as that village Mackenzie destroyed along the Red Fork of the Powder River. Nothing close to approaching the inconceivable size of that string of

camps Custer had pitched into beside the Little Bighorn. One
huge crescent of tipi rings after another Seamus and Grouard
had stumbled across as they probed north, anxious to provide
Crook with word of General Terry's and Colonel Gibbon's
columns operating south of the Yellowstone.

No, this wasn't a big village—but likely a dangerous camp,
what with the many young hot-bloods along for the adventure, those youthful holdouts who were likely to throw in
with the last chief to offer them this grab at fleeting glory.

But with help from men like White Bull, the hounds would
soon have that den of foxes surrounded, cowed, and on their
way back to the reservations.

He almost felt sorry for those Sioux out there—not realizing what they had coming at them: this army, its cavalry
spearhead, and these trail-toughened doughboys. Not to
mention their commander, a man driven, obsessed, to close
out a conflict no one else had been able to end.

Seamus felt a pang of regret for the enemy out there in
this cold, wet coming of dawn—realizing that, had the circumstances of his birth been far different, he would be out
there with them, sleeping in that camp with his wife and son,
fully prepared to offer his flesh and bone to protect their
lives. As it was, he was born in faraway Ireland, come as a
youngster to distant Amerikay. No longer a Patlander was
he—now Donegan realized he was as American as any, a
yonderer, a plainsman.

Some of the Cheyenne were stirring now, just yards away,
slowly getting to their feet, ripping up clusters of grass they
used to brush the drenching moisture from the backs of their
ponies before replacing the dampened blankets.

"Time for your husband to go back to work," he whispered, reluctantly taking the watch from where it had grown
warm against his ear. For a moment, he stared down at its
face, trying to conjure hers cupped there in both of his
hands—then he kissed the rain-splattered crystal, as if it really were her warm, wet mouth. And stuffed the watch back
inside the vest pocket where it would remain as dry as possible beneath his canvas mackinaw grown heavy with the relentless rain.

Recalling that incomplete map George Crook was forced
to use in last spring's campaign to the Rosebud, Seamus remembered that the country west of this creek vaulted itself

in a rugged divide separating the waters of the Rosebud from that of a series of streams called Tullock's Forks. They likely spilled on down to the Bighorn, if not the Little Bighorn.

As he stood slowly, becoming accustomed to the stab of damp pain in his joints from sitting too long on the cold, wet ground, Donegan wondered if the Sioux were returning to the seat of their glory—the Little Bighorn. Were they hurrying over these Wolf Mountains to drop down to that valley where they sent Custer and his five companies to their fates?

Or was he only trying to manufacture some dramatic climax for this Sioux War—wanting to believe that this last band of Sioux holdouts was racing back to reach that field of victory, there to make their final, glorious stand against the inevitable?

The men muttered and coughed around him now, grumbling at their sergeants for the lack of sleep, at the kicks from those boot-toes it took to get them off the soggy ground. The men stumbled bleary-eyed and soaked with sweat beneath their India-rubber ponchos to the edge of the brush to relieve themselves, to hack up the night-gather from the backs of their throats, then turning back to tighten cinches and replace bits on protesting horses and balky mules.

Seamus turned to gaze south after he had thrown the saddle blanket on the back of his claybank mare. Surely the Sioux could hear this army coming—so noisy was this band of wet, miserably cold, and weary fighting men. Miles would whip them into line, he figured, then move them out the way Crook kept his column marching through day after day of soaking rains last autumn. That ragged column had first stalked an elusive Indian village, fell to searching for a route to the Black Hills, then ultimately stumbled and lurched southward in hopes of finding its salvation before the men died of starvation, died of despair in the wilderness.

Yanking up on the cinch, jabbing it back down through the cold, steel ring, Donegan knew this army was different. Now they had a fresh trail. And they had Cheyenne trackers. Besides, they had Nelson A. Miles—an Indian fighter if ever there was one. While Crook and Terry might dawdle and ruminate and filly-faddle, the Bear Coat was a man who took the fight right to the enemy.

He was not the sort of man to order men into battle. Instead, like Custer, Miles was a man to *lead* his troops right into that fight.

"Mr. Donegan."

Turning, Seamus discovered the colonel's young adjutant approaching. "You found me."

"The general would like a word with you."

"Only me?"

The lieutenant's eyes flicked over to glance at Rowland. "Said you could bring along the squawman."

"Bill," Donegan called out. "Miles wants to see us."

Rising from the ground where he was retying his wet moccasins, the white man stepped over as the Cheyenne scouts looked on with great interest. "Likely the general's gonna give us our orders for the day."

As the new light emerged out of the east, White Bull led the other scouts south along the hills west of the Roseberry River.*

Behind him rode Long Knife and that gray-eyed *ve-ho-e* who possessed a good smile, the sort that caused White Bull to believe the tall one was a fair and open man. But there were enough lines at the corners of the *ve-ho-e*'s eyes, creases and crevices that ran from the edges of his nose into the hair on his face that led White Bull to realize the man wore a virtual war-map of his life. Each flaw a story of trial, tragedy, and eventual triumph.

Just the way White Bull was himself marked with the seasons of his life, all those joyous springs . . . and all those terrible winters.

Of a sudden he remembered Noisy Walking, his son who had chosen to die in the fight they all knew was coming when the soldier chief led his men to attack that village camped beside the Little Sheep River. It hurt anew to remember how a mortally-wounded Noisy Walking had begged his father for water that evening after the soldiers had been wiped off the earth, just as the Everywhere Spirit had promised. But White Bull could not grant his son that simple, yet precious, drink of cooling water. Now White Bull was scouting for the *ve-ho-e* soldiers who had killed his son.

Long Knife and the tall one returned from speaking to the

---

*Rosebud Creek

Bear Coat, declaring it was time for them to move out in advance of the soldiers. While Brave Wolf and a young half-breed rode through the spotty brush half-way down the hillside, White Bull led the others higher up, tracking just below the skyline so they wouldn't chance being spotted by distant eyes. After all, they were following a village of those who had once been old friends. Not just Lakota, but *Ohmeseheso* too. Those who had joined the *Mnikowoju* chief, Lame Deer, those refusing to go either north or south to surrender. Following this close on the enemy's back-trail, White Bull was sure Lame Deer would have wolves out in the hills, watching for the soldiers whom he had dared to catch his people unprepared.

At first White Bull grew furious with the Lakota chief for enticing the Shahiyela deserters to join his warrior band, for offering them a hollow, empty promise. Eventually, as the morning wore on, he grew saddened for those among his people who hadn't gone south with Little Wolf and Morning Star, for those who hadn't come north to surrender to the Bear Coat. He found his heart filled with a deep ache for those who once again had joined their hopes with another ill-fated leader.

Like those who had believed Last Bull in the valley of the Red Fork, assured the old way would live on, believing that the People would survive in glory and greatness, unable to realize their day was passing, unable to admit that the sun was setting on the magnificence and majesty that was the *Ohmeseheso*—

For a long moment White Bull wasn't sure what it was. Although not nearly close enough to smell Lame Deer's camp, the holy man drank a deep breath of air becoming drier already this morning. He glanced at the sun just then touching his left shoulder, rising in the brilliant blue sky. Yes, the air was nowhere near as damp as it had been yesterday and last night. Smoke might well rise rather than be weighed down, heavy and wet.

Turning to look downhill at Brave Wolf, he could tell his friend was just then spotting the faraway smudge against the hills himself. Brave Wolf gazed up at White Bull, pointing quickly.

He nodded at Brave Wolf, waving his friend up the slope as he halted. The young half-breed from the north country kicked his heels into his horse and followed Brave Wolf up the side of the hill, clucking at the animal as it struggled, lunging over the broken, brushy ground.

"Long Knife, do you see the smoke?" White Bull asked the squawman when he came up to join the rest.

Rowland said something to the white man and they both took what seemed to be a long time to study the distant hills.

"I cannot see the smoke," the squawman admitted. "Where do you see this smoke?"

Urging his pony closer to Rowland's, White Bull brought his left arm up and laid it against the squawman's right cheek, pointing to the faraway horizon. Then Rowland rubbed his eyes and muttered something to the gray-eyed *ve-ho-e*. The tall one said something to the two half-breeds. But both of them squinted, then shook their heads.

"Can't see it, White Bull," Rowland confessed. "How far away?"

He took but a moment to calculate the distance to the village as the red-tailed hawk would fly from where they sat atop their horses. Perhaps a long day's ride across broken country, without pushing one's animal too harshly—but a lot of climbing and descending. That, or winding along the tortuous curves of the Roseberry itself. If a hawk flew straight from here—

"Not quite a full day's ride," he concluded thoughtfully. "Not a half-day's ride either." Then in a swift gesture he tomahawked the edge of his flat right hand down upon the open palm of his left hand. "Half the afternoon."

When Long Knife turned to say something to the gray-eyed *ve-ho-e*, a smile was spawned across that tall man's face.

Chapter 33

6 May 1877

"Culbertson," Donegan called, waving the young half-breed closer. "Dig out them field glasses of yours."

While Joe Culbertson inched his horse closer to the Irishman, he twisted round in the saddle and yanked at the pair of buckles securing the flap to his off-hand saddlebag. All around them, the Indian trackers were talking quietly among themselves, a few pointing to the south, others gazing off left and right to study the nearby heights or glancing back to the north to assure themselves of the column's advance.

"Couple of the Cheyenne must've got themselves spooked," Seamus said as Culbertson held out the field glasses to him. *Want to make sure the army is close at hand, what with just spotting the enemy—*

"Donegan," Rowland interrupted him as Robert Jackson dragged out his pair of field glasses and brought them to his eyes, "Brave Wolf just said both him and White Bull can see ponies grazing on the hills yonder."

Seamus blinked his eyes, rubbed at them, then blinked some more, before he put Culbertson's field glasses against the bridge of his nose. *These damned Injins seen smoke, and now a pony herd off where I don't see nothing but those hills brushing the sky.*

As he slowly twisted the inner wheel, the far horizon ground into focus—right there where the green of those dis-

tant heights met the flawless blue sky. *Maybeso* . . . He gradually inched the field glasses down, there—a bit of a smudge
against the ridges—down across the countryside at the base
of the bluffs. But for the life of him, he couldn't make out
the horse herd.

"Can't see no ponies," he grumbled, tearing the field
glasses from his eyes and blinking them from the strain of
trying so damned hard.

Young Jackson looked over at him and instructed, "Look
for some worms crawling on the eastern hills." Then the half-
breed put his field glasses back against his eyes.

"Let Rowland have himself a look, Bob," Seamus requested as he positioned the field glasses for another look.

Worms, they said. Crawling on the hills. Worms.

He sighed, staring, concentrating again. When out hunting,
a man had to look for something that didn't fit. Something
out of place—only then would he spot his quarry: the deer,
elk, or antelope. Something that didn't quite fit.

Worms! By the bloody saints—it looked like a small cluster of bleeming worms!

"I see 'em, old man," he breathlessly declared to Rowland
without taking his eyes off the distant sight.

He had yet to spot any lodges, but hell, it didn't matter!
They saw the smoke, and there was the pony herd! Not a
big one, but no other band was going to be out hunting in
this country.

Rowland asked with a grim countenance, "So you see their
herd?"

"I saw the worms, yeah," Donegan replied as he took the
glasses from his face and smiled at the squawman.

"Smoke too?"

"Damn right. That too."

Rowland handed the field glasses back to Jackson, quickly
glancing at the position of the sun as it neared midsky.
"Smoke means they ain't moving for the day, Donegan. And
they got them ponies out to graze."

"They're still in camp," Seamus agreed. "Means they'll be
in camp 'least till morning—"

"*If* Miles can get this army anywhere close to that village
by sunup," Rowland interrupted with a doubtful wag of his
head. "We got some ground to cover afore then."

"I'll lay my month's wages this bunch'll do it," Donegan declared. "Just like Mackenzie done it."

For a moment Rowland chewed on his chapped upper lip. "But you 'member: Mackenzie had more men along when he come to jump that camp, Irishman. Even then, we rode in after sunup and got ourselves pinned down all day—"

"Miles is gonna get the job done, Bill," he shut off the squawman.

"Leastways," Rowland sighed deeply, "this time my wife don't have no family in there."

Reading the struggle there on the squawman's face, Seamus laid a hand on Rowland's shoulder. "Just remember, there can't be much of a fight come sunup. Only enough for them sojurs to capture the village and run off the herd."

"Said you'd bet your month's wages on it, eh?"

Asked to show his cards, Donegan swallowed. "Yeah, I will." And he held out his hand to shake hands with the grinning squawman. "Now, what say we get back down to tell Miles what his Cheyenne found?"

When Donegan announced the news, the colonel was beside himself, galloping on ahead of the column for that spot where the other scouts were waiting so he could confirm the presence of the enemy village for himself.

"By Jupiter, all I can claim to see is a fine mist, or cloud, against those hills," Miles admitted as he squinted into the distance. Holding out his hand to his adjutant, he took the field glasses from Lieutenant Baird.

Everyone waited breathlessly while the colonel studied the countryside.

"That's smoke all right!" he eventually cheered, clearly exuberant at this discovery. "And there! I see the herd! Their ponies!"

"Rowland and me, we figure they're laying in camp today," Donegan explained.

"Then we'll approach under cover of darkness," Miles declared. He looked through the glasses again, finally bringing them away from his face to say, "Four or five of you, I want to slip up on the village and learn what you can of their strengths, how the camp is laid out, where the herd is in relation to the tipis. Every intelligence you can bring back to me."

"I'll take White Bull and Brave Wolf," Seamus suggested,

turning at the sound of some hooves clattering up the hillside toward them. It was Bruguier. "I'll take Johnny too. Jackson here, and those two scouts. That should be enough to spy on them, bring you a count of the lodges so we can figure their fighting strength."

A clearly anxious Miles gazed through his field glasses a moment more, then said, "I can't emphasize enough that you must not be spotted, that you cannot alert the village."

"We won't, General," Donegan promised.

The colonel sighed and straightened. "Very well. I'll continue on upstream a few miles with the column, closing some of the gap on the village before we go into camp by the middle of the afternoon to await your return."

Nodding at Bruguier, waving at the rest, Donegan sawed his reins to the left. "C'mon, fellas. Let's go have ourselves a look at Lame Deer's camp."

Johnny Bruguier turned slightly in the saddle to listen to the squawman named Rowland talk with the Shahiyela holy man named White Bull, able to understand only some of what the two said as their words fell so fast about him.

"White Bull says this here is called Fat Horse Creek," Rowland explained. "What his people call it. Got its name because it's a favorite camping spot in the spring. Grass grows tall, ponies grow fat."

"This creek flows into the Rosebud?" Donegan asked.

"On down from the village a little ways," Rowland stated.

The seven of them lay on their bellies atop the lip of a ridge northeast of the camp, concealed in shadow and stunted cedar.

Then the Irishman said, "Bill—have your Cheyenne split up and go get as close to the camp as they can. Have 'em find out where the ponies are put out to graze. And tell 'em to count the lodges."

As Rowland turned to the Shahiyela, Johnny bellied over beside Donegan. "You want me stay here with you?"

"Yeah. We'll wait till them others come back."

Laying there with the Irishman and the two young half-breeds, Bruguier found himself watching the sun fall off mid-sky and slip rapidly for the west, hoping the others would get back before dark.

"I think the whites call this Big Muddy Creek," he declared out of the clear blue.

"Big Muddy?"

"Some white folks call it just the Muddy. If this is the one I heard tell about when I was in the Hills," Bruguier continued, "Goes into the Rosebud down there where the valley gets a little wider."

"But the Rosebud's a clear stream," Donegan said.

Johnny nodded, grinning. "Soon we know if this is the Big Muddy, eh?"

"Yeah, we'll know soon enough."

For a long time none of them talked, not uttering another word while they waited for the Cheyenne to return. The sun had set by the time the warriors slipped back up the ridge through a brush-covered draw to slip in among the white men and half-breeds lying there in the tall grass. White Bull spoke in hushed tones to Rowland as the air cooled and the last of day's light slanted off the chiseled, reddish sandstone bluffs.

"White Bull says he only counted thirty-eight lodges," the squawman explained.

"There's more than that in there," Donegan whispered harshly.

"Maybe he didn't see 'em all," Rowland defended. Then he turned to White Bull to talk again in the warrior's tongue. "He allows that maybe he didn't see 'em all—but what he did see, he counted."

"There's gotta be nearly twice that many," the Irishman said. "What with all them ponies too."

White Bull was talking to Rowland, motioning here and there with his arm, stabbing a palm with one finger on his other hand.

"He says there's two bands of horses," the squawman translated. "Small herd on this side of the creek. But it must've been the bunch we seen this morning what's on the other side. Farther away from the camp."

"East?" Donegan asked.

After Rowland spoke quietly with White Bull, the white man confirmed, "East. Upstream a ways." He started scooting backwards beside the holy man.

"Where you going?" Donegan asked.

The squawman said, "I think I'll take White Bull and go have myself a real close look at that village."

*   *   *

Near the Painted Rocks* White Bull led Long Knife out of
the brush and waded across the Roseberry, quickly disappearing again in the thick vegetation of a coulee that took
them up the heights where the pines would hide them again.
From twilight's shadows, the holy man gazed back downstream at the tall spires of those sacred rocks where ancient
ones had carved their history. This was a place of great
power, great mystery to both the *Ohmeseheso* and Lakota
who visited the valley every summer.

While some would say in the winters to come that he had
committed a great wrong by guiding for the Bear Coat's soldiers, White Bull knew he was doing what was best for his
Northern People. This war had to stop, and the killing must
end. He had to do all he could to see that what these bad
Lakota did would never be blamed upon White Bull's people.

Inside, this holy man of forty winters still stung at the
shame heaped upon him by Lame Deer and all the others
who called him a woman to surrender to the *ve-ho-e* soldiers
at Tongue River. Oh, how he wanted to see Lame Deer's
face when he was captured and made a prisoner after many
of his people were killed in the coming fight. Then he would
ask the Lakota chief, Which of us has done the best for our
people?

On the breeze tickling his nostrils that afternoon, White
Bull could smell the smoke rising from that camp. They were
cooking meat.

Earlier in their approach to the village, he and the squawman had come across a few gut-piles, along with the remains
of elk and antelope carcasses Lakota hunters had butchered
before returning to their camp. What slivers of meat had
been left on the bones hadn't had much chance to dry. Recent kills. The hunters were confident they would not be discovered. Or if they were, they were certain they would never
be disturbed.

---

*What the Cheyenne called today's Deer Medicine Rocks on
the upper Rosebud

"Look! There!" Long Knife whispered. He pointed into the mid-distance toward Fat Horse Creek.

By then the sun had disappeared behind the ridge. The string of riders they spotted were making long shadows across the tall grass. The horsemen led many ponies laden with bloody quarters of meat.

"Buffalo?"

White Bull nodded. "I think so, yes. Big meat. Must be buffalo. They have been out hunting."

Long Knife dragged the back of his hand across his mouth. White Bull knew just that feeling in a man's belly—that hunger for the rich, red meat when you had eaten nothing but the white man's beans and bread, and the poor meat of his pig or cow, for so long you had almost forgotten just how good gnawing on a buffalo bone could be.

"Their camp is near," he told the squawman. Rowland nodded in agreement. "We see the smoke, over there. Where the riders are coming back with their meat."

"Should we see how close we can get to the camp?"

Instead of speaking, White Bull gestured and they both moved out on foot, leading their horses through the trees along the back of the ridge to conceal themselves. Soon they crossed the trail of the buffalo hunters as they were returning to the village. And a ways beyond that, the two of them came to a narrow freshet spilling down the hillside. They drank their fill of the freezing water, then let their ponies nuzzle in the stream.

When the muted light once again chilled the air around them, the two dismounted again.

"We must crawl up there and look down," Long Knife whispered there in the shadows of the trees. "The village has to be right below us."

"Both of us cannot leave our horses," White Bull replied. "One of us must stay and hold them while the other climbs that rocky point to have a look. If we leave our horses, someone may take them away."

"All right," Long Knife agreed with a sigh, reaching inside his coat. "You must go."

The squawman pulled out a small tablet of paper and the stub of a wooden pencil.

"What is this?" White Bull asked as he took the tablet and pencil.

"Take these. And every time you see a lodge in the village,

make a mark on a page. When you get back here to the horses, I will add them up for you."

Stuffing the small tablet under his belt, White Bull clamped the pencil between his teeth and set out up the hill in a crouch. Once he reached the top, the woodsmoke slapped him in the face, and the distant smells of cooking meat made his belly rumble with hunger. From there he could see only some of the lodges. Then the holy man spotted a rocky outcrop where he might have a better view without being seen by those below.

Hunkering there on that high place among the scrub and boulders, White Bull began to count. When he had counted as many lodges as he had fingers, he took the pencil from his teeth and made a mark. Again he counted all his fingers and made a second, then a third mark. But the next time he had two fingers left over on one hand. So below the three marks he made eight smaller marks he would explain to Long Knife.

"That makes thirty-eight," the squawman said when White Bull had returned and handed over the tablet.

"We go back and find the Bear Coat. Tell him the size of this village is smaller than the half-breed White said it was when he visited it," White Bull explained.

"Wait," Long Knife said. "I must write a note to the Bear Coat about this."

When the squawman finished he stuffed the pencil and tablet away in his pocket and reached for the reins to his horse. "Let's go."

"Yes," White Bull said. "Night is coming fast."

Chapter 34

6 May 1877

"Them soldiers gotta come now," Johnny grumbled suddenly, having watched the fall of the sun and growing more nervous as time ground past. "General wants to jump the camp come sunup, they gotta come now."

"Hush," the Irishman told him. "They'll be back soon."

"You see that?" Culbertson asked, pointing.

"You mean them Lakota running races over there?" replied Robert Jackson.

"If they're having horse races over there, Johnny," the Irishman said, "they sure as heaven ain't worried about no sojurs coming."

Bruguier wagged his head. "But them soldiers won't have time to get here by morning."

Culbertson sighed and smacked his lips, sniffing the wind that hinted at rain. "I can smell them cooking buffalo. My, my!"

"Me too," Jackson added, drinking in the chill evening breeze with his eyes closed.

Hump jabbed an elbow in Bruguier's rib and said in Lakota, "Every afternoon after the ponies are brought in close to camp, they run races. This village does not know the soldiers are near, Big Leggings."

"You aren't worried about the soldiers getting here soon enough?"

Half-closing his eyes, the *Mnikowoju* chief replied, "Right now all I'm worried about is my empty belly. How I would like to have some of that buffalo meat they have killed today: a few fat-back ribs, hot from the coals and dripping red juices. This soldier food we have been eating since surrendering on Elk River, I say it is no good for a fighting man. Why, I am growing weaker by the day!"

Robert Jackson understood enough of that Lakota to laugh along with Hump, then said, "Tomorrow, maybe, we go down there with the Bear Coat and make peace with Lame Deer, and he will invite us to feast with him, eh?"

With a grim chuckle, Hump replied, "Lame Deer has vowed to his spirits that he will never make peace with the *wasicu*! If you eat any of his food tomorrow, it will be over his dead body."

Growing more and more upset that none of the others were concerned about how long it was taking White Bull and the squawman to return, Johnny scrambled to one knee. "Them two been killed! I know it," he snarled. "Now them Lakota come to kill us. They know we're here."

"Just relax," Donegan said, putting a hand on the half-breed's shoulder. "That village don't know we're—"

The snap of a limb nearly made Johnny jump out of his skin. The rest of them flung themselves to their bellies, their weapons out, cocked—everyone quiet as field mice and watching the twilit gloom for some movement.

Suddenly a faint, shrill whistle came from the darkness around that tight grove of lodgepole beyond them.

Donegan gestured to one of the Cheyenne and put his fingertips to his lips. The warrior understood, returning the whistle.

Bruguier's heart was pounding like it had only a few times before—when he had killed that man at Standing Rock, when he had stolen the horse in the Black Hills, and when he had gone riding into the Cheyenne's village back in February.

They waited, and watched . . . until the shapes and sounds took form out of the gloom. It was the Cheyenne holy man and the interpreter named Rowland.

"You get close to the camp?" demanded the Irishman as he stood and brushed the front of his canvas britches.

"We saw it. White Bull here counted lodges."

"We better get word back to Miles," Donegan said.

"I wrote out the number here," Rowland explained. "The count." He held it out for Donegan.

"Good you done that," Donegan declared. He looked over the rest of them, then suddenly dropped to one knee before one of the young half-breeds. "Jackson—I'll wager you're the smallest of us here."

"What's that got to do with bringing them soldiers up?" Culbertson asked, rising onto an elbow on the far side of Jackson.

"Bob here's got him a strong horse too," the Irishman continued. "Because of that, I figure he's the one what's got the best chance to get back to Miles on the double, bring up them sojurs quick as they can in the dark and get set for the attack by first light."

Jackson pushed himself up to a sitting position, straightened his pistol belt, and dragged his revolver out so he could spin the cylinder, seeing that every chamber carried a live round. "I'm on my way, Irishman."

"Ride low, friend," Donegan warned as he passed the piece of paper to the half-breed, who tucked it away in a pocket. "And bring up them sojurs quick."

Johnny watched Jackson scrunch back through the grass and brush in a labored crouch. Together the group listened after the young half-breed disappeared over the top of the timbered slope, hearing the faint snort of a horse, then the pad of hoofbeats as the animal headed off into the distance, carrying its rider north for the waiting soldier chief and his troops.

Brave Wolf whispered something, then Rowland interpreted. "He wondered if the half-blood was a good one to ride all that way back to the soldiers alone."

"He don't think Jackson's gonna make it?" Donegan inquired.

"Maybeso he's worried the half-blood won't make it back to bring them soldiers up," the squawman clarified.

For a long moment the Irishman stared at the top of that hill where Jackson had disappeared. Then he turned to gaze at the shadows of the enemy village in the valley. "What you think, Johnny?"

Quietly, Bruguier said, "He'll make it."

"Me too, Johnny," Donegan affirmed. "And so will Miles's boys. They'll be here by morning."

Now all they had to do was wait, Bruguier figured. Wait here in the dark, almost within pissing distance of all those Sioux who wanted Johnny's scalp.

Not long after dispatching his scouts to reconnoiter the enemy village, the infantry trudged up to rejoin the rest of Nelson A. Miles's command. After a brief rest for those foot-weary doughboys, the colonel put them all on the trail once more. For the next four hours they labored nonstop through an extremely rugged stretch of territory, battling steep slopes that dropped precipitously to the banks of the Rosebud on one side or the other, forcing frequent crossings of the snow-swollen creek. That battle against the terrain was clearly taking its toll on both man and animal alike.

Just past 2:00 p.m. that Sunday, Miles admitted he had to halt the march to recoup his forces. Having reached the top of a high, pine-covered ridge where he had himself a panoramic view of more than a hundred square miles of countryside, the colonel ordered the men into bivouac for four hours. They put their stock out to graze on the tall grass, then fell out on both sides of a narrow creek that spilled down the north side of the ridge where it wasn't very likely that roving hunters from the village would spot his command.

He had heard tales of Custer's ability to sleep anywhere, anytime, under any conditions, even when approaching the enemy. But for the life of him, Nelson Miles couldn't even sit still that long afternoon. Try as he might, the colonel wasn't able to make himself as comfortable as those who fell asleep where they landed, snoring away in the sleep of the innocent. Instead, Miles lumbered back and forth, walking up and down the stream, sometimes clambering back up to the high ground to have himself another look at the country to the south. Hoping to sight the returning scouts as the sun fell.

At six o'clock, he figured they had waited long enough. Four hours of grazing for the animals. Four hours of rations and rest for the men. From here on out, there might well be no halts until the battle was enjoined and victory was theirs.

"Mr. Baird!" he called out, lunging up the gentle slope toward his staff.

"General?"

"Officers' call, Mr. Baird!"

Edward Ball, cavalry battalion commander, trotted up at that moment. "We're moving out, General?"

"We've got an appointment at sunrise, Captain."

As soon as the rest of his cavalry and infantry officers had joined him that dusk, while the last rays of the sun faded from the slope, the colonel announced that he was taking both Ball's Second Cavalry and Lieutenant Casey's mounted infantry ahead with him to cover more of the intervening ground while awaiting the return of the scouts. They were to strip their commands down to only one pack-mule for each company, that animal burdened with two thousand rounds of carbine ammunition. In addition, company sergeants were to see that each soldier was supplied two days' rations carried in their saddlebags or haversacks.

Captain Dickey was to follow along with all possible dispatch with the three remaining companies of infantry and the remainder of the mules.

"In the dark, your foot soldiers may well cover the ground almost as quickly as we will, Captain," Miles declared. "Good luck to you."

Dickey saluted as the colonel took the reins of his horse from Baird and swung into the saddle. The animal pranced away to the head of the march whcrc the officers set their outfits into motion, departing in a column of twos.

Night quickly squeezed down around them, and once more the cavalry was forced to string itself out in single file, making a slow and agonizing crawl across the landscape. Then just past nine o'clock, Miles suddenly decided he needed to halt there in the darkness to await the scouts.

He was worried. Perhaps the trackers had been caught out in the open, discovered, forced to make a run for it, or were pinned down and unable to get word to him. That could be the only reason. After all, engineering officer Long informed him they had covered more than fifteen miles since leaving the foot soldiers behind. Something closer to sixteen miles. And that was more than the scouts' estimate of the distance to the village that very morning!

Something was wrong, terribly wrong. The scouts should have returned by now, and his command should have drawn close to the village after covering all that distance.

Throwing out a tight ring of pickets and assuring that their horses were hidden from discovery, as well as forbidding any fires, even the lighting of pipes because of just how close they might well be to the enemy—Miles tried to sleep.

Unable to rest out of fear for his trackers, the colonel instead sat in the cold mist and darkness with some of the cavalry officers, listening as the hours crawled by to the low sounds of conversation all around them, the murmur creeping up and down this creek that spilled eastward to tumble into the Rosebud. From time to time he heard a man snoring—jealous of that ability to nap here on the precipice of battle—

"Rider coming in, General!"

Miles bolted to his feet. "What the hell time is it, Mr. Baird?"

"Can't for sure read my watch—"

"Read the damned thing!"

"M-midnight, General."

Miles blinked and swallowed the taste of gall strong at the back of his throat. Less than six hours until sunup.

If this scout had left for the return trip near sunset, at about 6:00 p.m., then it had taken him six hours to get here from the enemy village. Damn! Miles realized that meant he and his men would have to cover that same ground in the dark in less than six hours to be in position for the attack.

As he lunged forward toward the sound of the voices and curious soldiers rising from the cold ground, the colonel hoped—no—he prayed it was the Irishman. Surely that Donegan was one man who could lead them on to the village in this rainy, coal-cotton night.

But the hope went out of him as he saw the rider loom out of the mist atop his horse. A slight figure that wearily kicked a leg over the saddlehorn and plopped flat-footed in his moccasins to the ground, stepping close enough for Miles to see his face in the dim starshine.

"Jackson."

"Yessir, General," Robert Jackson responded as he saw the soldier chief striding up. "May I have some water for my horse, sir?"

"By all means," Miles declared, wheeling on the others.

"Someone—take the man's horse and see that it's watered." Then he turned back to the young half-breed. "I was expecting your group back earlier."

"Sorry, General," he apologized with a gulp. "Turns out the village is farther away than the Cheyennes thought, farther'n we figured from what they said when they first sighted it this morning."

Disappointment was never plainer than it was at that moment on the face of Colonel Nelson A. Miles.

"F-farther away?" the officer croaked.

"Yessir," he answered. "I started back here at sunset."

"I was afraid of that," Miles groaned. "The rest, they stayed behind?"

"The Irishman, that one named Donegan, he sent me back alone," Jackson explained in a strong voice, drawing himself up. "Said I was the one small enough to make it back quick, since my horse was likely the strongest."

"Yes, I imagine that was a wise decision on the Irishman's part," the soldier chief agreed. "So, tell me—you saw with your own eyes what we're up against?"

"We did, sir. The old white man, and one of them Cheyenne went down the hills to get closer to the village than where we was hanging back," Robert began to relate his story. "They come back and that medicine man—"

"White Bull?"

"That's the one, General. He said he counted thirty-eight lodges. But the Irishman said there had to be more'n that."

"I'll go with Donegan on that one too," Miles echoed. "And the herd?"

"Two of 'em, sir. One on the north side of the stream, and the other south. Both on the far side of the camp from where your men will come in on their charge."

Miles clapped his hands once. "We'll make a sweep around and seize both herds, then they'll have to make their escape on foot." He loomed over the younger man. "Now, tell me squarely: can you get my cavalry back there by first light?"

Jackson felt his pulse leap, racing now at his temples. So weary, so damned weary. He quickly glanced from Miles to the other faces that had crowded close in that long, breathless moment while his lungs cried out for air. Robert gasped, swallowing down some of the mist and that night breeze tousling his long, black hair.

"Yes, sir. I can get your men back there before dawn," he vowed. "How fast can them soldiers be ready to follow me?"

"You grab yourself something to eat, Jackson," Miles instructed. "Get yourself a long drink from the stream there. I'll have these horse soldiers ready to march in less than an hour."

As it turned out, those troopers weren't ready to mount up until it was nearly 2:00 a.m.

Having stripped his attack force to light marching order, the colonel ordered that every man rid himself of unnecessary weight, then lash down every canteen, tin cup, or carbine sling that might slap or clang. It promised to be a very grueling march to make it to the village by sunrise.

"If the terrain permits," Miles instructed his officers, "we'll be in double time, gentlemen. All haste, all haste! Our enemy awaits."

As Miles finally climbed into the saddle and motioned for Jackson to lead them out, it was plain as sun the soldier chief could smell those Sioux in his nostrils the way a mountain puma winded his quarry unawares. Robert started them into the inky darkness as the mist stiffened, no more than a few stars pricking the black canopy behind them to the north.

"Mr. Jackson!" Miles called out right behind the young scout a few minutes later. "Pick up the pace!"

Robert nodded and without a word tugged the hat down on his head as those first cold drops of a chilling spring rain lanced out of the clouds, stinging his face as he tried to dip the brim of his hat against the onslaught.

If Miles wanted him to ride faster, then he'd do just that. Jackson hoped these soldiers could keep up. They had miles and miles to go, and a storm to fight now.

But by damn, he vowed, Robert Jackson would have these pony soldiers banging at Lame Deer's lodgedoor by first light!

Chapter 35

7 May 1877

As the hours crawled by and darkness deepened like the black blight on that final potato crop he had grubbed as a youngster in old Eire, Seamus grew all the more convinced he should have been the one to make that ride back to the column himself.

Not that Bob Jackson didn't have a heap of trail savvy. Not that he worried that the half-breed wouldn't make it to Miles with his report. Just that the young man might not be able to convince the general that the soldiers would have to double-time it if they were going to make it here by dawn.

No telling what these Sioux were going to do come sunrise. Those lodges might come down and they'd put to the trail, with Miles's column playing catch-up again. Especially if that camp suspected the army was close at hand.

Truth be, young Jackson might not have it in his power to convince the gruff, single-minded general that his soldiers had to be whipped and prodded into hurrying.

Seamus didn't want to consider the alternative: dragging this God-bleeming war out any longer.

They'd be caught an hour or two short of closing the noose around this last bunch of hard cases, letting the enemy slip right through their fingers. The sooner Miles and his men got the hostiles rounded up and driven back toward their agencies, the sooner Seamus could get south to Laramie, barter

for some more horses and fixings, then light out for the Montana gold-diggings with Samantha and little Colin.

Ten years late.

Beginning with that hot, dusty, parched July day on a bare,
windswept ridgetop above the Crazy Woman Fork, Donegan
had been staring at these Sioux and Cheyenne warriors down
the barrel of one rifle or another for more than a decade.
But now he could take Samantha and the boy north to Fetterman, up to Reno Crossing, on past the Pineys where Fort
Phil Kearny once stood, up to the crossing of the Bighorn
where he had endured a winter, a spring, then a fateful summer at Fort C.F. Smith. From there he would strike out north
across the fabled Yellowstone to reach the diggings at a place
called Last Chance Gulch—the mother lode those Montana
miners had described in rich and glorious hues late last summer.

To hold a small fortune in his hands at long, long last. How
it made his mouth go dry here and now in the cold darkness
as the wind soughed through the pines stabbing the under-
belly of the night sky as he lay on this bony ridge overlooking
the creek that the trail-breakers called the Big Muddy. Likely
he'd grub and sweat and grumble as the aging muscles in his
back complained—but he'd be able to buy Samantha more
dresses and another bonnet, along with all those things she
had been denied these past two years, since he dragged her
away from her sister in Texas, dragged her north from the
Staked Plain, dragged her right into another Indian war.

Sam and Colin deserved his very best, and Seamus swore
he'd claw at that Montana ground with his bare hands if he
had to just so he could give them all they were entitled to in
life. He'd eat salt-beef and moldy hardtack for a month of
Sundays if God would only grant him a little pay dirt. If God
would just smile down on this poor man wanting all the better for his little family.

After slap-dark as the clouds rolled in, his belly began to
rumble. Seamus crawled back to the horses, but didn't find
anything in his saddle pouches. Returning to the ridgetop, he
settled in among the others again, yanked off a glove between his teeth, and scratched around in his pockets. The
moment he touched it, he realized what he'd found.

From the bottom of that big patch pocket on his canvas
mackinaw, the Irishman pulled out the rat's-nest of soft yarn

just as the sky began to mist. Unable to see it in the cloudy darkness, he held the yarn under his nose, drinking in the fragrance of it. He imagined he could smell her, smell Sam's long-fingered white hands as she tied the yarn in knots around the brown paper and box. Sinking to his side as the mist became heavier and began to blow on gusts of wind, Seamus rubbed the yarn against his damp cheek, just as she might brush her fingertips down that very same skin.

And he began to weep in the cold.

He kept thinking on Sam and Colin, unable to sleep like the rest who dozed uncomfortably on the wet ground, curled fetally beneath the low branches of the cedar and scrub pine, out of the rain. He listened to the soft, wheezing breath of that soggy night, wrestling with his growing apprehension, until he knew he could struggle with it no more and must be on his feet, in the saddle—

"Bill!" he whispered harshly, kneeling over the man through the soppy grass.

The squawman jerked up, water sluicing off his hat brim. Seamus clamped a vice of a hand on Rowland's shoulder, sensing how the old man's muscles tensed.

When they relaxed, Rowland sighed, "You hear something?"

Donegan released his grip and wagged his head. "I'm going back. Can't wait no longer to know what's taking 'em so long."

The older man stared up at the thickening storm clouds, looked this way and that, finding neither the moon nor any constellation that would give him some idea as to the time. "How long I been sleeping?"

"Long enough I hope," Seamus replied as he stood. "You keep watch now."

Rowland scrambled to his feet too, held out his bony hand. "You be careful."

They shook and Donegan promised, "I'll be back by sunrise."

Then he was at the side of the claybank, slipping the bridle back into its mouth, yanking the cinch tight as he could on the mare, dragging down the stirrup fender and legging up. He was swinging the horse away even as his right leg was clearing the cantle, dropping down in the saddle and stuffing that right boot into the stirrup as the animal bolted off. Perhaps it sensed his anxiousness.

Seamus worried not so much about Bob Jackson or Nelson Miles or any of those soldiers hurrying their way right now, as he worried that if the column didn't make it back to the Big Muddy by dawn then all of his prayers would go unanswered for another month, another campaign. Another year of Samantha left to wait back at Laramie for a husband who was off doing all that he could to clear a path for his family right through the middle of the Sioux and Cheyenne's last hunting ground.

"Hep!" he husked into the claybank's ear as he leaned forward. "Hep! Hep-a!" The animal rocked into a rolling gait once down onto the bottomland.

Out of the night loomed boulders and monstrous stands of brush through which he weaved until he spotted a break in the valley wall. On the far side would be the Rosebud itself. Up, up he urged the horse as its hooves clattered across loose sandstone shale. Its iron shoes began to lose their grip as it scraped and clawed—

Slamming his boots onto the shifting ground, Seamus grunted. He landed on both feet, catching his balance on the loose rock, then looped the reins around one hand and clucked at the mare to follow him to the high ground. He was breathing so damned hard, feeling the reluctance of the animal at the end of those long reins, hearing its own dry, ragged breathing, that he wasn't sure if it really was worth the struggle by the time he reached the top of the ridge. Going cross-country like this to save miles and minutes took near everything out of a man—

Then he heard a sound as he stood there in the wind, bent at the waist heaving, sucking air, gasping like the mare beside him.

Squinting into the night, trying to see something in the misty storm, Seamus wondered if the wind were playing him the fool. Or did he just want this war to be over so badly that he—

There!

By the Virgin Mary—they were coming!

Damned if Miles and his cavalry weren't on the march already!

Down the slope, there in the valley of the Rosebud.

Quickly he turned, feeling the stab of pain in his back muscles as he did, looking to the east. No sign yet of any graying beneath those storm clouds. They might yet make it if he could hurry those horse soldiers on down the Rosebud and up those few miles of the Big Muddy by dawn.

Faint shreds of disembodied voices began to drift up from below, cold and spare against the bare rock of those timeless ridges. Orders were issued first, followed by curses as the word was passed back along the column. And finally the reassuring clatter of iron shoes scraping creekbottom stone. They were crossing the Rosebud to the east. Good, Donegan thought as he gripped the horn and heaved himself into the saddle, shorted his hold on the reins and jabbed the small brass spurs into the claybank's flanks, urging her down the slope toward the creek.

It didn't take all that much convincing—thirsty as the mare was by now, fully ready for a drink after that blow atop the ridge.

"Who goes there!"

"A friend!"

The trio of startled soldiers loomed out of the heaving mist as Seamus bolted into sight at the edge of their noisy gathering—the men watering horses on the bank, tightening cinches, chewing on hard-bread and cheap army tobacco.

"It's the scout!"

The mist was tapering off, perhaps the clouds were blowing over. Donegan asked, "Where's the general?"

"I'm over here!"

Out of the black emerged a half-dozen men strung out behind that big one in the center. At his elbow stood the slight, dark-skinned half-breed with the long straight hair and the old, shapeless, rain-soaked hat pulled down on his head.

"You made it, Jackson!" He stepped up past Miles to offer his hand first to the youngster.

"Is there trouble, Irishman?" the colonel demanded, grabbing the tall scout's upper arm. "Where are the others?"

"They're safe," Seamus declared. "But I come to say you've got some miles left to go."

Nodding, Miles pointed to the east. "We've stopped here only to give the animals a little water. No longer than that—"

"We're going to have to ride hard to make it, General."

The officer's lips closed and tightened into a long, grim

line of sheer determination. His eyes narrowed just before he spoke, "We'll make it, Irishman." Turning to his adjutant, Miles said, "Tell the battalion commander he has five minutes to finish watering up the stock." Then he wheeled on Donegan. "We're close?"

"You're damned close, General," Seamus smiled, feeling the sense of hope take wing in him once more. "These horse sojurs gonna be there by dawn."

"You heard the man, Lieutenant!" Miles bellowed at Baird who was still standing there, mouth agape. "Give the battalion commander my compliments and let's get this outfit moving!"

Minutes later as the colonel himself was climbing into the saddle, Seamus glanced over the officer's shoulder at the horizon.

"General, look."

Miles turned, some of the cavalry officers turning to look east as well. The sky was graying there beneath those swollen rain clouds.

"Sunup's coming," Jackson whispered.

Twisting back around to look at Donegan as the Irishman swung into the saddle, patting the neck of his own big chestnut warhorse, the colonel asked, "How many miles?"

"A handful. Maybe more."

"Lead us out, Irishman." And he flung an arm forward. "Bring them along, Captain Ball! Column of twos—on the double, goddammit! On the goddamn, ever-living double!"

Dawn was tinting the eastern sky to a bloody rose as Seamus signaled a halt to the cadre of officers riding hard on his tailroot.

Afoot, Robert Jackson lunged onto the flat near Donegan's big claybank, yanked there for the last two miles by the fierce grip he had on the tail of Private Charles Shrenger's mount.

"What happened to your horse?" the Irishman asked in a harsh whisper as he brought the claybank around, while the officers clattered to a halt.

Bent at his waist, Jackson cocked his head and peered up sidelong at the mounted scout, huffing breathlessly, "G-gave . . . out."

"How far back?"

"Long . . . long ways."

"Should've hollered for me," Seamus declared, at the same time angry and sympathetic with the young man. "I'd give you a ride behind me."

Slowly Jackson straightened, still wheezing like a winded animal. He was drenched in sweat, droplets trickling off the end of his nose, his wool britches soaked up past his knees from the damp brush they had plowed through in the last handful of miles. "I knowed I didn't w-wanna . . . be caught behind our lines where the Lakota might j-jump me. So I just called out . . . to this s-soldier here," and he gasped, jabbing a finger at Shrenger.

Miles's orderly nodded. "This scout started out hanging onto my stirrup as he run along aside me," Shrenger explained. "But after more'n a mile he was getting damned tired of that so he grabbed onto my horse's tail for the last gallop in here."

"I get left behind when the fight starts," Jackson growled, "them Sioux find me alone and chew me up."

"Damn," cursed Donegan, wagging his head as he pulled free the straps to one of his saddlepockets, dragging out a canteen he handed down to the half-breed scout. "Here, drink your fill. The first dance of the ball is about to begin."

Up in those heights to their left, William Rowland and the others had waited out the rainy night. Surely from there, those scouts could see the cavalry column as it stabbed out of the creek valley and came clattering to a halt in the new day's first light.

As Donegan tore the big, wet hat from his head and began to wave it at the end of his arm, the sky dribbled its last, the constant patter diminishing in those seconds as if the sky had just sighed itself into a sudden silence. He wasn't sure if the scouts had seen him as he dragged the hat onto his head and turned back to the head of the column with young Jackson.

Because Muddy Creek seesawed back and forth across the narrow valley, he had been repeatedly forced to ford the stream, with the horse soldiers following at every crossing. Now the troopers were coming to a halt on the north bank, upstream from these last of the Sioux, these hostiles who had dared the Bear Coat to catch them.

"General—you're within a mile of the outskirts of the camp."

"You said the village lies in a wide horseshoe?" Miles asked.

"That's right. A few lodges downstream are on the other side of the creek. But from here you won't have to make another ford."

Standing in the stirrups, Miles twisted about, his raspy voice raised slightly. "Bring up the battalion commander and his company captains."

The tension was something real, something tangible, there among those soldiers as Donegan grew aware of the first hint of woodsmoke. He turned to gaze down the valley. In the growing light, he thought he could spot the slowly rising pall of smoke, not near close enough to see any lodgepoles, much less any of the tipis. But make no mistake about it: that gray smoke was lifting far enough from the brushy valley floor to tint itself with streaks of vivid, newborn red as the sun continued its own climb.

He jerked about to watch the cavalry officers among their men as the ranks came front into line, spreading both left and right within the confines of the lush undergrowth bordering the north bank of the Big Muddy and the base of the jagged ridge.

"*Epa-havee-seeve!*"

Turning with a start at that Cheyenne greeting, Donegan watched White Bull and Brave Wolf slip out of the twelve-foot-tall willow thicket on horseback. Donegan raised his hand, smiling as he spotted Rowland on their tail-roots, the others close behind the squawman.

The group came to a halt just as Miles loped up with a big grin.

"By damn, you did get back by sunup, Irishman!" Rowland cried, his eyes darting back over the cavalry forming up.

"I give you my word, Bill," he said, then nodded his head back at the Cheyenne warriors. "What'd White Bull say to me?"

Rowland smiled, "He said, 'It is a good day.' "

"I s'pose it will be a damned good day now," Seamus agreed.

Dragging the back of his hand across his wet, hairless face, Rowland explained, "White Bull and the others—they wanted to get down here quick to tell the Bear Coat the women in that camp are starting breakfast fires."

"The camp is waking up?" Miles growled, glancing to the east at the brightening sky just then beginning to dome over the creek valley. "Captain Ball!" he bellowed angrily, turning back to his cavalry battalion. "See that your men are ordered to spare the women and children in our attack. I'll have Bruguier and the Cheyenne demand their surrender the moment we make the charge."

"*If* this bunch'll surrender," Donegan declared.

Both of the Cheyenne said something sharply to the squawman.

With an impatient gesture, flinging his arm at the village, Rowland bellowed, "General—White Bull and Brave Wolf say it's time for the Bear Coat's soldiers to strike!"

Growing nettled at the interpreter's agitation, Miles wheeled on his officers. "Mr. Casey, form up twenty of your Cheyennes over there with your mounted infantry. You will be the spearhead of the attacking column. Tell your scouts they'll be going after the herd."

"The herd, sir!" The young lieutenant saluted. "Yes, sir, General!" then reined away, gesturing at his warrior scouts.

The colonel wheeled on the cavalry officers. "Mr. Jerome, isn't it?"

"Yes, General Miles," said the young officer, urging his horse forward a few yards, coming to a halt close to Miles. "Second lieutenant."

The colonel asked, "H Company?"

"Right again, sir."

"You will follow on the heels of Mr. Casey's scouts, charging through the village, continuing downstream until you reach the herd. Together you will stampede them, drive them off so the hostiles can't recover them. Once that's done, you'll be in charge of those captured ponies. Your men are to secure the herd until I decide on their disposition."

"Very good, General," Lovell H. Jerome answered. "We're ready to follow Mr. Casey past the village!"

By then the rest of the officer corps had formed a ragged semicircle no more than an arm's length from the colonel, each one of them showing his own brand of anxiousness in these moments before their attack was launched. Kicking at the clumps of grass with a boot-toe, chewing on a lower lip, repeatedly rubbing at the end of a nose, fidgeting with but-

tons or a gunbelt, or re-creasing the shapeless crown of a
rain-soaked slouch hat.

"Captain Tyler," Miles said, taking a step toward the cavalry officer, "you and Captain Wheelan will serve as the attack squadron. As soon as Mr. Jerome and Mr. Casey are
away after the horse herd, you will follow immediately into
the village itself. I'm having your companies F and G ride
out front in the first wave."

"The fighting line, sir?" George L. Tyler asked. "Very
good, General!"

Then the colonel turned to the last of his cavalry commanders. "Captain Norwood, Company L, isn't it?"

"Yes, General."

"I'm going to hold your men in reserve," Miles explained.
"We'll see how things shape up in the first minutes of the
fight, and I'll throw your men in where they are needed."

Randolph Norwood saluted and said, "Yessir."

Now Miles turned to Bruguier. "Johnny, take Hump with
you. The two of you will ride in with Casey's scouts—tell the
people in that village that they will not be harmed if they
surrender. Tell the men their women and children are not in
danger. Remind them that we are attacking because they
have failed to go into their agencies. I want you both to shout
that repeatedly as you ride north through the camp."

"We tell them, General," Bruguier promised.

"Now, go catch up Hump and the two of you report over
to Casey's auxiliaries," Miles ordered.

Donegan watched the half-breed turn to go before he
glanced at Rowland and Culbertson. "General," he called as
he stepped up to the headquarters group, "since you've got
all them Cheyenne going in for the herd, what you intend
for the three of us?"

The colonel's eyes quickly flitted over the other two white
men who had come up to stand some distance behind the
Irishman. "I want you to ride with me. All three of you, Mr.
Donegan."

"Very good," Seamus said, then found himself saluting the
colonel. "Can't speak for them other two, but as for me, I
want to be in there to see for myself that this fight is the last
we'll have in this war with the Sioux."

Chapter 36

Moon of Fat Horses
1877

BY TELEGRAPH

The Russians Preparing to

Cross the Danube.

Investigating the New York

Postoffice Disaster.

DAKOTA.

The Surrender of Crazy Horse.

CHICAGO, May 7.—The official report of the surrender of Crazy Horse puts the whole number of surrendering Indians at 889, of whom 217 were men; 2,000 ponies were also given up, and 117 stand of arms and other firearms are known to be in their possession.

As the Bear Coat turned to take the reins of his horse from one of the little chiefs, White Bull grabbed Long Knife's elbow, spinning the squawman around to face him.

"You must tell the soldier chief I have an idea in my head!"

He was a holy man of the People. He had been given a gift, and that gift was to share what he could see, especially when it was something others could not see.

Sometimes, White Bull knew, a man put his feet on that trail where the Spirits directed, no matter what others might say.

"What? What idea do you have?" Rowland demanded, perturbed at the interruption now as the cavalry was forming up for its charge.

"I think I know a way we can get these soldiers in close enough to surround the village before the Lakota know the soldiers are there."

Long Knife wagged his head. "How are you going to do that?"

"When I was on the rocks yesterday at sunset, counting the lodges and making those marks in your little book," White Bull began to explain to the interpreter, "I saw two little streams coming into Fat Horse Creek from the hills. One reached Fat Horse Creek in the camp, and the other just below it. On that hill across from me—on the far side of the Lakota camp—there are many pines."

"To the east?" asked Long Knife.

"Yes. Tell the Bear Coat I know a way I can lead the soldiers up to that first creek I saw, slip all the way up that stream and over the divide, coming down to the other creek where the cavalry can be waiting to attack. His walking soldiers can charge up the main valley into the camp—"

"Why would the Bear Coat want his cavalry to be up there on the side of that hill?" the squawman interrupted.

"To prevent Lame Deer's people from running away," he explained.

Aghast at that, Long Knife shook his head violently and snarled, "No! I remember the Red Fork Valley fight! Here too we must let those poor people have a chance to get away!"

"Why?" White Bull demanded. "If we surround them and they have nowhere to run, they will have to surrender—warriors and the rest—and we will get them all."

"No! I will not tell the Bear Coat anything of what you've said," Long Knife whispered angrily. "You've brought these soldiers to the village. That's all you needed to do—now stay out of this and let the soldiers finish their job!"

"General Miles!"

He turned at the call from Captain Tyler. Several others in the broad front that was forming up were beginning to point at that hillside closest to the village.

There, he saw: one of the hostiles . . . on horseback.

"Has he seen us?" Nelson demanded as he lunged up to the front of the formation, watching that solitary rider make his way toward the tipis with no apparent haste.

"Sure as the stars in heaven," Seamus Donegan growled. "No way he could miss seeing your sojurs from where he was riding there on the side of the hill."

"A camp guard?"

"Maybe," Johnny Bruguier answered.

"For the life of me I can't figure out why he ain't running for the village," Donegan added.

Miles glanced at the east, saw how the light was growing beneath that swollen rumble of the previous night's rain-clouds. He turned on his heel suddenly and continued repeating the disposition of his troops to Adjutant Baird.

"Private Shrenger," the colonel called to his orderly, handing the soldier his big cream-colored hat. "Bring me my bandanna."

In a moment the young private was back with a huge white bandanna, which Miles folded in half, laid over his head, and knotted in the back. Stepping before the ranks of cavalry now, the colonel proudly explained to the cavalry commanders, "This white bandanna I've tied on my head will show your soldiers that I'm going into the fight with them."

Battalion commander Ball snapped a salute. "The Second Cavalry is proud to have you lead us into the coming fight, General!"

Private Shrenger started to move toward Miles with the colonel's big chestnut as Nelson felt the sour ball of sentiment choke him.

"General—you may want to see this," the Irishman called out.

When Miles stepped close, he looked where Donegan pointed at the edge of the village, and saw that solitary rider had been joined by a few other forms—all of them quickly loading up their horses with bundles. In a matter of moments the small group was on the back of their ponies and hurrying out of camp, heading back toward the hills where the lone rider had first been spotted only minutes before.

"I'm not going to worry about that handful slipping away, especially since they didn't raise an alarm in the camp," Miles told those around him, turning back to his cavalry officers and tucking in the knot on that white bandanna he wore. "Now we have the rest of these fish to fry."

Johnny had never done anything remotely like this.

Swept up, powerless, hurtled along with these soldiers racing right on the hooves of Casey's Shahiyela scouts, Bruguier found the noise of it deafening. Watching these mounted foot soldiers shout and bellow, unable himself to hear much for all the thunder of hooves, the screams of alarm and shock from the camp, the war cries of the Lakota men . . . then he realized he was shouting too; bawling and shrieking at any of the blurry forms that leaped into view as the charge swept this way and that past the lodges.

His throat hurt already—bellowing to these Lame Deer people that they must surrender to save their lives, give up to save the lives of their women and children.

"Do not fight the soldiers! Give yourselves up!" he cried as his horse raced past the rain-soaked lodges, skirting the north side of the encampment. "Do not throw your lives away!"

Despite his futile efforts, the women and children and those few old ones in camp were already on their way with no intention of surrendering.

Within heartbeats Johnny was glad these soldiers were such bad shots firing from the backs of their big horses. All this shooting, all that lead buzzing through the air, and it did nothing more than to hurry the escapees along.

Up ahead, more than half a mile beyond the village, he could now see how Lame Deer's people had put their ponies out to graze farther down the creek. While there were a few favorite animals tethered in among the lodges or grazing close at hand, the hundreds waited downstream. The Bear Coat ordered those ponies driven across the stream and away from the village.

But suddenly, looking close up at the tight, winding path of the creek, Bruguier realized how sharp and high were its banks. He doubted these soldiers would be able to make their charge across the stream in that same wide front the way they were sweeping past the lodges.

Off to Johnny's right, a pony soldier jerked spastically as he was struck with a bullet. Wheeling to the side, the man slid off his horse in a tumbling heap as the rest of the dis-ordered formation hammered past.

One dead man already. Likely to be more . . . if this charge got bottled up driving the herd across the creek.

Breathless, Bruguier twisted in the saddle, looking right, then left, finally spotting one of the white men whom Miles had ordered to lead his soldiers in this charge. The soldier rode close as he crossed behind Bruguier.

Since he didn't know what rank any of the bars or stripes meant on the uniforms, Johnny shouted, "Soldier chief!"

Against the racket of screams and gunfire and panic, the officer turned his head, his eyes finding the half-breed at the very moment Johnny heard the onrushing snarl of a bullet. As he watched, the side of the officer's jaw opened up in a deep red furrow slashed from chin to earlobe. Slapping one hand against the wound, the officer reacted by yanking back on his reins with the other.

Already the first of the Lakota ponies were leaping from the steep banks into the creek, lunging across.

In his next breath the half-breed was reining to a halt be-side the soldier called Jerome. "You can ride?"

At first all he could see of the man's face were those angry eyes above the glove he had fiercely clamped across his cheek. Then the soldier nodded. In a muffled voice he growled, "I can . . . ride."

"The creek!" Johnny started to explain as he pointed, yell-ing above the shouts and hoofbeats, the cries of fury and the gunshots. "The bank's too high! Slow down! Slow the sol-diers down!"

At that point it took but a moment for Jerome to look for himself where the ponies were being funneled together—slowing, rearing as they were forced off the steep bank into the narrow creekbed. Down in the churning water some were already stumbling across the slippery rocks as more animals were shoved into the air to come crashing down

into the stream where they slammed against those before
them.

"I see!" Jerome yelled, ripping the bloody glove from the
deep furrow along his jaw, crimson glistening his lips and
tongue. Already he was turning to the others, shouting wet
words at them about a file.

Johnny didn't understand what those orders were as the
others began to draw back on their reins, slowing, pulling
aside in two wide arcs, left and right. Just ahead of the soldiers the Shahiyela were forcing their ponies off the bank,
into the air in leg-thrashing arcs, plunging down to the water,
every man of them shrieking with joy at capturing the enemy
herd.

In the next moment Bruguier was at the bank himself,
yanking savagely on his own rein as the horse skidded to a
halt just before it no longer had any more ground beneath
its hooves. The pony sailed through the air, legs flailing, and
plunged into the creek on its back two legs with a jolt, churning its two front legs at the water, raising a blinding spray of
water as it side-stepped, snorting in fear.

Bruguier was barely out of the way, his animal lunging
sideways frightfully, when the first of those soldiers on his
heels lunged off the bank. Then a second, and a third—all
of them hurtling single file into the air to land in the middle
of the stream with him. One at a time the troopers righted
themselves in their saddles with a grunt, then yelled at their
mounts and each other as they kicked the horses into motion,
plunging through the rushing, belly-deep stream for the far
bank where the animals clawed their way onto the south side
of Big Muddy Creek behind the captured herd, great gushes
of water sluicing from every animal.

As he erupted out of the stream with the soldiers, Johnny
reined in among those who were streaming to the right while
others raced to the left, both wings fanning out to seal off
the Lakota ponies. No more guns fired at them. No longer
did these soldiers shoot back at the Lakota. All the gunfire
was back there in the village now. With much less noise,
Bruguier could make out the shouts of these soldiers as they
hepped and hawed at the frightened Indian ponies.

"We got 'em, by damn!" one of them cried happily as he
streaked past Bruguier, waving his pistol wildly in the air.

These horses are only the start of the fight, Johnny thought as the herd streamed toward the nearby bluffs, suddenly turned back on themselves by Casey's Shahiyela.

Only the start of this damn fight.

White Hawk awoke at dawn, slowly sensing his woman's bare skin against his leg beneath the blanket. Lying there in the ash-gray of early morning, he kept his eyes closed, concentrating on that feel of her skin against his, gratified in the way it made his manhood grow.

As he rolled over, the Cheyenne little chief pushed back the blanket so he could look at her sleeping naked. He gazed down at the earth color of that one exposed breast, its crimson nipple set in the center of that soft mound he so loved to clutch as he rode her, afraid he might buck himself off. Dragging the blanket off her hipbone, he stared at the dark triangle nestled there between the tops of her legs. Knowing that's where he wanted to be right then.

His eyes crawled quickly back up her belly, to that breast, climbing to her neck and finally to discover that her eyes were open. She had been watching him look at her body. When their eyes locked, he realized she knew what he wanted.

The woman gazed down at his rigid manhood, and smiled.

Rolling onto her back, she spread her thighs as she reached out and took his hardened flesh in her hand.

Groaning, White Hawk rocked onto his knees and went to climb between her legs.

They had come here several suns ago. Traveling with Lame Deer had given White Hawk's people a sense of protection as they went about hunting out the last of the cold weather, into the beginning of the wet days that heralded the Fat Horse Moon when the grasses grew tall and lush. At every camp White Hawk's people chose to raise their lodges off by themselves.

Here they were close enough to that village of Lame Deer's Lakota, but White Hawk's camp was out of sight, downstream, and around a hill.* His people would wander with Lame Deer as long as the hunting was good, as long as

---

*No more than one of the white man's miles

they managed to stay out of the way of the soldier columns that had to be stalking the land this spring. Especially after the half-breed named Big Leggings showed up at their camp on the Tongue and told them the Bear Coat would be on his way.

Sometimes White Hawk agreed with Lame Deer's nephew, Iron Star. Chances are they should have killed Big Leggings when they had him in their camp. Now only bad could come of letting that half-breed go, riding back to tell the Bear Coat how to find their trail, to follow their camp.

Most of the men in White Hawk's camp were Elkhorn Scrapers who owed this little chief their loyalty. Young men with no families, or whose families had gone south to surrender at the White Rock Agency. But, a few were men with wives and children like White Hawk—men who chose to stay free for the sake of their loved ones.

As his woman positioned his manhood against her waiting warmth, White Hawk heard the bark of a camp dog. He lunged, barely able to contain his anticipation for her.

More dogs joined the first.

He nestled himself deeper, moving slowly to savor what he knew would be over all too quickly. Back and forth, warming her, sensing the woman grow wetter at the same time, gazing down to see how she stared up at him with those eyes half-closed in exquisite feral pleasure.

Back and forth, back and forth he rocked, both of them groaning until he was able to plant himself fully inside her. She grunted as he drove himself against her violently, quickly locking her heels over the backs of his calves—

That gunshot came from downstream!

Another. And then a loud volley rumbled their way through the quiet, wet dawn.

Below him she jerked, having heard the shots too.

Now they could hear the distant screaming, and many, many more gunshots.

Outside the lodge, some of his people were shouting.

"The soldiers!"

Yanking himself from his wife, White Hawk lunged across the lodge for his belt and breechclout, tying them around himself as he stumbled for the lodgedoor and flung back the covering.

Outside all was pandemonium. Men were running about, catching up their horses. Children cried and the dogs ran round and round, growling while the women heaved their belongings out of the doorways. Young children climbed onto the shoulders of older youth to begin dragging lacing pins from the tops of the lodgecovers, while other children hunched over tall stakes, heaving this way and that to free them.

"The soldiers!" a woman yelled, her face looming in front of his suddenly. Then she was gone, dragging the long poles of her travois toward her lodge.

Something soured in his belly, telling White Hawk this was the end of his little clan. Perhaps the end of the last free Elkhorn Scraper warriors. The very end of the *Ohmeseheso* who had sought to live free, away from the agencies.

In the distance came more, louder cries of frightened women and the angry shouts of men, the cacophony broken by the rapid staccato of soldier gunfire.

The soldiers. Just as he had promised, the Bear Coat had come for Lame Deer.

Now all White Hawk's people could do was be gone before the *ve-ho-e* discovered they were here. Before they too would be forced to abandon everything they owned just to save their lives.

When he turned, White Hawk found his wife had pulled on her dress. She and their two children were stuffing a few belongings into rawhide bags.

The soldiers would always come.

They always had.

"We must run!" she sobbed, sinking to her knees in futility among their few possessions after all these seasons of destruction.

"Take only what you need," he chided her. "I don't care about those things. I want you and the little ones to live. Go now—to the Roseberry! On the horses and go!"

He watched them scurry toward the ponies like a small covey of flushed quail, then leaped back inside the lodge. Snatching up his rifle and gunbelt, stuffing the soldier pistol inside his waistband, White Hawk whirled back outside.

"Do not stay to take down the lodges!" he ordered the

other women. "Run downstream to the Roseberry! The soldiers will come and kill us all if you do not hurry!"

"Our lodges—it's all that we have!" a father and husband stumbled up to protest.

"No!" White Hawk said, grabbing the man's shoulders and shaking him brutally. "Get into the hills! There with your family, you will have all that is truly important!"

Chapter 37

7 May 1877

Heads poked from lodgedoors and disappeared; then half-naked warriors dashed into the dim light.

Spurts of flame jetted from the muzzle of each rifle, every pistol aimed at those Cheyenne scouts and Casey's mounted infantry as they galloped past the northern reaches of the village.

The village was fully awake by the time Tyler's F Company charged toward the lodges, Wheelan's G on their heels. In the graying light, more bright orange flamed from the muzzles of enemy weapons in the camp.

Among the first to reach the shallow coulee west of the village, Seamus watched three warriors emerge from the prairie itself—bravely racing toward the cavalry line as they shouted to one another, buoying their courage. He figured more would appear, but only those three came to fight. They dropped to one knee, aiming their rifles.

They look like cavalry carbines, he thought as Captain Tyler hollered his order.

Most of the troopers didn't wait to hear the dismount command echo from their sergeant. They were already swinging a right leg up and over the backs of their ass-numbing McClellans, leaping to the ground, huddling in fours as one among them snatched up the reins to the other three mounts. Only then did each trio hurry forward as the fourth man wheeled to the rear, tightly clutching the throatlatches securing his quartet of nervous horses.

A soldier went down noisily in the grass off to Donegan's left. He could hear him thrashing. Some men fell quietly, even without a sound, only to be discovered later by their comrades. But this one was not going to die without bellowing at the devil for his fate.

Over the front blade of his Winchester, the Irishman leveled the carbine high on a warrior's chest. Pulling the trigger, he felt the reassuring nudge against the socket of his right shoulder as the .44-caliber sphere hurtled on its way. Lead slammed into the Lakota, spinning him off the one leg he was kneeling on, back into the tall grass where he disappeared from view.

Now there were only two defenders who somehow held back the whole of Tyler's company as the captain rode among them on horseback, waving his service revolver in the air and crying out orders to advance toward the coulee.

"Forward! Forward, goddammit!" he was screaming at those Second Cavalry troopers as Donegan started for the depression in the bottomground that stretched up from the creekbank. "You don't go forward—they'll pin you down! When they pin you down, they'll cut you up! Forward, men!"

Seamus wanted to yell at them too, but instead he levered another round into the chamber of his carbine and turned to wave them on behind him. Perhaps they would see him and it would encourage them to scurry through the grass; now that they were dismounted skirmishers, now that they were no longer mounted cavalry.

He waved, watching the determined and the scared coming his way, each soldier's face carved deep with the terror of the battle just enjoined. Remembering the faces of another Second Cavalry. *Union* Second Cavalry. Men who were no longer. Comrades flinging their bodies at the cream of the Confederacy with wild cries and glittering sabers decorated with blood-red braided knots. Oh, for the glory of it those youths had offered up their flesh, bone, and blood—riding into the mutilating spray of grapeshot and the whine of a thousand minié balls.

How they had sacrificed to preserve the Union.

And in the end how they had fought to save their own lives, praying God above would spare them just one last time,

vowing to go back home to wife or sweetheart, to mother
and father. Some would live through the battle, live through
that day ultimately to break that vow and fight on with their
comrades of the Second in the charges and bloodletting to
come. Others would lie in the fallow grass, their bright, glistening blood daubing the emerald green until it dried to
black and the bodies bloated in the sun.

"Come on, you horse sojurs!" Seamus bellowed at these
youngsters, unable to contain a tangible swelling of pride
within him.

These were the Second Cavalry—no matter what the political changes or how their superiors had tinkered with it
over the years. These were the same fresh-faced soldiers who
had always ridden for the Second—whether stymieing the
Confederacy outside of Gettysburg, or riding into the gates
of Fort Phil Kearny behind William Judd Fetterman in those
last weeks before they all charged into hell together—this
was the Second-by God-Cavalry.

Always the first into battle. And always the last to ride
back out.

Already the women and children were spilling across the
deep creek, clambering up the south bank, soaked and lumbering in their blankets, racing toward the slopes in ragged
lines, these refugees screaming at the children, herding the
little ones through the freezing water, dragging the old ones
up the steep bank so they could keep up, keep up as they
headed for the timbered southern hillsides where snow still
clung in dirty, icy patches.

It was clear that the village hadn't been sealed off.

No matter, the Irishman figured. It would be like the Red
Fork when they had captured the ponies and driven the enemy into the hills. Then Miles would burn all that could burn,
destroy the rest, and butcher the horses. The survivors would
have nothing, left only with the choice of starving or coming
in to surrender.

He prayed this fight would not turn out like Reynolds's on
the Powder—the battle that started this Sioux War. The enemy had regrouped on the heights when part of Reynolds's
cavalry refused to advance in support of the rest and Egan
got himself pinned down beneath the warriors' crossfire. If it
hadn't been for Donegan leading Anson Mills's company
down the hill against orders, why, Reynolds would have had

himself more than four dead soldiers. And then the officers had ordered their men to pull back so suddenly, abandoning the bodies of their dead and dying to the enemy . . . Seamus vowed he would never again look down into the face of a young soldier who knew he was going to die, forced to listen to that soldier plead, "Finish me."

It was too much to ask a man to kill his brother-in-arms, to finish him off before he fell into the hands of a brutal enemy warrior who would torture and mutilate before killing.

"Forward!" Tyler was growling at them all over again as he came up behind the soldiers on his horse. "Toward the village! We got 'em on the run, boys!"

That much was true, Seamus thought, as he bolted out of the shallow coulee ahead of the rest, yanking down the lever and ejecting that hot copper case. They did have the village on the run. Very few warriors remained among the lodges. It appeared most had already scampered across the rain-swollen stream toward the hillsides where they were taking cover behind trees, firing at the soldiers lumbering through the scrub and sage, darting this way and that around the stands of trees toward the empty lodges where breakfast fires still raised their wispy fingers at the dawn sky.

One by one the warriors fled the village, darting from lodge to lodge until they reached the creekbank, leaped into the deep water, and struggled across the stiff flow to clamber up the far side, before sprinting for the nearby slopes. On those hillsides stood the women and children, crying out to their men, exhorting them with their brave-heart songs, encouraging the fighters as they raced across the open ground.

"We have the village!" hollered battalion commander Ball, wheeling his mount. As Captain Wheelan's company came up, the captain ordered them to make a careful search of the tipis to assure there weren't any snipers left within the camp. Then he stood in the stirrups to call, "Captain Tyler!"

The cavalry officer loped his horse over to Ball. "Sir?"

"Take your men across the creek and continue to drive the escapees into the hills. I don't want any of those warriors left close enough to the village to cause problems for the men searching the tipis. It appears the general is bringing his staff this way. Let's clear the slopes, Captain."

"Snipers. Very good, sir!" Tyler roared and spun his mount away.

When Donegan looked back to the west, he spotted Miles and his headquarters group headed toward the camp at a lope. Now that the village had been cleared of those last stragglers, it was safe to bring in the Bear Coat.

"Bring up the led horses!" Tyler sang out.

Nearly every one of the men in F Company took up that call. "Horse holders to the front!"

In moments the throatlatches were being passed off to the riders and snapped free before the men climbed into the saddle.

When most were ready, Tyler shouted, "Across the stream! Column of twos. It doesn't have to be pretty—just get there in one piece!"

They came off the bank into the Big Muddy with cockscombs of spray that drenched them all as the horses landed, found their legs, then began to hurtle their riders to the far bank where the animals lunged onto the grass. All of it was accompanied by the first sporadic rifle fire returned by the enemy who were just then reaching the nearby slopes.

The landing the claybank made almost jarred Donegan's teeth loose as a surge of bile flung itself against his tonsils. Swallowing down the pain in his groin and rising in the stirrups, Seamus urged the mare on across the stream in the midst of those shouting, clamoring troopers.

"Dismount!" came the cry from a sergeant with some faded chevrons on his blouse, the first officer to make it across among Tyler's men.

A soldier reached the south bank, clumsily spurring his mount onto the grassy slope on all fours, only to be struck by a bullet which toppled him to the ground. More bullets hissed past the Irishman.

"Dismount, goddammit!" the sergeant was hollering. "Horse-holders to the front!"

In the maddening confusion of men and animals whirling in all directions like a Kentucky reel, Seamus spun to the ground, dragging the horse behind him as he lunged for some tall willow. Hidden here where the warriors couldn't easily spot him, the Irishman knotted the reins to the brush then sprinted to a nearby stand of trees to begin firing at the hillside.

"There's Injuns behind us!"

At the cry, Donegan whirled around in a crouch. But there were only two Indians, then two more—all four of them bursting from the west side of the village, plunging off the steep bank into the creek.

"Sweet mother in heaven!" Seamus whispered, seeing how Miles and his staff were already across the creek behind Tyler's and Wheelan's men . . . headed at an angle directly toward those warriors.

From the sound of it, Miles was having Bruguier and Hump yell a message to the escapees. As Donegan started toward the bunch, his carbine hammer cocked, he heard Robert Jackson calling to Miles.

"General, that's Lame Deer!"

"The chief?" Miles asked, reining up suddenly, his chestnut raring slightly.

"Lame Deer!" Jackson repeated, pointing at the one wearing a long, double-trailer warbonnet, clutching a broken tree limb in his free hand. To the end of that stick hung a dirty white rag.

Hump was next to recognize the leader and shouted in Lakota at the four armed men angling away from Miles's group toward the closest hillside where their people continued to holler and bellow.

Miles bawled, "Tell them to halt, Jackson! Tell them I'll honor their white flag of surrender!"

Both Jackson and Bruguier cried out the Bear Coat's order. But only Hump urged his horse into motion just as two of the four suddenly peeled away from the others. With daring, Hump advanced on his two fellow Lakota, hand held out in peace there in that deadly middle ground.

Dressed in that bonnet of his battle acclaim, Lame Deer stopped, turning slightly to holler in reply to Hump. On the chief's heels came a second warrior, a younger man. Across the slopes the Lakota rifle fire trickled off.

Reining around, halfway between Lame Deer and the soldiers, Hump loped back toward the white men, stopping in front of Miles. He spoke, his words translated by Bruguier.

"This man is Lame Deer. He is *Mnikowoju*—my people. He asked me if the soldiers have followed him here to kill all of them in his village."

"Tell him I do not want to kill any more of his people," Miles replied.

Then Johnny interpreted, "Hump says Lame Deer wants to meet the Bear Coat."

"Very good," Miles replied, turning to indicate those he wanted to accompany him. "Let's go tell this Lame Deer face-to-face that he must surrender to me. I will look him in the eye and tell him that he is now my prisoner."

Nelson Miles nodded as Lieutenant Baird and his orderly, Private Shrenger, came to a halt near the rear flanks of the colonel's mount. "Here, Private," he said and handed Shrenger the white bandanna he tore from his head. "My hat?"

"Of course, General." Shrenger twisted in the saddle, pulling up the flap to his saddlepocket, and removed the wide-brimmed hat.

"Thank you, son. I want to wear it to meet this Lame Deer," Miles said as he re-creased the cream-colored hat before snugging it down on his head. Then he turned to one of the Second Cavalry officers. "Captain Norwood, please accompany me to our parley with Lame Deer."

"My pleasure, General!" the commander of L Troop acknowledged.

By the time he turned, Miles found two more warriors converging with the first two. Lame Deer waited for the pair to reach his side, then handed one of them the stick with that greasy scrap of towel tied to it, while the younger warrior at the chief's side passed off the reins of a lone war pony to the fourth man. Only then did Lame Deer and the younger man start alone for that open, middle ground some distance from the soldier lines.

"Perhaps that was Lame Deer's own war pony," Miles observed, tension rising in him like a spring flood. "All right, gentlemen—let's go."

He was going to meet this last war leader of the mighty Sioux, face-to-face! A warrior who had gone with Crazy Horse to whip Crook at the Rosebud, a fighter who had helped Sitting Bull crush his old friend Autie Custer. Last fall Miles came nose-to-nose with Sitting Bull himself when they parleyed at Cedar Creek. While he would always regret not having the chance to have himself a look at Crazy Horse during their fight at Battle Butte, here he was about to effect the surrender of this last wild band of hostiles on the northern plains.

Halfway across that open ground between them, Miles reined up, raising an arm for those eight soldiers behind him to halt.

"Careful of their weapons, General," Captain Norwood warned Miles with a growl as the four Sioux came forward, all of them warily looking this way and that.

"I suspect they're fearing treachery," Miles replied, reading the deep suspicion on their unpainted faces.

He watched the two in the rear start to slow their pace, not near so anxious now as they got closer and closer to the soldiers.

"Goddamn their red souls," Baird grumbled. "These bastards're the ones you can't trust, General."

The trio of warriors stopped a few yards away as Lame Deer continued on alone those last ten yards. Then one of the three stepped up close behind the chief's shoulder. That younger one was clearly nervous, agitated to the point of pacing, his rifle held at his hip, ready. His head twitched this way, then that, eyes trying to see everywhere at once as he watched the eight soldiers accompanying Miles, acting as if he were the chief's bodyguard.

"Lame Deer," Miles called out in English, remembering to smile. A moment ago he had pulled off his right glove and now he held his hand out so the chief could shake it. Then he remembered that Sioux word of greeting, the word for friend. "*Hau, hau kola.*"

Lame Deer stopped in his tracks to peer over the soldiers arrayed behind the soldier chief.

"No one will harm you," Miles said. "Tell him that, Bruguier. Tell him it is safe to shake my hand. He should shake the Bear Coat's hand."

The half-breed interpreted, instilling enough confidence that Lame Deer shifted the rifle into his left hand. Inching forward again, he stopped at the chestnut's side, holding up his empty right hand to Miles. They clasped, and the colonel squeezed firmly, wanting this enemy leader to feel the sincerity and integrity, if not the power of the soldier chief who had just conquered his village.

As Lame Deer pulled his hand away, Miles instructed, "Johnny, tell Lame Deer and the rest they must put down their weapons. Tell them to lay down their rifles, put them on the ground."

Again the half-breed interpreted. And the moment his words were finished the young man closest to Lame Deer began to yell at the chief, arguing, berating.

"That one," Bruguier warned, "Hump tells me his name is Iron Star, Lame Deer's nephew. He's causing trouble. Watch out: he's saying Lame Deer must not lay down his gun."

"Tell them they must all surrender their weapons," Miles repeated grittily, angry at the young warrior's intrusion, the hair bristling at the back of his neck as he closely studied that anxious warrior a few yards behind the chief, seeing how agitated Iron Star had become, pacing a few steps in one direction, then a few steps in the other, holding his rifle exactly as would a sentry on guard duty.

Lame Deer turned from Iron Star to look again at Miles. The chief knelt, laying what Miles recognized was a Spencer carbine on the ground. But as he did so, the chief cocked the hammer, and positioned the weapon so the muzzle pointed at the colonel.

While Iron Star continued to talk louder and louder, more of the Sioux on the slopes began to holler. The women wailed, the children cried—terribly dismayed by their chief surrendering his weapon.

Miles swallowed, his heart thundering, then he began instructing, "Tell Lame Deer that all of his men must come forward and surrender their weapons to us. His warriors are to bring in any ponies we haven't captured."

He waited a moment while Bruguier translated, but through none of those words did Lame Deer appear interested in listening with his full attention. Instead, the chief had turned slightly, as if to better hear the calls from the hillside.

A suspicious Robert Jackson urged his horse closer to the chief, halting a few yards to Miles's right so that he stood on the other side of Lame Deer, leveling his Springfield carbine at the Sioux chief.

"Don't frighten him, Jackson!" Miles barked. "Get back!"

"He won't listen to you good unless he's scared for his life, General," Jackson explained. "Be on your guard—this Lame Deer don't act like a man going to surrender."

At that moment White Bull came up and halted at Miles's left elbow, tapping the colonel's leg with his moccasin toe. When Miles glanced over at the holy man, the Cheyenne gestured at the Spencer carbine Lame Deer had laid down, crooking his thumb to indicate that the hammer was cocked.

"I saw," Miles told the Cheyenne in English. "Not a good sign."

Nodding, his lips pressed in determination, White Bull urged his horse into motion, moving past Lame Deer toward Iron Star.

"Mr. Baird, go with the Cheyenne," the colonel ordered.

As his adjutant jockeyed by on his left side to follow White Bull, Iron Star started to wave his rifle menacingly at Miles, placing the butt against his hip and swinging it this way and that, all while he was muttering angrily.

"He's saying this is his country," Bruguier translated nervously. "Says you killed an old woman this morning. You killed his grandmother. You do not belong here—this is his land. He's a soldier on his own land and he shouldn't have to give up his weapon to no man—"

"Tell him he must surrender his rifle—"

Bruguier interrupted, wagging his head apprehensively as he continued, "He keeps saying he is a soldier, walking on his own land. He won't give his gun over to no one."

Somehow White Bull must have understood enough of that Lakota for he wheeled his horse up suddenly and leaned off to grab the muzzle of Iron Star's carbine, being brandished in the air.

And now Lame Deer was yelling, Bruguier hollering his translation, "My nephew is only a young man! Only a young man and doesn't know any better!"

In the blink of an eye, Lieutenant Baird reined up on the other side of Iron Star, reaching over to seize the warrior's forearm. Struggling for a few moments between the lieutenant and White Bull, Iron Star bellowed a warning, causing the two warriors behind him to turn and flee.

As the struggle continued the half-breed Bruguier kept on bellowing his translation, "My nephew doesn't know any better!"

Miles growled, "Get the weapon away from that red son of a bitch and tell him to surrender *now*! Tell him to look at all the women and children in the hills—"

"That bastard's gonna shoot someone!" Captain Ball cried.

"Mr. Baird, get that rifle from the son of a bitch!" Miles bawled angrily. "Get it now and tell him to surrender! Bruguier—"

White Bull struggled to hold onto the muzzle of that carbine Iron Star was waving around so menacingly. Suddenly lunging back with his elbow, the Lakota knocked Baird aside, then brought his left hand up to clasp around his rifle's forestock.

With a startling crack, the weapon exploded, its bullet ripping a hole in White Bull's coatflap, causing the holy man to release the carbine, flinging it aside as he jerked away in the opposite direction.

Lame Deer was yelling at the young warrior, snarling at the soldiers. Behind Miles, he heard his officers cursing, warning.

From the far right side of his vision, the colonel spotted a flicker of movement and spun quickly in the saddle to find Lame Deer lunging for the Spencer on the ground.

The word leaped from his throat, "No!"

But the Sioux chief yanked the carbine up to his knees in one smooth arc and pulled the trigger.

That muzzle spewed orange flame, belching a puff of dirty gray gunsmoke as Miles listened to the whine of the bullet that carried his name.

Chapter 38

7 May 1877

With the way Miles jerked aside as Lame Deer's carbine exploded, Donegan was certain that bullet had killed the colonel.

In that next instant came the sound of lead smacking against flesh and bone like a flat hand slapping wet wall putty. Barely a yard behind Miles, Private Charles Shrenger pitched backward off his side-stepping mount. His hat flew off in the opposite direction as the young soldier spilled out of the saddle into the rain-soaked, trampled grass.

"Son of a bitch!" one of the officers shrieked.

In firing that shot at White Bull from his own weapon, Iron Star freed his rifle from the Cheyenne's grip, then whirled about to start racing for the nearby slope where the Lakota from the village once more sent up a howl. But after only two steps he suddenly stopped and wheeled, dropping to his knee, the carbine jammed against his shoulder.

One of Norwood's sergeants had spurred his horse forward, leveling his pistol at Lame Deer at the same moment Iron Star found that sergeant in his sights. The .45-caliber army bullet missed the Lakota chief, sailing on to strike one of the two warriors fleeing up the long slope. The Indian pitched forward into the grass, a'sprawl, then lay still.

Iron Star's bullet hit its intended target. With a startled grunt, Sergeant Sharp keeled to the side out of the saddle, his left boot tangled in its hooded stirrup as his frightened horse pranced in the midst of all the hubbub.

Havoc was loosed like a swarm of maddening wasps. Down the hill toward that open no-man's-land raced more than a dozen warriors. Every soldier and Sioux with a gun was firing, some in what might soon be a deadly crossfire that could well have soldier killing soldier.

Baird and Norwood rushed forward to reach Miles as the colonel began to pat himself, trying to find a wound, discovering nothing but a bullet hole in his wool coat. Another pair of soldiers dropped to the ground to see to Shrenger, finding the young orderly already dead.

In the confusion, Lame Deer rejoined Iron Star where the bottomground met the rising slope, no more than two hundred yards from where Seamus now spun out of the saddle, flipping the reins twice around his left hand to steady the claybank. Laying his repeater over the saddle to steady his shot at Lame Deer and the nephew, Donegan figured those impressive bonnets of eagle feathers with their long trailers sweeping the ground behind them would make fine targets.

Behind him Seamus could hear an exasperated Miles yelling orders along with the rest now. Wounded or not, the Irishman thought, the general ain't dead yet.

When Seamus fired the carbine, his bullet struck Iron Star low in the back. He watched Lame Deer's nephew falter, then straighten to courageously keep on scrambling toward the slope.

At that moment it seemed the whole right flank came alive with a fusillade of gunfire aimed at the escaping pair. That sound of the soldier weapons became a thunderous roar. This time Lame Deer faltered, dropping his Spencer carbine as he collapsed to one knee. Then slowly the chief struggled back to his feet, turning to find Iron Star down on hands and knees.

In the midst of that noise, Lame Deer yelled at his nephew. Though bleeding terribly himself, the chief looped an arm around the younger man's waist, pulling Iron Star onto his feet.

"He's telling Iron Star to turn and fight!" Bruguier announced. "Telling him to fight until they're dead!"

Arm in arm, the two Lakota whirled about, with Iron Star struggling to raise his weapon, having trouble leveling it at the soldiers as bullets sailed at them. Lame Deer fought to maintain his balance each time a new bullet shocked through his body. Brazenly, bravely they both turned their backs to the enemy and started up the hill, trudging wearily, both bleeding terribly from their wounds.

What gallantry, Seamus thought. Instead of fleeing for their own safety, both warriors struggled to save the life of another. What courage in the face of certain death.

They were both done for, Donegan figured, dragging his carbine off the saddle and chambering a fresh round with the lever. Those two can't make it up the hill to safety—not with all those soldiers concentrating their fire on them, even shave-tail soldiers who didn't practice their marksmanship.

Seamus stood there in amazement as the pair trudged farther and farther away as the soldier line roared away. After a few more yards Lame Deer dragged a pistol from his belt and waved that last weapon back toward the soldiers. Crazily, he fired, and fired again, unable to aim the weapon, the explosion of each round a small puff of muzzle-smoke. Yet each bullet did nothing more than smash into the rain-sodden earth a few yards behind the chief.

Another last act of bitter defiance in the face of death. Lame Deer's last courageous sneer in the face of the enemy.

It was plain the chief couldn't last much longer, not with so many wounds.

Finally, the strength seemed to flush out of Lame Deer. He stumbled and pitched forward onto all fours. Iron Star fell backward beside him, rolling onto his side and crumpling into a ball.

Off to Donegan's left, Robert Jackson kicked his horse into motion, bursting from that group of officers protectively surrounding the colonel. Hunched over his horse's neck, Jackson galloped east toward Captain Wheelan's company.

Shrill shouts drew Donegan's attention back to the escaping pair. Up the slope, Lame Deer was squatting on his knees, trying to yank Iron Star off the ground when he was struck with another bullet that rocked his whole body. Slowly the chief keeled back onto one elbow, then sank for the last time.

Iron Star slowly rolled aside, lumbering to his feet to stand over his dead uncle, one arm clutching his belly wounds and the other dragging the muzzle of his rifle. Surprising Donegan with his stamina, Iron Star lurched around sharply and continued to trudge desperately up the slope.

As Seamus looked aside to find Jackson among Wheelan's men, the troopers started to move out toward the far side of the narrow spur Iron Star was climbing. In moments Company G would be in position on the far side of the low ridge—waiting for the Lakota warrior, nephew of the fallen chief.

The wounded young man appeared to grow more weary the higher he climbed, struggling step by step, one foot falling in front of the other, dragging his weapon by the muzzle as if it weighed as much as a horse.

Already, White Bull and Brave Wolf were hurrying forward, hoping to reach Lame Deer's body, preparing to strike first coup on this enemy who had once been their comrade-in-arms.

What dogs war makes of us, Donegan thought as gunfire erupted from the far side of that spur where Wheelan's men had disappeared to lay in wait for Iron Star.

More desperate cries burst from the far slopes where the women and children watched. They must be able to see it, Seamus thought—to watch Iron Star cut down.

Leaping atop his horse, Donegan kicked it into motion, heading for the far side of the spur. He reached the rising ground just in time to watch Iron Star settle heavily into the grass as if he were merely sitting. There he leaned forward slightly, attempting to reload his rifle from some cartridges in his belt.

By then Robert Jackson was the first to burst away from Wheelan's line. He covered half the distance between the troops and Iron Star before he reined up suddenly and spun out of the saddle. Dashing forward a few paces, he suddenly knelt and took aim, gripping his pistol in both hands.

Iron Star's head popped back violently, his headdress slipping off to the side as the Lakota slowly lay back in the grass, his legs twitching for a moment before the body ceased moving.

Already on his feet, the young half-breed was shouting, sprinting for the body as renewed rifle fire came from the hillside above them. After making no more than a few yards toward his intended quarry, Jackson wheeled about and beat a hasty retreat.

"No scalp's worth losing your own!" Seamus bellowed, spurring his horse up so that he provided some cover for the young half-breed.

"Not just that! I want that headdress too!" Jackson huffed as they both came to a halt among Wheelan's soldiers. "Soon as we start mopping up and burn the village, I'll get that bonnet off that body."

"Time enough for taking your trophies later," Donegan reminded sourly. "For now, the general's got his work cut out for him clearing these hills."

"They're having a time of it!" the young infantryman yelled exuberantly to the others all up and down the line of pack-mules.

"I'd say, my boy," replied an older foot soldier. "Just listen to 'em banging away at them red-bellies!"

The sounds of battle were well carried up the valley that dawn as this escort struggled to reach the village with their precious ammunition lashed to the mules, struggling over the open ground.

He had already been blooded, as the old files with the Twenty-second called it. Assigned to the Glendive depot last summer, he was with Otis's bunch when the Sioux jumped them on their way with that long bull-train of supplies bound for Miles's Fifth at the mouth of the Tongue.* He was blooded already, by damned. Seen men hit, watched army bullets strike the enemy. Heard their shouts and screams and blood-curdling shrieks. He was blooded all right. Not no wet-eared, shave-tail recruit no more.

"Gonna make short work of it, them boys are!" cried a voice, cheery and lustful, as they marched along to a certain victory over these last of the warrior Sioux.

For some time he kept expecting to reach the battle scene, listening to the booms of the big guns rattling closer and closer, the cracks of the smaller carbines the Sioux used. The minutes and yards crawled by as the soldiers struggled to push the mules up and down the broken landscape, stumbling themselves each time they had to cross and re-cross the narrow stream, as it meandered from one side of the valley to

---

A Cold Day In Hell—vol. 11, The Plainsmen Series

the other. After all this time and all that fighting, after all
the miles of trying to catch up . . .

Disgruntled, he grumbled, "We gotta be getting close—"

"Sweet mother of pike!"

At that exclamation from one of the civilians walking
ahead of the column, they all jerked to look up at the high
ground, just as the first screams and shrieks burst from the
throats of the warriors. More than a dozen of them, perhaps
as many as twenty.

"Jesus God!" he whispered, filled with sudden panic as the
Sioux swept down on them.

Half of the Indians were on foot, the others racing ahead
on ponies.

He could see the puffs of smoke from the muzzles of their
guns. Had to be Springfields, he thought, captured from dead
soldiers.

Then came the first sound of bullet striking bone, the
sharp, pained, wordless cry of one of the men up ahead.

Already the mules were balking, yanking this way and that
on their leads, tugging against the men, yanking away from
one another as if an artillery canister had gone off in their
midst.

"Shoot 'em, goddammit!"

A few of the men were yelling at the others; likely the
sergeant and some older ones, the youngster thought as he
dropped to his knee beneath one of the nervous mules who
had gone stiff-legged there on the trail, frozen in fear. He
wondered if the mule would piss on him as he huddled there.
Then worried if he would piss on himself.

The horsemen swept sideways across the sodden slope
above them, firing wildly, full of fury at the soldiers, while
those warriors on foot came running straight downhill for the
mule-train, shrieking and flapping blankets. The mule he
hunkered under shifted sideways, enough so that he was no
longer within the cavity of its legs, then the animal suddenly
bolted, *hee-raw*ing as it thrashed spraddle-legged into the
brush, snared by the wide ammunition boxes in making its
escape.

A bullet hissed past, slamming into the mule's rump.

He looked down at his crotch. "Damn," he muttered as
the warmth spread.

No matter, he decided. None of the others gonna notice I

pissed on myself. They're too damned busy right now anyway. Blooded was he, but it was still hard to keep from puking as he heard that dying man thrashing, saw the civilian with the lower half of his face blown off, gurgling in his own blood. Drowning slowly, noisily.

He hoped a bullet would find him quick so that he didn't have to go slow and painful like that.

"Hold them goddamned mules, you sonsabitches!" some man ordered.

Another voice bellowed, "You heard the sarge! Hold onto 'em!"

Then a new order, "Save the bloody ammo! Save the bullets!"

He suddenly heard all the voices around him, each and every word distinct, able to put a face to each voice—wondering if that clarity meant that he was going to be all right ... or if such clarity came to a man only in those final moments before he was killed.

Either way, he decided, it was going to be fine by him.

"You gonna shoot that rifle of yours today, soldier?"

Jerking about, he found the old corporal looming over his shoulder, grinning. By damned, the man was grinning.

"Y-y-yes, I will—"

"There's plenty of them red buggers for targets," the corporal bawled, some of his front teeth gone, the rest a pasty brown from his chew. "Pick you one and blow his eggs off!"

The corporal settled in beside him, gave him a wink, and put his Long Tom to work.

By damn if it wasn't gonna be fine now, the young soldier thought as he set his rifle against his shoulder and peered down the barrel at the backs of those warriors who were scampering back up the hill now that the soldiers were getting themselves over that initial shock, beginning to rally and put up a stiff defense.

On either side of them the few on ponies swept by, pouring this way and that, then upon reaching the streambank, they circled back toward the slope. Mules grunted. Men cursed, doing their best to hold onto the frightened, balky animals carrying that precious ammunition, doing their best to hold their urine, to hold back their gorge that threatened to make them puke.

Men who knelt there among the pack-train doing their level best to hold back this ambush.

He knew they would do it. As the minutes crawled by, the Sioux grew less and less brassy and bold. Less willing to take a chance and get too close to those Long Toms these infantrymen carried. He knew they would do it.

If worse come to worst, he figured, they could hold out till just this side of forever with all this ammo. Leastways till them horse soldiers with Miles heard this gunfire and come running to raise this siege.

But that would have to wait for now and he would have to find another target, to hold off these red hellions for a while longer. The cavalry with Miles had their own fight going and until it settled down, none of the horse soldiers was about to hear this little fight going on a valley or two over.

"That'a way, son!" the corporal cried as one of the warriors on foot stumbled and pitched face forward onto the grass.

Two men on horseback saw their companion fall at the same time, wheeling about to rescue the wounded warrior.

The corporal clapped and hooted, "They make a fine target of theyselves!"

The young soldier yanked up the trapdoor of his rifle, ejecting that hot copper cartridge. Stuffing his trembling hand down into the black leather pouch at his belt, he pulled another shell from his kit and stuffed it into the breech. Slamming down the trapdoor, he dragged back the big hammer and nestled the rifle into his shoulder again.

If they were going to be here for a while, he might as well keep himself busy.

Chapter 39

7 May 1877

"Dear Jesus, help me hold 'em back," whispered Private William Leonard, L Company, Second U.S. Cavalry. "Just help me hold these red bastards back."

So angry he was close to tears, the young soldier wanted to curse himself for forgetting the prayers taught him in his youth. He dwelled on his mother and father, how they always saw he got to church on Sunday mornings. The remembrance made his eyes smart, and that made Private Leonard even more angry at himself. He swiped at his bleary eyes and shoved his cheek back down on the stock of his Springfield carbine.

Damn if he didn't have all the luck—dragging himself out of one scrape just to plop into another. From the frying pan right into the fire.

How he had looked forward to getting in some fighting with the Sioux hostiles before this war was over. Just like the over-riding eagerness felt by all the others in those four companies of horse soldiers who had followed Major Frank "Grasshopper" Brisbin east from Fort Ellis in April, assigned duty with General Miles's campaign punching south of the Yellowstone. All those rough miles of up and down in the last two days as word along the column had it they were getting close to the village. Then just as Miles had them moving at a trot toward the enemy camp in the dark that morn-

ing, his saddle started to slip off the backbone of his big bay
gelding.

Quickly Leonard reined out of column and leaped to the
ground as the rest poured past in a throbbing, thunderous
wave, following Miles's scouts toward the coming dawn.
Goddamn that cinch! Why now?

Busted but good, the stitching worn loose. It was almost
enough to make a man want to cry. The private stood there
with a loose end of that cinch hanging in one hand, staring
at the tail end of the column as it disappeared down the creek
valley. Damn, but they were going to have themselves a daisy
of a scrap. The last scrap there might well be out here.

Forlorn as a man ever was, he felt angry, bitter, and despairing that he wasn't going to get in on the fighting now.

It was to have been a glory ride! Sweeping in at dawn on
that last Sioux village to thumb their noses at the army and
their Indian agents. Likely the last chance the Second Cavalry would have to cloak itself in honor for a long time to
come, what with the Indian wars coming to a close both south
and north. Then it would be back to having nothing more to
look forward to than endless days of fatigue duty until his
enlistment was up.

As the sounds of his comrades faded downstream, Leonard
collapsed right there beside the trail, ready to bawl from frustration, when he had a prick of inspiration: he'd do what he
could to repair his saddle. He had his folding pocketknife
after all, and he might just improvise enough to get that cinch
re-attached to the saddle. A few long whangs might work.
He could cut those narrow strips of leather from the saddle
cover itself. He only needed a half-dozen of them to make
his repair, just enough to keep the saddle and cinch together
until he made it into that village and that last glorious fight.

So he had gone to work there in the growing light of that
cold spring dawn, struggling to drag his pocketknife through
the thick latigo leather, carving out the first of the narrow
strips. By the time he started on the third one, the distant
gunfire had become all but steady. Those sounds and the
growing frustration he began to suffer spurred him to work
a little faster.

He was poking holes through the braided sisal fabric of
the cinch, matching holes in the saddle leather, when he
heard the first yelp.

Snapping his head up in surprise, Leonard couldn't believe his eyes. A half-dozen warriors on foot, and another three on ponies, had just reached the top of the ridge behind him— and peering down had discovered the lone soldier. Without losing a step they came rolling toward him, shrieking billy-be-hell and eager for his scalp!

He stood up so suddenly the pocketknife tumbled off his thigh. Leonard scooped it up, clumsily closing the blade as he stuffed it into a back pocket on his wool britches. Already the bay was skittish. Maybe the scent of 'em on the wind. More likely all their hollering.

He hurriedly dragged up the blanket and saddle as one and flung it on the back of the horse. Untying the rein from the brush, he swept up his carbine. Only then did he wonder where the hell he would go. It had to be quick, and it had to be close, because he was heading there on foot. Still couldn't cinch that saddle down, but he prayed it would stay on that bay's back long enough to get him somewhere he could fort up.

"C'mon, girl!" he bellowed as he yanked the horse away, heading sidelong up the slope.

If he could reach the top, he would have the high ground and a good field of fire. Not that he had ever had to worry about having a field of fire before; he and the others never had themselves a good dirty scrap with any Injuns. Could have, if Iron-Britches Custer had decided to take Brisbin up on his offer of these same four companies, back when the Seventh marched away from the mouth of the Rosebud to its destiny. These same four companies that marched east to go campaigning with Miles.

Time now to see if all that stuff they'd filled his head with back at Jefferson Barracks was worth a damn . . . at least worth one poor soldier's life.

High ground, he huffed almost out loud. And recognized the paunch-water sounds of the horse behind him as it rattled up the slope.

Turning, Leonard glanced back to see that the saddle was still there, bouncing along on the gelding's broad back. Damn if he didn't need what was in them saddle pockets. Hell, if it come down to it, a man might figure that saddle cost him his scalp, Leonard thought as he neared the crest of the hill.

Then again, if he didn't lose his extra cartridges, that saddle might just save his life too.

While hanging onto the gelding's tail for all he was worth, the horse dragged him up those last few yards to the top. He spun around, looked, and gulped. No trees. Only some scrub brush. Nothing big enough for the bastards to hide behind and slip up on him—

He heard the slap of lead. The bay whinnied, twirling and kicking, flinging off the saddle so that it tumbled into the tall grass. A big hole bubbled in its chest, red and glistening, spewing froth. Done for, goddamn.

Leonard dropped his carbine, wrapping both hands around the reins as the horse struggled against him, shoving at first, then pulling the private as he dug in his heels to keep the animal from bolting. Up here in the open, he still needed that gelding.

Lashing the reins around his left hand, the soldier yanked back the mule ear of his holster and dragged out his service revolver. Snapping back the hammer as the horse lunged to the side, Leonard felt all the strength oozing from that arm the gelding had nearly popped out of its socket. The bay almost knocked him over as he leaped close, jamming the muzzle just below the ear, clenched his eyes shut, then yanked on the trigger.

The gelding settled on all fours, then gently keeled onto its side, legs facing the top of the hill.

Snapping off two quick pistol shots at the horsemen who were the closest to him, Leonard spun on his heel and scuttled for the saddle down the slope. Snagging hold of it in his left hand, the private whirled and started back to the dead horse. A bullet whined past him, ricocheting off a small boulder he hurdled in midstride. Skidding in between the dead animal's legs, he dragged up the carbine. Now he had some ammunition, enough to reload his pistol four times, and a hundred rounds for his Springfield.

There wasn't that many of them, so Leonard figured he could hold them at bay long enough with what ammunition he had. Here between some shin-high rocks and this carcass, he hunkered down, settling in to return their fire. Listening to them yell for his blood.

As minutes crawled past, the morning began to wear on and on. Those warriors wouldn't stop yelling, and the distant shooting in the village continued. Neither of them were good signs, the lone private figured. The others wouldn't know he was missing, wouldn't hear his carbine—not with all they had to deal with then and there.

So, he reminded himself, clenching his teeth in resolve, it was going to be up to him for the next hour or so until help came along.

Beneath that cloudy sky as the wind came up, it seemed as if time slowed, then stood still. After what must surely have been an eternity of holding the warriors at bay, he heard the distant rifle fire trickle off, and it grew quiet on down the valley.

Each time the warriors started to get in too close, Leonard did his best to force them back with the long-reaching carbine and its .45-caliber bullets. And the few times they were foolish enough to attempt rushing him, the trooper used the .45-caliber bullets in his pistol.

When next he stuffed his hand into the saddle pocket to pull out some long copper cases for the Springfield, Leonard stared down at his hand. He held the last of them now, with no more than five rounds left in his pistol.

"Save the last for yourself, bunkie," he said sourly. "Don't let 'em take you alive, not these red devils."

He figured he would use the Springfield to keep them as far away as he could for as long as he could, then fire the last four shots in the pistol as they rushed in closer the way they had threatened to do all morning.

And when he had only that one last bullet left—

Leonard jerked around as if yanked by a rope. Surprised to hear the voice. Like an answer to his prayer.

Three of them appeared there just this side of the creek, down by the brush at the bottom of the slope.

He couldn't tell what they were yelling, if they were yelling at him or shouting at others who were coming behind—but did those three ever look good to him!

Doughboys! Foot-goddamned-sloggers! Walk-a-heaps! No matter what folks called 'em, they damned well looked like angels of salvation to Private William Leonard then and there.

They were pointing up the slope as more of those uniforms joined the trio. Then there was a horseman. Had to be an officer. The man stood in the stirrups, yanking his horse around, flinging his arm up the slope, bellowing like a stuck pig as two dozen or more of those foot-sore doughboys started out in a dead sprint up the side of that hill toward Leonard.

Tears streaming down his face, the private stood, slamming the carbine into his shoulder and finding the broad, brown back of one of the retreating warriors who were whooping it away on the double. He fired, missed, and cursed his foggy vision. Quickly he ejected that scalded shell and rammed home another. One more shot at the bastards who came close to getting his scalp, the bastards who almost made him use that last bullet on himself.

"Holy mother—" one of the first doughboys exclaimed as he huffed breathlessly to a halt, leaning slightly on his Long Tom rifle to peer down at Leonard. "How . . . how the hell long you been holed up here?"

"A l-long time," Leonard croaked, surprised he could speak around the bitter ball that clogged the back of his throat.

"I hope to shout, soldier," one of the others commented as the rest began to gather close, gazing down at that litter of strewn copper casings for themselves.

A third one stepped to the side and propped one of his feet on the flank of the dead gelding. "You done you a piece of work here, horse soldier. A fine piece of work."

"You don't mind," Leonard said quietly, "I'd 'preciate you taking your boot off my horse."

That third infantryman suddenly looked down self-consciously, realizing his foot was resting on the dead horse, and dragged it off. "I-I'm sorry, trooper."

"If it weren't for this horse a'mine," Leonard explained as he knelt beside the gelding's head, "I'd been red soup long afore you boys come to save my hair."

"Didn't mean no disrespect, soldier."

Leonard blinked and nodded at the apology as he turned to watch more of the foot soldiers coming into view now. "You was the fellas stayed with the packs we left on the Rosebud?"

"That's right," answered the first man. "That down there's Captain Dickey. Coming out of that brush is Captain Poole."

The third man stepped around the carcass and pushed back his kepi, saying, "Heard us a ton of shooting. Brought us on the double. Didn't figure to find only one poor horse soldier needing rescue—"

"Listen!"

When one of them snapped that command, they all went silent, rigid, listening. Sure enough, just beyond the next rise, they could hear some rifle fire. Not near enough to be a big fight in the village. But surely more than a half-dozen guns.

"You suppose them Injuns we run off got some other poor horse soldier pinned down?" asked the first infantryman, spitting a brown dribble into the grass.

"I s'pose it could be," Leonard said, stuffing the near-empty pistol back into its holster.

Downhill Dickey and Poole were barking orders, shaping their men back into line as the soldiers descended the hill with that lone cavalryman and his carbine, leaving behind the bay gelding and his busted saddle atop a lonely little hill above the Big Muddy. They were moved out again at a trot, settling into a pace the foot soldiers were told they would have to endure for another mile or so, just long enough to reach the sound of those guns.

Leonard swiped at the drop of sweat hung pendant from the end of his nose and jogged alongside the doughboys in the muggy dampness of that morning.

Damn if that wasn't the way it was with this army.

Officers always yelling at their men to ride to the sound of the guns!

The young infantryman swore he could smell the dead civilian's blood on the chilly breeze that morning.

He had been forced to listen to the mule-whacker gurgle and thrash his last there in the trampled grass beside the creek. Between each shrieking charge of the warriors, between each loud boom of his Long Tom, the man went noisy. And finally died, coughing and gurgling no longer.

That morning wore on and on, and at times the soldier swore he heard gunfire from upstream to their right. But each time he listened, he just figured it was a random echo from the fight downstream to their left, off in that village he might never get a chance to see. Just some echoes as the cavalry mopped things up and drove off those what they couldn't kill in their fight. Those horse soldiers would never know the mule-train was pinned down here until they needed more ammunition.

At the start of this dirty little scrap, the warriors managed to get off with two of the mules, scaring the animals enough that they bolted free of the pack-string, heading tea-kettle-over-biscuits downstream with their boxes of ammunition slapping and rattling like dice in a bone cup. But the old soldiers and the young recruits leaped up and got control of the rest, and with the help of the three other civilians they managed to keep the rest of the mules from running off each time the blankets flapped and the whistles cried and the red-bellies shrieked, close enough he was sure he had only to reach out and yank a breechclout clean off one of them.

Then he had glanced down at his own itchy wool britches, self-consciously, and was relieved to see that the dark stain was fading from that pale blue cloth. He'd leave the warriors their breechclouts, if he just didn't have to display his britches until they were dry.

"Lookee thar'!"

The old corporal poked a fist at his shoulder, pointing off upstream.

"Ain't that the purtiest sight!" someone else called.

"Doughboys!"

"It's Dickey! And Poole's boys!"

Sure if it wasn't. Trotting into view came Captain Dickey. And right behind him came a double column of shuffling foot soldiers struggling to keep up that numbing, ground-eating pace.

"Wasn't they back at the Rosebud when we left 'em?" he asked the corporal.

"They was, son. They was," he answered thoughtfully, his old eyes beginning to brim. "But, like any good foot soldier, they come a running when they heard there was trouble."

"C-come a running," he repeated in amazement, thinking back on all those miles these doughboys must have put behind them, "Come on the double."

"That's right, soldier," the corporal added, dragging a hand beneath the dribble at the end of his nose. "Man can allays count on 'nother good foot slogger come to pull your fat out of the fire: no matter how far, no matter how long it takes."

Chapter 40

7 May 1877

T hough the village had been put to flight and the warriors driven into the hills, the bloodiest fighting of the day was yet to come.

Nearby, Miles and Captain Ball quickly formulated a plan to prosecute their advantage now that Lieutenant Jerome's H Company and the Cheyenne scouts had returned to the camp with the captured ponies. The colonel put Jerome's men in charge of both the village and the horses while he had battalion commander Ball form up his cavalry for a full-scale assault on the heights. Many of the Cheyenne scouts were already making calls on some of the Sioux ponies, in addition to picking out some of those larger cavalry horses and government mules discovered among the herd.

As the three companies dressed right and left into formation for this attack on foot, their horse-holders stepped to the rear, ready to advance right behind the skirmishers. In the center stood the men of Norwood's L Company. On the left flank stood those troopers of Wheelan's G, and to the right, Tyler's F Company. With their mounts arrayed behind them, Ball shouted the order.

"Advance!"

As the troopers moved out at a walk, Seamus Donegan turned to find Miles watching the dismounted cavalrymen advance. He loped over to the colonel.

"General, permission to ride along behind formation?"

"By all means, Irishman!"

He quickly saluted, jabbing heels into the claybank and burst away.

At the center of the horse-holders of Company L, Seamus dismounted and dragged his mount behind him. He joined the movement up the slope about the time the warriors unleashed a furious barrage.

"Hold steady, men! Hold steady!" Ball hollered behind them on horseback, moving first to the right flank to encourage Tyler's men, then loping to the left past Norwood's men to cheer on Wheelan's company.

As soon as the enemy fire became intense, the company commanders and the noncoms were in among their men, moving them by squads, each platoon firing a volley as the others came up behind them, then went to reloading while another squad knelt, aimed, and fired at the enemy concealed among the brush and trees up the slopes. Leapfrogging up the gradual slope, yard by soggy yard.

"Put 'em on the run!" hollered F Company's Second Lieutenant Alfred M. Fuller who was waving his revolver, bringing up the laggers. "We've got 'em routed now—"

The bullet struck Fuller squarely in the right side of his chest, spinning the man off balance so that his pistol flew in one direction as he toppled backward out of the saddle in another, landing under the hooves of the first of that company's horses. Seamus was on the ground with lightning quickness, along with a private who fell out of formation the moment the bullet struck his lieutenant.

Coming to a halt, the horse-holders clustered around the scene protectively.

"That's a bad one," someone in the group declared quietly.

"Hush yer goddamned mouth!" another snapped.

"Get something on it so the man don't bleed to death—"

"The rest of you!" hollered their sergeant, prodding them all into motion. "Keep moving! Keep moving! The lieutenant don't need none of you to help 'im! He just needs you to flush them bastards off the hill!"

"How I get him back down, Sarge?" asked the private.

The noncom looked up at Donegan. "Mayhaps this man'll help you."

"Sure as sun, I'll help," Seamus volunteered. "Bring my horse over, sojur."

The young private wheeled to go for the reins. As he brought the claybank near and steadied it, the noncom said, "Lieutenant, Lieutenant Fuller? Can you sit?"

When no reply came from Fuller, the sergeant looked up at Donegan and said, "Don't think he can sit your horse, Mister."

"We'll throw him over the saddle. The man's in bad shape. Better we get him back to one of the doctors fast as we can."

They had Fuller slung over the saddle in no time and Donegan had started back to the rear with the private, while the sergeant continued up the slope with the rest.

Miles already had doctors Brown and Eman marking out their hospital in a small horseshoe of the stream, across the creek from the village. Two men were already there, John O'Flynn of F Company, and that other form stretched out on the ground beneath a gray army blanket, Private Charles Shrenger.

"This man needs help!" Donegan hollered as he trotted up with the horse.

Assistant Surgeon Paul R. Brown and a steward dashed up to help pull Fuller from the back of the mare, gently laying the lieutenant out to inspect his serious chest wound.

"He gonna make it?" Seamus asked.

Brown looked up, and slowly wagging his head he said, "Odds don't look good right now."

"Then do what you can to make him rest easy, Doc," Donegan requested. He stood and took up the reins to his horse.

Swinging into the saddle he brought the animal around and started at a lope for the side of the hill where Norwood's soldiers were all but stopped in their ascent. His L Company had the toughest part of the battlefield to cover: ordered to climb where the slopes were the steepest, to defend themselves and advance offensively, all while struggling to maintain their balance and not slip backward each time their boots lost a grip on the wet, grassy hillside strewn with loose rock.

Back among the first line of horse-holders who had clattered to a halt right behind the fighting men, Seamus watched Tyler's men continue their dogged climb on the west side of the ridge. A yard or two at a time they managed to scramble forward, forcing back the warriors who were putting up a stiff resistance, giving ground only when the odds finally tipped in the army's favor. But despite the intense pressure the Lakota faced from three sides, the warriors managed to keep Norwood pinned down and Wheelan's G struggling to advance up the ridge a foot at a time.

Of a sudden the first handful of Tyler's front ranks broke over the crest, seizing a firm foothold on the top where they began to lay down a murderous crossfire against the warriors who had forced the other two companies to take cover. A cheer went up among Tyler's horse soldiers as more and more of F Company reached the heights, concentrating a devastating fire on the enemy.

With what little ammunition they had begun the morning with, the warriors had no choice but to start falling back, some of the young men on horseback and others on foot fleeing over the top of the ridge where the slope descended into the valley of the Big Muddy. Most hurried upstream, their blood boiling from the rout. In their flight some of them would fall upon the pack-train, while others pinned down a lone horse soldier struggling to repair his busted saddle.

But on the east side of the ridge, where most of the women and children had gathered behind a few of those stalwart warriors making a valiant stand, the story would play itself out to a sadder end.

There the warriors slowly retreated along the heights, clinging to the brush and trees, covering the retreat of the women and children until the slope eventually gentled to their right. Terrain that would allow Wheelan's Company G to remount and charge down upon the screaming, fleeing Indians.

"Horse-holders to the *front*!"

Seamus turned, the hair on his forearms prickling at that order. How many charges had he made with saber? How many had he been part of against these red horsemen of the high plains? He stood with the others in Norwood's company to watch as Wheelan's horse-holders rushed forward with the mounts, quickly passing off throatlatches. Men snapped carbines onto their slings, flung the Springfields to their backs, and leaped into the saddles as G Company went stirrup to stirrup.

"Front into *line!*"

That second command gave him a cold shiver across the broad scar streaking down the great muscles of Donegan's back.

"*Charge!*"

And Wheelan's men were off with a deafening roar as those half-a-hundred scared, worked-up men jabbed their tiny brass spurs into the flanks of more than fifty matched grays. Whooping and hawing, they raced uphill after the Indians scattering on foot like a flock of wrens with a hawk swooping down.

There on that gentle, open slope turned to killing-ground, Donegan watched it happen. The older ones, those not able to keep up with the strong warriors who ran, turned and fired, then ran again, were the first to fall beneath the onslaught of Wheelan's charge.

"No!" Donegan bellowed, feeling like he'd been gored himself as he watched the slaughter from afar.

There, midway across the slope, he spotted the old gray-head, not sure if it was a man or woman at first. Then as the form stumbled, he saw it was an old woman, gray braids flapping as she scrambled back to her bare feet in her muddy, soaked dress.

A trooper was upon her in the next breath, swinging the barrel of his revolver at the back of her head as he loped past. With the power of that blow, the woman went sprawling. While the soldier yanked back on his reins to wheel his mount in a skid, the stunned woman lurched to her hands and knees, still crabbing up the slope where others called to her.

But the soldier reached her first.

Leaping out of the saddle as the woman continued to labor up the slope on all fours, the young cavalryman lunged over her, grabbing the woman by the braids, and yanked her around.

Surely he had to see she was a woman—not a warrior! Seamus felt the angry bile rising in his throat.

For a moment the soldier held his pistol out as if he was going to slash it across the old woman's face, but instead he flung the woman's head about as he stepped around her and began dragging the old one across the slope to a small copse of stunted pine a few yards off. There he threw her down against a tree, watching how she cowered and peered up at him, blubbering pitiably.

When the soldier turned his back on the old woman, walking away a few steps, Seamus breathed again with relief, his lungs aching while he held his breath.

But the soldier suddenly wheeled, took deliberate aim, and fired a bullet point-blank at the woman's head.

Biting his lower lip in fury, Donegan felt the warmth of the blood ooze across his tongue as his eyes began to sting with rage.

Quickly he turned to look right, twisting to look left—had anyone else seen the murder? But there was no one close enough at that moment for him to grab, no one he could shout to, no one else to protest that killing. Breathing deep while his heart pounded in his ears, a calm started to wash over him as he looked on all sides again, seeing how the officers and their soldiers were intent upon other concerns.

A soldier was a soldier, while a murderer was a beast. A deep gulf existed between the two, a gulf that could never be breached.

Seamus knelt, placing the carbine against his shoulder, bringing up the front blade and seating it within the notch of the back-sight, finding that anonymous, faceless soldier striding back to his horse without a whimper of remorse for what he had done.

Donegan held high, right at the brow-band of the trooper's slouch hat, knowing the bullet would drop some in its travels uphill. Watching the soldier move toward his horse . . .

Blinking, Donegan suddenly glanced again at that old woman's body. Moving only his eyes he squinted one-eyed at the murderer, placing the front blade against his faceless target. Here was a bastard who brought shame to the Second Cavalry. A blight who had shamed a century of good soldiers.

No one would know. He'd be just another casualty. Another soldier killed by the Sioux. A victim of war like the old woman—they'd say she was just a worthless old Injin woman anyway, he brooded. No one would give a good bleeming damn about her, about any of the non-combatants who had been killed in this last decade of brutality.

The fury in him began squeezing down on that trigger. But the rest of him revolted, preventing that finger from moving, resisting to the point where he found his hand, his whole arm shaking, his vision blurred.

No one would ever know—just one more dead soldier. A dead murderer. A merciless butcher who killed old women, likely slaughtered children too . . .

An image of Colin bloomed in his mind. What would his boy think of him if he ever knew his father had killed another white man in a battle against Indians? How could he expect his son to look up to him if he sank as low as those who killed for the sake of killing?

Dropping the blade slightly, Donegan squeezed off the shot a yard in front of the soldier's toes. That bullet made it with the cavalryman's next step forward, slamming into the ground inches in front of the horseman's boot, making him leap back, vault toward his horse in panic, then lunge atop the saddle. He kicked furiously, spurring the animal down the hill.

Seamus was grinning with satisfaction when he crawled off the ground, following the soldier's path—fully intending to run down the soldier and pummel the man until his face was a sodden rag of wounds. But just as he did so, the cavalryman reached the forward edges of Wheelan's company. A solitary horseman mingled with half-a-hundred horsemen, every last one of them swirling about, reforming in knots.

G Company swallowed that lone soldier, sweeping him away in the murderous frenzy of battle.

Grinding his teeth in fury, Donegan wondered if he was crazed, gone insane after all these years of fighting, after leaving a war against Confederates to leap into a war against the red men of the plains. Didn't war, after all, have everything to do with killing? Was he a demented, soft-brained creature to think that there must be some honor to the way a man conducted himself in battle?

Too many times this war had been waged against the helpless, against those who had committed no wrong, while time and again the guilty, bloody-handed warriors escaped.

Captain Ball was loping up behind Wheelan's company in that next moment, bringing Norwood's L sweeping behind him. In a matter of seconds, Ball had them all on their way in a broad front, making for the hillsides where the women and children shrieked as they whirled about, fleeing over the top of the ridge, making for the Rosebud. Behind them came that thin line of warriors to do what they could to slow the cavalry's advance up the hill, to cover the retreat of their loved ones.

Back, back, back the Sioux men fell as the horsemen thundered toward them.

Of a sudden it grew stunningly quiet as the cavalry swept over the crest and was gone from sight. Down the hill he could hear a soldier groan as one of the doctors worked over him, likely jabbing his probe into a bullet wound. The man begged for whiskey, laudanum, anything to put him past the point of caring.

Seamus sank on the hillside, the carbine erect between his knees as his head collapsed atop his forearms.

After more than a decade of fighting Sioux, the Irishman prayed for God Himself to give Seamus Donegan anything that would put him past the point of caring.

Chapter 41

7 May 1877

His horse soldiers had the village on the run.

And he had the pony herd intact.

Nelson A. Miles hadn't felt this good in a long, long time.

It made no difference to him that the warriors made off with a few horses, the ponies they kept close at hand in the village.

And it really was of little consequence that the village didn't stand and fight when he had hoped they would—just as Crazy Horse had tried to do at Battle Butte.

What really mattered is that the gunfire was fading over the ridge as Ball's battalion ran the escapees down, and that Miles could now begin the destruction of nearly everything these Sioux owned. Just as Mackenzie had destroyed the Northern Cheyenne in the Bighorns last winter.

Miles was overjoyed—he had just crushed the last of the hostile Sioux bands still roaming the Northern Plains. He was closing the book on the Great Sioux War. None other than Nelson A. Miles!

Sherman had to give him his star now. That, or Miles might well carve himself out an important chunk of territory in Washington City one day real soon.

"You wanted to see me, General?"

Miles turned at the voice, finding young Lieutenant Jerome rigid, saluting.

"Mr. Jerome," he sang out, flush with excitement, standing here where he had established his headquarters close by the site of that fateful encounter with Lame Deer. "First of all, my compliments on your splendid work capturing the herd. Commendable!"

"Thank you, General."

"While some of your men continue to maintain a corral around those Indian ponies, I want the rest to begin preparing the village for destruction."

"We're going to burn what belongs to the enemy, sir?"

"Everything," he replied, wiping one palm quickly over the other. "But first, I want your men to stack everything so my adjutant can make an accounting for the record: weapons and ammunition, meat and robes, along with anything else that might be of interest to our government officials."

"I'm not sure I understand you, General."

"I want to know if your men come across anything like feed sacks, flour bags, or the like. Anything that might indicate some of these people recently fled their reservations."

"Understood, sir."

He returned Jerome's salute. "Very good, Lieutenant. You have your orders."

While some ten of H Company joined Casey's Cheyenne scouts in keeping herd on more than 450 Sioux ponies, the rest split up to start rummaging through more than sixty abandoned lodges. From them the soldiers pulled a wealth of buffalo robes, at least thirty tons of dried meat, along with some two hundred saddles and other horse equipment. Besides some powder, lead, and fixed ammunition, the troopers discovered a number of Springfield carbines. In addition, they ran across quite a few Henry repeaters—seven in one lodge alone. Still, it was plain that the warriors managed to flee with most of their firearms.

Then the scalps began to show up—brown, blond, and red, a few long enough, curly enough, that they might even belong to women. And with each new discovery, Jerome's men cursed and Miles boiled. How it reminded him of the atrocities committed against the German family down on the Southern Plains in '74. While his own men, led by Frank Baldwin, had managed to recapture the two youngest sisters in a daring wagon-charge on one camp, it was some time before Mackenzie's Fourth accomplished the release of the older two.

White prisoners, white scalps.

"General Miles, I have a report on the number of enemy dead abandoned on the battlefield."

Nelson set his jaw. "Very well, Mr. Baird."

"Besides Lame Deer and his nephew, Iron Star, there are twelve bodies accounted for."

"That's all?"

"As you yourself have taught me, they probably dragged off most of their dead."

"Of course," Miles replied bitterly, struggling with the immense dissatisfaction. "Fourteen dead warriors."

Baird cleared his throat. "Not exactly sir. Th-they weren't all men."

"Women too." The colonel wagged his head. "I hate hearing that. It always makes the warriors fight harder, makes it tougher for those in the village who want to surrender, to make peace."

At that moment, Jerome brought his horse out of the creek, bounding onto the bank with a rush of water. "General Miles? I've got some things I thought you might want to see."

"You brought them with you?"

The lieutenant pointed. "Across the creek, sir."

Miles remounted and with his headquarters staff, followed Jerome back to the village where soldiers came and went in frenzied activity. Stopping near a small pile of goods outside a cluster of hide lodges, the lieutenant slid to the ground. He picked up a pair of leather gloves, clearly of eastern manufacture. Inside the gauntlet, their owner had scratched a large letter *C*, and beneath it, *7th*.

"And these watches, sir." Jerome's men held up more than half-a-dozen pocket watches.

Next came the small cabinet photos, and pocket diaries of those men who fell with Custer, the blank pages of which showed the talents of a few fledgling Sioux artists transcribing their battle exploits in crude ledger drawings. In addition, Jerome's men discovered a few items made from the leg portion of black cavalry boots, along with various pieces of army clothing, some stained with blackened, crusty blood that had never washed out, no matter how hard a squaw had tried. In the end, the troopers came across curry combs and brushes bearing regimental markings too.

"And we've counted more than a dozen of Custer's horses among the herd," Jerome declared. "They're all branded, sir."

"Captain Ball's returning, General!"

At the sentry's call, Miles turned with the others, gazing to the south to find the first of the battalion coming over the ridge.

"I want half of Captain Norwood's men to report to Lieutenant Casey to act as guards for the herd," he explained minutes later as the officers gathered about him. "And half of Lieutenant Wheelan's men will join Lieutenant Jerome's in preparing to burn the village. The rest will take up positions there and there, to the east and west of camp—to protect those high points from being regained and used by the enemy."

"Do we have our dead accounted for?" Ball inquired.

"Five so far, Captain. Perhaps as many as nine more wounded. They're being cared for right over there," and the colonel pointed out the field hospital established nearby in that tight loop of the stream.

Wheelan asked, "Will we bury our dead on the field?"

"Yes," Miles replied. "I think it would be a fitting tribute for those who gave their lives in this fight to rest here for all of eternity." Then he pointed to a spot about two hundred yards away to the southwest. "Captain Ball, you'll see that a burial detail begins digging those five graves over there, against the bottom of the slope."

It was some time before the horse soldiers reappeared on the top of the ridge. A number of them whooped and cheered when they came in sight of the village once again after returning from that hot running fight, chasing the fleeing warriors.

As things had turned out that morning, the attack came at just the right moment for seizing the pony herd.

Rowland explained, "The Cheyenne, they said they could tell the herder boys just brung out the ponies to graze up in that meadow by the stream, 'cause them herder boys was headed back to camp."

"So if we'd attacked a few minutes earlier," Donegan commented, "the ponies would've still been in camp."

The squawman nodded. "And if we'd come a few minutes later than we did, the herder boys would've been in camp to warn the village."

Shortly after noon that Monday, Dickey and Poole arrived with their infantry battalion and Private William Leonard in tow. That reunion was no small cause for celebration as Lieutenant Jerome held the first firebrand against a pile of robes, blankets, and clothing. Everything the soldiers did not rescue for personal souvenirs—beadwork, tomahawks, and knives—now went into the bonfires. By early afternoon there were more than a dozen greasy black spires climbing into the damp spring sky.

From time to time in the distance, the Irishman believed he could hear the wails of the dispossessed, the keening, anguished cries of those who had lost everything but their own skins, moaning in torment and fury. As the sun began to fall off mid-sky, knots of warriors took up positions among the hills, staying in one location long enough to fire a harassing volley at the soldiers in camp before fleeing in the face of a squad sent to drive them off. A while later, the warriors would return to fire into camp again, having set up shop atop another ridge.

"That coffee of yours any good?"

Seamus looked up to find Joe Culbertson coming up, soot-stained and mud-caked from the trail. "Does it really have to be that good for you to drink it?"

"Nawww. Only hot, Irishman."

"Sit down, young man, and pour yourself a cup."

The half-breed was doing just that when a new series of gunshots rattled into camp. While many of the soldiers dived this way and that with each new volley from the snipers, most did not. For one unlucky private, Thomas B. Gilmore of Jerome's H Company—a man determined to cook his bacon no matter the danger—that midday meal came at a high cost.

At a fire near Donegan's, Gilmore continued to squat beside the flames as others scattered, persevering with his chores until a bullet clipped his elbow, causing him to drop his frying pan and spill his meat into the ashes as he tumbled backward.

"Goddammit," the soldier cursed as he gripped the elbow

in a hand, dark ooze seeping between his fingers. "There goes my breakfast!"

"You're a tough old hide, aren't you now?" Seamus asked as he leaped over to help the soldier scoot back from the fire, where he had made a good target of himself in the dancing light. "Someone needs to get one of the docs over here."

"Shit—it's gonna be tougher to kill me'n it was to kill that ol' chief of theirs," Gilmore grumbled as Donegan leaned him back behind some saddles.

"Saw that for myself," Seamus replied as he squeezed down on the wound, doing his best to stop the bleeding, knowing that arm would have to come off before morning. "Took some shooting to bring Lame Deer down."

Wagging his head, the soldier grumbled, "I counted seventeen holes in him, my own self. You know that? Seven-goddamned-teen!"

Donegan slid aside as Dr. Eman knelt beside the soldier. "You're tougher, by the saints."

In small groups, the curious had gone up to view the bodies of both Lame Deer and Iron Star. A few laughed profanely but most were struck silent as they viewed the corpses of the men who had almost killed their commander. As soon as White Bull could safely get up the hillside, he scalped both the dead Sioux himself. He explained that although he wasn't claiming the kills for himself, he nonetheless was counting coup on these defeated enemies.

Close to twilight that evening, Robert Jackson moved about the camp showing off his trophy: Iron Star's feathered bonnet. He was especially proud of running the tip of his finger through the bloody notch at the base of the brow-band to boast on the accuracy of the head shot he made to finish Lame Deer's nephew.

While the random sniping slowed some after dark, the warriors nonetheless persisted in one place or another right on until dawn. *Perhaps they're hoping to find a weak spot in our lines*, Seamus thought as he fitfully tried to doze through the infrequent rattle of rifle fire from the hillsides, each outbreak accompanied by the curses of frightened, angry men and always answered by the nervous bawl of army mules. Perhaps those warriors would dare to slip in and recapture some of their ponies from Casey's Cheyenne scouts. Maybe the Sioux were even attempting to hasten the army's departure so the warriors would rush in from the hills and salvage what they could from the smoldering ash heaps of what had once been their wealth.

A long time after dark, Miles summoned White Bull, Rowland, and Donegan to visit with him. It was clear the colonel was a happy man, satisfied with the job his men had done that day, relieved that he had been spared the fate of Private Shrenger.

"There's an old soldiers' saying I'm sure you've heard of, Mr. Donegan," Miles began as the men settled in the fire's light. "It has to do with a soldier's destiny, and the bullet that may one day find him."

Donegan scratched at his chin, then said, "I think I heard that saying a long time back, General. The belief that every bullet has its billet."

"That's the one, Irishman," the colonel sighed. "Twice now, I've had a bullet aimed at me pass by to take another man's life."

"Where was the first?" Seamus asked.

"Spottsylvania Court House," Miles explained. "The Richmond Campaign. Lee threw everything he had into that fight."

Blowing on his coffee, Seamus said, "I remember hearing of a piece of ground there called the 'Bloody Angle.' "

"That's the fight. Bullets and canister falling around us like bees," Miles declared, then went pensive. "I received my brevet of brigadier general of volunteers for gallantry in that battle. And I've never come so close to death in all these years since . . . until Lame Deer fired at me this morning."

"As you said, perhaps fate didn't truly mean that bullet for you," Seamus said.

"Perhaps Lame Deer's bullet wasn't really meant for me," Miles replied. "I suppose I'm to believe that I was meant to live, and Lame Deer was meant to die."

After taking a cup of coffee from Lieutenant Baird while Rowland translated, the Cheyenne holy man turned to the Bear Coat and said, "I want to give you something—a gift from one warrior to another."

From his belt White Bull pulled one of the two fresh scalps and held it out to the soldier chief.

Miles didn't say anything at first. Instead, he swallowed hard, and finally asked Rowland, "Which one is that?"

"Iron Star," White Bull replied.

Then Rowland explained in English, "Among the Cheyenne people, it's good manners for a warrior to offer a scalp to the leader of his war party. It's an honor for you to accept it."

Wagging his head, the colonel apologized, "Tell White Bull I appreciate his offer to share his war trophies with me, but I want him to keep both scalps. They are his to give his children, to his grandchildren."

After taking a sip at his own coffee, Miles settled on a log next to the Cheyenne holy man.

"White Bull, do you remember what I told you when you agreed to become a scout for me?"

"The Bear Coat promised me horses," Rowland translated White Bull's answer.

"Yes, I promised you horses. Now you can have your pick of these horses we have captured. My soldiers will need a few for our trip back to the Yellowstone, but I give you your pick to give away to the other scouts who have helped my soldiers win this great victory."

Rowland's eyes narrowed thoughtfully, "You aren't going to kill any of the captured ponies, General?"

With a shake of his head, Miles answered, "No. I decided not to. The horses belong to my good friends, my Cheyenne scouts now." Then the colonel reached over and tapped the Springfield carbine the holy man had carried since leaving Tongue River Cantonment on their campaign. "And this rifle—I want you always to keep this gun that you've been shooting at our enemy."

Patting the dark wood of the stock, White Bull said, "I will keep this rifle, and the ponies too. My people will know the Bear Coat as a man of his word."

With a smile, the colonel asked, "What else can I do to repay you for all the help you have been to me and my soldiers?"

The holy man was pensive for some time, then Rowland translated for him. "I do not need much. But I will say that the only thing I want more than what you have already given me is for my people to continue to live on in this northern country."

Miles nodded. "Tell White Bull this: I will do everything in my power to give him what he wants for his people, to give them a home where they can live now in peace."

Chapter 42

8 May 1877

BY TELEGRAPH

A Finding and Sentence in the Reno Court Martial.

WASHINGTON.

The Reno Case—Verdict of Dismissal Modified to Suspension.

WASHINGTON, May 8.—Following is the result of the proceedings of the court martial at Fort Abercrombie, which recently tried Major Reno on a charge of having made improper overtures to the wife of Captain Bell, and taken means to cast slurs on her character:

WAR DEPARTMENT, May 8.—The proceedings in this case having been forwarded under the 106th article of war to the secretary of war have been most carefully considered, and have been submitted to the president, who approves the finding and the sentence, but is pleased to mitigate the latter to suspension from rank and pay for two years. Major Reno's conduct toward the wife of an absent officer, and in using the whole force of his power as commanding officer of the post to gratify his resentment against her, can not be too strongly condemned, but after deliberation upon all the circumstances of the case as shown on the record of the trial, it is thought that his offenses, grave as they were, don't warrant the sentence of dismissal, and all its consequence upon one who has for twenty years borne the reputation of a brave man, and has maintained that reputation upon the battle fields of the rebellion and in contests with the Indians. The president has modified the sentence, and it is hoped Major Reno will appreciate the clemency thus shown him, as well as the very reprehensible character of the act of which he was found guilty.

Signed, G.W. McCrary,
secretary of war.

That show the colonel's doughboys put on the next morning was the best—and most bruising—entertainment Seamus had seen in a long time.

The afternoon of the seventh, as the destruction of the village began, Miles ordered that two hundred of the very best of the captured ponies be selected so that he could mount his foot soldiers for the return march. Yet the animals would serve more purpose than mere transportation back to the Yellowstone. The colonel had designs on forming a permanent mounted battalion composed of four companies of his Fifth Infantry.

After the strongest and fittest of the captured horses were separated out, and after White Bull, Hump, and the other warrior scouts had picked over the rest to take what they wanted as the spoils of battle, Miles reversed himself and began the destruction of the remaining animals.

While the arriving infantrymen helped pull everything of value from the lodges, the officers instructed their men to separate every usable saddle and halter for later use before the leaping flames began their growling destruction. At sunup that Tuesday morning, as more robes and lodgepoles and blankets were tossed on the smoldering ash heaps from the day before, the circus began. Those recaptured cavalry horses branded with *7th U.S.* on their rear flanks had been assigned to soldiers who had little or no experience on horseback. But the rest of the infantrymen? Why, they were about to have themselves the ride of their lives.

"You ever wonder why a soldier enlists for the infantry instead of the cavalry, Mr. Donegan?" Miles asked as he came up to stand beside the civilian, sipping at a cup of coffee.

On either side of them in a great arc stood the officers, Cheyenne and Lakota scouts, along with those cavalry troopers watching this indoctrination of the foot soldiers to the frightening, unpredictable world of a half-ton of mean-spirited animal.

"I s'pose that foot soldier don't want to have him nothing to do with a horse, General?"

Miles nodded with a grin bending one side of his face. "These lads never knew they'd have me volunteer 'em for the Eleventh Cavalry!"

That joke the colonel made referred to the fact that there were only ten official regiments of cavalry. This so-called "eleventh" was the oft-tried, but most times ill-fated, attempt of infantry commanders to put their men on the backs of captured horses and mules, perhaps as a means of saving wear and tear on the doughboys. But in the end, such a decision usually meant more in the way of pain, bruises, and bloodied wranglers.

"Prepare to mount!"

Those laughing at Miles's joke quieted and watched as the long lines of foot soldiers draped their Long Toms off the right sides of their Indian saddles. Short loops of rawhide rope taken from the captured lodges were used to suspend the long Springfield rifles from the tall horns adorning the Lakota saddles. In hopes of giving his newly mounted infantry a chance at controlling the contrary animals, Miles had ordered each of Captain Ball's cavalrymen to donate one of their brass spurs to an infantryman.

At this moment the two-hundred-some soldiers stood stiffly beside their wary mounts, ready to put their one spur to use, nervously awaiting the next order. At least one, and sometimes two, cavalrymen assisted by holding onto the bridles as the infantrymen prepared to—

"Mount!"

In ragged order the doughboys stuffed a foot in those Indian stirrups, clumsily pulling themselves atop the Indian saddles strapped around the bellies of those Indian ponies.

Miles bobbed his head, saying, "So far, so good."

Eventually every man got himself up. Some of the ponies did not stand still in formation for long. In fact, that formation didn't last but a heartbeat or so until the first two dozen horses coiled up their backbones like the cocking of a gunspring, then unleashed their fury on their hapless, unprepared riders. Far too many of the infantrymen figured the spur's purpose was to help them hold on to their thrashing, convulsing animal—they dug in all the harder with that brass spur.

To the roaring laughter of the officers and cavalrymen alike, hats flew from the heads that snapped up and back, up and back. Those Long Tom rifles suspended from the saddlehorns pistoned up and down with deadly accuracy, battering not only the ponies' front flanks, but smacking the doughboys in the face, along the sides of their heads, and right under their chins.

The hapless foot soldiers began to fly right off what Miles had hoped would be their transportation back to Tongue River Cantonment. Catapulted into the dawn sky that eighth of May, the colonel's infantry landed in heaps among the grass and sage as the ponies bolted, heading in as many directions as there were routes of escape.

But Lieutenant Casey had foreseen this disintegration of the Eleventh Cavalry and had positioned his Cheyenne scouts here and there around the circus grounds. He used Miles's warriors to race after the escaping ponies, returning them to that field of battle between man and animal before setting off to recover another horse making for the hillsides in a wild burst of freedom.

All across that meadow beside Big Muddy Creek, foot soldiers began to peel themselves off the ground, hands held to heads or on hips, depending on just where a soldier collided with the damp Montana soil. One by one the runaway horses were returned to the infantrymen as their officers goaded the soldiers to remount. This time both pony and rider were even more wary of one another. Big, saucer-sized eyes glared back at the bruised doughboy as he once more climbed atop the animal and settled into the crude saddle, only to feel the pony come uncorked again as he dug in with that one spur and the other mud-soaked brougham, clutching the reins, saddlehorn, even the horse's mane to prevent another brief flight through the air.

Again the crazed ponies bounded stiff-legged into midair, twisting and thrashing as those men put to flight screamed, then groaned the instant they smacked the ground.

What a sight to behold: some four hundred men darting and dodging this way and that across that patch of meadow, every one of them attempting to catch and restrain, subdue or remount those two hundred horses!

Donegan laughed until his sides ached, then turned back to the colonel's fire when Miles returned to his breakfast, giving instructions to captains Charles Dickey and DeWitt Poole.

"Gentlemen, Mr. Casey's scouts have already separated off the captured ponies that we won't be herding north," he began, stuffing a thumb inside his waistband. "By midday, I hope to have the newly mounted battalion secure enough that we can assign your men to the destruction of those horses."

"Destruction, General?" Dickey repeated.

"That's correct. We need to kill what animals we aren't taking with us for the mounted battalion, those that Casey's scouts don't want. The poor, the lame—I don't want a one of them falling back into the hands of Lame Deer's warriors."

Poole asked, "Where do you propose we conduct this . . . this destruction, sir?"

For a moment, Miles considered it, then pointed. "There, across the creek in the narrow pocket formed by those two fingers of the ridge. It should be easy enough for your troops to throw up a cordon across the fourth side of that natural corral, while some of your men commence shooting the remainder of the captured herd."

As the two captains departed for their units, Seamus realized he had to be gone from there before the killing began. He'd seen enough Indian ponies slaughtered to last him half-a-dozen lifetimes. And although he knew that putting a mounted warrior on foot was the surest way to bring this long fight to a close, the Irishman had simply endured enough of the eerie, humanlike screams and cries of the horses as they fell . . . one by one by one. Their carcasses left to lie in heaps as the predators—both four-legged and winged—came to feast, drawn here by the stench. Until there was nothing much but piles of bones to bleach beneath the endless seasons of sun and snow, the only monument to mark this sacred patch of ground where the Sioux War whimpered to a close.

"General, could I have your permission to draw upon your stores for enough rations to get me back to Laramie?" Donegan asked.

"You're not going to travel with us to rendezvous with the bull-train we left on the Tongue?"

"No, sir," he said. "Figured I'd head south from here."

Miles set his cup down. "So this is something you've got to do today?"

"You're planning to get underway this afternoon, aren't you?"

The colonel nodded. "Yes, just as soon as the ponies are killed and everything else is burned. Of course, just tell Quartermaster Douglass you have my permission to draw what you need for rations and ammunition for your weapons."

"I don't need much, sir," Donegan explained. "Didn't get in that much shooting—nothing near what your men did in driving the Sioux into the hills."

Turning to his adjutant, Miles declared, "Mr. Baird?"

"Yes, General?"

"Prepare me a pay voucher for Mr. Donegan," he said. "Something this scout can present when he returns to Laramie."

"How much should I make it for, sir?"

And as Baird stood waiting, Miles gazed at Donegan for a moment, before he said, so quietly it was almost a whisper, "I don't suppose we'll ever see one another again, will we, Irishman?"

"Don't seem likely, General—now that you've brought this country to rest."

"What will you do now?"

"I plan to hug and kiss my wife, then hold my young son, Colin."

Miles suddenly turned to Baird, "I hired Mr. Donegan at forty dollars a month and found, didn't I, Lieutenant?"

"Yes, sir. More than your other scouts—"

"Yes, well, I suppose I did that because Mr. Donegan has a family to support."

"Then I should make the voucher for twenty dollars to cover him for the last two weeks of duty time?" asked Baird.

"Make it for fifty, Lieutenant."

"Fifty?" both Donegan and Baird echoed at the same time.

"Yes," and Miles stared at the Irishman. "He did just as he promised he would do. He came north to help me fight one more dirty little battle, to finish the job others had botched all along. I think Mr. Donegan's due just compensation for the time he spent on the trail coming north, and for the time he'll spend returning to his family—don't you, Mr. Baird?"

"Of course," the adjutant replied, glancing quickly at the civilian before he turned away to kneel beside the colonel's oak field desk, raising the lid to remove a small sheet of paper and the ink bottle.

Seamus didn't know quite what to say. "That's very generous of you, General—"

"Would you, just for these last few minutes we'll have together, call me Nelson?"

"Of-of course . . . Nelson."

"More coffee?" Donegan shook his head. The colonel stared at the fire a moment, then looked up at Seamus with studied concentration.

"You'll see your family before I see mine, Irishman," Miles said wistfully. "In fact, you've seen them more in the last year than I've seen mine—not since I left Leavenworth last summer just after Custer . . . just before Terry and Crook bungled everything. Those two could have put the cork back into the bottle a lot sooner."

"You're returning south soon, General?"

"No," Miles grinned, his eyes crinkling, "I'm bringing my Mary north on the first steamboat next month. Cecilia, my little princess, will come too. And Elizabeth Sherman, Mary's sister—the general's other niece. They'll all be arriving on the first paddlewheel of the season."

"Trust me, sir, I know how you must feel anticipating that reunion."

Miles sighed, dragging a hand beneath his nose, a distant look in his eye. "Nothing but male voices for far too long. It will be like angels' harps to hear their sweet voices, Mr. Donegan."

The Irishman looked away, a little embarrassed to hear that crack in the colonel's voice. "The life of a fighting man isn't the easiest road for a man to walk."

Looking up, Miles grinned and blinked. "You know, I've been giving some thought to pursuing another line of work."

"You? Leave the army, General Miles?"

The colonel snorted, "Silly of me, isn't it? To think of leaving after all these years, all the advancement, just to jump into a life of politics—"

"Right here is where men like you belong, sir," Donegan pleaded. "That's a life of back-stabbers and double-tongued two-talkers back there. You're a real rarity in the army, a straight-shooting man who doesn't mince words and does just what he says he'll do."

"That's one more thing we have in common, Mr. Donegan," Miles declared. "You vowed you'd return for our spring campaign—and you kept your word."

"I'll never let a friend down."

The colonel's eyes narrowed as Baird got to his feet and started their way. "You do . . . consider me a friend?"

"I'm honored to call a straight-talking, steely-eyed, honest-to-bullets fighting man like you my friend, General."

Miles reached out and grabbed the voucher Baird stepped up to present him. His eyes poured over it quickly, then he said, "Your back, Lieutenant?"

The adjutant handed the colonel a pen, then held up the glass inkwell as Miles dipped the quill into it. Baird turned so the commander could press the paper against the back of his shoulders to sign the pay voucher.

"There," Miles said, handing off the pen and blowing on the bottom of the voucher. "Fifty dollars. And I trust you'll take all the ammunition you can carry in your saddlepockets."

"Only what's fair, sir," he replied as he took the paper and folded it for the coat's inside pocket.

Miles held out his hand. "Let's just hope we don't bump into each other on another battlefield anytime in the next decade or two."

"I don't plan to do no more Injin fighting, General," Seamus declared as they shook hands, then he stepped back. "I want to find me a nice little vein of gold up there in the Montana hills, stake my claim, then take care of my family with my labors. Maybe have some more children, if God's willing."

"No more fighting, eh?"

"Not if I can help it," Donegan vowed. "I'm fixing to take my wife and boy up where we're nowhere close to Injin troubles."

"God speed, Irishman." Miles's voice cracked slightly again. Then he took a step back and saluted. "I trust you'll watch your back-trail, Sergeant Donegan."

He felt the sour ball rising in his chest as he blinked away the sting of hot moisture. He saluted. "General, it's been an honor—"

Seamus immediately turned on his heel and stomped away before the two of them betrayed any more of that strong sentiment that since the beginning of time had bonded fighting men who shared the same battlefields, shared the danger, shared the nearness of death.

Men with that same sense of duty to country and to family. Men dutybound to honor above all.

Epilogue

Late May
1877

THE TOWN OF "MILES."

General Miles has sent a communication to Governor Potts, of this Territory, advising his action upon Miles' proposition, some time since submitted to the War Department (but not yet acted upon) in favor of the permanent establishment of the town of Miles upon the Tongue River [military] reservation. The town is growing; stocks of goods are there, and the citizens now have a representative here who visits the Governor asking the organization of Custer County, in which the town is located. That a large population will this season locate upon the Tongue and Big Horn cannot be doubted, and with such settlement the construction and occupation of the posts and offensive movements against the Sioux, we cannot question that the end of the Sioux war is at hand. The new posts will be built of hewn logs, matched and lined with building paper, for the construction of which 600 carpenters are now on the way up the Yellowstone.

Army and Navy Journal
12 May 1877

After saddling up the claybank, Seamus had walked the mare over to present himself to Lieutenant Samuel R. Douglass, quartermaster for the campaign, packing up fifteen days' rations of coffee, hard-bread, and some salted beef in case he might run through a stretch of country bare of game, or might just have to avoid firing his rifle for fear of attracting attention. If he was lucky, he'd only have to aim his rifle at a mulie buck, maybe a curious antelope.

Shaking hands and slapping the backs of the officers and line soldiers who had been his comrades-in-arms for two cold, wet campaigns, the Irishman snorted back the dribble at the end of his nose and rose to the saddle. He yanked aside the reins and gave the claybank the business end of those spurs strapped around the heels of his stovepipe boots.

Half-a-hundred yards away he slowed to a halt, dismounting beside the ashy scars of what had been five fresh mounds the burial detail had scratched among the ruins of the Sioux village, there beside the banks of Big Muddy Creek. To protect the bodies from predators, and to prevent the camp's survivors from returning to dig up the bodies after Miles had pulled off to the north, late last night Jerome's detail had torched a large pile of blankets, robes, and dried meat over the graves.

Tensely gripping the reins in his left hand, Seamus dismounted to stare at the blackened ground, then brought his right hand up to the curled brim of his big hat, saluting those soldiers fallen in the line of duty in a stinking little war too often forgotten by the folks back east, ignored by their own government, overlooked even by those army leaders who sent the faceless ones off to fight an unknown enemy in a distant land.

As he stood there, his heart weeping, Donegan watched the ghostly faces of so many old friends parade past his memory in grand review—men fallen in battle, gone to their eternal reward having earned a hero's sleep.

These were men who had borne the ultimate price as their nation entered its second century. Men who would never again return to hearth and home, return to the kindred spirits of family, the kiss of a sweetheart, the warm embrace of wife and children. Men who would forever sleep beneath the green shroud of this great land they had come to fight over.

By nightfall, he knew these five graves would lie alone in

this valley as a mournful silence swallowed the land. A land abandoned by both the army and the Sioux. Those unmarked graves would be left to the ages and the endless wind that came to whisper with the turn of the seasons.

Recrossing the creek Seamus started away south by west toward the far side of the valley where Jerome's burial detail was lowering the last of the fourteen Indian dead into a long mass grave dug there against the bottom of the ridge some two hundred yards southwest of the streambank. Here, on another part of yesterday's battlefield, the soldiers had lashed the bodies in blankets then laid them side by side in that shallow hole where Donegan stopped and peered down.

"You here to get you a scalp," one of the cavalrymen said, "them Cheyenne took 'em all."

Wagging his head, Seamus looked at the corporal who had his sleeves rolled up, reddish dirt caked all the way up his sweat-stained forearms and replied, "No. I'm not here for no scalps."

He waited as two young soldiers looped the ropes beneath the last faceless, blanket-wrapped shroud and dragged the body over the yawning hole, lowering it inch by inch to join the rest.

"Which one of 'em was Lame Deer?" he asked the soldiers as the ropes were pulled up and three more cavalrymen started to rise from their perches on the rocks, dragging their shovels behind them.

"Don't rightly remember," the corporal answered.

"It don't really matter anyway," Seamus said, reaching down inside the deep pocket of his canvas mackinaw. As one of the men stabbed his shovel into the fresh dirt beside the grave, the Irishman asked, "If you fellas don't mind, gimme a minute here before you throw that dirt back in."

Not a one of them spoke, curious were they all, as he pulled out his small waxed pouch of army tobacco. From the corner of the plug he bit off a large chunk and with his fingertips began to grind the tobacco into flakes. Just as he would do if he were lighting his pipe. Maybe the way a warrior might fill his own pipe and offer a prayer over a fallen comrade.

Slowly, as he inched down the long side of that mass grave, Seamus Donegan sprinkled the tobacco over the blanket shrouds. Then he bit off a second hunk and sprinkled it too as he moved back along the other long side of the grave.

"Now what you do that for?" one of the young soldiers asked as Seamus stuffed the rest of his tobacco away in a pocket.

"Yeah," said another. "I figured the general was crazy to ask us to bury these goddamned bodies—but you gone and wasted good tobacca in that buryin' hole!"

A third man snorted, "Should'a just left 'em for the coyotes, what we should'a done!"

Then they all fell silent, expectant, as the tall man with the long hair tormented by the chill breeze now touched each one of them with his gaze.

"I just figured these folks don't have 'em no one to say some words over their graves, like folks said when you buried your friends back there in the village."

The corporal swiped his forearm across the bottom of his face, smearing the red dirt over his mouth and chin. "Never thought 'bout it that way, mister."

"Man what fought and died for what he loved most," Seamus explained, "he ought to have folks say a simple prayer over his resting place. Man died protecting his land, his family—should have someone say a prayer."

The soldiers stood motionless as Donegan swept up the reins to the horse and climbed up to the saddle.

The corporal loped over and came to a stop beside the horse. His brow knitted in consternation, the soldier asked, "Wasn't you gonna say a prayer before we throwed the dirt in on them bodies?"

"I already did say the prayer, Cawpril."

"You-you did?"

"With that tobacco," Seamus said, tapped heels against ribs, and turned the animal, moving off at a lope.

Putting the battlefield at Big Muddy Creek behind him.

Putting the Sioux War behind him too.

Pointing the mare up the valley, south by west for the Tongue, then the Powder. Heading home to loved ones waiting back at Laramie.

Now the three of them could set out immediately for the gold diggings of Montana Territory, for Last Chance Gulch where the future beckoned him, where after a delay of more than ten years an old soldier could at last get on with his interrupted life.

Praying that he would die an old man. That he would die in bed. That as he closed his eyes for the last time, he would be holding Samantha's hand while he took that final breath and crossed over.

Prayed there would be someone to sprinkle some tobacco on his grave, someone to say a prayer over his resting place, maybe even sing a hymn, perhaps a drinking song or two. But mostly he prayed he would never again have to die on such a lonely, forgotten patch of ground as he was leaving behind. And then he prayed he would never again have to point his weapons at another Indian.

Begging God above that he would find himself a little peace for his family in this wild, unsettled, and tortured land.

Afterword

It had to gall Nelson A. Miles something fierce as the seasons turned to discover how the Lakota and Cheyenne were detouring away from him and choosing instead to surrender into the arms of George C. Crook.

The lion's share of those *Ohmeseheso* bands, not to mention the Lakota who Spotted Tail found in the Little Missouri country, and especially that camp of the famed "Crazy Horse people," had all rebuffed Miles's straight-talk. While he refused to play Crook's game of promising what he could not guarantee, the end result of coming out second-best in that undeclared war of nerves with his gray-bearded nemesis must have irked Miles no end, as winter whimpered to a close on the high plains and spring began to flourish.

Compared to what numbers were surrendering almost daily down at the Red Cloud Agency, very few put their trust in the unvarnished truth the colonel spoke at the Tongue River Cantonment. He could promise them only one thing for certain: if they did not go in to surrender, he would continue to make war on them.

As events turned out by late spring, all of Miles's direct, eye-to-eye negotiations with both the Cheyenne and Lakota delegates at his post—in addition to his unheralded efforts at second-party peace feelers by sending Johnny Bruguier and Old Wool Woman to the combined *Ohmeseheso*/Crazy

Horse village—essentially reaped little reward when compared to Crook's expert sleight-of-hand. Not only did Crook poise his handpicked subordinate, William Philo Clark, at center stage that crucial spring, but with even greater effect the gray-bearded general played the strongest ace in his deck: Spotted Tail.

Miles didn't stand a chance.

There was no way he was going to convince the village that Crook could not guarantee all that he was promising if the bands surrendered to him in the south, especially when Crook's pitch was made by the revered Spotted Tail. While Miles told the bands the truth rather than what they wanted to hear, Crook's political posturing through Spotted Tail meant that Miles lost the honor of bringing in the hostiles, while Crook's dishonest duplicity won the day.

You have to give old gray beard credit for coming up with his highly successful initiative to send Crazy Horse's uncle to deliver that package of pie-in-the-sky promises. By the fourteenth of April, those *Mnikowoju* and Sans Arc bands Spotted Tail had visited in the Little Missouri country, before marching west in search of the Crazy Horse village on the Powder, were already straggling into both the Red Cloud and Spotted Tail agencies. Some two weeks later the Little Wolf contingent of the Northern Cheyenne appeared at the White Rock Agency. In short order Morning Star's and Spotted Elk's camps trickled in to Camp Robinson.

To his credit, Miles doggedly forged on with his plans for the campaign against those bitter-enders who refused all entreaties from north and south. Perhaps it was his grizzly-sized ego, if not his all-consuming desire to salvage something out of those herculean efforts he had made to induce the hostiles' surrender, which compelled the colonel to push on in the face of such a humiliating personal and professional defeat at the hands of the double-dealing Crook.

Miles is to be admired, while Crook should be despised for joining the ranks of those "peace-makers" who lied to the warrior bands down through history. Crook's actions in the spring of 1877 become all the more despicable when one takes into account the admirable efforts he had made in recent years to get to know his enemy, the lengths he went to in dealing honestly with his foes.

Another great source of aggravation for Miles had to be

the fact that the eastern press—savvily kept by Crook in his hip pocket—was busy that spring reporting how Crook's successes were eclipsing those of Miles. Back east journalists were reporting and re-reporting that the reason for that spring's success in securing the surrender of so many of the Cheyenne, not to mention the impending surrender of Crazy Horse himself, was no less than Crook's defeat of the Dull Knife Cheyenne. Nearly all of the eastern papers failed to factually report that the Dull Knife defeat was due to the field commander who actually made the attack on the Red Fork village: Colonel Ranald S. Mackenzie of the Fourth U.S. Cavalry.

This extremely politicized and slanted coverage had to put the intemperate Miles at a slow burn since he already regarded the press as conspirators who refused to put the credit for the surrenders where the credit was due—the tenacious war efforts of the Fifth U.S. Infantry and its commander.

It must be remembered that Crook did nothing but bring in the camps that had been recently defeated by the Fifth at Battle Butte (see *Wolf Mountain Moon*—vol. 12, The Plainsmen Series). It was Miles's relentless winter campaign that had given a rebirth to the peace faction in the villages, convincing tribal leaders that their best route lay in suing for the best possible terms of surrender. In my estimation, it was Miles's promise that he would continue to bring war to their doorstep that eventually convinced the headmen that they should negotiate with the Bear Coat rather than continue their fight-and-run tradition.

To counter all the good that Miles had accomplished in the field that bitter winter, it would take what this writer considers was no less than underhanded chicanery on the part of Crook and his subordinates.

What Miles had worked long and hard to accomplish, it took no time for Crook to undo. The Indians Crook brought in were in actuality seduced away from the lower Tongue, where they had been poised to give themselves over to the Bear Coat. Even with his success in stealing most of the hostiles away from Miles, Crook would not wait patiently for history to take its course with the rest of the warrior bands. Anxious, undoubtedly worried that something with his nefarious plan might yet go awry to turn Crazy Horse back into the arms of Colonel Miles, Crook sent none other than Red

Cloud himself to smooth over any last minute hitches that
might deter the Oglalla war chief from completing his sad
journey to Camp Robinson.

The final miles of that surrender march, especially the final
months of Crazy Horse's life, once he turned himself over to
"White Hat" Clark and began to suffer the jealousy and in-
dignities of the other Lakota chiefs, I will tell in a forthcoming volume in this Plainsmen Series: *The Broken Hoop*.

In the end, history would wait close to a decade before it
took its retribution on George Crook, before history finally
rewarded Nelson Miles for what he accomplished not only
with the last of the warrior bands in that spring of 1877, but
with the surrender of Geronimo's Chiricahua Apache in Arizona. But that too is a story I will leave for another time,
another adventure for Seamus Donegan.

While the commander of the Fifth Cavalry was consumed
with pressuring the Northern Cheyenne and the Crazy Horse
Lakota to surrender to him on the Yellowstone as spring
began to flower on the northern prairies, Miles did not neglect his other arch-rival, Sitting Bull. Throughout the waning
of that long winter he continued to do his best to gather
intelligence on the mood and movements of the Hunkpapa
leader's hostiles clinging to the Missouri River country.

Late in April, in fact, when resupply from downriver made
renewed campaigning possible, just prior to departing for the
Rosebud, Miles dispatched two companies of the Fifth Infantry under Second Lieutenant Hobart K. Bailey to scout
north of the cantonment from the Sunday Creek area to the
headwaters of the Big Porcupine (east of Fort Peck), circling
back to the Yellowstone opposite the mouth of the Rosebud.
Unable to locate any sign of the Sitting Bull village, Bailey's
battalion returned to their post on the sixth of May.

That same day, Crazy Horse led his people in to Camp
Robinson.

The following morning Miles had his fight with the last of
the holdouts under Lame Deer.

And sometime in that first week of May 1877, Sitting Bull
took his people across the *chanku wakan*—the medicine
line—into the Land of the Grandmother.

There was good reason Bailey's battalion was unable to
find recent sign of the Hunkpapa village in that last sweep

of the Missouri River badlands. Sitting Bull had abandoned the fight and fled the United States.

The Great Sioux War was all but over.

In constructing our map of the May seventh fight to accompany this book, like historian Jerry Greene, I have consulted an invaluable resource in the map drawn the morning after the battle by Sergeant Charles Grillon. A member of H Company, Second Cavalry, Grillon served as battalion topographer, performing various cartographic duties while on campaign. The sergeant's map is astounding in its detail, including the night route of the advance down Muddy Creek to begin their attack at dawn; the locations where two of the cavalry soldiers were killed; the point where the pony herd was located near camp and the point across the river where that herd was finally halted and corralled by Lieutenant Casey's men; as well as the exact dispositions of the individual cavalry companies as they went in pursuit of the fleeing Lakota in their chase that lasted some eight miles, all the way to the Rosebud.

For the inveterate researchers among you, this map can be found among the papers of General Frank D. Baldwin, housed in the William Carey Brown Collection in the library at the University of Colorado in Boulder.

Among the few accounts we have of the Lame Deer fight there exists some minor variations in the number of lodges that comprised the village. In his count made at the edge of the village late on the afternoon before the battle, White Bull showed William Rowland his tally of only thirty-eight lodges. The only way I am able to explain this too-small, incorrect number is that the Cheyenne holy man did not see the entire camp from where he was in hiding as he made his count. From Sergeant Charles Grillon's map of the village, as well as my own roadside visits to the area, I can logically deduce that with the twists and bends in Muddy Creek (now renamed Lame Deer Creek), as well as the knotting of willow and undergrowth clotting those twists, that White Bull simply was unable to see the entire village.

Beyond the holy man's tally of thirty-eight, there were two other incorrect counts recorded for history. One record gave the number of lodges as fifty-one, while another listed sixty-three, somewhat minor inconsistencies one must admit when considering the *sixty-one* lodges most historians generally accept as the number of "tepees" in the camp. At the same time you must remember that this figure did not include those brush bowers the bachelor warriors used for sleeping—young fighting men who had forsaken their south-bound families in giving allegiance to Lame Deer.

The site where the village stood that spring day in 1877 is now all but obliterated, covered by a hodgepodge of mobile homes on the south edge of the Cheyenne community, fittingly named Lame Deer.

Here along what is now BIA Route 4, Cheyenne historian George Bird Grinnell tells us that the hillside where Lame Deer fell is some fifty to sixty yards up the slope from (that is, to the southeast of) a shallow coulee that scars this narrow creek valley. Today, as on the day of the fight, one can gaze up the slope to locate a little red knoll above the coulee. Just beyond that, to the south-southeast, rises a taller knoll strewn with dark rocks lying among some stunted trees. It was on this higher point where Lame Deer was buried.

Twenty summers after the fight, Grinnell himself visited the site, watching as Lame Deer's daughter mourned beside his final resting place. National Park historian Jerry Greene confirms that Lame Deer's remains were later interred at that site Grinnell described: a sandstone cave on the heights overlooking the village site, close to the place where he fell.

No more than forty yards farther up that ravine lies a slight prominence dotted with some taller trees. Reports have it that this slope is where Lame Deer fell, just south of that coulee, collapsing sideways in death across a pine sapling. Greene records that at a point just west of where the chief was killed, there is that sandstone rock formation referred to by the Cheyenne locals as "Lame Deer's Tomb."

Robert Jackson, the half-breed Blackfoot scout, was among the first to examine Lame Deer's corpse that fateful day, counting seventeen bullet holes in the Lakota chief's body from that devastating barrage fired at him as he sought to escape.

Another half-breed army scout, Joseph Culbertson—although not near the scene when Lame Deer was killed—later maintained that the chief was finished by a shot from fellow scout Robert Jackson. But a contemporary account in the *New York Herald*, dated June 11, 1877, confused matters all the more by ascribing Lame Deer's killing to Private Henry

L. Davis of L Company, Second Cavalry. Muddying the discrepancies all the more, the newspaper account states that Davis reportedly presented the chief's headdress to Miles later that day. Additionally, Private Anthony Gavin, who declared he was one of the first to reach the body, recalled for the same *Herald* article that it was Robert Jackson, and not White Bull, who scalped Lame Deer, declaring that Jackson took "ears and all," and kept the war chief's scalp on his bridle "for over a week after the fight."

Just as we noted in the killing of Dog Soldier chief Tall Bull at Summit Springs in 1869 (*Black Sun*—vol. 4, The Plainsmen Series), there is no little argument on who might have fired the shot that killed Lame Deer's nephew, Iron Star. Intriguing too is that we have two separate accounts among Indian recollections recounting the Lame Deer–Miles episode that state the agitated nephew on the scene was actually named Big Ankle (or Big Ankles) instead of Iron Star.

Private David L. Brainard of L Company, Second U.S. Cavalry (later an army colonel who came up through the ranks), did indeed witness the killing of Lame Deer. He did not, however, watch the death of Iron Star with his own eyes. According to Brainard's report:

> When the old man fell, Iron Star escaped over the hill through our left, and ran into the face of G troop under Wheeland [sic], and was shot by Wheeland, who used a pistol.

The private's statement nonetheless does corroborate that a pistol was used to kill Iron Star—an important detail that Brainard likely could have heard from the lips of those who did witness the killing. In the same manner, he might well have overheard the reports from Wheelan's men that credited their company captain with making the kill, rather than credit the coup to a half-breed scout.

Private Brainard would later receive a commission in the Second Cavalry and begin his climb through the ranks, late in life becoming a noted explorer who served in the Arctic with Adolphus Greely.

For the record, the reader should understand that the incident involving a Second Cavalry trooper murdering the old Lakota woman on the slope of a hill just beyond the lodges has not been manufactured by me. It happened the morning of the fight, and is not a product of my imagination. Rather, it is recounted by Jerry Greene in *Yellowstone Command* and provides a tragic counterpoint to the brief but hot fight at that moment raging between the soldiers and the camp's warriors.

Was this an isolated incident? I feel safe in stating that such a cold-blooded act was a rarity in the frontier army.

A murder committed by a soldier worked into a lathered blood lust? Perhaps. We know for certain that this anonymous trooper hadn't seen any action during the Great Sioux War while other units were either getting in their licks or getting licked by the "savages." Most probably he was a member of that squadron of four companies of Major Frank Brisbin's Second Cavalry, which Lieutenant Colonel George Armstrong Custer refused at the fateful meeting aboard the *Far West* on June 21, 1876, before he marched up the Rosebud with his Seventh Cavalry. Now that this trooper was in the thick of it he might well have been helpless—his emotions running at fever pitch—to make any distinctions between a fleeing warrior and a noncombatant.

For most of the soldiers who saw action on the western frontier, more often than not there was no practical distinction between the fighting men and those in the village. All of the hostiles were the army's enemies. In fort barracks and around campaign fires the old files and veteran frontiersmen often repeated an old saw that had much basis in fact: in the heat of battle, in any attack on a village, the women as well as old men and young boys could be every bit as deadly as the battle-proven warriors. Truth was, most women could wield a firearm, club, or knife, could fire a bow with accuracy.

Forgetting that fact, or ignoring it through either the softness of his heart or the white man's cultural deference to a female, might just get a soldier killed.

Not an attitude found among the plains tribes. One has only to read the record concerning how an attacking tribe might well kill every one of the defeated enemy, no matter their age or sex. The reader can refer to the Northern Cheyenne destruction of a small camp of Shoshone just prior to Mackenzie's destruction of the Dull Knife village in the fall of 1876 (*A Cold Day in Hell*—vol. 11, The Plainsmen Series).

No matter the soldier's mind-set, no matter the era—that killing was a murder. Pure and simple. A murder made all the more tragic because the killer went free.

In his recounting of the fight many years later, Brigadier General William Carey Brown stated that the army casualties were four killed and seven wounded. However, I was able to locate an accounting of *eight* wounded in Jerry Greene's landmark study of the Fifth Infantry on the Yellowstone. And with some more digging, I located two more wounded soldiers listed in a contemporary article of the well-respected *Army-Navy Journal*, bringing the total of wounded to *ten*!

In regard to the enemy dead, however, the official report listed fourteen Sioux killed and abandoned on the battlefield, of which two were Lame Deer and Iron Star. Beyond the army's record, however, discrepancies arise upon checking other sources. George Bird Grinnell notes that only six Sioux were killed in the fight. And White Bull himself later declared that he knew of only five Sioux dead: three men and two women.

At that time the Cheyenne holy man stated "others may have been killed above," perhaps meaning on the hillside above the village site, or in the running fight beyond the top of the hill, but he did not personally know of any.

In addition, White Bull stated for the record that he recalled two soldiers were killed in the fight, along with hearing that one other person—either civilian or soldier—was killed while with the pack-train.

On the morning after the battle, during the mounting of Colonel Miles's "Eleventh Cavalry," Lieutenant Lovell H. Jerome watched in bemused horror as the infantry's doughboys were catapulted into the air by the captured Indian ponies they were attempting to mount. Jerome records that he hurried to the colonel's side and:

> ". . . told Miles that [the horses] were mostly squaw ponies and that the squaws mounted from [the] right side and that if the men would try to mount in the same way they would have less trouble. They did this and got along with them all right."

For the duration of the Fifth Infantry's tenure at Tongue River Cantonment, a seasoned number of Miles's foot soldiers would put those Lakota horses to good use in the months to come as they completed the final mopping-up of the northern plains.

Upon their return to their Yellowstone post, Miles would recommend several of the cavalry and his own infantry officers for brevets awarded for their performance in the fight: Captains Ball, Wheelan, Norwood, Tyler, Dickey, and Poole; along with Lieutenants Jerome, Casey, Fuller, and Cusick.

Upon the colonel's commendation, five enlisted men received Medals of Honor for their conduct in the battle: Corporal Harry Garland, Farrier William H. Jones, Private William Leonard (who held out in that lonely seige behind his dead horse), and First Sergeant Henry Wilkens, all of Company L, Second Cavalry; in addition to Private Samuel D. Phillips, Company H of the Second Cavalry.

It is also of interest to note that for many years White Bull kept the army rifle (perhaps a shorter cavalry carbine?) given him by Miles at the time he volunteered to become a scout for the Bear Coat in that spring of 1877. He managed to hunt with that weapon until the summer of 1905 when it was destroyed, as his home on the Northern Cheyenne reservation burned to the ground.

In those minutes before the soldiers began to torch the lodges, White Bull and some of the other Cheyenne scouts rescued pounds of buffalo meat and what they called "white grease" from the flames. It's only conjecture on my part, but the army pork they had been eating as rations would have rendered a "gray grease." Perhaps these former roamers of the plains were starved for buffalo "fleece," that layer of fluffy white fat lying just below the skin. Could this be what the holy man would later describe to an interpreter as "white grease?"

Remember that Johnny Bruguier had killed a man on the Standing Rock Reservation just before he fled to settle in with Sitting Bull's Hunkpapa?

Although he did not come along on the Lame Deer campaign and would not return to the upper Yellowstone until much later that summer of 1877, Luther S. Kelly recounts that subsequent to the Lame Deer fight,

Brughier [sic] gave himself up to the courts, where he was defended by that brilliant genius of the law, "Bill" Erwin, the famous criminal lawyer of Minnesota, and cleared of the charge held against him.

More than fifty-five years later in the August 30, 1932 issue of the periodical *Winners of the West*, General Hugh L. Scott also wrote about Bruguier and his brush with the law:

Johnny Brughiere [sic] killed a man at Standing Rock Agency in the early seventies and ran off to the hostile Sioux where he could not be reached and was a clerk for Sitting Bull.

When tried for murder at Fargo, in December, 1879, General Miles and Baldwin went to his trial. He was found "Not Guilty." He was finally murdered in Poplar, Montana.

I was unable to locate any mention of the journey General Scott said Miles and Baldwin made to that trial in Fargo, Dakota Territory. Would they have made that trip merely as curious spectators? More likely, the two of them would have gone to testify as to Johnny's character in Erwin's defense strategy once the half-breed was getting his day in court. Remember that Bruguier helped Baldwin time and again during his search for Sitting Bull in the fall of 1876 (*Wolf Mountain Moon*—vol. 12, The Plainsmen Series). And you've just finished reading my account of how invaluable the half-breed was in delivering Old Wool Woman and the Bear Coat's message back to the wandering camps.

I don't find it difficult to believe that both Miles and Baldwin would have made that journey to Fargo for the sole purpose of assisting in Johnny's defense, especially after the colonel had promised he would do all that he could to get the charges dropped. After all, in his memoirs, Miles is quoted describing Bruguier as "the man to whom I am largely indebted for the success of my campaign against Sitting Bull and Crazy Horse."

You might recall that as Seamus Donegan was taking his

leave of the battlefield, Miles explained how he understood the Irishman's anxiousness to be back in the arms of his wife. He told Donegan how he was planning to have his wife, Mary, visit him at Tongue River Cantonment. Not only did she and their daughter, Cecilia, visit the Yellowstone post in the summer of 1877, but the following August of 1878 found Mary and the wives of other officers taking an extended trip into the field to visit not only the Lame Deer site, but also the Custer battlefield.

On the ground where the soldiers fought Lame Deer's Lakota some fifteen months before, a member of the entourage later reported in the September 15, 1878 issue of the *New York Herald*,

> "We ... found the rifle pits, empty shells, bones, clothing, ornaments and clothing of several Indians ... [One member] was particularly fortunate in finding the breastplate worn by Lame Deer himself, and in having it identified by some of the Sioux Indians in the party who knew that warrior. To the ladies of the party this little excursion was exceedingly interesting, as it was where nearly all their husbands had risked their lives and the first battle ground they had visited."

As I have done before in the afterword to these Plainsmen novels, I want to list the sources I used to write this compelling story of the peace negotiations, the personal and political struggles within the Cheyenne and Crazy Horse camps, as well as the bloody climax in that crushing of Lame Deer's bitter-enders. For those of you who want to read more on this tragic and triumphant winter waning into spring, you can read:

A Good Year to Die—The Story of the Great Sioux War, by Charles M. Robinson, III

Army and Navy Journal, Volume 14: May 12, 1877

Army and Navy Journal, Volume 14: June 16, 1877

Autobiography of Red Cloud, War Leader of the Oglalas, edited by R. Eli Paul

Battles and Skirmishes of the Great Sioux War, 1876–1877—The Military View, compiled, edited, and annotated by Jerome A. Green

Black Elk Speaks, Being the Life of a Holy Man of the Oglala Sioux, as told through John G. Neihardt

Cheyenne and Sioux—The Reminiscences of Four Indians and A White Soldier, compiled by Thomas B. Marquis

Cheyenne Memories, by John Stands In Timber and Margot Liberty

Crazy Horse Called Them Walk-A-Heaps—The Story of the Foot Soldier in the Prairie Indian Wars, by Neil Baird Thompson

The Crazy Horse Surrender Ledger, edited by Thomas R. Buecker and R. Eli Paul

Death on the Prairie—The Thirty Years' Struggle for the Western Plains, by Paul I. Wellman

The Fighting Cheyennes, by George Bird Grinnell

Frontier Regulars—The United States Army and the Indian, 1866–1891, by Robert M. Utley

A History of the Cheyenne People, by Tom Weist

Indian Fights and Fighters, by Cyrus Townsend Brady

The Indian Wars of the West, by Paul I. Wellman

Joseph Culbertson: Famous Indian Scout Who Served Under General Miles in 1876–1895, by Joseph Culbertson (and F. Delger)

Journal of the United States Cavalry Association, Volume 10: June, 1897

Lakota and Cheyenne—Indian Views of the Great Sioux War, 1876–1877, compiled, edited, and annotated by Jerome A. Greene

Lakota Belief and Ritual, by James R. Walker (edited by Raymond J. DeMallie and Elaine A. Jahner)

The Lance and The Shield—The Life and Times of Sitting Bull, by Robert M. Utley

My Experiences in the West, by John S. Collins (edited by Colton Storm)

Nelson A. Miles—A Documentary Biography of his Military Career, 1861–1903, edited by Brian C. Pohanka

Nelson A. Miles and the Twilight of the Frontier Army, by Robert Wooster

North American Indian Anthropology—Essays on Society and Culture, edited by Raymond J. DeMallie and Alfonso Ortiz

People of the Sacred Mountain—A History of the Northern Cheyenne Chiefs and Warrior Societies, 1830–1879, by Father Peter J. Powell

Personal Recollections and Observations of General Nelson A. Miles, by Nelson A. Miles

Phil Sheridan and His Army, by Paul Andrew Hutton

The Pitman Notes on U.S. Martial Small Arms and Ammunition, 1776–1933, by Brigadier General John Pitman

Sharps Firearms, by Frank Sellars

Sioux Indian Religion—Tradition and Innovation, edited by Raymond J. DeMallie and Douglas R. Parks

The Sioux—Life and Customs of a Warrior Society, by Royal B. Hassrick

The Sixth Grandfather—Black Elk's Teachings Given to John G. Neihardt, edited by Raymond J. DeMallie

Spotted Tail's Folk—A History of the Brule Sioux, by George E. Hyde

Vestiges of a Proud Nation, edited by Glenn E. Markoe

War Cries on Horseback—The Story of the Indian Wars of the Great Plains, by Stephen Longstreet

We Are The Ancestors Of Those Yet To Be Born, by Bill Tall Bull

William Jackson, Indian Scout, by James Willard Schultz

Wolves For The Blue Soldiers—Indian Scouts and Auxiliaries with the United States Army, 1860–90, by Thomas W. Dunlay

Wooden Leg—A Warrior Who Fought Custer, interpreted by Thomas B. Marquis

Yellowstone Command—Colonel Nelson A. Miles and the Great Sioux War, 1876–1877, by Jerome A. Greene

To close, I want to restate that this long and protracted campaign against the warrior bands of the Northern Plains impacted far more than the 408 lives accounted for in the official army record of the Great Sioux War. Killed were 283 officers and men (which included Indian scouts), most of whom died at the Little Bighorn. Only 125 were wounded. But those are not the whole of the costs.

In the midst of recovering from the devastating costs of the Civil War, finding itself staring squarely into the teeth of an economic depression, the battered federal government accounted for $2,312,531.24 it spent defeating the Lakota and their allies. As author Charles M. Robinson points out in his book *A Good Year to Die*, the full impact of this much money from that era could have built at least nine large steam warships, fully armed and equipped, ready for the sea.

Without argument, the Indian losses for the duration of the conflict are impossible to determine because of the removal of the dead and wounded from the battlefields by their comrades. However, author Robinson explains that a reasonable figure based upon the subsequent testimony of warrior participants places the number at approximately 150 killed and no more than ninety wounded. That means that in some fifteen months the government spent over $9,600 to kill or wound each one of those Lakota and Cheyenne.

Likewise, we have no solid count of those civilians killed outside of the many skirmishes and battles: teamsters, mule-whackers, cattlemen, and prospectors. Nor do we have firm figures for the casualties among noncombatants in the villages attacked by the army during the Great Sioux War. Not only were women, children, and old ones killed in the fighting, but even greater numbers died of starvation or exposure to the brutal temperatures of the Northern Plains.

Perhaps even more telling, for those who survived an attack to escape into the wilderness, their villages and most of what they had owned had just been destroyed. By any reckoning, the economic loss in lodges and robes, blankets and kettles, clothing and weapons was nothing short of devastating.

Their way of life had been brought to an end, crushed forever.

The eventual fate of those who were conquered depended much upon where they chose to surrender. As you've seen, many of the *Ohmeseheso* who turned themselves over to Miles enlisted as scouts and were therefore allowed to remain along the Tongue River where they kept their weapons and ponies, serving the frontier army faithfully across the next two decades.

On the other hand, those Cheyenne who followed Little Wolf and Morning Star south to surrender to Crook at Camp Robinson were not near so fortunate as their kin to the north. Despite their steadfast belief that they would receive a better deal from Three Stars Crook, they were quickly marched to Indian Territory. The removal of those Cheyenne bands created misgivings among the Camp Robinson Lakota who began to suspect that they were next, regardless of Spotted Tail's professions that he had struck an unbreakable deal with Crook.

For some time Congress did in fact resist regional pressure to send the Lakota to Indian Territory, adopting instead a course only slightly less detestable in Lakota eyes: relocation of the Red Cloud and Spotted Tail agencies to the west bank of the Missouri River, near the town of Yankton where it would be far easier to supply the defeated peoples by river steamer.

At the same time, the Ponca Indians, a small band long friendly to the government, were uprooted and removed to Indian Territory so their reservation could be given over to the new Lakota agencies transferred to the Missouri. The very thing that Spotted Tail had feared and struggled so hard to oppose was now a reality.

By that May of 1877, as the last of the northern hostiles were escaping into Canada or surrendering at the Nebraska agencies, and as Miles was mopping up Lame Deer's bitter-enders, far away to the west there were rumblings of trouble with the non-treaty Nez Perce of Joseph, White Bird, and Looking Glass. The first group of transferees from the Spotted Tail Agency was being shipped east to the new agencies on the muddy Missouri. However, it is interesting to note that many were allowed to remain at the old agencies for the time being. There, confronted with growing despair and more broken promises, they looked to Crazy Horse to lead them anew. But other Lakota, exhausted by war and the ruin of their culture, feared the Strange Man of the Oglalla.

All around him at the Red Cloud Agency were chiefs growing jealous of the powerful hold Crazy Horse held not only among his own people, but over the white agency and soldiers alike.

It would not be long before the army was forced to turn much of its attention to Idaho and Yellowstone National Park, chasing the courageous Nez Perce into Montana Territory as they fled pell-mell for Canada. While the soldier chiefs turned their attention to catching Joseph's people, many of the powerful Lakota leaders would turn their backs on Crazy Horse.

Both of these are dramatic, and ultimately tragic, tales I will chronicle over the next three years in forthcoming volumes of the Plainsmen Series.

Because of the collection of rundown trailers scattered across the ground where Lame Deer's village once sat, because so little remains that would allow me to visualize how the site appeared 120 years ago, I went exploring the countryside around the tiny community of Lame Deer, Montana. While the creek the frontiersmen originally called the Big Muddy is now named in honor of Lame Deer, less than a handful of miles west of the town I ran across present-day's Muddy Creek as it ambled and twisted toward its junction with the Rosebud.

It was there I found hills and a valley closely matching those in that 1901 L.A. Huffman photograph of the battle-site. I turned off the blacktop and onto BIA 209, a gravel road that led me toward the far slopes where it wasn't hard for me to visualize the women and children, the old ones, and eventually the warriors all fleeing in escape that chilly spring morning.

Down in the bottom I crossed the last few yards of the Muddy and turned off to follow the faint parallel tracks of a four-wheel-drive road meandering beside the contorted creekbed. Here in Montana it has been an unusually wet year, so I found the stream running high as I brought the truck to a stop and sat still for a few minutes, stunned at the sudden, all-consuming quiet.

Nothing like that ground where the mobile homes now sit, there beneath that hillside where Lame Deer's bones rest for eternity.

Here, I could step over to the side of the Muddy and settle down in the grass beside the whispering water and the freshly killed carcass of a wild turkey. No downwind tainted smell, the turkey hadn't been here for more than a day. In time the noisy magpies quieted their protests and returned to their feast.

Once more I was struck with the feeling that I was the interloper here. Some critter had killed that fat bird, eaten its fill, then moved on.

Perhaps, I thought, it's part of what I'm being told.

These moments of such quiet are far too rare. Here beside this creek I listen for the whispers of ghosts from that last fight of the Great Sioux War.

Each time the breeze died in the tall grass that brilliant, sunny day as the hours passed, I could once again hear the gentle gurgle of the Muddy across its pebbly bed, make out the trill and whistle of the birds in the brush all around me.

And in those voices of the earth warming, I made out the voices of those who wanted their stories told—stories of this place . . . tales of a time that was, never to be again.

> —*Terry C. Johnston*
> *Muddy Creek*
> *Montana*
> *May 7, 1997*

*In his thrilling saga of the Nez Perce War,
Terry C. Johnston combines unmatched authenticity,
fascinating details, and a broad tapestry of vivid
characters—to make frontier history come alive
as never before.*

LAY THE MOUNTAINS LOW

A PLAINSMEN NOVEL

TERRY C. JOHNSTON

To the U.S. Army the Non-Treaty Nez Perce tribes
were an inconvenience—soon to be eliminated from
Idaho's Salmon River territory. But the soldiers discovered that their enemy was a skilled and ferocious
opponent, and that the war had only begun . . .

**"Johnston is a skilled storyteller whose words ring
with the desperation, confusion and utter horror
of a fight to the death between mortal enemies."
—*Publishers Weekly***

**"Johnston's books are action packed . . . lively,
lusty, fascinating."
—*Colorado Springs Gazette Telegraph***

AVAILABLE WHEREVER BOOKS ARE SOLD FROM
ST. MARTIN'S PAPERBACKS

LML 12/00

About the Author

TERRY C. JOHNSTON was born on the first day of 1947 on the plains of Kansas, and has lived all his life in the American West. His first novel, *Carry the Wind*, won the Medicine Pipe Bearer's Award from the Western Writers of America, and his subsequent books have appeared on bestseller lists throughout the country. He lives and writes in Big Sky country near Billings, Montana.

Each year Terry and his wife, Vanette, publish their annual "WinterSong" newsletter. Twice every summer they take readers on one-week historical tours of the battle sites and hallowed ground Terry chronicles in volume after volume of this bestselling Plainsmen Series.

All those wanting to write to the author, those requesting the annual "WinterSong" newsletter, or those desiring information on taking part in the author's summer tours, can write to him at:

Terry C. Johnston
P.O. Box 50594
Billings, MT 59105